QUANTUM GIRL NEXUS

BEING THE THIRD PART OF
THE QUANTUM GIRL TRILOGY

BY

DONALD KIERAN AUSTEN

AND

PEYTON ELISE HERRON

INNER SPACE MEDIA
2022

QUANTUM GIRL NEXUS, Volume III of the Quantum Girl Trilogy
Copyright 2022 by Donald Kieran Austen and Peyton Elise Herron

Published by Inner Space Media
10325 Donna Avenue, Porter Ranch, California 91326.

Quantum Girl Nexus / Donald Kieran Austen, Peyton Elise Herron
    p. cm.

ISBN 978-1-7377812-3-3 (pbk. : acid-free paper)

Library of Congress Control Number: 2023918204

1. Science *Fiction*[1].   2. Superheroes   3. Alien Civilizations
4. Time Travel   5. Parallel Dimensions   6. LGBTQ
7. Bullying   8. Teen Suicide   9. Self-Harm

122024

Cover design by Donald Kieran Austen

Printed in the United States of America

---

[1] So stated as science *fiction* for the sake of Library of Congress Card Catalog classification and search engine visibility, though, most assuredly it is not.

to

Anya

ever for Anna

*the inspiration for a universe
filled with hope and possibilities*

Quantum Girl Nexus

FORWARD

The most important question about existence is, why does anything exist at all, and, if it didn't, how could there just be nothing? There have been numerous explanations from both philosophers and scientists alike. The philosophical or religious view holds that a deity, whether it be God or Vishnu or Gaia or Khii, created the world or the universe out of nothing. Never is the question asked how the creator came into being. To do so would be a denial of the faith that undergirds the unquestioning belief. Conversely, science (or, at least, modern science) contends that the universe was created from a massive explosion, which its adherents have named the Big Bang, describing it as a quantum process that not only created both matter and energy, but spacetime as well, and contend that the effects of the expansion of the latter is continuous, and has caused its size to more than double since the putative explosion occurred. It gives no reasonable explanation for this but contends that there is some yet undiscovered force (effectually, a contention, based upon *scientific* faith) called dark energy. But neither faith nor science explains what came before that explosion, nor how neither space nor time can have a beginning nor an end. When I was little, I used to wonder about such things. I would envision the end of the universe as an endless brick wall. But then, I wondered, what was behind it. Now I know, and, soon, so will you, dear reader. All of this will be explained by the time this, the final book of the Quantum Girl Trilogy, ends.

Endlessly yours,

PEYTON ELISE HERRON

CHAPTER I

Jordan

From the Original Timeline
In the Alternate Reality
On Rendenaaar
Trillions of Universes in the Past

I was phasing back in time at breakneck speed, chasing after Dargra-Tol, when I lost sight of her in the *Jaaathara* Period. I stopped abruptly and hung midair, two hundred meters above the surface of the primitive landscape replete with its giant flora. Beneath me, a herd of *soltraaad* trudged slowly through a shallow swamp. Then, as if out of nowhere, a *waaark*, beating its massive wings, swooped down upon a juvenile *soltraaad* that had fallen behind, wrapped its wings around the poor creature, and sunk both its claws and its razor-sharp teeth into its flesh. The infant let out a blood-curdling wail as it attempted to fight for its life but all odds were against it. The *waaark* was far too large and powerful for its prey to escape. A few of the adults looked back in horror, but even their primitive brains recognized that it was all too late for anything to be done; and so they continued on their path, as the *waaark* sucked out the azure blood from its helpless victim. Such is the praxis of nature whichever universe one is in.

The gods of Rendenaaar had yet to be born and the creatures that populated its lands and its seas were left on their own to survive. It was kill or be killed for the predators; escape or be

1

eaten for the herbivorous kind; the topography showing no mercy. Vast open plains of grassland offered no protection for those that could digest only grass, although many, by the rungs of evolution, had developed armor or other defenses similar but far prefatory to the later dinosaurs of the Earth. Yet here walked the predecessors of our great civilization, precursors to the Gaaalthaaarans[2] that would one day declare their race superior to all, even those yet to be born. Here on this planet, long before it had ever been named, breathed the living stock that had, step by step and herd by herd, softened the ground of our world so that those who followed could tread more gently upon soil that had been thoughtlessly sculpted by the footfall of a trillion animal feet. Even in my time, their echoes still remained, reverberating endlessly within the metal sphere upon which we breathed.[3]

The pursuit for naught, I phased back to my time to my house, to stare out the window toward the mountains in the distance, wondering what I would have done had I caught her—she who was so much more powerful than me—she, who had led me on a not-so-merry chase, unaware that she was even being pursued. My mother and aunt had warned me against such recklessness, but I was still young and lacked the wisdom not to test to foolish ends—the god-stones filling my head with the false belief that I was somehow immortal. My name is Jordan Katherine Herron, I was thirteen years old in Terran years at the time of that pursuit, but was born in a universe, trillions upon trillions of eons in the future if such a measurement can even be made. At the time, I possessed just one god-stone in my head, a quantum gem of almost limitless power that had endowed me with superhuman abilities. I was known on my world as Zhardaaan, which was how the Gaaalthaaarans were able to pronounce my name.

---

[2] What we called ourselves.

[3] The iron core of Rendenaaar constituted nearly three-quarters of the planet's mass with a relatively thinner mantle than Earth's.

Both I and my people had but one great adversary and that was Dargra-Tol, an artificial lifeform that resembled the humanoid inhabitants of my planet, one of millions created by my people. Dargra-Tol and her kind were known as *Thaaagrans*, meaning *Those who did not exist*, and had pre-determined lifespans of roughly six Terran years. Such did not apply to Dargra-Tol, however, for she possessed another god-stone; one far more powerful than all of the rest. Hers was the mother stone, which she had stolen from my aunt, Khattaaara Gaaalthaaara in an act of great deception. How my aunt had rued the moment that had ultimately brought Rendenaaar to its knees. Despite all her efforts and years of attempts, she was never able to defeat her *Thaaagran* adversary, for the mother stone was far too strong. When I turned sixteen, she gave me all but the violet one; holding onto it, perhaps for protection from attack, perhaps because she did not wish to grow old, and the stone was an elixir against both.

"Five are all thou shalt need for now," she would tell me. "When I am dead and gone, thou mayest take mine," but, of course, that wouldn't happen for a thousand planetary cycles or more, and I wasn't around when it did.

As a child, though, I was treated as if I were a *yaaargh*-severed *Thaaagran* by those who should have been my friends.[4]

"Thou hast not the *yaaargh*!" they would chant again and again, till I would clap my hands over my ears and race back home to my mother's lap. "*Thaaagran, Thaaagran!*" I would hear in my brain, echoing into my dreams.

Poor *Thaaagrans*, who had their *yaaarghig* excised. Poor me as a child, for the relentless teasing, being compared to them, I who was next in line for the Gaaalthaaaran throne, bullied for my unchosen humanity.

---

[4] The *yaaargh* was a tail-like sexual and reproductive organ of the Gaaalthaaaran race and of the more advanced lifeforms on the planet. See the previous two books for further explanation.

3

There were so many times that I came home and wept bitterly, but my mother would always come to me and comfort me and stroke my hair and sing to me a song called *Smile*, which she said had been composed by a man named Charles Chaplin in the universe whence we came. "Smile, though your heart is aching, though with each tear it's breaking." I can still hear her voice to this day, across the endless sea of time and the vast ocean of space. She and my Aunt Khattaaara were the kindest women I had ever known.

Dargra-Tol had proved a most formidable opponent. She had used her powers to band her kind together in order to murder or enslave as many Gaaalthaaarans as she could. My aunt, as *Zhaaagur Scraaa*,[5] did her best to stave off Dargra-Tol's attacks. Regardless, our world—our very civilization—had fallen into ruin. The god-stones were gone; at least from that place where they would have best served our people, and there was no way for my Aunt Khattaaara, to put them back.

Anyway, *yaaarghless* though I was, and doomed to be a girl no matter what, I had the best teacher to help me learn to use my powers; at least the ones she was familiar with. But there were others I discovered on my own because each of the god-stones was slightly different from the next. I could project my consciousness into other Gaaalthaaarans, though only those I had come in contact with. I could create objects with my mind, though nothing mechanical unless I knew precisely how the thing worked. I could morph into any living creature. And I was able to read minds including those of animals, though, in the case of the latter, it was just images and emotions and sounds, but not words. What I could not do that Auntie could, was cause objects to become transparent. It was what she called X-ray projection. Oh, well…

---

[5] As explained in QGs, *Zhaaagur Scraaa* means Quantum Girl in Gaaalthaaaran.

I suppose having all of the powers given me by the god-stones was some slight compensation for my being an outcast among my peers. No one ever asked to date me. I wasn't capable of mating with anyone. And, I suppose, I was considered somewhat of a freak, especially after the time when others my age chose which sex they wanted to become. As a female, I must have seemed hideous to most males. Being human, I had neither a *yaaargh* nor pointed ears, and only one pair of breasts. Beyond all that, my eyes were a shade of blue unseen in Gaaalthaaarans or in either of the other humanoid races on the planet or in any of its colonies off-world.

It was something I learned to live with. Oftentimes, though, from a very young age well before I was gifted the five god-stones, Auntie would lend me one god-stone, so that I could duplicate myself, and have all the playmates I might ever need. Even so, it seemed lonely sometimes, because no matter how many of myself I created, they were all still just me. Beyond that, she and my mother taught me games to play that no child on Rendenaaar knew, like hide and seek, hopscotch, Simon Says, red light/green light, blind man's bluff, red rover, and tag to name a few. And both taught me English; well, tried to, but, without years of training, their vocal cords had a difficult time pronouncing the words. To compensate, Auntie would briefly pull herself apart, so that Auntie Payton, who was fully human, could emerge.

Regardless, I wished so much that I could have met my father, though I often thought, *One day, perhaps I will.* But he was in another universe so far into the future from where I was that I felt it was just an errant wish of mine.

It was on my twenty-fourth Earthday (that's what my mother would call the Terran anniversaries of my birth) that Auntie entered my room and sat down on the edge of my bed.

"'Tis time that thou goest back whence thou came," she said in the Gaaalthaaaran tongue, as she gently stroked my hair.

I sat up and stared at her. "I cannot think to leave thee, Draaaya.[6] You are all I have left in the world. You alone are the very heart in my breast," I proclaimed.

"Thou art a grown woman now," she replied, "and the world you left behind needs you. You have the five god-stones that I gave you, that thou might search for the sixth in the distant future; that one which is still in the Payton half of me. There thou shalt find three Quantum Girls and, perhaps, thy father as well."

"But what of Dargra-Tol?" I asked.

"There is nothing to be done of her," she replied. "Thou hast pursued her to no avail. She has the mother stone for which the other six together are no match, no matter what thou might think. Forget this *here and now*, my *Graaadral*[7], and find thy place on Earth."

As I began to rise from my bed, she took hold of my arm. "Shouldst thou meet thy father, Liam, tell him that his sister had a happy life and that his beloved Phee and I raised his daughter well."

How tragic it had been for my mother, who, with her every breath still loved him endlessly. Gaaalthaaaran that she had become, she never took another male to husband; nor female, for her broken heart could never mend. To have such a love as to traverse the boundaries of space and time, one would think could only be found in fairy tales, but there it had been in my mother's breast—my mother who now breathed no more.

And so, later that day, I bid my farewell, blessed my *Graaadra's yaaargh*[8] and she blessed mine as was our way, and then I phased forward through time.

---

[6] The Rendenaaaran equivalent of *Auntie*.
[7] The Gaaalthaaaran equivalent of *niece* in the most endearing way.
[8] The blessing of the *yaaargh* was meant to wish happiness, long life, and prosperity on someone.

CHAPTER II

Ophelia

From the Original Timeline
In the Alternate Reality
On Rendenaaar
Trillions of Universes in the Past

I do not think that anyone can imagine the horror I felt; not only having been turned into an alien creature but then abandoned in a long-extinct universe on a planet filled with beings such as I had become, who spoke a language I didn't know. The only comfort I had was knowing that I was with Payton, regardless that she, too, had become one of *them*. And then there was Jordan, though why should she, just an infant, have been dragged into the madness of the hell my life had become? Peyton never returned, and I wondered to myself if something had happened to her, or if perhaps the timeline had changed so that she couldn't find the one I was in or, worse, that she had never been (or, rather, never would be) born. Regardless that I refused to look in a mirror or a reimager as they called it, I still saw reflections of myself whenever I looked at Khattaaara or Payton—I didn't know *what* to call her, I was so confused. I would vomit ten or more times a day, even when there was nothing in me. And I tried to kill myself more times than I can remember. But Khattaaara (I needed to finally call her that) was always there to save me, to hug me, to be there for me when I needed to vent or to cry. There was so much denial in me. I felt that my life was over. My God, I was eighteen years old, taken from my family, taken from my supposed to have been *forever love*, and turned into some

7

abhorrent abomination of I didn't know what. *Where was God?* I asked myself more times than I can remember. But then God wasn't a part of this universe if He existed at all. In the beginning, God created the heavens and the Earth, but apparently, this was long before the beginning, and, thus, He did not create Rendennaaar!

Then there was Jordan. I envisioned her as destined to have a troubled life; dear Jordan, so different from everyone else, the only human, not only on this world but in this universe. As an infant, she looked much the same as others her same age. But as she grew, whilst the other children appeared androgynous, their sexes having not yet been chosen, her features were decidedly female. And then there was the matter of her voice. Having human vocal cords, she could not emulate the Rendenaaaran tongue, which had an almost reptilian sound to it combined with clicking tones, which, try as she might, she couldn't replicate and thus took on the brunt of mockery from the other children in her circle. The adults looked upon her as some sort of malformation. Supposedly learned physicians attributed her difference to some undetected burst of god-stone radiation from when they were taken from their sacred vault. It was the only way they could explain how each of her cells was encoded with two strands of nucleic acid, rather than three, for, of the more than ten thousand planets in the Gaaalthaaaran Empire, no other living creature's cells possessed what they concluded was an anomaly. Neither did any protein in them match any others that were known, which had the most fortunate effect of making her immune to any and every Rendenaaaran disease. And, despite that she, my blonde-haired, blue-eyed child, was strikingly beautiful all by human standards, on Rendenaaar she was a freak. As she grew into womanhood, her ears remained those of a Gaaalthaaaran male, a feature, which lent discomfort to unaccepting Gaaalthaaaran eyes. There were, of course, a number of the population that had been pricked to become a sex they did not want to be; but none of them, despite even surgical attempts to change their appearance, even remotely resembled Jordan. Doctors and scientists alike refused to believe that she was from a universe other than theirs. Meanwhile, the pious nicknamed her *Gaaarleff*, the Rendenaaaran word for god-stone.[9]

Jordan grew up to be extremely smart; I think smarter than any of us. Perhaps it was due to the heavily-oxygenated air on the planet, or perhaps to an effect from traveling through the quantum fabric, but I have always liked to think instead that it was Liam's and my chromosomes combined, which, by all logic, shouldn't have combined at all, since our molecules were mirror images of each other. Oddly enough, the scientists here found that the DNA of each pair of her chromosomes coiled in opposite directions from its mate. How this might or might not have affected her intelligence is unclear to me; regardless, it has always been my hope that it was the result of our union and our love, unscientifically romantic as that may seem.

I don't know how smart it was, though. for Khattaaara to have given Jordan a god-stone at so young an age (I had to get used to that new/old term for what Peyton and I called a quantum seed). It changed her. I don't mean for the worse. It just changed her. All things considered, I suppose it was for the best. The poor thing suffered from a lack of companionship, and so, with the aid of the god-stone, she would duplicate herself to create playmates. One time, though, when she was about six Earth years old, there were just two of her playing in her room. I was in the kitchen making

---

[9] The Gaaalthaaaran concept of the universe did not bode well with the idea that time was mutable, or even that space was anything but infinite. Indeed, the words of Krotaaarak were scoffed at, until, when she was two and a half cycles old, a costumed Jordan named herself Gaaarleff (It was easier for Gaaalthaaaarans to pronounce than Quantum Girl) and saved the world from destruction by freezing in time one of Rendenaaar's moons that had been pushed out of orbit by a resistance group, and then nudging it back into place.

up lunch. Things were more mundane on Rendenaaar ever since the god-stones were stolen. Gaaalthaaaran had to actually do things for themselves. Anyway, I suddenly heard another voice—older—and wondered if it might have been one of the neighbors' children that Jordan had let in. When I went into her room, though, I discovered another one of her; only that one was fifteen or sixteen years old by my guess.

"Hello, Mother," the teenager said as she looked up at me after I had entered.

"Jordan?" I said. It was half a question and half astonishment.

"I phased back in time," she said.

I suppose I should have taken it for granted that she could, and, one day, might. It wasn't that, though. It was the memory of Peyton that put me on pause for just a moment. The younger ones were laughing, as they had been when I had entered, but the elder held up her hand toward them in a gesture of silence, and they immediately stopped.

"Art thou all right?" she asked of me. "I did not wish to startle thee. I only meant…"

"I know," I said, but the room was spinning from the rush of emotion, and consciousness was abandoning me as blood seemed to drain from my head. I stumbled my way to the bed to try and lie down, just before I passed out, and that was when the dream began.

I was still on Rendenaaar, but it was years (Earth years) earlier—nighttime—and I was a young child, trying to catch the equivalent of fireflies with a young Khattaaara. The insects had butterfly-like wings that glowed either azure or magenta, and both of us had *waaardram*, which were hoops about a foot in diameter from which extended long handles. The *waaardram* were powered by the god-stones. Waved over one or more of the creatures, the insects would instantly be transported to either my or Khattaaara's *draaadrum*[10] in our home. As I stared at the tiny creatures, playfully jousting against the *waaardram* in Khattaaara's hand, it suddenly struck me that she was my twin sister and that my name was Klothaaara.

"Thou shalt not beat me!" I proclaimed, laughing. "I shall capture more than thee for my *draaadrum*!"

"Nay!" came the response. "Victory shall be mine!"

"In thy dreams, Thaaaraklo!" I shouted.

"*Thy* dreams shall be nightmares, Taaarakatt!" she cried out and then lunged forward in such a way that we both tumbled to the ground, laughing so hard that it hurt.

I looked at my *waaardram*'s handle. "Forty-seven by its count!" I proclaimed breathlessly.

"Alas," sighed Khattaaara, "I have only forty-six." She paused and then lifted her free hand, and threw two more through the hoop so that her count went up to forty-eight. "I win!" she announced, victoriously.

"Thou cheated!" I proclaimed. "The rules are that the *flidraaas* (yes, that was their name!) must be caught by the hoop and not by the hand!"

"Where does it say that?" Khattaaara demanded.

"By the book in my head!" I said as I fell back onto the soft *voraaax*.[11] "I am the eldest, and my rule is law!"

Khattaaara threw herself on top of me, propping herself up with her arms. "Thou art only my elder by two *rogaaaran*.[12] 'Twas just by chance that thou emerged from our mother's *yaaargh* before me!"

"Thou impudent girl! It was Khii, who chose me to be born first!"

Then, suddenly, I felt a sharp pain in my head. Khattaaara saw

---

[10] A small confinement of air, held together by a force field.
[11] A type of grass.
[12] Roughly two minutes.

the expression on my face and realized my distress.

"What is wrong?" she asked, concerned.

"I do not know," I replied and then screamed out from the agony that I felt in my brain.

Khattaaara began to rise, but my hand caught her arm and held her back. "Prithee, do not go!" I begged. "I wanted to tell thee, but I feared thou wouldst treat me differently." I paused from the pain I endured and then went on as it subsided just a bit. "Dost thou remember when I fell on the ice and hit my head?" I said. "Thou asked if my head had damaged the ice. Thou said that my skull was hard as stone."

"It was childish of me," Khattaaara replied with great apology. "But I waited for thee whilst the medicians took stock of thine injuries. They pronounced that it was but a concussion."

"It was," I replied. "But there was more. Whilst they made their examination, they discovered a growth inside my head. They gave me but three *vaaaralan*[13] to live, but I fooled them. It has been six, and I fear I must now bid thee my leave."

Khattaaara's face turned pale. "Nay," she begged. "Nay, do not speak so. I shall go find a medician. I shall wish us both to one of them now."

"Thou speakest from the heart," I said back, "and not the head."

"Thou canst not leave me!" she said and wept out tears. "Thou art my dearest dear. We shared our mother's *yaaargh* next to each other. We shared but one bed till but..." and her voice dropped, as she realized, "six months ago." It was then that she laid her head down upon my breast. "How can I go on without thee, my Klothaaara, my Thaaaraklo?" and her voice faded off into nothing, for I think that at that moment, I died.

It was then that I awakened. The older Jordan was sitting beside me where I lay.

---

[13] Meaning months.

12

"I put my younger self to bed," she told me in the most gentle voice. "Mother," she went on, "there is something I need to know."

"And what is that?" I asked as I tried to sit up in bed, though Jordan urged me back down upon the pillow that she, I assumed, had laid beneath my head while I was unconscious.

"I need to know everything that happened before we arrived here," she said.

"And why did thou not ask myself from your time?"

Her face took on a serious look. "Because," she said, "there was no one *to* ask. Thou didst take thine own life but one *vaaaralan* ere I left to come here. My coming back had twofold reason— to learn the truth, and perhaps to change what is to come."

"But if thou dost succeed in the last," she replied, "then the reason for thou to come back would be gone, and time would loop forever on this world."

"Not so," she proclaimed, "for I stand protected by the god-stone I possess. There will, of course, be another of me from the rewritten timeline, but I can merge myself into her when I return."

I smiled to myself at the young woman my daughter was soon to become. Then I bid her lay down next to me, and, as she rested her head against me, I told her, hour by hour, the events of my life on both Earths.

CHAPTER III

Daisy/Dargra-Tol

From the Altered Timeline
In the Alternate Reality
On Earth I
Earth-Date: 2025

Fuck me! The words echoed in my head. I now had the *rhaaarghag-flaaarg* that I got from Theresa merged with the same one from trillions of universes in the past! *Rhaaarghag-flaaarg? What the hell? Where did that word come from?* I wondered. *Shit!* There was now this other weird-ass language in my brain, along with Russian and Chinese. Add to that my own command of English and French. I guess that would have made me a cunning linguist! *Hah!* I remember laughing about that play on words at the time.

It was strange, though, having to accept the fact that I was not all me, but also someone named Dargra-Tol who was an artificial life form from a planet called Rendenaaar from a different universe. *What the fuck!* I thought. *How can there be another universe? Oh*, I realized. *I get it now. Hmmm.* I suddenly knew so much more than before she or it or whatever had become a part of me. But then part of me was her thinking, too. I was now Daisy McKenzie *and* Dargra-Tol. I was trying to figure it all out. *It was sort of like when I was part of the hive mind,* the Dargra-Tol part of me thought. *but all the rest of the Thaaagrans are long dead.* And while the Daisy part of my mind thought it weird-ass fucking strange to say the least, to see myself now with four breasts, pointed ears, and a fucking tail, the Dargra-Tol part was weirded

14

out by the fact that I still had a vagina. Vages were not part of the anatomy of anyone on Rendenaaar, whether biological or synth, but the synth half of me was not weirded out by the dual pleasure that I/we/whatever could achieve when our *yaaargh* began to stimulate our vag, which is what I/we spent doing for it must have been two weeks, till I/we dragged me/us out of bed, pulled off the bedding and threw it all in the washer. Then I (needed to come to grips with the fact that there was just one of me) dragged myself into the kitchen and searched around for something to eat. My now-dead-mother's cat, Gia, stared at me, hungry for food.

"Here, kitty, kitty," I purred at the irritating creature.

The feline thing approached and then stopped as it saw my *yaaargh* lift over my head and point at it. The cat's tail in turn went up as though to counter mine and then it hissed at me. I hissed back—It must have been the Thaaagran in me, the synthetic part, that did—and, as I did, my tail shot forth toward the furréd beast, and, in an eye-blurring instant, pricked its neck. All at once, the thing fell in a heap onto the floor, quivered a bit, and then breathed its last. Hungrily, I snatched up the now limp mass, sunk my teeth into its fur, ripping off a large part of it, and then began to devour its flesh and the organs that had lain hidden beneath. Its heart was still warm, as it went down my throat. No, I was no longer just Daisy McKenzie or Flower Power as I had ridiculously thought to call myself on a moment's whim. I was so much better than just that. I was Daisy 3.0.

I hadn't gone out since my *transformation*. I could never think of another, better, word for what had happened to me, so much had gone down. First, there was Theresa—poor, poor Theresa, now rotting in the grave I had dug for her. But—kind thoughts—she had awakened within me my sexuality, and I have always been grateful to her for that, despite our *falling out* in the end. Then there was the matter of the *rhaaarghag-flaaarg* that I took from her after she pegged out (my mother was so weirdly into

15

cribbage with her friends). And two weeks ago, wet and naked in the shower came the last *change*—merging with Dargra-Tol. I remember stretching out my arms at the thought, my nipples (all four of them now) stunningly erect as I reminisced on my affair with Khattaaara—Khattaaara, the trusting fool who had allowed me to have stolen the mother stone. Yes, that's what it meant— *rhaaarghag-flaaarg*—mother stone! Then it dawned on me. Blessed Hell! Peyton was Khattaaara reborn! Now, I'd have to fuck her ere I killed her! So Lady Macbeth of me! She was a lesbian, Lady Macbeth! She had to have been with that impotent husband of hers! Or was I Coldheart come to life from her fairy tale? *Speaking of tails,* I thought to myself, as another overwhelming urge toward hedonism overwhelmed me and sent me back to the bedroom where I satisfied myself once more with thoughts of Peyton Herron naked in my arms, fucking her for hours till I pricked the life from her with the tip of my furry *yaaarghl*. Or perhaps, I thought, I would just choke her to death with it.

Dressing proved a bit of a dilemma. I tended to wear somewhat short skirts, but there was the matter of my *yaaargh*. I couldn't very well go out with it sticking out in plain sight, and I definitely was not about to cut it off. Seriously, was I supposed to go to some Beverly Hills plastic surgeon, and have him excise my newfound sexual organ? Not in a million billion years! It took a bit of focus, but the Dargra-Tol part of me was able to flatten it to near ribbon thinness and wrap it around my hips. As for my breasts, I had to band the lower pair. My ears proved the simplest—easy enough to hide beneath my hair. The fact that I now appeared a bit older was explainable by the fact that I had been through so much, what with my parents' demise, and then poor Theresa, who (with my help) had taken her leave.

Not to label myself as having a one-track mind, I wanted Peyton Herron in bed with me; the matter of fact was, I was obsessed with her. I suppose it was in part that the Dargra-Tol part of me that had been with Khattaaara, and, while that was all an act in that Dargra-Tol was a *Thaaagran* with no real emotions, all of the erotic moments with her were now ingrained in the human part of my brain that was anything *but* emotionless. I wanted her sexually and spiritually. I wanted her to want me. Killing her could wait until things got old between us. I had everything material that I could ever want. I had godlike powers. All that was left to be had was the satisfaction of my ego and my sexual needs. And forget the superhero crap. I was a god! No costume! My vestments were white flames that licked my body and singed my hair. These were the trappings of an immortal. Daisy McKenzie had been filled with human frailties. There would be no more fairy tales. There would be no more fear. I had become special and unique. *Who,* I thought, *could even begin to challenge me?* Daisy had been a flower, but flowers wilt with age. It was time for a new beginning. Daisy McKenzie would be no more. To the world, then, from that day forward, from that moment on, I would be known as Dark God. Dark God, the All-Powerful. Dark God, the Merciless. Dark God, the omphalos for a new religion for all mankind!

CHAPTER IV

Sarabeth

From the Altered Timeline
In the Alternate Reality
On Earth I
Earth-Date: 2029

I could still feel the rope around my neck. Death haunted me in my dreams. Mom brought me up to be religious and to believe in God and the Bible and Heaven and Hell, but when I died, there was just nothing—no white light, no host of angels—just oblivion.

The fact remained that I wasn't looking for any resurrection. I just didn't want to live; even afterward. I mean, there were moments when everything seemed okay. I was even asked to be on the cheerleading squad, but then there was Theresa Martinez again. It was like there was no end to her wanting me to suffer. I wondered what I had ever done to her. But because of her and the potential threat of her, I had to be yanked (pardon—phased) four years into the future. The only friends I had were Phee, who was no longer my same age, and the older version of me, who was now filthy rich and Quantum Girl.

Peyton told me what had happened after I died and how everything had just fallen apart. Dad became an alcoholic and caused both him and Mom to die in a car crash, and Phee became a drug addict; heroin or meth, I don't know. But it made me think how much damage I did by taking my own life. It was fortunate for them that someone went back in time and changed things; kind of putting things back to normal, if there is such a thing.

18

I go to a public school now. No uniforms or dress codes. It's totally different from the private schools I'd gone to. In my previous life, I was never alone. I had Phee. Born only minutes apart, we were inseparable. But then, suddenly. while I was still a freshman in high school, Phee was already in college. We'd always talked about how we'd go to the prom together with our dates, and how we'd graduate side by side. I sure messed up that one, though.

Anyway, the first week I was there, after I got settled in, I went to Mrs. Langford, who was the head school counselor, and asked her if I could set up a group during lunch for kids to come and talk about things that were bothering them emotionally, and she agreed to let me have one of the classrooms to use, as long as I got one of the faculty members to sit in. It took a bit of asking around, but I finally convinced Miss Wakefield to accept the role. Miss Wakefield taught tenth-grade English and used the time to grade papers. Actually, as it turned out, it was *her* classroom that we used.

In order to make things known, I put up posters that I designed, handed out fliers, and got the word broadcast over the P.A., though I had to kiss Eric Stoller on the lips to get *that* done. Eric Stoller was what was referred to as a computer geek. I made him swear not to tell anyone. Little did I know he had a camera set up that recorded the entire upchucking affair, including the part where he managed to thrust his tongue into my mouth! To make matters worse, he uploaded it to YouTube. That pretty much backfired on him, though, as when the school found out, they made him take it down, apologize, and then agree to upload the unedited version that showed me literally gagging as I pulled away. The agreement was that it remain up for one week for everyone who had viewed the original to see; then that, too, the unedited version, was taken down. I assume there are still copies out there. I kept all of that hidden from Phee and Peyton, as I didn't want Peyton to go back in time and change things; not over this! Bad decision on my part it turned out, as all too many people said that I looked a lot like Peyton, but by then, too much time had passed with all too many possible consequences for her to prevent the video from ever being recorded.

The meetings went well. Initially, only a handful of students showed up, but, over time, the group averaged around twenty or so. Back ten years ago, there were a lot of suicidal thoughts among high school kids as a result of all the Covid shutdowns and masking. In our groups, some of the kids talked about problems with alcohol and drugs; some about bullying. One girl had been date raped just the night before. She hadn't told anyone until the meeting. It had really shattered her. I took her by the hand to Mrs. Langford and got permission to bring her to the hospital for a rape kit exam. The school paid for the Uber there and to her home. I wound up spending the night there. Halfway through the night, I felt her spoon me from behind. I remember feeling her tears on the back of my neck. One of her arms wrapped around me, and I took hold of her hand, interlaced my fingers with hers, and then went back to sleep. When I woke up (I had set my phone alarm to six a.m.) I found myself alone in bed. I dragged myself, wearily, out of it and then went to the bathroom to do what it is one does in a bathroom, but when I switched on the light, there she was on the floor in a pool of blood, having slit her wrist. I screamed out for help. Both of her parents and her little sister rushed in, I took hold of the girl and turned her head away, as their mother tried to stop the bleeding while their father called 911. It was fortunate that I'd found her when I did because she managed to survive. We are all so fragile when you think about it. But it was then and there that I decided that I wanted to be a doctor someday. I mean, why not if I could never become Quantum Girl? Anyway, the peer group, which met on Thursdays, lasted the entire time I was there at that school. In the end, I felt proud of myself for that.

20

CHAPTER V

Peyton

From the Original Timeline
In the Alternate Reality
On Earth I
Earth-Date: 2029

How incredible was it that when I had left Rendenaaar, which was to me only moments ago, Jordan was still an infant? Now, standing before me, she was an adult, years older than me, endowed with quantum powers even greater than mine. Stranger still was her expression when she saw Phee descending the stairs; not her mother, of course—the Phee from the altered timeline—but still…

Her mouth formed the word, but the realization of who this other person was came before it was pronounced.

"Is it safe to come down?" Phee asked as she nearly completed her journey. "It sounded like a war was going on."

"It was Khattaaara," Sarabeth chimed in.

"Khattaaara?" Phee said, looking confused. She looked at me. "I thought *you* were Khattaaara?"

"The Khattaaara from Liam and Li's dimension," I said to clarify things.

"Hello," Phee said as she noticed Jordan in the room.

"You look remarkably like…" Jordan said. Her head tilted. Her eyes fixed themselves upon Phee's face.

"She is," I interrupted. "There was a time overwrite." I then turned to Phee. "This is Jordan," I announced, "all grown up."

"I am beyond confused," Phee proclaimed. "There are four

versions of you in this room, and now an adult version of what is supposed to be a small baby?"

Before any of us could explain, Phee saw Payton lying unconscious on her couch, and rushed over to her, dropping to her knees. She looked at Payton's face, felt her forehead, and then turned her head back toward the rest of us.

"She's burning up," she said.

"Emma could only do so much," I replied. "Khattaaara injected her with some sort of venom. Rendenaaaran toxicology, sadly, is not one of her specialties."

"What if you could make an antivenom," Pay chimed in.

"Which requires getting a sample of the venom itself," I said then shrugged. "I suppose I could go back to Rendenaaar."

"Not possible." That was Jordan,

"Why not?" I asked.

"Because I placed a quantum barrier around that universe."

"Why would you do that?"

"So that you would not go back and rescue my mother and me, and undo our timeline. You need me here as an adult. I have five quantum seeds in my head, not just one."

"And that was your mother's wish as well?" I asked.

"Would that it were," Jordan lamented. "My mother was murdered by Dargra-Tol just days ago for me. 'Go thou, my child,' my poor mother said with her dying breath as I held her in my arms. 'Follow her to Earth, and help my dear sister and our once-departed-from world. Tell my Peyton that I forgive her for never coming back. Would that I had but a lock of her soft hair to have caressed my cheek at night. Kiss her for me and thy grandparents that I loved and missed them both.' And with those words, all breath left her, and she was gone. Dargra-Tol had put an end to her and then fled. All that was left of my family was Khattaaara, who stood beside me, watching as her once sister shed her mortal skin."

22

Afterward, Dargra-Tol came back and stole her corpse as it lay in state. When I tried to pursue her, she escaped using the quantum thread that brought us all to Rendenaaar—a thread that shall no doubt lead her here.

"Why not go back to your world?" young Liam broke in, entering with Li from the kitchen. His eyes were fixed on Pay. "That's where the Rends are. You could get some venom there."

Our attention turned toward him, as he stood at the landing of the stairs. By this time, Li had gone up to Pay and was hugging her. Pay, in turn, put one arm around her.

"He always eavesdrops," Li said.

"Do not!" Liam shot back.

"I think it's a good idea," Pay said.

"But we need to stay here as well," I added.

"Agreed," said Pay.

Then the three of us, Jordan, Pay, and I, divided; Pay and myself into Quantum Girls, and Jordan into a non-Quantum Girl version of *her*self. That was the first time I actually saw her face, revealed from her mask, so strikingly beautiful, with so much of Phee in her. The room became crowded when the four parents returned from wherever they had been. All of them showed concern the moment they noticed Payton, but the three of our Quantum Girl selves phased to Earth II, before any words were ever exchanged, and left any and all explanations to Sarabeth and our other selves.

It was rather dismal, phasing into the Herron home, although I suppose more so for Pay. After all, this was the house where she grew up in a time when life, even in the big cities, seemed pleasant and calm. It wasn't exactly the same as the world in which Demi or Payton (or whatever one might call her) had grown up, but it close. The Earth in that dimension had always reminded me of what I perceived life must have been like on my Earth in the 1950s. The people there still listened to records, watched television on dismally small black and white cathode-ray tubes, and either mowed their lawns on Sundays or else went to picnics after church. There remained, however, a segregation of the races, though it must be acknowledged that as negro families remained together as a unit, crime among black males was substantially lower than among whites. But now all of that was gone. The world had all the makings of the Invasion of the Body Snatchers, only here the people themselves were being turned into Rends.

"What do we do now?" Jordan asked, breaking the awkward silence.

"Hang on," Pay said, and then she phased from the room. A moment later, she returned, holding an unconscious adult Rend female, whom she laid down on the floor. "You wanted venom. Here's one source."

"Yes, but how do we extract it?" I looked at Jordan for an answer.

"There's a retracted stinger at the end of her tail. Beneath it lies a venom sac. You can milk it as with a snake."

"We're going to need something to put it in," I said.

Jordan looked at me. "Hold out your hand," she said, "Palm up." Her eyes turned orange, as she stared at my palm. Slowly, then, a test tube with a membrane across its open end materialized on it, along with a rubber stopper.

"That's one trick I *can't* do," I said as I wrapped my fingers around the glass cylinder.

"We'd better act fast," Pay interjected. "I don't know how long she'll be unconscious. I used a tranquilizer dart on her that I got from the zoo," she said and paused. "What used to be the zoo."

As Jordan took hold of the female's *yaaargh* and revealed a single fang that lay hidden beneath the soft blue fur, I pierced the membrane with the fang. That action, or perhaps the pressure, coaxed a green florescent venom out and into the tube. That done, I pushed the stopper back and handed it to her.

"We need to get it back ASAP," I said.

"It's already done," Jordan replied as the vial vanished from her hand. "I phased it to the self I left behind. The antivenom is being created as we speak."

It was at that moment that the transformed now conscious female, seeing an opportunity, attacked. With the help of her *yaaargh*, she sprung to her feet. Then, *yaaargh* held high and pointed, she faced us, turning this way and that, as the three of us encircled her.

The creature hissed at us, thrashing her tail this way and that at us. But she was not the same as that Khattaaara, who possessed a quantum seed. Violent as she appeared, she was in fact still mortal.

As her tail was about to strike me, Pay yelled out to her.

"Claire!" she shouted. The Rend heard her and stopped. "We're not going to hurt you. We just needed some of your venom to help save the life of our friend. Khattaaara poisoned her. Please. We don't want to fight!"

"Pheeelja?" Claire hissed from her Rendenaaaran throat. "You saved her with my *kaaatach*?"[14][15]

"No," Pay replied. "Not her. We saved another version of me." She broke off, steeled herself, and then went on. "Claire, we used to be best friends. Don't you remember? I was to be the bridesmaid at your wedding."

"I was to have a baby," Claire hissed at her, "till Pheeelja stole Leeechaaam away! No matter. He had a very small *yaaargh*!"

"You don't just stop loving someone," Pay insisted.

"Leeechaaam stopped loving *me*!" she said back. "And my baby is gone!"

"You can have your child *back*," Jordan interrupted.

---

[14] Venom.
[15] Claire's words were barely understandable, but for the reader's sake, they have been written in clear English.

"How?" Claire asked. Her tone had softened. It seemed that Jordan had struck a nerve.

"*I* can't do it," Jordan admitted, "but the mother stone in Khattaaara's head *can*. We just need to capture her."

"Will you come with us?" Pay asked.

"You were like a sister to me," Claire replied. "If you think I might have my little boy—it was a boy—I will come."

"You won't try to sting anyone?" Pay asked, staring into her eyes.

"I will not," she replied. "You have my word."

And so we phased back to my dimension, to my Earth, back to my home, merging back into just one of each of us, as the now Rended Claire looked on in awe.

CHAPTER VI

Claire

From the Altered Timeline
In the Alternate Reality
On Earth I
Earth-Date: 2029

My life was not what it once was. I was in another dimension, or so I was led to believe. It was confusing, to say the least. How odd it was to accept that Payton, a girl I had grown up with, now had superpowers and that there were four of her. Was it any more strange that I was no longer human? *Is this real or is it a delusion? Was I strapped down somewhere in a mental asylum, and all of this is nothing more than the canvas of a mind gone insane?* All of this crossed my mind.

I was confined to a room that looked like the exact same one that Liam and I had shared, though the furnishings were not the same. I was standing, staring out the window when a young girl, whose name I later learned was Li, entered unannounced. Sensing the door opening, I began to turn toward it, whereupon the girl, seeming frozen in her footsteps, began to scream, waking up the entire house, with everyone rushing in to see what was wrong. It was both frightening and bizarre, as two identical sets of Liam's parents, a young boy, and a younger-looking Peyton rushed through the door, while two other Paytons, one with dark hair, Pheeelja, and that other one, Jordan, appeared in the room out of thin air. One of the Mrs. Herrons went over to Li, and embraced her from behind, as the girl turned around and hugged her.

It was the young boy who courageously strode up to me, and

looked me up and down.

"It's not Khattaaara!" he said with great affirmation in his voice as he glanced back toward the girl. Then he turned again toward me and stared me in the face. "Who *are* you?" he demanded to know.

"Her name's Claire," the blonde Payton told him. "Claire Salinger. She's my very best friend. Or was." And then she, Payton, turned to face me.

"That's not Claire Salinger!" Li proclaimed. "Claire Salinger's ten years old like Liam and me, if she's still alive!"

I quickly stared at the boy. He did look like a younger version of my Leeechaaam —well, what used to be my Leeechaaam.

"She's out there somewhere!" young Leeechaaam insisted. "Anyway, this isn't her!"

"Liam's always had a crush on her," Li announced.

"So what if I did!" he shot back, glaring at her.

"Children!" the dark-haired Payton said in a stentorian tone. I stared at the two young ones, as some memories began to return.

"Leeechaaam?" I said and then turned toward my Payton. "How is it possible?"

"They're from Earth III," she explained. "Time moves more slowly there."

"And there is one of me there, too?" she asked, "As a child?"

"It would seem so," Payton went on. "Or there was. Khattaaara and her kind leveled the entire planet. Only a handful of people seem to have survived."

"We need to go after her," I insisted. "To save her."

"First we need to defeat Khattaaara," the dark-haired Peyton said.[16]

"There's another concern." Those words came from Jordan. "There's another threat. Her name is Dargra-Tol."

The correct spelling of Peyton's name is written here for the sake of preventing confusion.

28

"Who's Dargra-Tol," said Sarabeth, injecting herself into the mix.

"She's from Rendenaaar," Jordan explained. "She has the mother stone from her dimension. She's what we called a *Thaaagran*, an artificial lifeform created with the help of the god-stones by those who intended her and her kind to serve as docile servants. Khattaaara—our Khattaaara—after she had been merged with Payton's spirit, was tricked into giving it to her. The mother stone is more powerful than all the others combined."

"How could she have found the Earth?" Pay asked.

"There are residual threads within the quantum fabric that can be viewed through the god-stones if one knows how. Dargra-Tol followed the thread that Peyton took when she brought me and my mother to Rendenaaar. And I followed her here. I had been going after her with a vengeance ever since she murdered my mother."

"There are four of us now." The words came weakly from Payton who had just entered the room.

All of us turned toward her. Some color had returned to her face.

"The antivenom has done its work," Jordan said. "She just needs to rest."

The Peyton with dark hair vanished and then reappeared (they called it *phasing*) next to the Payton who had just come in, catching her as she started to collapse. Then she phased her onto my bed, sat down facing her, and stroked her hair. "We were all so scared you would die," she said.

"Hey," she said back, trying to force a smile. "I'm a diehard, remember?"

"I guess you just proved that," the dark-haired Peyton replied, smiling back.

"Have you found Liam?" the injured one asked.

"We haven't had a chance to look yet," the one beside her

answered.

"Well, now you do have time," I said. "Leeechaaam is the father of my baby that Zhaaardan said she would bring back."

"You need to wait until we have the mother stone to bring back your child," the Zhaaardan replied.

"I want my baby," I insisted. "I shall name him Eetaaan. It was my father's name."

"I think she means Ethan," Pheeelja chimed in.

Then my Payton spoke. "Seriously. Jordan. Is there anything we can do to change her back?"

Jordan thought for a moment, phased off, and then phased back a few seconds later. It was almost as though she was never gone, and there was just a momentary blur of her form. She then projected a three-dimensional ghost of me before the change, which she then laid over me. All at once, I felt something and then I was human again. I looked down at myself, felt my ears and my breasts, glanced back to see that I no longer had a *yaaargh*, and then turned to my Payton. We took steps toward each other and then I fell into her arms. "You were there for me all along," I said.

"You're my best friend," she said back, pulling me close to her, "like the sister I never had."

I pulled back a bit to look into her eyes. "Like the sister-in-*law* you never had," I said.

"We can work on that," she replied with a smile.

I shook my head. "I don't know if Liam loves me anymore. I don't even know if he's still alive."

"He's alive all right. Remember, I can go back in time."

"I still can't believe that you're now Supergirl."

"Quantum Girl," she reminded me.

I looked at the Peyton from this world and the Payton on my bed at my Payton and at Jordan. "And Quantum Girl and Quantum Girl and Quantum Girl and Quantum Girl," I sighed. "It's all so confusing." Then I looked at Jordan again. "Thank you for saving me." She just nodded and smiled. I turned back to my Payton. "Can I get some food?" I begged. "I'm famished!"

"Chinese takeout?" she asked.

"Please!" I begged. "Nothing Chinese! How about a cheeseburger?"

Suddenly, she phased us both to the back of an In-N-Out Burger. I looked around at the sudden change. "I hope you're buying," I said. "I left my purse on the other world." We each had a Double-Double, fries, and a shake. Regardless of how I felt before, it was good to be human again.

CHAPTER VII

Payton

From the Original Timeline
In the Alternate Reality
On Earth I
Earth-Date: 2029

When an ordinary person is stung by a Gaaalthaaaran, death comes fairly quick. My quantum seed, however, protected me; at least it protected my mind. Whether my body had grown pale or limp or quivered, my thoughts remained intact. My mind bounced from one person in the room to another, each for only a second or two, so it was doubtful that any of them noticed. But I viewed the room (and my unconscious self) from each of their perspectives. Then I was out of them entirely and it felt as though everything went insane. Suddenly, I was back in my dimension, on my Earth, and my mind went from person to person—hundreds, thousands, millions, maybe billions in a matter of seconds, and yet it seemed as though it were years to me, catching a glimpse of each person's life, one after the other. For the most part, it was tragic, what had been done to the people on my world. Then, all at once, it stopped.

I was outdoors. It was midday. The sun was directly overhead, and it was hot—really hot—and I was sweating, naked from the waist up and I was a man, or at least I was in the body of a man. By whatever cause, for whatever reason, I had lost my powers. They were gone. I no longer felt the quantum seed in my head. I was mortal again, and holding a pickax, gripping it with both hands, coming into consciousness in this body mid-swing just as the metal slammed hard against its stone target. The palms of my hands burned. They were cut and blistered and hurt like hell. I was in a strip mine, and there were hundreds of other men, each with a pickax of their own, each chipping away at the living rock. If any worker paused, a guard from one tower or another would aim a rifle at him that would fire rings of blue energy that had an almost crippling effect, so that the man would either continue to work as a result of and despite the pain, or else simply collapse, at which point the guard would intensify the burst, and the man or his corpse would disappear.

The work was backbreaking, even for my now male physique. Ladles of water were brought to us periodically by Chinese women wearing large straw hats. I later learned that the rocks contained cobalt, which was used in the production of lithium-ion batteries among other things. Anyway, it wasn't until the sun began to set that we were allowed to quit, at which point, I was ready to drop. There were no showers, but each man walked past a fire hose, held by Chinese men. There was no soap though, so, despite the forceful water, the men all stank from the sweat that remained on each of them. From there, we progressed to a mess hall filled with rows of long tables with benches on each side, but the men first formed lines at either of two food service tables, where Asian women doled out a thick gruel disguised as food. Each man was served a plate of it, along with a bottle of water and a spoon. The girl who gave me mine was around eighteen and pretty and looked shyly downward when I made eye contact with her.

Food and drink in hand, the men went to whichever table we so chose. Those at the table, beside and across from me, all ate greedily at the disgusting masses on their plates. I balked at mine and then laid down my spoon. The man across the table glanced at me as he ate.

"Better shovel it in, boy," he said, "if you wanna live."

He was right, of course, and so I brought one spoonful into

my mouth after another, forcing all of it down my throat. Seriously, it tasted as though I were eating ground-up worms, and, all things considered, that just might have been the case.

After dinner, we were ordered into the barracks; however, once inside, I had no idea where to go. The room was lined with what must have been a hundred metal-framed bunk beds, but which one was supposed to be mine, I had no idea. My thoughts were to wait and find out which bed was left vacant. All I could do was shove my way back and forth through the rows of beds, and hope that I would find the one I'd been assigned. As the ceiling bulbs blinked, prefatory to lights out, a strongly built male Russian guard spat out words to me in his native tongue. Oddly enough, I understood him. He was ordering me to my bed. I told him that the heat had made me forget things. He shook his head to himself, called me stupid[17], lifted my left arm on which were tattooed numbers, and then forcibly led me to the bed with numbers that matched.

It was a bottom bunk. The top was filled (literally) by a very rotund white man in his mid-forties—dark eyes, large nose with large nostrils—who looked like, had he been able to have become pregnant, he would be in his ninth month—wearing the same-style wife-beater that all the men wore when out in the quarry. His arms were matted with dark hair that sprung up past the low-cut neckline of his filthy cotton undershirt. Ethnically, he had a Middle Eastern look about him—maybe Sicilian. Anyway, that was my take on him, as I climbed into my bed. Once there, looking up, a fear took hold of me that if the man moved too much, both he and the mattress that supported him would come crashing down on me and that would be the end of me or whoever's body I was in. The labor of the day had taken its toll on me and it wasn't long before I fell into a heavy sleep. It seemed only a moment later, though, that I was awakened by a female

---

[17] Дурак (pronounced Do' rock) was the word he actually used.

voice with a thick Russian accent that came over a loudspeaker.

"Good morning, comrades," it announced. "Welcome to a brand new day that will allow you to further contribute to your new Rendenaaaran world. Feel free to enjoy fifteen minutes of bathroom privileges, then proceed to the dining area for a nutritious breakfast."

Wearily, I rose from my bed, watching all the others do the same. Then I followed the crowd to what turned out to be a group latrine that smelled like a sewage spill. In that, until the day before, I had been a total *girl*, I had never seen or been in a men's bathroom, though I assumed that they were far different from what I had observed. The room was large and offered two long troughs for men to urinate into and a row of toilets for defecation. The combined odor was overwhelming, to say the least. All were given plastic safety razors with which to shave.[18]

Breakfast was much the same as supper had been, my meal again served by the same Asian girl, only this time she attempted to smuggle a couple of strips of bacon onto my plate, covering them up with the slop I was to eat. Her actions, however, were noticed by one of the guards, who confronted her, and then backhanded her really hard. Upon seeing this, the blood seethed in me, and I launched myself at him, bringing him to the ground, and beating him with my fists. Suddenly, I felt a surge of electricity throughout my body. I didn't know if it was from a TASER or some other sort of weapon, but I collapsed on top of him. Two other guards, who had come to his rescue, lifted me to my feet, whereupon the guard I had attacked began to beat me, wielding blows as hard as he could to my gut and to my face, until I finally passed out. When I awoke, I was in a small, dank cell. Regardless that I was in a man's body, beneath it all, I was still a girl. I had never been beaten in my entire life, let alone like that.

---

[18] As a side note, I found it interesting to be able to urinate through an appendage I previously lacked, and while standing up no less.

I lay in fetal position on my side, hugging my legs. Sobbing uncontrollably for what must have been hours. I don't know how long they kept me there—days or weeks. There was no way to tell. There were no windows. There was only darkness. Food was shoved into the room through a slot near the floor. The only way I had to judge time at all was first by the stubble and then by the beard that had grown on my face. I laughed hysterically—a girl in a man's body, judging time by the beard on her face. Finally, the door opened, the daylight blinding to my unadjusted eyes. Two guards came into the room and ordered me to stand. I rose on legs that were cramped and weak and was led back to my cot and told to lie down until morning when work in the quarry would begin again.

When night finally came and the other men were asleep, I heard a voice whisper in my ear. It was the girl I had tried to protect. She held her index finger to her lips to urge me to be silent; then she raised her arms, unfastened her dress, and let it fall to the floor. Without the slightest hesitation, she climbed into my bed, wrapped her arms around me, placed her lips on mine, and began to kiss me. Then she undid the cord that served as a belt for the loose-fitting pants that I wore, and slipped her hand inside, wrapping her fingers around the now male part of me, arousing it and me. Thus, it came to pass (Gods, that sounds so Biblical!) that we made love. It had been so long since I had been intimate with a girl, but there was more to that. It was her way of saying thank you. It was my way of admitting that I needed someone in my life to love. I dozed off afterward, and, when I was once more awakened by the voice over the loudspeaker, she was gone. But thank Gods I am a lesbian, or our encounter would have been awkward, to say the least. From that moment on, though, I could say in totality that I knew what it was like to be a man—not just to walk in his shoes, but to live in his skin.

CHAPTER VIII

Dargra-Tol

*From the Altered Timeline
On Rendenaaar
Trillions of Universes in the Past*

It was what we had waited for, ever since the first *Thaaagran* had been created for the servitude of the *Gaaalthaaar*, the ruling class of Rendenaaar. I, or, rather, we, now had one of the god-stones in our possession. I knew it was a source of power, but what the full extent of it was I had no idea.

Chronologically, I was less than one cycle old when I took the stone from Khattaaara, and while I was born with a supposedly mature mind, emotionally I was not prepared for the sexual indoctrination I received from her. At first, things were *ordinary*. I cooked, I cleaned, and I attended to the day-to-day needs of both her and Thara-Klo. The first impression I had of my mistress was that she was quite ruthless. She paid little attention to me, treating me as though I possessed no sentience, but, rather, was a well-put -together machine, designed to look and act like one of them. For myself, I carried on the pretense that I was nothing more than that. One day, however, she changed. She became different. It was as though there was a whole new personality in her, and her attitude toward me took on a whole new direction. Before, I had been viewed as nothing more than an automaton, programmed to assist her with the menial tasks in her life. Then, suddenly, she appeared to accept me, not only as a love interest, but as her equal, and it wasn't as though it was only for sex. She appeared to care about me, constantly displaying genuine affection. What she didn't understand—what none of them understood—were the dynamics of the *Thaaagran* hive mind and its shared consciousness, the creation of such having been implemented by our manufacturers as a safety measure. By linking all of us together through the aid of the god-stones, it allowed the creation to install a kill switch wherein they could shut each and every one of us down simultaneously with a single command. Unfortunately for them, the god-stones were no longer in their possession. More to the point, I was (and, therefore, we were) now in control of one of them.

It took time, but through trial and error, I learned the power of the stone. I could move through time or space. I could stop or start time—even reverse it. I could throw out energy blasts, and I could morph into anything I chose. Perhaps, I thought, there were other abilities I had not yet discovered, but these were enough for my purpose at the time.

There were more than a million of my kind on Rendenaaar. We were laborers, domestic servants, and sex slaves. Some were assigned dangerous tasks; others were dissected "for scientific purposes." We had no control over our lives. Khattaaara was the first Gaaalthaaaran to allow me any measure of freedom, though it was toward a selfish end, as was the case with the rest of her kind. The only difference was that Khattaaara was not cruel; at least not after the change had taken place. Regardless, I decided that there must be consequences for selfish acts, which, in and of themselves, are the basis for evil. Was it then criminal that we should have chosen to cut off the *baaagragh's* head?[19]

The revolt began at the stroke of midnight in *Laaarghdaaar*, the capital city, when most Gaaalthaaarans there lay asleep in their beds. Many we bludgeoned or stabbed or slit their throats. We watched as the azure blood fled from their veins. Others were

---

[19] A *baaagragh* was a creature on Rendenaaar, more or less equivalent to a serpent on Earth.

strangled as we choked the breath back into their lungs until they died from asphyxiation. We cut off their *yaaarghig* and kept them as souvenirs or else threw them in piles and burned them. It was an odd thing about dismembered *yaaarghig* in fire. While the *naaahnra*, the furry end simply catches fire, the hollow air-filled *yaaargh* explodes, splattering *graaam*[20] in all directions. *Thaaagrans* were considerably stronger than their creators, so, for the most part, it was easy for them to overwhelm and kill their taskmasters. Gaaathaaan children shrieked and cried, as they saw what had become of their parents. Azure blood spattered across rooms and dripped down walls. The children, however, were dealt with more mercifully. Each was given a drink to make them sleep. The liquid was derived from a drug frequently used by Gaaathaaans to enhance or delay orgasms, but in its concentrated form would quickly stop the heart from beating.

That is not to say that the insurrection had been a total success. Not all of the ruling class had been asleep. The Rendenaaaran population was divided among Gaaalthaaar, Koalaaar, and Preataaara, the three continental land masses, each of which rose majestically from Haaarataraka, the great ocean that was said to have been filled by their creator's tears when the world grew angry and breathed fire from its belly and swallowed up so many of her children. But this was just a legend that gave explanation as to what had happened when internal forces caused the planet to rapidly expand. Regardless, those on other parts of Rendenaaar were not so easily taken by surprise, with the result that my kind incurred many casualties. In those regions, individuals gathered together to form factions. Each armed itself, and thus the war that would last for nearly three cycles began.

It was to our advantage that the Empire no longer had the god-

---

[20] Unlike humans, the *yaaarghig* of both male and female Gaaalthaaarans produce thick, azure-colored fluids that intermix. That of the male contains the equivalent of sperm, while that of the female contains from one to four eggs.

stones to allow its people to either communicate with each other or teleport from one location to the next. We, on the other hand, with our hive mind shared one consciousness. Meanwhile, I had the ability to teleport to any location where my newfound abilities were needed.

While our first objective was to take control of the cities, our second, and of equal if not greater importance, was food. The entire population of both Gaaalthaaarans and *Thaaagrans* and whatever others remained had relied on the god-stones to replicate our sustenance. With the god-stones gone, the threat of starvation became a reality. But while the Gaaalthaaarans struggled to gather up their livestock and farm their crops in the midst of battle, we set up processing centers into which the bodies of Gaaalthaaarans, after being stripped of their clothing, mostly dead, but some still living, were fed into machines with bladed, rotating cylinders, from which a paste was derived. The paste was then molded into small, edible bricks that were distributed to our kind to stave off hunger. That in and of itself served another purpose—clearing the buildings and streets of the decaying corpses that would have otherwise bred diseases capable of infecting our kind. The rains that fell heavily in the growing season, worked to wash away the blue and pink stains that came from both their and ours.

Prior to the theft of the god-stones, there had been no relationships between *Thaaagrans* because we shared a common mind. Neither did we possess what might be called self-esteem in that we had been indoctrinated with the false belief that we were manufactured and not divinely created lifeforms. All of that quickly changed after the revolt began. The first issue that needed to be addressed was our relatively short lifespans. This would not have been of particular relevance before, since, being of a hive mind, our memories and our consciousnesses were all shared, and, thus, preserved; the death of any one *Thaaagran*, therefore, was of no particular consequence. However, as the insurrection had the effect of shutting down all *Thaaagran* manufacturing facilities, without replacements, our entire race would have soon become extinct. Realizing that, the Gaaalthaaarans had quickly acted to destroy as many of the plants as they could. It was indeed fortunate that I had managed to save and take control of one.

For the last thousand or more cycles, *Thaaagrans* had been manufactured from one of only a dozen molds, meaning there were only six different *models* of each sex. For clarification purposes, the hive mind worked on two separate levels. While thoughts were spread within and throughout the entire population, physical sensations were shared only between similar models. None of this had been the intent of our creators, but, rather, an attribute that had come about more or less by accident through the workings of the god-stones. When the stones were stolen by Khattaaara and her cohorts, all of that came to an end. It was like suddenly becoming colorblind and tone-deaf and not being able to taste or smell anymore all at once. The initial shock had been nothing short of madness. Within moments after the god-stones had been purloined, *Thaaagrans* began to attack their owners. They became physical and violent. I can only surmise that I was unaffected because my *yaaargh* had been left intact and so I alone was able to bring some small measure of sanity back to my kind once the god-stone was in my head. It allowed me to link my mind to the rest and enabled my people to learn to exist as individuals, frightening as that prospect at first seemed.

It was at that one remaining *Thaaagran* factory that I first met Solgaaart in person, though his thoughts had been a part of mine until *The Upheaval*, as it was later referred to, meaning the end of the *Thaaagran* hive mind. Solgaaart, who was nearly at his lifespan's end, had been forced to work in a lab that extracted radium from uranium ore. The work, which was lethal to Gaaalthaaarans, caused only skin burns to our more resilient bodies. Given his proximity to death, however, those effects had painted upon him a rather tawny complexion, caused the loss of his hair, and taken away much of his body mass, leaving him with a gaunt physique. Adding to that was a slight facial tick and a tendency to mumble to himself; this last as a result of a hive mind misconnect, later defined by some Gaaalthaaaran medical term. With time, it wore off, but at that moment, it made communication difficult.

"Hast thou been able to fabricate any method to disburse radiation through the atmosphere?" I asked.

"Coelaaanth," he mumbled incoherently, "regarded the prospects of lengthening the workload by two *baaagtran,*[21] which would increase the mean production rate by fifteen percent." Then he glanced at me. "No," he interjected and mumbled on. "Having trouble with *yaaargh* now always stimulated, gets in way, and annoys. *Graaam* contaminates radium. Clogs apparatus. Cannot concentrate as before."

This was a problem from my having used the stone to restore their *yaaarghig.* He glanced at me but was at a loss for more words.

"Doth thou wish to copulate with me here and now?" I asked.

I recognized that sexual madness had been affecting his mind; one orgasm building upon the next. The thought came to my mind that were I to achieve orgasm with him, I could synchronize my brain with his, and allow me to suppress the excitation from his newly-restored member.

I grabbed him by the shoulders and forced him to look at me.

"There will be no other thoughts," I insisted. "What we do, we do for a purpose. It will put an end to the insanity."

"Art thou certain?" he asked.

"I am," I replied. "Now penetrate my *yaaargh* with thine."

I released my hold on him. He nodded and then shook his head, ending with erratic motions. *If his behavior were the case*

---

[21] The Gaaalthaaaran equivalent to hours.

with most Thaaagrans, I thought to myself, *we would be hard-pressed to win.*

CHAPTER IX

Khattaaara/Payton

Payton from the Original Timeline
Sharing the Mind of Khattaaara
In the Altered Timeline
On Rendenaaar
Trillions of Universes in the Past

It was just hours before Judgment Day (if I may be so brazen as to steal that term) that I sat outside the house with Ophelia, staring out at the night sky on the bench that sat to the side of the palace entrance. Before I had stolen the god-stones, a mere thought from anyone could have billowed us up into the clouds; now only I had the power to do so. I had stolen from every Gaaalthaaaran the gift that had put magic into the world, and I had no way to put it back, especially with the mother stone gone.

We watched as a lone *kadaaarak* sailed through the air, cutting across Padraraaag, the larger of Rendenaaar's moons. The silence of the nighttime was broken as Jordan began to cry. Phee, who had been cradling her, rocked her in her arms.

"You're so fortunate," I said staring out into the night. The English words took their toll as they passed through my Rendenaaaran throat, as they did through hers.

"How so?" she asked. "I don't feel fortunate at all. I miss my Mom and Dad and Peyton. And I miss Liam, who would never want me now."

"I know it's difficult," I replied.

"How would you know?" she said back. "I used to believe in God, but not anymore." She took her eyes briefly from Jordan to

44

glance up at me. "But then, you're going to turn evil someday. I don't know when or how or why, but you will."

"I don't believe so," I said. "Not anymore."

"What makes you think that?"

"Because I'm no longer just me," I said and then used the power of the stone to separate the Payton half from me.

"Hello, Phee," the Payton me said.

Phee stared at my Payton half and gasped. "How?" she asked. The words seemed to fall from her lips like the tears that had begun to drip from her eyes.

And so my Payton half told her what had happened; how after she had put the quantum seed in Theresa's head to save her life, Theresa awakened with powers but with no memory and confused her with the Peyton she had tormented at school, and how, in her anger, she had thrown Payton's mind back in time to mix with my own.

"So that's why everything changed back home," Phee said.

"What do you mean?" Payton and I asked as though with one voice, truly with one mind.

My Payton half and I stood in awed silence, as she explained all that had gone on, how the timelines on both worlds had been overwritten, and how so much had changed in both dimensions. While I knew about how the other version of me from what they had named Earth III had created a Soviet takeover on Earth II and how she and others had been transformed, this was the first I had heard of the overwrite of time. But it was the Payton half of me that reacted the most.

"Let me back in!" she sobbed to me bitterly. "I can't believe that I was responsible for all of this!"

And so I pulled her back into me, and the two halves of me dealt with it together. The Khattaaara half had no feelings either way about the fate of two worlds I had never known. But the Payton part; that part was filled with regret.

Suddenly, there was a loud clap. Looking up in the distance in the direction of the royal palace was a mushroom cloud.

"Oh, my God!" Phee exclaimed as she saw it.

Immediately, I jumped to my feet and threw a quantum barrier around the house to protect Phee and Jordan from any radiation. Then I divided into two of me—one garbed as my Rendenaaaran version of Quantum Girl, who phased off an instant later.

"Where did you… she go?" Phee asked.

"To the bomb site," I told her.

"Why?" Phee gasped out. "It's an atomic bomb! It's filled with radiation! Your alter ego dropped a bomb on L.A. not long before I left. *Your* L.A.! On *your* Earth! We had to hide in bomb shelters till the radiation was gone."

"She'll be all right," I replied. "The god-stones will protect her."

"But why did she go?" she asked.

"To undo it all," I said.

"Can she do that?" she questioned.

I took hold of her shoulders and looked her in the eye. "She and I, we're Quantum Girl," I said and smiled.

Phee offered a faint smile in return and then stared back at the cloud that had formed on the horizon.

Up close, the view was not the same. The cloud, by the time I had reached it had spread to nearly sixty miles in diameter, the top of which was more than forty miles high. The heat alone would have burned me up in less than a second had I not been protected by the stones. Intense radiation bent all around me, but none of it came near, nor did the blinding light impede my vision, despite that it was like looking at a thousand suns. The destruction was spectacular. It had destroyed everything in its path for three miles—and the radiation spread for twenty more. I tried to phase back in time to prevent it, but this was not from a bomb blast—at least not a cased bomb. I tried phasing back to the moment before

46

it exploded, but there was nothing there. Then, all at once, there was a hole in the atmosphere that burst out in all directions, throwing me to the edge of the initial blast, and rendering me unconscious. When I finally opened my eyes, I was on the ground, staring up at myself about to go phase back in time. Everything around me had been leveled. There was no sign of life. The city had been utterly destroyed.

Standing up, shaken, I phased up to the edge of the cloud and duplicated myself tens of thousands of times until I was able to surround it. Then I caused time within the circle I had created to reverse. It was a strange effect, the light from the blast being absorbed back into itself, the cloud itself shrinking in size, until, finally, it collapsed into a small sphere and vanished. I then placed a quantum field at that spot to prevent it from happening again. As all of that occurred, the city and its inhabitants sprung back into existence. Buildings were undestroyed, burnt clothing and flesh uncharred themselves, my subjects peopled the streets once more, and all became as it had been before the blast had occurred with none of them aware that anything had ever happened. Phasing back into my other self, there sat Phee, cradling Jordan in her arms.

"I don't feel fortunate at all," she said. "I miss my Mom and Dad and Peyton. And I miss Liam, who would never want me now."

"At least you have Jordan," I said. "And me," said my Payton half that I had pulled apart from me once more. That one of me smiled at her and she smiled back.

CHAPTER X

Claire (from Earth II)

From the Altered Timeline
In the Alternate Reality
On Earth I
Earth-Date: 2029

I looked her up and down. "Fuck!" I replied, "You're serious." I was human again, but I was left with all the memories of what I had been. It was like a nightmare. I was vain and cruel, and I had had sex (if one could call it that) with another monster, for I was one, too. We all have our dark sides, but this was like that book that Roberta Louise Stevenson had written more than a century and a half ago. I was Madame Hyde, the wretch of a woman, brought into existence from a frothing drink.[22]

This was all too strange. Payton, my best friend since we were children, now had superpowers, and mine was not the only Earth. After I had rested, Payton came into the attic where a cot had been set up for me. I was lying on my side, awake and staring at an antique spinning wheel that had fallen into disuse, probably before the Civil War. Had there been a Civil War here, I wondered? This wasn't my world; at least that's what Payton had said. Hard to believe. What was I supposed to do, though? I had been transformed into some alien creature and then brought back. I remembered eating *worms* and enjoying them slithering in my mouth. I remembered the sex. I remember blaming that girl,

---

[22] Claire was from the parallel, where certain sex roles were reversed. There, the Strange Case of Dr. Jekyll and Mr. Hyde went even further, to turn Henrietta Jekyll into a murderous harlot.

Ophelia, for stealing Liam from me. But no one can steal from you what you don't really have. If Liam really truly loved me, he wouldn't have turned from me. The fact that he had was devastating to me. It didn't seem fair. I loved him so, so much!

I was the one who spoke first. "Where's Liam?" I asked, trying to sound like I didn't really care.

"We don't know," came the response. "A lot's been going on."

"How so?" I asked, sitting up in bed.

"Things have changed," she replied. "Our world is under attack. What they did to you, they're doing to everyone."

"My Gods!" I exclaimed. "What about my parents? I need to go back."

She gently urged me down as I tried to stand. "The three of us will go look for Liam… and your parents."

I threw my feet over the edge of the bed. "I'll get dressed," I said.

"I didn't mean you," she replied. "I meant the other two Paytons and me."

"What are you talking about?" I said. "Other two Paytons?"

"Don't you remember?" she replied.

"I thought I was dreaming," I said.

"They're from others, dimensions, realities," she replied. "It gets confusing."

"And you all have superpowers," I said, half-concluding.

"All except Sarabeth," she replied. "She's very upset about that."

"Are there other ones of me?" I asked.

"Not sure at this point," she replied, "but I'm sure if there are, there's just as beautiful as you."

"That's so sweet," I replied, "but creepy when I think about it." I paused, thought for a moment, and then went on. "So, which dimension is ours?"

49

"Earth II, revised edition," she replied.

"Huh?" I said. I was so confused at that point.

"There are three parallel dimensions that I know about and two timelines. You've heard about the acorn effect? A time traveler goes into the prehistoric past, picks up an acorn, puts it in his pocket, and then brings it back to the present. Only that acorn was supposed to grow into an oak tree that would have survived the mass extinction that wiped out the dinosaurs. Without oak trees, primitive primates weren't able to survive, and so he returned to a present where humans didn't exist. Kind of the same here. Something happened in our dimension and in this one that caused reality to be overwritten. One of the other Payton's is me in the original timeline and in that one, I was a diehard sapph."

I looked her up and down. "You're serious."

"Stop undressing me with your eyes!" I said. "In this reality, I'm a total sparrow."

"Sorry," I replied. "You do know I'm bi."

"And *you* do know," she said, "that I've turned down your offers, not your sheets."

"You'll never know you don't like something," I replied, "until you've tried it at least one time."

She cast a frown at me. "My original is in the other room," she said, "near death from some poison from Khattaaara's tail. She—Khattaaara—she's from Rendenaaar, from that third dimension. She's the one behind all the transformations."

I stood up from the bed and then turned away, thinking. "Kind of hard to take all this in at once," I said.

Payton nodded.

"So, who was I before things changed?" I asked.

"I don't know," she replied. "I don't know if we were friends. I don't even know if you existed."

I turned back to face her. "But... how did I get here from another dimension, and how will you... and the other Peyton...

Wait! The other one I remember seeing... She looked younger."

"She's part of the overwrite of this dimension, only she killed herself when she was fourteen, and the Peyton from this dimension's original timeline brought her here through time after she was resurrected."

"God!" I said, "All of this would make a whole lot more sense if it turned out that I was lying in a coma somewhere, after having been hit by a car, and this is all some weird-ass dream."

"It's not a hallucination," she insisted. "All of this is possible because the three of me—the older ones—we're all Quantum Girls."

"Quantum Girls," I repeated. Then she turned into one, right in front of me, the room taking on a strange purple glow. And that was when I fainted.

When I finally came to, I was on the bed again on my back. Payton was sitting on the edge facing me, daubing a cold compress against my forehead. But now there was another person in the room, the younger version of her. My eyes went from one to the other in the half-light.

"This is Sarabeth," Payton announced. "She took the name, to avoid confusion."

"Hello," that one said in a younger Payton voice.

"So, you're the beautiful girl who tried to kill herself," I said.

"Did," came the reply. "But I'm alive again, and there won't be any repeat. I have a lot of friends now, even if some of them are other versions of me." She paused and then went on. "I'd like to be your friend, too, if you'd let me."

"Of course, I will," I replied. "Why don't you sit down on the bed and tell me your story, and later Payton can let me know how she wound up becoming Captain Marvel."

"I'll leave you two alone to talk," Payton said and then she left to go downstairs.

"So, Sarabeth Herron," I said. "Where do you want to begin?"

CHAPTER XI

Peyton

> *From the Original Timeline*
> *In the Alternate Reality*
> *On Earth I*
> *Earth-Date: 2029*

Peyton Herron might have been a wanted woman, guilty without trial of supposedly murdering a federal agent as Quantum Girl, number one on the FBI's most wanted list in the former timeline, but Katara Drall was not and never was. The fact of the matter was that in this new timeline, Katara Drall stood impressive on stilettoes as one of the richest, most powerful women in the world, and I was Katara Drall.

I arrived at the 2029 MET Gala with Mara Delacroix, my occasional girlfriend, who, at twenty-seven still looked fabulous. Granted I was barely pushing nineteen and there was no future in it for us, but with being rich, at least in my case, came the desire to *en*rich, especially with all the shit that had gone on in my life, and, considering all of the unmarked time I had gone through after experiencing the Big Bang, in reality, I was billions of years her senior. Regardless, the two of us strode up the red carpet and its seemingly endless stairs hand in hand; she, wearing a barely covering sheer gown that had sewn on just enough Swarovski crystals to feign modesty, while I myself sported a lipstick red McQueen with a four-foot puffed train, held up by a loop with my left wrist. The neckline, if one may call it that, plunged down past my waist, front and back, while around my throat was wrapped the ruby and diamond necklace by Fred Joaillier, that Julia

Roberts had worn in *Pretty Woman*, that I'd purchased two weeks before for two mill and change.

While the event was ostensibly non-political, the crowd in attendance most assuredly was, and so woke that they could have served as a substitute for caffeine. For myself, I found it all hypocritical—celebrities flying in on private jets with a/c units in their mansions so large they could cool the Gobi desert, causally, and with feigned concern, discussing global warming and climate change. Everyone there, of course, was on the A-List, including me, in that I was affirmatively the wealthiest woman on the planet, having parleyed Dhraaal's millions into more than one hundred billion by stock market purchases carefully made by phasing into the past, and buying significant shares in Amazon, Apple, Google, Starbucks, and Xerox—just to name a few—when they first went public.

The Gala was more of a mug gallery than anything else with nearly everyone vying for photo-ops to be on the web and on the covers of mags hardly any of them would ever buy, but which all displayed so bright and bold at supermarket checkout stands. No one there really cared about anyone but themselves. As for me, I had an agenda. Governments listen to celebrities, no matter how obtuse they are, because they, celebrities, all have their oh-so-influential on-stage personas to compensate for their intellectual deficiencies. The fact was that there needed to be R&D for the Rendenaaaran virus that had yet to hit our world but *would* eventually. Khattaaara had found out how to invade our dimension, and so humanity's very existence lay at stake.

And so, I mingled. I moved around. I had to. I was more than just someone celebrated in this crowd. I represented money and power. I was glommed onto. Everyone wanted a piece of me from the paparazzi, who salivated for photographs, to the producers and directors, who hungered for financing, to the actors and actresses, who would prostitute themselves to be seen with me. And then there was Harvey Weinstein, who had been released from prison on a technicality only a few months earlier, who only wished to fuck me. No photos, no financing, no smothering me, and "What part of 'Get your filthy hands off of me,' didn't you understand, Mr. Weinstein?" Besides, I had a mission.

Thus, I quietly spread the word (but cautioned each one I told to keep it on the down-low) that there was another virus that had just been "accidentally" released from a lab in China called RenTran-26 that was a hundred times more deadly than Covid.

The reaction was mixed, but I managed to stir sufficient panic in enough of them that within two days I was getting calls from Statesmen, as well as various members of the Fourth Estate. The questions were all pretty much the same. *How did I know? Did I have any proof? Who else was in the loop?*

Mara, who apparently began to notice my mingling after she returned from the ladies' room, glided up to me, wrapped her arms around my waist from behind, and whispered to me.

"What's all the jabber about?" she demanded in a pouting voice, as she nibbled at my ear, her other hand sliding down toward the that-which-should-not-be-touched-in-public part of my anatomy.

I gently slapped the back of her hand away, and whispered, "Not here! Not now!"

"The editor from Vanity Fair is over there," she cooed with a stare in that direction, her cheek set against mine. "I want to talk to him about us doing a shoot together. Some high fashion. Some scandalously nude. You don't mind taking your clothes off for the camera, do you? I mean, your body is to die for."

"Tell me about it," I replied with a hint of sarcasm that flew its way right past her.

"Come on, then," she said letting go of my waist, and intertwining one of her arms with mine, lacing our fingers together. "I want to show you off to him."

"You *do* know he's gay?" I said glancing toward her.

"They *all* are, Jellybean. It's so *in* these days. But this is all about the regard." She paused only to turn and stare at me with puppy dog eyes. "Please?" she begged. "Please, please, please. I promise to be beyond attentive to your needs tonight."

I shrugged with the affirmation of a smile, excused myself to the couple I had been speaking with, and then let her lead me to her destination like a young girl being led to her first visit to the gynecologist, only the ob-gyn in question cared absolutely nothing about vaginas; at least not the way Harvey Weinstein did. The man in question—more of an ob-omg—was in fact Aaron Wentworth, the fashionista/editor for Vanity Fair, who was dressed in a tux, the cloth of which was made entirely of sterling silver thread. Wentworth stood around six feet, bleeding fortyish, with chiseled features and slicked-back jet-black hair.

"Darling," Mara cooed at him. "This is my significant, Katara. Don't you just love the name? And look at her. God made her an angel so that we could worship her, although sometimes I think He made her just for me. You should see her naked. I was thinking… the two of us in your December? Haute couture on the cover and naked within. She is, after all, the richest…"

"And you are after all," Wentworth interrupted with a hint of gay affect, "the bitchest."

Mara offered back a scowl worthy of Vivian Leigh in Streetcar. "Surely, Aaron, darling, you don't *mean* that?"

"No, of course not," he replied, his gaze fixed on me. "It is an honor to meet you," he said to me, "I have read so much."

"I try desperately not to live up to my press," I said with a smile.

"We can't pay you anything commensurate to your worth," he said. "But, if you like, we can donate the money to whatever charity you prefer."

"Done," I replied, instantly feeling Mara's fingers tighten

around mine. "I'll have my assistant contact yours on Monday."

"I will consider it a privilege to work with you," he replied. Then he turned to Mara. "You, I will tolerate," to which, in response, Mara stuck out her tongue at him. Then back to me, "She's always been beautiful," he half whispered, loud enough for Mara to hear. "The trouble is, she knows it. But I must be off now. This event," he quietly proclaimed with an upward glance, "is self-reflection at its worst," Then he sighed, "I'm only here to cater to all the narcissists in the room, but my salary forbids me to complain." And, with that, he took his leave to mirror smiles in rooms that were filled with fakery.

"You are so fetching," Mara said squeezing my hand once more. "I am going to totally exhaust you tonight."

"I can't," I said. "Not tonight."

"Tomorrow then," she replied.

"Tomorrow," I agreed.

"Starting with a warm bubble bath together."

"And champagne," I added, "but I have some work to do during the day." The work had to do with preparing for the other Khattaaara. Mara Delacroix had not the hint of a clue that I was Quantum Girl and I intended to keep it that way— sometime lover or not. All that aside, I wasn't quite sure which direction I wanted my future to take. Immortality can have its regrets, and I wanted as few of them as possible.

CHAPTER XII

Dark God

> *From the Altered Timeline*
> *In the Alternate Reality*
> *On Earth I*
> *Earth-Date: 2025*

The illusion that was my costume covered my body up to my chin in shiny black, snakelike scales. Having projected myself far above the Earth, I stared at the sun and then at the stars. One day, all of this would be mine—all of the universe for all time.

From where I floated in space, the Earth looked fragile and small. It was as though if I reached out my arms, I could crush it and all of its inhabitants in my fist. How would they react if I did, I wondered? Like ants, scurrying around after someone disturbed their nest? Or would they try and attack, like a swarm of bees, whose hive has been disturbed, prepared to give up their lives to protect their queen?

The only one who stood in my way was Quantum Girl who might or might not have been the one who called herself *Zhaaagur Scraaa* back on Rendenaaar. Regardless, I needed to eliminate her but to do so, I had to find her first. Theresa had said that she met up with Quantum Girl the day she resurrected Peyton Herron but she never told me just when that had occurred. My only thought was to go to the cemetery the day she showed up at my home and let time unfold around me.

Nothing much changes at a cemetery, even when viewed in reverse. A few scattered mourners come and go every day, walking backward. A grave is undug and then the casket it holds is lifted from the ground and placed back in a hearse that is driven back toward the mortuary from which it came. The sun and moon arc across the sky from west to east. Trees pull back their leaves into their branches. Withered flowers, left on graves, spring back into life, to be taken away by the grieving, whose tears stream back into their eyes. This was how it went: day after day, night after night, until *kaboom*! Dirt and broken headstones came crashing down onto the ground, to be restored to the restful setting that once had been. This was the moment. This was where Quantum Girl had to have been. And so I went forward in time. Shrouded in the dust that filled the air were three figures: Theresa (unconscious)... Peyton Herron, brought back from the grave, and Quantum Girl! I was tempted to synchronize my motion through time with theirs and battle her there and then, but I feared the consequences of altering this timeline to one where I would never have gotten the stone. Instead, I chose to follow her, as she projected herself to the Herron home, watching invisibly until, to my great surprise, she changed into an older version of Peyton Herron! *What the hell!* I thought to myself. *What the hell! If she was Peyton Herron, who the fuck was the girl in the bedroom who looked just like her?* Words listened to at accelerated speed are like trying to make sense of the buzzing of a fly in the room with you. But by brief pauses, I learned that this was an alternate timeline and that the Quantum Girl Peyton was from the original one. That brought sense to all the ramblings that had come from Theresa about seeing another version of herself. So, she wasn't batshit insane. Fuck! But as I accelerated through time there, to see what would eventually happen, suddenly both of them—both Peytons—were gone!

Following the thread brought me four years into the future, but I overshot just a bit to their bedroom, Peyton's and Phoebe's or whatever the hell her name was. But where there were two of her before, now there were four, three of whom were Quantum

Girls; not the same one split into three, but each with a different quantum thread. It was all confusing. All I was certain of was that I had to think things through before formulating a plan of attack.

I projected myself back home after that; home in this future time. The house, however, was in shambles. Abandoned for four years, it had been turned into a haven for the homeless. Most everything was dirty or torn up. There was the repugnant smell of human feces. Upstairs, the bedrooms, as well as the maid's quarters, were filled with vagrants—drug addicts and alcoholics. There was even the stench of a dead body that had been dragged to my parents' bathroom and dumped face-up in the tub. The fetor was unimaginable, especially to my now heightened senses. I shook my head in anger, turned back into as much of Daisy McKenzie as I could, and then strode out of the bathroom, out of my parents' room, and into my own, where there was a naked black man in his late twenties fucking a pretty, blonde, emaciated white girl, who appeared to be perhaps eleven or twelve years old, her pupils so dilated I could barely make out the color of her eyes. Whatever the alien in me thought about this situation, the human part of me flew into a rage. I jumped onto the man's back and plunged my fingernails into his eyes, blinding him. The man screamed, lifted himself up, and tried to pull me off, whereupon I twisted around to face him and then plunged the fang of my *yaaargh* through the back of his neck to have it emerge out the back of his throat. Beyond him gagging, within seconds, the venom paralyzed him, at which point he dropped to the floor in a heap. Empty sockets stared up at me as I dematerialized the illusion of my clothes, and stood above him, revealing myself as the alien-human hybrid that I now was. I pulled back my hair to reveal my pointed ears. Then I hissed at him like a cat ready to pounce. "Dost thou believe in God?" I spat at him all so Biblically. "My father is Lucifer, Lord of Darkness, and thou shalt spend eternity in Hell!" And with those words, I projected him into orbit above the Earth. *Let future astronauts find his miserable corpse!* I thought to myself. That done, creating the illusion once more of human clothes, I went over to the girl, turned her light as a feather, lifted her into my arms, and projected us both to the Cedars-Sinai emergency room, where I left her in the care of the staff.

"You'll be all right now," I said to her before I left. "And if anything goes wrong, you say the name Dark God to yourself, and I'll hear you. Do you understand?" Drugged though she was, she nodded her head. "No one will ever hurt you again." Then I gently squeezed her hand, kissed her forehead, and vanished before her eyes.

Back to the house. Room by room, I projected each and every one to the Pentagon; all of them, alive and dead. Let the military brass deal with them and try to figure out how they got there! *O Ye of great esteem, let ye solve the problem of homelessness when it lands smack dab in your backyard!* I laughed out loud at the very thought!

All of that aside, my house—my home—was a disaster. There were hypodermic needles scattered all about, human excrement, trash, graffiti on the walls, broken dishes, and destroyed rare antiques. *Fuck it, I thought to myself,* and so I just left—walked out as casually as could be, morphing into Dark God as I did— and caused the entire building to implode behind me, swallowed up into a microscopic black hole. A subtle smile of satisfaction on my face, I went half a year into the past, scoured the Internet for a cool place for sale to live, and then projected myself back to the present to the downtown loft that I determined I would buy six months ago.

I'd gotten used to time travel by then. The place was furnished to my liking, all by me. I would, of course, go back into the past and buy it and then hire some decorators to remodel and furnish the place. But that was for tomorrow or the day after that. For the moment, I settled myself into a nice warm bubble bath, dried myself off, fell onto my silken bed, and, with the help of that newfound *tail* of mine, fucked myself to sleep. Traveling back again in time to make all this happen would come sometime the next day—after a blissful sleep!

CHAPTER XIII

Sarabeth

From the Altered Timeline
In the Alternate Reality
On Earth I
Earth-Date: 2029

Hello. Some of you may know me. Some may have seen me in the halls or in class. I'm fairly new to this school. My name is Sarabeth Herron, and I just did something that, hopefully, will turn into something good. I started what I call the Live Again Movement here at Brighton [23] *The Live Movement is for those teens who have thought about ending their own lives. I started it because four years ago, my would-now-have-been older cousin, took her own life. Her name was Peyton. She was fourteen years old, the same age as I am now. I followed in her footsteps. It was a hard, bad decision but I'll get to that in just a bit.*

Some people might think that a fourteen-year-old is not one to give advice, but I've been there myself and had those same thoughts. I know what it's like to feel so alone that you go to bed wondering why you were ever born. I know what it's like to feel so desperate that you take a razorblade to your arm and cut through your skin just to feel something that isn't emotional pain. Nearly a quarter of all American teens and young adults contemplate suicide. Roughly fourteen out of every hundred thousand succeed in taking their own lives. More girls attempt suicide than boys, but more boys wind up actually taking their own lives than girls. Think about it. If you're a teen and you're

---

[23] This was the speech given at my new high school.

with three of your friends, chances are that one of you has seriously thought about ending your own life.

I grew up in a good home with loving parents, I had a good childhood. I didn't want for anything, but I wasn't spoiled by any means. And then it happened. I was bullied. It hit me like a bolt from the blue. Well, actually, the bolt was orange in the shape of a basketball that had been hurled at my head by the girl who was bullying me. I won't tell you her name, but the basketball was a Spaulding.

When you're a small child, when something's wrong, you go to your parents for help and protection. But when you get older, you feel that it's expected of you to handle things yourself. Parents often don't see the warning signs. Mine didn't. They didn't know until it was too late. I took my life by hanging. I didn't say almost. According to the paramedics, I was clinically dead, before I was brought back to life. And, let me tell you, dying isn't easy. Your mind may decide that it wants to end things, but your body will fight against it. Your heart will want to continue to pump. Your lungs will want to continue to breathe. Hanging myself was the most painful experience I have ever had to endure. I still have scars around my neck from the rope. And when I finally blacked out, there was no white light. There was no music or angels welcoming me to Heaven. There was nothing. It was like I'd been knocked unconscious. Not even the hint of a dream. Death is like that. But when you kill yourself, it isn't just about you. It's about everyone who knows you—everyone who loves you even though you think they don't when they do, and it leaves them with scars.

It would be great if everyone had a crystal ball to be able to see what would happen—what the effect on their family and friends would be-if they died. Perhaps that would make them think twice.

I want each of you to look around the auditorium and realize that a quarter of you, and maybe you yourself, has at some point *wanted to die. But I want you to do something for me. I want you to believe that it isn't just one-fourth of everyone, but everyone, and I want you to turn to the person next to you and say, "I want you to live," and I want you to mean it. And if you don't know the person sitting beside you, I want you to introduce yourself right now, and say, 'I'm John or I'm Heather or I'm Bill or I'm Jane, and I'm here for you no matter what, and I want you to mean that, too, because each of us is different and unique and special, and whether you believe that we're here on this Earth because of God or Nature, life is precious and irreplaceable. Trust me, I know, because I nearly caused my life to be taken away. You just need to understand that in this life and on this planet and in this universe, there is no one else like us, and there never will be. Maybe you're not the most beautiful or the most handsome or the most athletic or the smartest or the most popular. None of that matters. All you need to be is the most giving, the most understanding, and the most kind. We need to love our commonalities and cherish our differences. Think of us all as snowflakes, each made of the same stuff, but unique, and that's what makes us special. We need to work together, because—we, you and I and everyone on this planet—we're all in this world together, and each other is all we've got.*

CHAPTER XIV

Claire (from Earth II)

*From the Altered Timeline
In the Alternate Reality
On Earth I
Earth-Date: 2029*

I felt so alone. Gods only knew what had happened to my parents. Liam was gone from my life. My world had been taken over by aliens from some distant past from another dimension. My best friend was now a super being. Mr. and Mrs. Herron were here with me and I knew they loved me and had wanted Liam and me to get married and there was the grandchild they thought they would have. But now it just seemed awkward since our relationship had broken down and I'd lost the baby. Meanwhile, the alternate Payton was still in a coma, and I know they were torn about how they were supposed to feel about *her*. I mean, she wasn't the daughter they'd raised because reality had changed, but she was identical to my Payton—their Payton—and how could they *not* feel her pain?

This was not the time to go to them for comfort, and Payton, my Payton, was busy trying to rescue Liam and save our world with the Peyton from this dimension and with Ophelia's grown-up daughter from the past. Added to the mix was the other set of Herron parents and Sarabeth, Peyton's younger self, who physically reminded me so much of what Payton was like when she was that age, but in terms of personality, was a totally different girl. All told, it was enough to make one's head spin.

I had to get out of the house for a while if only just to clear my head. Normally, whenever I would become upset, I would pick up a book to read, but in this dimension, everything was backwards, so that reading was too much of a chore.

I went out and just started walking. It was late afternoon. The air was brisk and sent a chill through the sweatshirt I had on, enough so that I pulled the hood up over my head. It was Superman blue and had the large UCLA letters sewn on the back. It was Ophelia's but just like the one Liam had that I often borrowed when he was off somewhere, just to make me feel as though he were near. I really wasn't paying attention to where I was headed or, maybe, subconsciously I was, as when I finally awakened from the reverie I was in, I found myself back in my old neighborhood. *My parents' home would be only a few blocks away*, I thought, *if both dimensions were the same.*

My pace quickened as I walked the four blocks to Euclid Street, where I had grown up. It was getting dark by the time I finally arrived at what in my dimension had been my home. I stopped in front of it—the exact same house, with the same white stucco front, the same red tile roof, and the same curtains in the window, through which I could see that the lights inside were on. Taking one long deep breath, I walked toward the front door, ascended the two stairs to the wooden porch, bared my knuckles, and then knocked on the door. Surprisingly, a young girl, perhaps twelve years old, answered, looked up at me, grabbed my hand, and pulling me inside.

"Mona is so upset with you," she said with an Aussie accent. "All the guests are here." She looked me up and down. "Why on earth are you dressed like that? Come on!" she insisted, dragging me by the hand toward what in both dimensions was my bedroom. She half glanced back at me as we went. "You *did* remember to pick up the tickets? I told all my friends we were going to go."

Once in the room, she shut the door, marched to the closet, and picked out a pink chiffon dress, which she handed to me.

"Off with that rag," she ordered, and so I pulled it off, over my head, and then handed it to her. She held it out at arm's length, staring at the university letters on the back. "Ucla!" she groaned, pronouncing the letters as though they were a word. "Uh! I intend to go to Smith after high school!" She sniffed the sweatshirt, made a face, held it out and away from herself as far as she could with her index finger and thumb, and let it drop unceremoniously to the floor. Then she turned back to me.

"Oh, my God!" she exclaimed. "Just look at your hair. Sit down at your dresser, and I'll fix it. Did *you* just come from a football game? Honestly, what would you ever do without me?"

And so I sat on the dresser chair, facing the wood-framed mirror that hung over it, watching as the girl began first brushing my hair and then maneuvering it this way and that by means of a rat-tail comb.

"Seriously, I know that you're head over heels about Ryan Scofield, but this is Mom and Dad's silver, and the very least you could do is show up on time and groomed."

"And just *who* are you?" I asked.

"Very funny!" came the reply. "I am her Serene Highness, Chloë Anne Salinger if you must know. And you, older sister, if I don't manage to get you looking royal..." at which point she tugged at my hair.

"Owww!" came my reply.

"will be summarily removed," she went on, tugging this way and that, "from the line of succession, leaving me and my progeny the obligation of carrying on the Salinger name. Matriarchs that we are, my husband and future servant will be obligated to take on *my* last name rather than I his. There!" she concluded, setting down her tools, and admiring her work. "The make-up will have to do. Now, get into your dress. And you might want to do a pit stop with some roll-on. We don't want a reputation. I'll be out on the patio," (she paused for a deep sigh) "making excuses as usual!" And with that she left the room, shutting the door behind her. Then, through the door, I heard her shout, "And kindly step into the dress. Don't pull it on over your head, so you don't mess up your hair!"

As I began putting on the dress, I paused. Everything *wasn't* the same. Most of the people were, I guess, but there were differences. My mother had gotten pregnant when I was seven years old, but then she and Dad were in a car accident, and she'd lost the baby she'd been carrying. But not on this world. In this dimension, maybe the accident wasn't as severe, or perhaps it hadn't happened at all. They might have left the house just ten seconds later and avoided it entirely, and so Chloë'd been born. I'd never had a little sister. Precocious thing, this one. But I wondered to myself, why did she have an Australian accent, and where was the other me?

There were about twenty people in attendance, most of whom I knew as friends of my parents, but there were also a few strange faces. The patio was lit with Japanese lanterns, and there was a table that had been set up with food off to one side. Many of the attendees had drinks in their hands. I'm not sure if any were alcoholic, as Dad had had a problem with it back in the day, and having alcohol available to a recovering alcoholic would have been bad form. It was Mona, my mom's best friend, who came over to me as I appeared, greeting me with what I would call half a hug. Drink in hand, her arms made a small gesture to embrace me, just grazing my arm, as she was careful not to drop or spill the food or liquid in her grasp.

"Claire," she proclaimed in a somewhat graveled voice that boasted years of cigarette consumption, "you look absolutely radiant!" Then she turned to a woman, who stood talking to a couple of men about ten feet away. "Francie, come over here and meet Ed and Joanne's oldest child. What *am* I saying?" she added as the woman drew near. "She's a grown woman now." She threw a smile at me and then turned to the woman as she came over. "Isn't she just ravishing?" she said to me then added, "Your parents must be so proud!"

Suddenly, there was the sound of a car pulling up into the driveway. "Quiet everyone," Mona cautioned the crowd. "The guests of honor are about to arrive."

We could hear a car door slam once and then again. There was the click of the front door lock opening. It was Chloë, who met her parents as they came in and then urged them out to the patio. The lights that had been briefly unplugged went on again, and all who had been waiting yelled out, "Surprise!"

I don't know whether the reaction from my parallel's parents was genuine or feigned, but there came smiles and a din of congratulations and good feelings all around. Dick Waldman, one of my father's coworkers came up and slapped him on the back.

"Well, man," he said all so jovial. "Twenty-five years in the ring! Only fifty more rounds to go!"

"This was all Chloë's idea!" Mona told Mrs. Salinger. Chloë smiled broadly and received a hug from her mother in return.

"Claire helped!" Chloë said looking up at her.

Mrs. Salinger looked over at me as I stood watching and then mouthed, "Thank you," invoking a nod from me in return. Suddenly, there was the sound of the sliding door being opened. "What's going on?" one voice said, followed by, "Who is *she*?" at which point silence muffled the air, for there, not ten feet away stood the other Claire Salinger, the one from *this* world, wearing a blue silk dress, her hair caught up in a top knot.

It was a jaw-dropping moment. Everyone in the room stared at the two of us, as the glass fell from Mona's hand, and went crashing down onto the patio. The other Claire walked over to me and looked me up and down. I remember how we stared at each other, neither of us taking our eyes off the other.

"Mom?" I heard Chloë say, at which point her mother pulled

69

her in closer.

"Who the fuck are *you*?" the other Claire shouted. The guests at this point all began to whisper amongst themselves.

"I can explain," I said defensively. "Can we go inside and talk?"

"No!" my doppelgänger shouted, or was it me who was the doppelgänger to her? "I want to know now, *right* now!" she screamed. "Who the fuck *are* you?"

It was at this point that I just felt cornered. "I'm from a parallel world," I said.

"Bullshit!" my lookalike screamed. She then began to circle around me, looking me up and down. "What?" she announced. "Did you see my posts on TicTok, and decided to try and take over my life because you *look* like me? Between you and me, I'm much prettier!"

She took a hold of the hem of the dress I was wearing and lifted it up. I immediately pushed it back down. "I'm telling you the truth," I said as I looked from her to Chloë, who clung to her mother.

"You are *so* naïve!" the other Claire laughed. Then she turned to the rest of those there. "You are all so fucking naïve!" Suddenly, in front of everyone, another figure began to emerge from her, literally pulling out of her, as though she were a breakaway suit. The figure, that emerged was Khattaaara! The other Claire appeared utterly spent from the ordeal, and dropped to her knees, catching herself with her left arm. It was at that point that Chloë ran up to her and embraced her. Khattaaara then turned toward me.

"Did you think you could escape so easily?" she laughed. "You were a Rend once, and you loved it!" Then looked up at the crowd, "You! Every one of you shall people this world with my kind!"

All of them watched in abject horror, as she then lifted her tail—her *yaaargh*— from which a blue mist began to appear, as it moved this way and that, dispersing it in all directions. Then she vanished into thin air.

"Hold your breath," I told Chloë and the other Claire. Then urged Claire up to her feet and the three of us rushed back through the sliding doors and out the front door. Finally, when we made it as far as the middle of the street, the breaths we had held, burst from our lungs. It was then that Chloë pulled away from both of us.

"What's happening?" she screamed, as tears gushed from her eyes.

The other Claire looked first at her and then at me. "I'd just picked up my dress, and figured I'd use their change room to save time, when *it* appeared."

"Khattaaara," I interjected.

"She knew my name," the other Claire went on. "I guess she thought I was you. Then she merged into me, but it was like I was trapped inside *her*."

"I'm going back to find Mom and Dad!" Chloë sobbed.

"No," the other Claire and I cried out as though with one voice.

"They're gone!" the other Claire said.

"What do you mean they're gone!" Chloë sobbed out.

"I shared her mind," the other Claire said, glancing at me. "She, it, whatever, is from some other universe from some parallel dimension. She's here to turn us all into beings like her."

"I know," I replied.

"So what are we going to do?" Chloë sobbed, her cheeks wet with tears. Her sister walked over to her and held her to calm her down.

"We'll figure something out," she assured her.

"I know a place we can go," I said, "but it's a bit of a walk from here."

"We can take my car," the other Claire said as she reached into the small clutch that she had been holding all along, took out her keys, and tossed them to me. "You drive," she said. "We'll ride in back."

CHAPTER XV

Payton

From the Original Timeline
In the Alternate Reality
On Earth II
Earth-Date: 2029

It seemed like there was no way out of this situation. I had no idea how to escape this labor camp or the body I was now in. And if the work wasn't bad enough, it began to pour rain during the work shift. The rain, in turn, turned the dirt into slippery mud, which made it difficult to maintain a foothold. Had I been on the ground, it would have been difficult enough, but I, like many others, was sent to work on one of the elevated rows of the mine. As it was, nearly half a dozen men had slipped and fallen, either to their death or were crippled and then shot by the guards. I had no idea where that place was, but most of the work slaves were Americans.

Each of the workers was given a pickax and a canvas knapsack. Ore found was placed in the sack. When a sack was full, the man who owned it would shout out for permission to carry it over to a low-set open train car to empty it. Whenever I had filled mine, I would turn to the nearest guard, and call out, "Sack off, Boss!" to which the guard responded, "Sack off!" at which time I headed for the nearest train car. The filled sacks were quite heavy, perhaps a hundred pounds, and were carried by slinging them over one's back, emphasizing the fact that this was backbreaking work.

After dumping the ore, as I turned around to return, my foot splashed in a shallow pool of water caused by the rain. Lifting my foot out from the puddle, as the ripples in it began to settle, I could see my reflection. Cautiously, I bent down, pretending to tie my boot. As I stared at the now-still water, my heart stopped. The face that stared back up at me was Liam's! How it had happened that my mind had occupied his body I did not know. Or why? As the guard called out to me to get back to work, as I rose once more to my feet, a sigh of relief rippled through my brain. No matter what had happened to put me here, at least I knew he was alive. Mom and Dad were safe on Peyton's Earth, and Liam was alive! But where in Gods' names was his consciousness? *And where in the world was this place,* I wondered, *so that I could rescue him when and if my spirit returns back to my physical form?* I had to find out. I had to know.

How does one communicate with someone who doesn't speak one's language? How does one communicate with the deaf and dumb? All three of those attributes described the girl I had tried to save. I had no idea how she had lost her ability to hear or to speak. I had seen her read the lips of the other Chinese around her, as well as those of the guards, but English was all too foreign to her, and I spoke not a single word of Chinese. I named her Jasmine because that was what her skin smelled like to me.

Jasmine was a gentle creature, and I began to gradually fall in love with her. Every night, she came back to my cot and laid down beside me, and every night I made love to her. She appeared to be around my age, perhaps a slight bit younger, maybe sixteen or seventeen, but love knows neither age nor words. Despite that the nights were cold, her naked flesh felt warm against mine. Her body was soft like velvet, as were her lips, but my fingers read the pain she had suffered at the hands of her masters. Ripples of scars on her back defiled her otherwise smooth skin; the marks of whips that had cracked down upon her, had, undoubtedly, when they were inflicted, produced wounds of unbearable pain to an innocent, who could not scream.

To love someone is to need them. To love someone is to want them. To love someone is to realize that their life is more important to you than your own. My heart pounded in my chest when her breast lay against mine. My sex grew emboldened when I tasted hers. She had become my hedge against insanity in the madness of this world, and the drudgery of the days was lessened by the thought of her there by my side at night. Her kisses imbued new strength in me. Her breath awakened my soul. But I needed something more. I needed to know where I was so that if my mind ever left his body I could find him. I needed to ask her, but she was both deaf and dumb, so it became a matter of how.

Having given it much thought, as she lay on her back beside me, I drew a circle on her stomach and she laughed her silent laugh. But I held up my hand, splayed out my fingers, and widened my eyes a bit. Even in the half-light to which our vision had become accustomed, she could see that this was something even more serious than our love. She stared at me with intensity and then shook her head. Then she propped herself up just a bit. Again, I drew the circle around her belly, pointed to the ground, and then looked in all directions. The abilities to hear or speak are not indicators of intelligence. Jasmine was a smart girl—smarter than most, I would think. She mouthed the word, Congo. Then she mouthed Lubumbashi, which turned out to be a city there. I smiled at her, kissed her, and then held her in my arms. When the night had nearly gone, as always, she rose from the bed, donned her shirt and slacks once more, and disappeared into the distance of the room. In a few more moments, I fell fast asleep. It was nearly two months later when I was out again working the mine, thankfully cooled by some passing clouds, that everything began to spin. A moment later, the world around me went dark.

I awakened alone in the guest room in Peyton's house. It was night and the lights were out. I was dressed in pajamas that, along with the sheets I lay on, were drenched in sweat. I rose from the bed, dragged myself to the bathroom, stripped, and then stared at my reflection in the mirror above the sink. I was me again. I turned on the faucet in the tub, pulled up the lever to turn on the shower, and then stepped in. The warm water beaded down on me, on my head, on my breasts, and on my back. After six months of having to endure the stink of my own flesh, it was like dying and ascending to Heaven. *Poor Liam*, I thought to myself. *I have defiled his body with a stranger of a girl*. But he was my twin brother. I'm sure he would understand. I turned off the water reluctantly, dried myself with a towel, turned into Quantum Girl, and then phased to Peyton's bedroom in her estate. Peyton sleepily opened her eyes, as the purple light from my glow filled the room. She saw me and instantly sat up.

"Oh my God!" she exclaimed. "You're ok! We thought we'd lost you."

"I know," I said. "It's been so many months."

"What do you mean?" Peyton replied. "Khattaaara just stung you yesterday!"

"Not for me," I said. "It's been half a year and more. But I found Liam. I know where he is. My mind was in his body. I just have to follow the quantum trail to the moment that I left."

"I'll go with you," she said starting to rise from the bed.

"No need," I replied. "I'm Quantum Girl again. I can find him and bring him back. But I want to get something to eat first, and I have to catch my breath."

CHAPTER XVI

Jordan

From the Original Timeline
In the Alternate Reality
On Earth I
Earth Date: 2029

The fact was that I only had one living relative in the new timeline and that was my Aunt Peyton, who at the time was actually a few years younger than me—at least physically. The Katherine and James Herron of that world were both from the rewrite and had no recollection of either her or my mother, who had been murdered a trillion or more universes ago. For the most part, I felt disconnected, and I could only imagine how Aunt Peyton felt when she returned to a world that did not remember her. I suppose there was an upside for her, though, as with the restricted timeline, she was no longer a fugitive from the law, and, aside from our immediate family. no one had ever heard of Quantum Girl, so she remained Earth's secret weapon. On the other hand, my somewhat cousin, Thara-Klo, never survived childhood on Rendenaaar to have, as an adult, traveled to this universe.

Aunt Peyton, as my supposed younger sister, Katara, had put me up at her mansion. The Herron home was by then all too crowded, and I had nowhere else to go. We had pleasant conversations, sister Katara and I, interspersed with plans of action for how we were going to save our world and Payton's from her namesake from Earth III.

"It's hard for me to conceive," she admitted, "that your mother was forty-two years old when you left—when she died."

"She missed you," I told her. "Of all those in her past, she missed *you* the most."

"I've missed her, too," she replied and then asked, "Why didn't you ever cure your mother the way you cured Claire?"

"I couldn't reverse time around her," I explained, "when that spacetime was in a universe that had yet to exist."

"I intended to go back just after I had left her and you," she replied, "but even if the two of us went back together now, restoring her would create a paradox and perhaps an irresolvable loop in quantum time. My poor, poor sister. I feel that it's all my fault. If I hadn't hanged myself…"

"Then you would never have become Quantum Girl," I replied, "my mother and father would never have met and fallen in love, and I would never have been born—at least that's what my mother said."

"Still," she sighed, "I feel responsible for everything that's gone on."

"Don't be," I told her. Then I used a new power that I had learned.

CHAPTER XVII

Peyton

> *From the Original Timeline*
> *In the Imagined Timeline*
> *On Earth I*
> *Earth-Date: 2025*

I had been talking to Jordan in my library when all at once I was back in my old bedroom. It was morning, and my head was filled with sleep. Suddenly, I felt the side of my bed tilt downward just a bit. I looked up to see Phee sitting on the edge of the mattress facing me. *My God!* I thought to myself. *She's fourteen again! And human!*

"Happy Birthday!" she exclaimed in her inimitable way.

"Thank you, I think," I said totally confused. I stretched out my arms. "What year is it?" I went on.

"It's fourteen years after we were born," she said seeming exasperated. "What universe did *you* just wake up from?"

"Hopefully, not the one with Rendenaaar," I said back.

"What the heck is Ren*dar*in?" she replied. "Anyway, I have your present!" she went on, all so enthusiastic. That was how Phee used to be. But where the hell was I? I wondered. I sat up in bed, still trying to focus. Phee held out a small box in her hands.

"Happy birthday!" she repeated.

I took the box from her with a smile—the same box she had given me before on my other fourteenth birthday, strange to say.

"Open it!" she insisted.

"Just a sec," I replied, "I need to pee." Then I jumped out of bed and rushed to the bathroom, closing the door behind me.

Inside, I stared at myself in the mirror. The image that stared back at me was fourteen years old. I couldn't believe my eyes. I touched my face to check if it was real. Then I stretched out the neckline of my nightgown and stared down at breasts that had not yet blossomed, so to speak.

"What are you doing in there?" Phee called out from the bedroom.

"I'm almost done," I called back. Then I flushed the toilet and went back into the bedroom.

"You need to stop drinking so much before you go to bed," Phee admonished. "Will you open your present now?"

"Of course," I said with a smile.

I went over to the bed and picked it up. It was wrapped in the same black paper as before with the same silver and gold stars, once again neatly tied with a braided silver cord.

"Read the card first!" she exclaimed. Her voice—her words—were an echo from the past. Once again, I pried loose the gold foil seal and then pulled out the card on which she had written, "Happy Fourteen! To the best twin sister ever!" I looked up at her and smiled with a hint of tears. God, I loved her so much! I opened the box to reveal once again the meteorite. "Thank you, thank you, thank you," I said. I paused and then announced, "Your present's in the closet in my change bag." *If things are still the same*, I remember thinking.

Phee rushed to the closet and emerged a moment later with a somewhat large box that I'd wrapped in handmade paper that was colored red, white, and blue with gold splatting. She laid it on her bed. First, of course, she picked up the blue envelope and then took out the card inside that was decorated with plastic jewels. Opening it up, she read it aloud. "Happy Birthday to my Phee-nominal sib. Love Peyton." Then she turned and hugged me. That hadn't happened last time.

Suddenly, we heard Mom calling us from downstairs.

"Peyton! Ophelia! Breakfast!"

"Coming!" Phee called out as she turned her attention back to her gift, carefully opening it, so as not to damage the wrapping. Phee was OCD about things like that and had kept all of the paper from all of the gifts she had ever received from age five, stored in a black artist's folder that she slid under her bed. Inside the box I'd given her was a realistic, hand-painted statue of Gal Gadot as Wonder Woman, sword and shield in hand, golden lasso at her side. Phee was the ultimate Wonder Woman fan. She would have been her if she could have. Alas, she wound up with Quantum Girl for a sister instead, which, in another four years would mark her emotional and physical doom. But she was so happy and so beautiful at that moment. She took the statue out of its box, stared at it as she sat on her bed, and started to cry.

"What's wrong?" I asked.

"Nothing!" she wept. "But all I got you was some stupid rock!"

"What do you mean?" I said kneeling down before her. "That *rock* is older than the Earth. It came from outer space; maybe the asteroid belt. It's probably four billion years old!" I opened the hand that still clutched it to show her.

"Really!" she said through her tears.

"It's the best present I ever had!" I assured her.

"The man in the store," she replied, "said it might be from Mars."

"I don't know," I said and smiled. "It's been a while since I've been there."

A laugh burst from her lips.

Then came Mom's voice again, echoing through the halls. "Peyton! Ophelia! Come down now!"

"We're on our way!" I shouted and then rolled my eyes at Phee. "Come on," I said, knowing what was about to come next. "We don't want to keep Ma*ma* and Pa*pa* waiting!"

"No, we don't," she said so Bette Davis-like. I remembered that we had watched *All About Eve* the night before. We both went downstairs together, holding hands, to the kitchen where at least Phee was greeted with the surprise that I already knew about from my previous go-round. Mom and Dad were there along with a cake with candles that read, "Happy Birthday, Ophelia and Peyton!" It was the same cake as before—white with blue icing— quite delicious, as I remember, especially for breakfast. And they say you can't have your cake and eat it, too! What do *they* know? We both blew out the candles at the same time. I watched again, as Phee closed her eyes so tight, making her wish. I wondered before what it was. This time I asked.

"I know you're not supposed to tell," she said, "but I guess it's all right since we're twins. I wished that Theresa the Terrible would stop bullying you."

"Don't worry," I assured her. "I know how to take care of her violent streak."

School was as I had remembered it, though I failed miserably on a pop quiz that Mr. Chatterjee handed out in physics class. If I had had my quantum powers, it would have been a snap, but I was just Peyton Herron again. At gym class, there was a redo of basketball although this time, when Theresa Martinez hurled the ball at my head, knowing that it was coming, I caught it.

"Bitch!" she spat at me, as she came up to me, and took the projectile from my hands.

"After school," I said back. "Just you and me. In back."

"Fine!" she sprewed out in anger. "That's when I'll be able to bounce your head off the blacktop!"

When school let out, I met her outside. Everyone always left through the front. No one else was around. Theresa came up close to me and then pushed me with the palms of her hands.

"Wait!" I said and then walked up to her, our faces inches apart.

"You plan on chickening out like the bird you are, *Herron*?" she asked.

"No," I replied.

"Then what?" she said. We were so close I could feel her breath on my cheeks.

"Just this," I replied and I moved in close and kissed her on the lips. Her eyes went wide, but she kissed me back. Her arms gripped my shoulder. I could taste her tongue in my mouth. A minute or maybe two, the kiss ended, both of us breathless.

"Look," I said. "I'm not into girls. At least not the way you want. But I want to be friends. Is that okay?"

"How did you know?" she asked, dumbfounded.

"I just did," I said. "Is it okay?" I asked again. "I mean, I think you're beautiful and all, and maybe we can mess around once in a while, but I'm not a total…"

"Dyke," she interrupted. "I get it. Okay. I'm sorry about all I put you through." Then she extended her hand toward me, which I took.

"How about lunch tomorrow in the cafeteria?" I asked.

"Your sister, she's not going to pounce on me?" came the reply.

"I'll clue her in on the truce," I assured her.

"You're a strange one," she said after staring hard at me. "I never figured you as bi."

"People change with time," I told her, "and I've had a long time to change. Today's my birthday. Wish me Happy Birthday."

"I'd do more than that," she replied, "if you'll ever let me."

This was the Theresa I'd eventually gotten to know. This was a different timeline, a different existence. I had no superpowers; at least not yet, but I wondered where things would go from there in that things had changed.

CHAPTER XVIII

Khattaaara/Payton

> *Payton from the Original Timeline*
> *In the Rewritten Timeline*
> *On Rendenaaar*
> *Trillions of Universes in the Past*

The battle for Rendenaaar was fought from the sky. It was a legion of Gaaalthaaaran Quantum Girls battling against Dargra-Tol. As was the case with Thara-Klo on Earth, she did not appear to have the ability to duplicate herself, but she could morph into anything or anyone she chose. The reason was that shortly after Ophelia had arrived, Dargra-Tol disguised herself as her. I was at dance practice, when who I thought was Ophelia appeared.

"I was bored," she said, "so I decided to come here to watch thee perform."

"I welcome thy audience," I said back to her and then added, "but prithee, where is Jordan?" I glanced around the room. "I see her not," I proclaimed.

"What dost thou mean?" Ophelia answered in Gaaalthaaaran. "The babe is here in my arms."

Then, all at once, it seemed, her arms were cradling Jordan. The only problem was that Ophelia did not speak Gaaalthaaaran; at least not at that time.

"How didst thou come hither?" I asked. "The god-stones have been purloined, and no longer allow teleportation."

"I chose to walk," she replied.

"On foot?" I inquired with feigned astonishment. "Of a certain, thou must be tired, for the distance is more than eighty *ghov.*"[24]

Realizing that she had been discovered, the child disappeared from her arms, and what had only an instant before appeared to be Ophelia, changed into Dargra-Tol. As there were others around, I immediately phased back home to make certain that Ophelia and Jordan were all right and then phased the three of us to the then-deserted palace, a short distance removed from where we needed to be, to make certain that we were, in fact, alone and in no danger from any *Thaaagran* stragglers. Safe to say, there were none, nor any other Gaaalthaaarans than myself, a fact that pierced me down to my very soul.

It was strange to see the ancient building devoid of every living person but us. The polished granite walls, stained with eons of history, echoed our passage down the Great Corridor. Huge marble statues lined the walls with the likeness of great personages in every direction. At one end, the path down which I led Ophelia, were the crystal thrones of the Divine Emperor and Empress. On either side stood likenesses of the first of our line, who had brought peace and rule to our civilization more than twelve thousand cycles ago. To the left was Paolondaaar the Uniter, while to the right, Gatharnaaara, his consort. The two semblances of our civilization's founders each stared out through sightless eyes perhaps one hundred feet above the floor, while the rest of my ancestors filled the empty corridor behind them, each generation of emperor and empress, shoulder to shoulder and hand in hand, farther back then the eye could see. The stone effigies of my parents stood at the very end, far in the distance. To think, had things gone differently, behind them would have been carved likenesses of Dhraaal and myself, and, behind us, in time, ones of Thara-Klo and whoever she would have chosen as her mate.

Whereas the floor near the thrones was made of dull granite,

---

[24] A *ghov* was a unit of measurement equal to about seven miles.

the rest was made of glass or crystal or diamond, perhaps, through which could be seen a vast deep chasm illuminated by a purple phosphorescence.[25] That, along with the glow from my Quantum Girl persona, served as the only source of light. The torches that were interspersed among the statues, were untended, dark, and cold.

"Where are we?" Ophelia asked.

"The north corridor of the Royal House of the Gaaalthaaara," I told her. "It has been the home of my ancestors for twelve thousand cycles of recorded time. I, Khattaaara Gaaalthaaara, am the last of my bloodline, though it may not matter since all of my people are now facing ruin thanks to me."

"What do you mean?" she asked.

At first, I was ashamed of what I had done, but I realized that she had a right to know. And so I told her how I had been betrayed by my synth, and how, because of my foolishness, my kind lay on the brink of extinction. I thought about a passage from the Bible that my Earth mother once said. "He that troubleth his own house shall inherit the wind." I guess that Ophelia's mother had said it as well.

Father's throne that our band of thieves had moved in our quest for power, had been pushed back over the hole where Naraaag-Tal had disintegrated the granite floor. Perhaps that had been done by Dhraaal and his cohorts after I had left, but that was mere speculation on my part. Regardless, since no one else knew the location of the god-stones or that anything beneath the throne was amiss, I decided to keep that bit of information and speculation to myself. Wearied of both mind and heart, I sat down on the throne and bade Ophelia sit beside me on the one that had belonged to my mother. Just as she did, though, Jordan began to cry.

"She's hungry," she said. "I tried breastfeeding, but it made

---

[25] Beneath the floor upon which the thrones sat was a natural column of stone.

her ill. She needs human milk or formula. The old woman, your servant, said I should feed her what she called flaaargh,[26] but how can I do this to my child? I don't know *what* to do. I was sure that Peyton would have returned by now."

I thought for a moment and then had an idea. "Set her down," I told her, and then come over here.

Carefully, she laid Jordan down on the throne and then walked over to me, as I rose to meet her. "Give me thy hands," I said. She held hers out and I took hers in mine. "This will only last ten minutes, perhaps less. I don't know how long I'll be able to hold your pattern."

Ophelia looked at me with puzzlement in her eyes, as I focused my concentration on her. I had never done this before—at least not to anyone other than myself. The purple glow that radiated from me seemed to burst *from* me and then wrap itself around *her,* changing her back to human form.

"Do it quickly," I urged, trying desperately to maintain my concentration. "Feed her now."

Ophelia looked down at herself and then up at me. Then she turned and went over to Jordan, lifted her into her arms, sat down, and began to breastfeed her. It was just over ten minutes when I could no longer hold onto the matrix. My focus snapped. The glow faded from her and returned to me, and she became a creature of Rendenaaar once more.

"We're going to need to find some other way," I said. "I don't know if I can do this a second time."

"So strange," she said. "to have felt human again." She stared up at me, the whites of her eyes, blue with tears. "If you looked at my back, you would see where I pricked myself to try and end my life. But then they gave me Jordan, and I knew that I had to live for *her*."

"I'm sorry," I replied. "I wish I could undo it all."

---

[26] Regurgitated food, such as birds feed their young.

"I'm eighteen years old!" she sobbed. "Liam and I—we were going to be married! Now, I'll never see him again!"

"He was my brother," I said. "at least the Payton part of me. And my best friend, just like Peyton was yours."

"How do you do it?" she said wiping tears from her cheek with the back of her right hand, her left arm cradling Jordan. "How do you accept what has happened, and go on?"

"You just do," I said staring off into the distance. "Life is what we make *it*, not what *it* makes *us*. I don't know why we exist—why any of this exists—but it *does* and so we go on." I shrugged. "Why did it happen? What more could we have done? We're all like grains of sand in a hurricane and the only thing that keeps us alive is fighting against the wind."

"And when it stops?" she asked. "What then?" She stared at me through her tear-stained eyes.

"Then we die," I said staring back. "The calm at the center of it all is death, so pray that the winds never cease. Whether you know it or not—whether Gaaalthaaaran or human—you, Ophelia Jane Herron, are a beautiful creation and I love you as the sister that I will have one day and as the best of all possible friends."

Suddenly, I heard a sound from down the hallway. Ophelia's Gaaalthaaaran ears perked as well, for she pivoted her head in the direction from which it came. Turning toward her, I held my finger to my lips and divided into two, one of me then phasing over to where I thought whoever or whatever made the sound might be. There, behind one of the statues, huddled a young, pretty female about one and a three-quarters cycles old,[27] holding onto a *goraaag* that appeared to be her pet. The girl trembled. The *goraaag* growled and bared its teeth at me. As I reached out toward the girl, the *goraaag* attempted to bite me, but I momentarily phased my hand out of sync, so that it chomped down right through it and bit down on empty air, causing it to

---

[27] Roughly twelve Earth years.

cock its head in apparent confusion. I then squatted down, and asked her, "What's your name?"

"Dulallaaah," she replied in a timid voice and then added, "*Her* name is Chaaargh," casting a glance at the dog-like creature. "She is my protector."

"Where is thy family?" I asked.

"I do not know," she replied. "They just disappeared."

"What dost thou mean?" I pressed on.

"They were there, and then they were gone."

"Vanished into thin air?" I asked.

Dulallaaah nodded. "Then Chaaargh and I fled. The doors to the Palace were open, so we hid in here." The girl craned her head to one side, as she stared at me and around me. "Why dost thou glow with such light?" she asked.

"I am known as *Zhaaagur Scraaa*," I replied. "I have special powers. Yonder at the royal throne sits my dear friend Pheeelja with her infant daughter Zhordaaan."

"Thou does prevaricate," Dulallaaah insisted. "There is no such thing as an infant girl. One cannot be girl or not girl till one is scratched on the neck with one of their parents' *yaaarghig* at the time of decision. Such was told me by my mother, and my mother only spake the truth."

"This may be," I replied, "and what thy mother has told thee is correct, but only for those children of Rendenaaar. Zhordaaan is not, for she is a child of Urtaaah, a planet far from here. Stand up," I said, "hold thy pet against thee, and take my hand,"

As my fingers wrapped around hers, I phased us back to the throne. Dulallaaah stared with astonishment at my other self and then at me. "There are two of thee!" She proclaimed.

"Nay," I said as I merged back into one. "'Tis just one of my powers to make more of me." I turned then to Ophelia. "Ophelia," I said in English, "this is Dulallaaah and her *goraaag*, Chaaargh. Dulallaaah," I said in Gaaalthaaaran, "this is Pheeelja, and the little one is Zhordaaan."

Dulallaaah walked over to Ophelia, looked her over once, stared down at Jordan with curious eyes, and then turned back to me. "Thou does try and trick me," she said. "'Tis like any other infant on Rendenaaar!"

I shrugged and went to Ophelia, loosened the diaper that was taped to Jordan, and then removed it. Dulallaaah held her nose and turned her head away.

"What is that foul smell?" she exclaimed.

"'Tis the *proaaagh*[28] of huymaaan children," I replied.

"Then I am glad," she proclaimed, "that I was never a huymaaan child!"

"Still, look on," I insisted, as I lifted Jordan up with both hands.

Dulallaaah, glanced reluctantly, still holding her nose with her hand, but then dropped it, as her glance turned into a stare. "She has not the stub of a *yaaargh*, and what is that fold in the front 'twixt her legs?"

"'Tis called a vaaachinag," I explained. "'Tis from there in adulthood in females that infants emerge when born."

"Not from the *yaaargh*?" she exclaimed

"Nay," I replied. "Such is the way of her kind."

"And how did she arrive here on Rendenaaar?" she asked.

"She was brought by my twin," I replied. "Not that one thou didst see just now, who is but a part of me. Nay, a reflection of me from the future."

"Would that Chaaargh would bite me," she exclaimed, "so that it might prove that I am awake!"

Such was my first encounter with Dulallaaah—and Chaaargh—who would play a significant role in days to come. Little did I realize what the consequences of that role would be.

---

[28] The Rendenaaaran word for excrement.

CHAPTER XIX

Dark God

> *From the Altered Timeline*
> *In the Alternate Reality*
> *On Earth I*
> *Earth-Date: 2025*

The United Nations was in session when I materialized mid-air inside the General Assembly Hall just in front of the large Great Seal that was just behind the rostrum, where sat the U.N. president. The Great Seal was mounted on an obelisk roughly fifty feet high, both of which were faced in gold. High on each side, were television monitors, giving the appearance to the whole of some great religious cross. I suppose that my *hanging* in front of it gave it the appearance of a crucifix, which was fitting considering that I was to become their new god.

Once I appeared, whispers began to spread from one ear to the next. Voiced alarms went up within the gallery, until, at last, the sounds within the chamber were like the droning of a swarm of bees. One and then another security guard aimed their guns at me never realizing how useless their bullets were against me.

How sacrilegious! I thought to myself as I turned both the guards and their weapons into dark matter.[29] Then I grew to nearly

---

[29] Dark matter is a term for what astrophysicists described as a hypothetical form of matter, undetectable by conventional means, which accounted for 85% of all mass within the universe and had been said to be responsible for the movement of galaxies and stars. The truth is that while normal matter consists of quarks paired in threes, dark matter consists of single and paired quarks, which renders them undetectable, but still has the effect of being able to warp spacetime.

the full height of the room. As the members of the council, one by one, realized the extent of my power, the droning stopped and silence ensued. One woman, though, got up and ran for the door. I caught her with a force field and then pulled her up to face me. I thought, *How small she is in comparison to my new size!* There was terror in her face, tears drenching her tightly shut eyes. I could hear her heart beating like a kettle drum. I could smell the urine as it fled from her down to the floor. I could feel her tremble. I could have killed her there and then but instead I eased her to the floor and then stared at the assembly.

"I am Dark God, Destroyer of Planets," I said as my voice boomed throughout the hall. "Dark God, the Feared and the Formidable, and yet," and I paused staring down at the woman as she cowered in fear, sprawled on the floor that was wet from her fear, "I am also Dark God, the Merciful and the Just." My voice echoed through what now appeared to me to be a tiny room. "But to be clear," I went on, "as your Bible says, 'Thou shalt have no other gods before me.' Each of you here are to inform your leaders that they are to surrender themselves to me in this chamber by midnight tomorrow or I shall lay waste to their lands."

One of the men in the assembly called out in a Jamaican accent, "What will happen to the leaders?" he asked.

"They shall sacrifice their lives for their people," I replied.

"You will kill them?" he went on. "Murder them?"

"Theirs shall be a noble death," I said in return. "unlike yours," at which point I caused all of the atoms in the man to degrade into dark matter as I had with the guards. Those remaining in the room mumbled, mostly in fear.

"What assurances do we have," the Australian ambassador asked, "that you won't destroy us regardless?"

Poof! He too met the same fate.

"Any more questions?" I asked. Crickets could be heard, as silence once more filled the room, and the amazing part of it all was that it only took four of them to be sacrificed before they finally caught on that they didn't have a choice in the matter.

There is something very revealing about leaders when it comes to self-sacrifice. In the Navy, it has always been a point of honor that the captain goes down with his ship after saving all of the passengers and crew. Most mothers would sacrifice their own lives for their children. Political leaders are what were once described as armchair warriors, men who sent others into battle to risk their lives, while they stayed safely at home. So, to ask the leaders of nations to willingly sacrifice their own lives to save countless millions is like asking the Cowardly Lion to show courage. When midnight came the next day, of the one hundred ninety-six member nations, only twenty-three showed up—men of dignity and honor—heads of smaller nations. Those I let live. The others, including the President of the United States, I uncreated wherever they were. One day they may find their claim to fame in a display case in some alien museum. But to those I spared, and to the ambassadors of the coward nations, I gave a message: "From this point forward, there is but one god to worship and that is me. There shall be no more Bibles, or Qur'ans, or Vedas, or any other religious books. Those who minister religion shall only preach the worship of me. Those who defy this order shall learn that the knowledge of death may come all too quick." And with those words spoken, I teleported each of them back to their homeland, so that I might find peace within an empty hall.

CHAPTER XX

Claire (from Earth II)

From the Altered Timeline
In the Alternate Reality
On Earth I
Earth-Date: 2029

In this dimension, Peyton Herron and Claire Salinger barely knew each other. And then there was the matter of Chloë, who did not exist in mine. That was a point of regret for me, and I have often wondered what it was that caused her to be born here. Chloë was radiant, with shoulder-length dark hair cut with bangs and with blue eyes the same as mine. She was sharp as the proverbial tack and very loquacious. It was almost as though she never ran out of breath or words. Her sister, on the other hand, was a lot like me, though it was strange to suddenly find myself with an identical twin. So odd, too, that she drove the same car as me—a red Toyota Corolla XLE with black leather seats. I drove us all to the Herrons', which seemed a lot closer when not having to walk. I could see through the rear-view mirror, Chloë glancing again and again from her sister to me.

"I still don't understand what's going on?" she sobbed. "What happened to Mom and Dad and everyone else, and why do you two look so much alike?" She wiped away tears from her cheeks with both hands, stared at my twin, and threw herself into her arms sobbing bitterly. The other Claire held her, resting her cheek against the top of her head—holding her as though she were all that she had left in the world, and perhaps there was truth in that.

"Do you want to tell her," the other Claire said, "or should I?"

94

"You go ahead," I replied. "You're her sister."

Hearing that, Chloë pulled away a bit and looked up at her. "Are you like twins? Did Mom give one of you away? I mean, I saw *Parent Trap*, and that's what Annie's and Hallie's parents did."

"No," her sister told her. "She's another Claire from another dimension."

"I don't understand," Chloë said trying to dry her tears. "What do you mean, 'another dimension?'"

It was then that I pulled into the driveway at the Herron home, turned off the ignition, and turned to face her.

"I'm from another Earth," I said, "one that's nearly identical to this one."

The other Claire continued. "You saw how that *woman* pulled herself out of me. She's not only from another dimension but from another universe. She mistook me for *her* and merged herself into me until she realized her mistake and then decided in a fit of anger or, perhaps loneliness, to change everyone in the backyard into one of her kind—from her world. It was called Rendenaaar, but its people died uncounted trillions of years ago."

"But why does she want to hurt *us*?" Chloë asked.

"She wants her planet back," I said, "her people, her civilization. She wants her race to be reborn."

"How do we stop her?" she asked, looking up at her, begging for an answer.

"Quantum Girl," the other Claire said. "She's afraid of her."

"Quantum *Girls*," I corrected. "There are four of them. Three are Peyton Herrons from this and my dimension, and the other one, I'm not too sure of, but I think she also came from Rendenaaar. Her name is Jordan. Her mother is Ophelia, Peyton's sister."

"Ophelia Herron was on my swim team at school, till she suddenly dropped out," the other Claire interjected.

"Let's get inside," I suggested.

We all got out of the car and went to the front door. I'd been given a key, so I let us in without having to ring the bell. Sarabeth, who had heard our car pull up, looked through her window and then raced downstairs to meet us.

"Holy crap!" Sarabeth exclaimed when she saw me with the other Claire. "Don't tell me—another time rewrite."

"No," I replied. "She's just the Claire from this dimension."

"Isn't that…" my doppelgänger started to say. She was going to say, Peyton.

"Sarabeth," I interrupted and then turned to the resurrected one. "Sarabeth," I said, "this is Chloë, Claire's sister. Chloë, this is Sarabeth. Why don't you two go upstairs and play with your Barbies or something? Claire and I need to talk. Privately."

Sarabeth stared at me gaping. "Barbies?" she exclaimed. "What *world* are you living in?" Then she turned to Chloë. "Come on. I'll introduce you to Liam and Li. They're pretty cool for their age. They're from Earth III."

Chloë turned to *her* Claire with a wide-eyed stare like, *What the hell have we gotten into?* Her sister threw back a nod and an upward head motion in return. Chloë took a deep breath, shrugged, and then turned and followed Sarabeth upstairs. Once the two of them were gone and we *twins* sat down on the living room sofa and an overstuffed armchair respectively, I started the odd conversation that was to follow.

"You weren't startled by my appearance?" I asked her.

"Not in the least," she replied. "I know—knew—all about you long before you showed up at my house. Shared consciousness with that… creature. I know how you were turned into one of her kind, and how you mated with that brute of a Gaaalthaaaran male. The only thing I can't figure out is how you managed to become human again."

"One of the Quantum Girls, Jordan, found a way to reverse

the transformation," I said.

"How?" she asked.

"One of her powers," I said. "We're living in a whole new world."

"Tell me about it," she replied.

I remember smiling. "Anyway," I said, "one good thing came from it."

"What's that?" she asked.

"Having you and Chloë as kind of sisters," I said.

"This Jordan you mentioned," she went on with focused seriousness. "Where is she now?"

"Not sure," I replied. "Why is it important? She'll show up eventually."

It was at that moment that the cat that Sarabeth had recently adopted walked up to me, looked at the other Claire, put up its tail, and hissed at her. Claire glared at the cat, curling her lip. The cat reacted, growing fierce, and seemed about to pounce, when a tail flew out from behind Claire, and stung the animal, causing it to moan and drop to the floor in a heap.

"What the fuck," I gasped. I jumped to my feet. The other Claire did the same and then morphed into Khattaaara. "Where's Claire?" I demanded.

Khattaaara shrugged off a laugh. "Please! Do you think I wanted her alive, while I pretended to *be* her? As for you, you're coming back with me to become Gaaalthaaaran again!"

"Like hell, she will!" Sarabeth said from the staircase, Chloë at her side a few steps up. By the time I turned to look, Sarabeth already had a whistle in her mouth and was blowing it. All at once, Payton, Pay, and Jordan appeared in the room. But there was no battle; not even a fight. Khattaaara saw that she was outnumbered, and vanished from the room.

"What happened?" Pay asked.

"I brought her here," I tried to explain. "I thought she was my counterpart in this dimension but it was just Khattaaaara pretending to be her."

"Where's Claire?" Chloë screamed with tears in her throat. "Where's my Claire?" She raced down the stairs and looked in every direction.

"I'm sorry," I said. "Claire's…" and I paused. "She was never here. That was Khattaaara all along."

"No!" Chloë wailed. "No! No! No!" I took her around and held her close. She had no one left, but me, and we weren't actually sisters. Not really. But I made up my mind there and then, that I would *try* to be, from that moment on.

CHAPTER XXI

Payton

> *From the Original Timeline*
> *In the Alternate Reality*
> *On Earths I and II*
> *Earth-Date: 2029*

It was stressful to think that Khattaaara had been to Peyton's parents' home again and that she, for a second time, had fled. Mentally, however, I was not prepared for that on top of everything else. For the moment all of my thoughts and concerns were focused on Liam and rescuing him. Unfortunately for me, there was no GPS on my Earth, but there were maps. Lubumbashi is a small city at the southern tip of Katanga, which in turn is or had been a part of the Democratic Republic of the Congo in central Africa, and that, according to Jasmine, was where Liam was being held. After a few misses, I phased right next to him as Quantum Girl, midday at the mine.[30]

"Hello, brother," I said. "Sort of brother. I'm not exactly the sister you grew up with, but..."

"You're from the other reality," he said interrupting me. "The reality that Phee is from. How is she? Is she all right?" Just like Liam! His concern wasn't for him but for her.

"It's a long story," I said. "First, I need to get you out of here."

It was at that moment that one of the guards noticed me, and

---

[30] I need to make clear that it was necessary for me to phase to Liam months into the future, after my soul (or ka as the ancient Egyptians called it) had left his body, fearing that to do otherwise would create a paradoxical time loop since my having been able to find him was predicated on my having learned where he was while in his head.

shouted out something in Chinese. He repeated it again and then called out to the other guards. All of them aimed their rifles at us. When we failed to comply, they fired. Their bullets hit the quantum field that I had projected around us, disintegrating into small bursts of light as they did. Then I phased us back to the Herrons' home, the very instant after I had left.

"Liam!" Claire called out startled and then froze, as she saw Ophelia descend the stairs.

Liam glanced at Claire, noticed Ophelia as well, and then rushed toward her. Ophelia backed off from what was about to be his embrace.

"*Excuse* me?" she said in a preemptive tone. "Do I *know* you?"

Phasing back into me, I rushed over to intervene. "Liam!" I said. "That's not her!"

"Different version," echoed Pay.

Liam, shirtless, sunburned, weathered by months that must have seemed like years, turned toward Pay's voice and then back to me, looking desperately confused.

"What's going on?" he begged.

If the labors from the work camp and the desolation he felt didn't hammer at his mind enough, this was too much for him to take in—at least all at once. He sank into one of the armchairs and stared around the room. There before him and around him stood not just two, but three Paytons. Chloë, at Sarabeth's behest, retreated back upstairs to keep young Liam and Li from adding to the madness that must have engulfed *this* Liam's brain.

It was Claire, who finally broke the silence that had ensued, rushing over to where Liam sat, and taking hold of one of his hands with both of hers.

"It's going to be all right," she said. "It's going to be all right."

"I thought you were done with me," he asked, staring off at her, "that we were done with each other?" Then he glanced back at Phee.

"Love isn't something you take back," she said almost whispering the words.

"I think what Liam needs right now," I said, "is a shower and some rest."

Claire let go of Liam's hand and backed up a bit to give him some space.

"He can have my room," Sarabeth added. "I can stay at Kat's Landing—at least that's what I named it. All large mansions deserve a name. Jordan can take me—phase me—there."

"Thank you," I mouthed at her. Then I looked at Jordan, who nodded a smile at me.

It was Pay, who then walked over to Liam and knelt down in front of him. "Hello, Brother," she said in a soft voice and then smiled. "I'm the Pay*load* you grew up with." She looked toward me briefly and then returned her gaze to him. "She's from another reality." Liam glanced at me and then turned back to her. "Look," she went on, "I know this is all a lot to take in, but we're all together now. We rescued Mom and Dad. They're both safe, but they're staying somewhere else. We have a lot to catch up on. You know we were all so worried about you. But we've got you now. You get some rest, then we'll talk later."

Liam nodded. Pay rose to her feet and then helped him to his. Sarabeth went over to him and took his hand. "I'll take him to my room," she said then she led him upstairs.

"I never had a brother before," she said to him. "I hope you're not into Barbie dolls," then shouted back, "This isn't 1960, you know!"

Liam used the shower in the room that had been his on our world, but here it was Sarabeth's, she having given up her (and what had also been Phee's) room to the twins. After washing off half a year's worth of sweat and mud, he laid down in Sarabeth's bed and promptly fell asleep. There was sand in the shower when

I looked in on him; sand and dirt. So exhausted, he lay like a corpse in the bed. His skin, which had been so smooth and pale, was now dark and leathery, scorched by the burning sun, day after day. His hair had grown more blond, touched with gray, his face more gaunt. The layers of sweat and grime had been washed away, but the toll the ordeal had taken on him was indelible. He was never quite the same afterward, Phee sadly confided to me. She and Liam were two lovers who were literally star-crossed, separated by both circumstance and rewritten time and to each of them it was as though a part of them had been ripped away, never to be seen again. Claire was still there for him; her love for him would never fade. He had been the most special part of her life, and she was good and kind and forgave him for his indiscretions, perhaps realizing that Fate had tricked all of them into a life that was so unkind. And Liam loved her back, but there was never the fire between them that he had felt for Phee, and so it seemed to me at the time that his love for Claire, and hers for him, was bound more in friendship than great passion. But perhaps I overreached in that regard, for that part was theirs to tell, not mine.

CHAPTER XXII

Peyton

> *From the Original Timeline*
> *In the Imagined Timeline*
> *On Earth I*
> *Earth-Date: 2025*

The following day, school had let out early. Three girls had been killed in a car crash on their way there in the same car that nearly ran into Phee and me the day I first learned of my powers. Two died instantly, and the third, en route to the hospital, possibly because it had taken so long for the ambulance to arrive. Tragically, knowing what was about to happen, I tried calling 911 but couldn't get through. None of this, of course, was discussed at school. It was something just whispered about in the days that followed.

Everything in my life appeared to be going along swimmingly, as Phee would say, but this time I didn't try to kill myself and, as a result, I never became Quantum Girl. The scene then flashed to a studio, where I was the subject of a modeling shoot. I was flustered by the sudden change, and the photographer, a somewhat beautiful woman in her late twenties, stopped.

"Something wrong?" she asked.

"No," I replied, trying to orient myself.

"Well," she said, "let's get on with it. I'll need a couple dozen more shots before the wardrobe change." She turned to one of the men in her crew. "Carl, could you use a board to add just a bit more light to the left?"

The man complied, and the woman began to shoot again.

"All right," she went on to me. "I want you to close your eyes, and pretend like you've just had the best orgasm imaginable."

Then, it all changed *again*. I was naked in bed with someone. The lights were dim, as I opened my eyes. I was with her, the photographer. She had her mouth to mine. I could feel her tongue probing inward, while one of her hands, her fingers, worked their way in and out of my… *sex* to put it in more decorous terms, but all of it was producing pleasurable results, and, for whatever reason, considering that to my mind this was a total stranger, I did not resist. I suppose that the gentleness of her kisses and the thread of ecstasy that came from the action of her hand lulled me into compliance with the sexual act that was being played out. *Besides*, I kept telling myself, *this is all just a dream.*

Only what if it wasn't? I wondered. *What if Jordan had actually changed reality? What if whatever this was, was real?* It was as I was having that thought, mid-orgasm, that I heard another voice in the room—Theresa!

"What are you doing!" she cried out, as she flicked on the lights. "How could you do this to me?"

Immediately, the woman, who was with me, rose from the bed, taking the sheet with her, and leaving me naked. Theresa began throwing anything and everything she could find at her. It was then that I blacked out again to suddenly find myself in a courtroom filled with people. I was sitting at a table, facing the bench, alarmingly dressed in an orange prison jumpsuit. Beside me sat a woman in her mid-thirties in a dark business suit, a laptop and a folder on the table in front of her. Suddenly, a man's voice rang out from one side.

"Here ye, here, ye, Court is now in session!" he called out. "All rise! The Hon. Judge Edward Flynn presiding!"

Everyone stood up as Judge Edward Arthur Flynn emerged from behind the wooden panel that held the state seal, went to his chair, and sat down.

"You may be seated," the bailiff's voice went on, and so everyone sat back down.

The judge looked down at his docket and then up toward the two wooden tables in front of and slightly below him. As I said, I sat at one of them, with what turned out to be my public defender, while a lawyer from the district attorney's office and his assistant, a pretty, twenty-something woman sat by his side at the other. "Good morning, counselors," the judge said in a pleasant voice.

"Good morning," your honor, the two lawyers said almost in unison.

The judge stared down at his docket with a frown. "Case number 26CF1879, the People of the State of California versus Peyton Elise Herron on two counts of murder in the second degree." He glanced up. "Are both sides ready?"

"Yes, Your Honor," said my lawyer.

"Yes, Your Honor," said the ADA.

"Counsel," the judge said, "will you and your client please rise?"

My lawyer stood up, and urged me, with a glance, to do the same.

"Peyton Elise Herron," the judge went on, "you are charged with the murder of one Theresa Maria Martinez Moreno in the second degree, which is punishable by fifteen years to life. You are further charged with the murder of one Miranda Louise Harrison in the second degree, which is punishable by fifteen years to life. How do you plead?"

"Not guilty by reason of insanity, Your Honor," came the response from my lawyer.

Tears began streaming down my eyes. "What are you talking about?" I cried out. "I didn't murder anyone!"

The bailiff took several steps toward me. The judge remarked, "Counselor, you will constrain your client or I will have her removed from the courtroom."

"My apologies, Your Honor," she replied. "It won't happen again."

Suddenly, everything seemed to shift, and I was face down on the floor, handcuffed, with one of the deputy's knees on my back. My head, turned to one side, I could see my lawyer on the floor, her eyes staring vacantly toward me, red marks around her throat, as though she had been choked to death.

The scene then shifted again. To be honest, it was like when I would phase from one place to the next. This time I found myself before the same judge, but now there was a man in a dark suit standing beside me, and I was both handcuffed and shackled, with a chain connecting both.

"Peyton Elise Herron, it is the consideration of this court that you be remanded to the custody of Napa State Psychiatric Hospital for such time as, and until, you are deemed fit to stand trial."

And then it happened once more, This time, still garbed in the same orange jumpsuit, I found myself strapped to a gurney in what turned out to be a hospital room. I struggled to get up and then called out, "Hey! Someone let me out of this!" but no one came, despite my shouting again and again. Half an hour later, a black nurse entered, wheeling a small stainless steel cart.

"The guards say you've been making quite a racket," she said.

"Why am I strapped down?" I asked, pulling against the restraints.

"You needed to be controlled," she said. "Girl, you stabbed your friend, Daisy, when she came to you on a visit, or are you pretending not to remember again?"

"What are you talking about?" I replied. "How is she?"

"She's dead," the nurse answered. "And she was the only one you had on your side."

"What happened?" I asked.

"All I know," she replied. "is they say you lunged at her with a broken plastic spoon and plunged it into her neck so that she bled to death." She shook her head. "Katara, Katara, Katara, what *are* we going to do with you?" She rolled up my sleeve a bit, swabbed me with some disinfectant, and then picked up a hypodermic needle.

"What are you doing!" I said trying to pull away.

"Just a little nighty-night to calm you down," she said.

"Ow!" I exclaimed as she stuck the needle in my arm. All at once, my head began to spin. "And why did you call me Katara?" I tried to say, but I had lost consciousness before I could get out the name.

When I awakened the next day, it was already afternoon, and I was still restrained. This time, however, there was another woman strapped to a gurney to the left of mine. "Finally awake," she announced. She was a chubby woman with short dark curly hair and thick eyebrows. "Came to L.A. from Birmingham, I did," she went on, with a cockney accent "and they put me in here because I ran into a colored man, a blackguard 'e was, too. At the shelter. 'ad his trousers down beyond 'is arse, so I calls 'im on it, and 'e looks at me with eyes like Satan 'imself, and say to me, 'e says, 'You looks like yous could use a good fuckin','e does, so I kicks 'im 'ard in 'is twig an' berries,[31] and 'e starts to scream like a basin o' gravy. Then 'e pulls out a drum an' fife,[32] an' olds it up towards me, wavin' it around like 'e intends to cut me, so I did the only thing I could. I picks up a lion's lair[33] and smacks 'im over the head and down he goes for the count. As for me, I starts dancin' a jig around 'im. Then I 'ears 'im callin' me a bitch through 'is pain, so I hikes up me dress and spends a penny all over 'im. Thank God I ran out of me knickers the day before or

---

[31] British slang for male genitals.
[32] British rhyming slang for a knife.
[33] British rhyming slang for a chair.

I'da gotten 'im all wet with piss." She paused and then asked, "So what d' they got you locked up for?"

"I don't know," I replied. "I don't know how I got here or even where I am."

"You're in Napa State Hospital, Luv," she said, "for the criminally insane. But I like yer alibi that you gots amnesia. Woulda used it meself if I'd thought of it."

It was then that a doctor came into the room with the same nurse as before. There wasn't much about him other than his white coat, pale complexion, and the bristly hair, that ran its course everywhere on his head other than the top, which reminded me somewhat of an octopus I had seen at the aquarium when I was eight years old. The doctor approached the gurney I was on and then lifted the clipboard that was at its foot, near my *naked* foot, which I caught a glimpse of craning my neck with some difficulty. He glanced up at me over his half-frame glasses—or whatever they're called—and spoke.

"Good morning, Katara," he said. "And how are we doing today?"

"Not very well, thank you," I replied. "and my name isn't Katara."

"So, you're not Katara Galthara, Divine Empress of Rendenar and all Known Worlds, as you've maintained for the past thirty-eight years?" There was sarcasm in his voice.

"Thirty-eight years," I gasped.

"And you don't remember murdering Theresa Martinez, grabbing her, and then ripping out her throat, just to name one of your victims?"

I tried to make sense of what he was saying. "My name is Peyton Herron," I maintained.

"And how long have you been Peyton Herron?" he asked.

"All of my life," I said.

"And how long is that?" he asked.

"Fourteen years," I replied. "That's how old I am."

The man glanced at the nurse. "The ECT[34] appears to be working. Schedule her for another session this afternoon." Then he looked down at me. "We're making progress. In another six months, we'll have you well enough to stand trial."

"I need you to call my sister," I said. There were tears in my eyes. "She'll tell you who I am."

"We know who you are. You're Peyton Elise Herron, born September 24, 2011, at Cedars-Sinai Hospital. Parents, Katherine and James Herron, both deceased. Sister, Ophelia Jane Herron, died of a drug overdose, July 12, 2028." He replaced the clipboard and then left the room.

"2028?" I repeated. "This is supposed to be 2025!" Then, for the first time, I looked over to my right. There was a dresser against the wall with a mirror above it. I stared at my reflection, and my heart began to pound in my chest. "What year is it?" I asked. "What year?"

The nurse looked down at me. "It's 2066," she said in a calm voice. Then, looking down toward my legs went on, "I'll get a couple of the nurses to change the sheets."

I could feel the wetness and smell the pungent odor as it wafted up to my nose.

"Ask for a bedpan next time," she went on. "It will save us all a lot of work."

---

[34] Electroconvulsive therapy, a medical treatment that involves running an electrical current through the brain—also known as electroshock therapy.

CHAPTER XXIII

Jordan

From the Original Timeline
In the Alternate Reality
On Earth I
Earth Date: 2025

On Rendenaaar, for the most part, growing up alone, I learned to be very meticulous about things. It was, therefore, unlike me to just appear somewhere without first knowing *about* the somewhere. My mother had told me much about the Earth, about how things were, and how people lived, but hearing about life is not the same as experiencing it.

When I first appeared in Peyton and Ophelia's bedroom, it was not my first moment on Earth. My initial phase point was September 24, 2025, the day it all began. But how and where and when it began was not my final goal. It was just where quantum reality had first folded itself when Dhraaal resurrected my Aunt Peyton when she was fourteen years old and sent her, first forward and then backward through time.

Knowing what had just happened, but not wanting to upset the course of time's new trajectory, while curious about the Earth—my Earth—I quickly phased to the East Coast—the Upper East Side of Manhattan to be specific—phased what I was wearing into what appeared to be an outfit I saw one woman around my age dressed in, and then went into a pawn shop to exchange one of a small cache of diamonds I had brought with me from Rendenaaar. The somewhat gruff-looking man, who sat behind a barred window, insisted that I give him a driver's license or ID, which, of course, I did not have. It took me having to go into several more such establishments before I found someone willing to pay me cash without any identification, though for half of what any of the others had offered. Attempts to rent an apartment met with similar concerns. It didn't matter how much cash I now had. In addition to identification, they demanded proof of employment, W2s (whatever those are), a bank account, and references, none of which I had. Exiting the last place, a sign in the window of one business caught my eye: "Help for Immigrants and Aliens," so I walked inside and approached a woman in her early fifties, who sat behind the desk nearest the door. That proved fruitless as well. Apparently, I was the wrong kind of alien. When night fell, I wound up sleeping on a bench in Central Park.

Just as I had fallen asleep, I was awakened by the slurred voice of a man who came with an unwashed aroma. "That's my bench!" he yelled. "Everyone knows that bench belongs to Shoeless Willy, and that's me!"

I opened my eyes to see a man dressed in rags, looking to be in his late fifties, haggard and gaunt. His face was weathered with what must have come from decades of alcohol and sunlight, his jawline shortened by his lack of teeth.

"Get off of my bench!" he railed on.

I shook my head to cast off the few bits of sleep I had gotten and then sat up. "I thought this was a public bench," I said.

"Goll durn it! It ain't no public bench!" the man snapped back at me. "I've been sleeping on this bench for more than twenty-five years!"

"I'm very sorry," I replied. "I had no idea."

"Well, now you do," he said and he stomped his foot.

I glanced down to see that Shoeless Willy was wearing shoes. "Why do they call you Shoeless Willy?" I asked.

"Because," he replied, "years ago, Bar'foot Eddie stole my shoes whilst I was asleep. Danced around in 'em when I woke up, then run off, not to be seen agin by me for nigh on twenty years. But I got back at him, I did."

"What did you do?" I asked.

"I stole these here shoes right off his feet whilst he was drunk, I did," he said gleefully. "Then I tied up his ankles with the laces, so he couldn't catch me if he woke up before I got away!" He gave out a cackle of a laugh. "Stole his socks, too! He styled hisself Gentleman Eddie before, but he's Bar'foot Eddie now!"

I laughed with him. "Why don't you sit down next to me?" I asked.

Shoeless Willy looked me over after he had sat down. "You sure are a pretty 'un," he said. "Reminds me of my Helen."

"Who's Helen?" I asked.

"She was my wife," he said. "She was the most beautiful girl I ever did see. Hair as black as coal and eyes as blue as the sky on a cool spring day."

"Where is she now?" I asked.

"She died back years ago," he replied. "Hit by a white panel truck, she was, just as I was comin' back to her. I was in the mil'tary, and had just returned from Afghanistan. I was respectable back then; Lieutenant William Leonard Morrison. That was me, and I was gonna surprise her at her work. She was a sec'etary at an accounting firm Mid Town. But then the truck hit her on her way there, and that was it for me. She's buried in a cem'tery out yonder," he said with a motion of his head. "I couldn't even bear to go to the fun'ral. I hit the bottle hard after that and been here ever since."

"You really loved her, didn't you?" I said.

Shoeless Willy began to cry. "She was the only thing ever meant anything to me in my whole life," he wept, "and I couldn't do nothin' ta save her. Now, I'm just a never-was."

"What's that?" I asked.

"It's someone that no one cares 'bout," he replied, "that it don't right matter if they'd never been born."

"I care about you, Willy." I said.

Shoeless Willy looked at me shyly with a sideways glance. "You do?" he asked.

"Of course, I do," I said. "Tell me, what do you want the most?"

"Well," he said, "I don't need shoes or socks no more."

"I mean, in your heart," I replied.

"Well," he said again, "I never got up the courage to go to her grave. I just wish I could see her one last time, even if it were just the photo on her headstone if there be one there."

"Maybe we can do better than that," I replied and stood up, facing him.

"What all do you mean?" he said.

It was at that point that I stood up and turned into Quantum Girl.

"Are you an angel?" he asked.

"My mother thought I was," I replied, "unless I got into trouble. Let's just say that I'm your fairy goddaughter. All right, stand up now," I said and he did. "We need to clean you up a bit." Then I looked up to the sky and caused a downpour. It soaked us both. Willy began to dance in the puddle that had formed at his feet. I lifted my arms up into the air, tilted my head back, and enjoyed the heavy rain.

"There was never anything like this on Rendenaaar!" I shouted.

I laughed as the water from above trickled into my mouth. Then I caused the water that clung to us both to disappear. Barefoot Willy rubbed his chest with the palms of his hands and then ran each hand down his sleeves one at a time.

"I do feel refreshed by that," he said. "Can't remember the last time I bathed."

"That was quite apparent," I remarked with a smile. "Now,

tell me, where and when was Helen when she was killed?"

"It was on March 22nd, Twenty Ought Two," he replied, "at the intersection of Broadway and 23rd. She was on her way to work, and it was at around eight forty-five, as the cab I was in was being held up by rush hour traffic. I remember looking at my watch."

"All right," I said. "Give me your hands. We're going to take a trip."

"Where to?" Willy asked.

"Not just where," I replied, "but when," and I phased us to that exact same intersection.

Willy stood amazed. He glanced at me, now changed back to my street clothes. Then, all at once, his face turned pale, and he pointed toward a woman at the corner across the street, waiting for the light to change.

"That's her!" he said, excited. "That's my Helen!"

As he spoke, he saw the truck he had described heading toward her and made a frantic dash in her direction. As the truck was about to hit her, he pushed her out of the way, and the truck hit him instead, as the truck driver screeched to a halt. A crowd quickly gathered around Willie. Helen pushed her way through.

"That man," she said. "He saved my life!"

A short distance away, a yellow taxicab pulled to a stop and a good-looking man in uniform emerged. Both Helen and Lt. William Leonard Morrison appeared to notice each other at the same time. Helen Morrison once again broke through the crowd and raced toward him, as he raced toward her, falling into each other's arms when they met. After a brief embrace, Helen stared up into her husband's eyes and said breathlessly, "Oh, Will, there was an old man I noticed rushing at me. I thought he'd wanted to hurt me, but then he pushed me out of the path of that truck, only to be struck by it himself!"

Will Morrison looked in the direction from which his wife had just come and then took her by the hand. "Come on," he said. "Let's go see if he's all right." He led and she followed.

I was already there. The last time I saw Shoeless Willy, there was a smile on his face. He had saved his Helen, and, in doing so, had saved himself.

"What's going on?" Will asked the crowd. He glanced at Helen. "I thought you said there was a man?"

"There was," she said as taken aback as *he* was.

"The man was there as plain as the nose on my face," a man declared. "Then he just vanished!"

"Are you sure he isn't under the truck?" Will asked, bending down to look.

"*No*, sir," the man went on. "He just up and disappeared. If I didn't see it with my own eyes, I'd never have believed it, and I almost don't believe it now."

Will shrugged and then turned to Helen. "Come on, Babe, let's go home."

"But what about my work?" she asked.

"You can call in sick," he replied. "This is enough for one day."

And I guess it was enough for me as well. I'd had a new perspective of my home planet. I'd seen desolation and pain, but I'd also seen self-sacrifice and love and a miracle that brought a tear to my eye before I left. A moment or so later found me in my grandparents' living room just after the start of the war; not the war for the survival of nations, but the war to save all mankind.

CHAPTER XXIV

Peyton

> *From the Original Timeline*
> *In the Imagined Timeline*
> *On Earth I*
> *Earth-Date: 2025*

Electroshock therapy is not as bad as it has been made to appear in movies like *One Flew Over the Cookoo's Nest*. I was given a general anesthetic prior to the procedure. When I awoke, I found myself in a small padded cell but this time it was different. It was as though someone else was in charge of my body and I was just an observer. I had no control over my movement. I began clawing at the cloth on the walls, screaming. *"Jogaaarth Khattaaara Gaaalthaaara, Kkitaaai Taaargoth naa Rendenaaar anaaagh teraaa Hooolraaa Chaaargin! Jogaaarth Khattaaara Gaaalthaaara, Kkitaaai Taaargoth naaa Rendenaaar anaaagh teraaa Hooolraaa Chaaargin!"*[35] again and again, until there was blood on my hands.

Two guards rushed in to restrain me, while a nurse, brandishing a hypodermic needle bunched up my sleeve and injected me with some sedative. As I began to lose consciousness, I couldn't help but notice my arm. It was old and thin and frail, with age spots and bulging veins. And then I woke up; woke up for real this time. I was back in my home, still standing facing

---

[35] "My name is Khattaaara Gaaalthaaara, Divine Princess of Rendenaaar as decreed by Hooolraaa Chaaargin (the Sacred Council)! My name is Khattaaara Gaaalthaaara, Divine Princess of Rendenaaar as decreed by Hooolraaa Chaaargin (the Sacred Council)!"

Jordan.

"How?" I asked, staring down at my once-again young arms and then rushing over to a mirror to see myself as eighteen again. "How long was I gone?"

"Less than a second, our time," she said, "but I was there, watching you all along. I wanted to show you what your life would have been like if you had never become Quantum Girl. Ophelia and others would be dead because you didn't have the strength you'd achieved from your quantum seed to fight off Khattaaara when she took over your head. And I would never have been born. The world, dear Aunt Peyton, is a far better place, because of the path you chose. You and I are here today, because of it, and with me and your mirror selves, together we will save three worlds!"

CHAPTER XXV

Chloë

> *From the Altered Timeline*
> *In the Alternate Reality*
> *On Earth I*
> *Earth-Date: 2029*

"Stay in the room with Liam and Li." That was Sarabeth's command. She was only two years older than me, but it was, after all, her house, so I stayed, despite all hell breaking out downstairs. It didn't matter. I didn't care about anything anymore. I'd just lost both of my parents and my big sister, my absolute best friend. I remember sitting on the floor with my knees drawn up to my chin, my back pressed up into a corner when both Liam and Li came over.

"Are you all right?" Li asked. I could hear the concern in her voice.

"I'm all alone," I answered, sobbing.

"We were alone, too," Liam said. "Our parents were murdered by an alien."

"Khattaaara," Li added. "Payton's parents took us in, though right now we're living with Sarabeth's till they get settled. They're over at the other Peyton's mansion."

"They're from a parallel dimension," Liam added. "We are, too, but not the same one."

"Why is everything suddenly all about parallel dimensions and aliens?" I sobbed. "Why can't things just be normal like they were?"

"I don't think you'd like that very much," Liam said.

"Why's that?" I asked.

"Because from what I understand," he explained, "time got overwritten, and before it did, your sister was an only child. Look, I know it's hard, but we're here for you if you want us to be."

"Thanks," I said trying to wipe away my tears with my sleeve, "but I need to go back and try and find my folks."

"What if they're dead?" Liam asked.

"They're *not* dead!" I shouted through my tears.

"But it's dangerous out there," Li said, "and you're just a kid. We all are."

I climbed to my feet. "I'm not a kid!" I insisted. "I'm twelve years old!"

"Well," Li said, "you can't do it without help."

"Are you two wanting to tag along?" I asked.

"Maybe…" Liam said.

"That's not what I meant," Li replied. Then she nudged Liam, and said in a low voice, "Give her the other stone."

"I thought we were keeping it for one of us?" he replied.

"She's the one who needs it now," Li insisted. "She can always give it back."

"All *right*," Liam grumbled. Then, reaching into his pocket, he looked at me. "But this is just a loan."

"What is?" I asked.

"This," he replied revealing what looked like a tiny red glass marble that he held out in the palm of his hand.

"What is it?" I asked.

"The Peyton from this dimension said it's called a quantum seed," Liam explained. "We saw what the other one we had did for the Payton from Earth II."

"That one was green," Li interjected.

"They came from the aliens on our world when Khattaaara murdered them," Liam went on. "We didn't know what they were until Payton looked at it real close."

119

"Then it went into her head," Li added.

"And?" I asked. "Like a bullet or something?"

"No," Li went on. "It was like it melted into her."

"So, you want me to have this one melt into *my* head?" I looked at them like they were insane. "What happens afterward? Are my eyes supposed to glow red or something?"

"No," Liam said. "Do you honestly think we'd do anything to hurt you?"

Li gave me a look after glancing at her brother. "He thinks you're hot."

"Do not!" Liam insisted.

"Then why do you keep mumbling her name in your sleep?" she replied.

"You're crazy!" Liam snapped back, though I could see his face turning red from embarrassment.

"I may be crazy," Li replied, "but at least I'm not *in love!*" singing out the last two words.

"Hey!" I said. "Can we all just focus? What exactly happens if this thing goes into my head?"

"It'll give you superpowers," Li replied. "It will turn you into a *Quantum Girl*."

"What's a Quantum Girl?" I asked. *Superpowers!* I thought to myself. *This isn't a comic book!*

"It's what all of the Peytons are and Jordan," Li said.

"Jor…?" I started to say.

"All except Sarabeth," Liam interrupted. "She's from the overwrite."

I glanced at each of them, cautiously took the quantum seed from Liam, and slowly brought it up close to my eyes. Then, all at once, it began to spin. It was scary. I tried but I couldn't take my eyes off of it. I watched as it spun faster and faster, and grew smaller and smaller until it was barely a point of light. I tried to hold onto it. I pressed my fingers tighter and tighter against it, trying to hold on to it but there seemed to be hardly any of it left. Suddenly, it jumped out from my hand to my forehead like a laser beam—and then it was gone! I felt a slight chill where it touched—and then nothing.

"What the fuck!" I exclaimed.

"I wouldn't say that in front of Peyton's mom," Li said. "She's a Christian!"

"There aren't any left in our dimension," Liam added. "Literally!"

"It went into my head!" I said.

"That's what it's supposed to do," Li replied.

"How do I get it out?" I asked, half shaking.

"Why would you want to?" she asked.

"Because it's in my head?" I replied.

"What my *blonde* sister means is," Liam interjected, "is that you're now a Quantum Girl."

"Oh my God!" I shot back at them. "What the fricking frack is a Quantum Girl?"

"You now have superpowers," Liam said.

"Seriously…" I replied. "Like Superman…"

"No," Liam said. "Superman is a total wuss compared to what you can do."

"You two are cuckoo," I said, shaking my head. "Do you know that?" Except as I said that, my voice echoed.

"Really!" said Li, folding her arms and assuming a posture of superiority.

Looking to my right, I saw another one of me. I mean, looking to my left, I saw another one of me. I mean, there were two of me!

"Holy shit!" both of me said at once.

"Told ya," Liam said.

"And how am I supposed to get us back together?" both of me asked.

Liam shook his head. Li did the same.

121

"Grrrr!" both of me said through clenched teeth. "I didn't ask to become twins!" both of me said at once. Each of me then turned to the other, exclaiming, "Shut up!" followed by, "Ugh! This is so exasperating!"

"Try thinking of becoming one again," Li suggested.

I did and it worked. I went and hugged her. After the hug, Li looked over at Liam who stood frowning.

"I think Liam would rather you have hugged him," she said.

I shook my head to myself. "Come here," I said to Liam. He shyly came over and I hugged him, too. As I did, I could hear his heart pounding like a sledgehammer. *Another power?* I remember wondering at the time. "Is this why there are three Paytons?" I asked.

"Four," Liam answered. "You haven't met the Quantum Girl from *this* dimension yet. But they're all different people."

"Sort of," Li added. "Sarabeth is a younger version of Peyton because she time-traveled here from four years in the past. She's part of the rewrite, the same as the Payton we gave the other quantum seed to."

"This is way too much to take in," I said. "So, because of the quantum seed that's now in my head, I have superpowers?" I stared at both of them. "What else can I do?"

"You can pop around space and time and different dimensions," Liam said. "And you can put force fields around yourself."

"Our Payton—well, she's from Earth II—has a green quantum seed, and the other two have purple ones. I don't know about Jordan's, but I think they all work different."

"Differently," Liam said, correcting her.

"When they're *different* colors, I mean." Li went on with a harsh glance at him.

"I wouldn't tell the others that you have one, though," Liam said. "The one we just loaned you; we've kept it a secret."

"You might want to hide who you are when you use your powers," Li suggested. "Like a costume. All of *them* have one. Our Peyton told us, she could will hers onto herself just by thinking about it."

"So if I think about myself wearing a costume, it'll just appear on me?" I asked.

"That's what Payton says," Liam replied. "First you should just see if you can make all your clothes disappear."

"Shut up!" Li said as she poked him really hard.

"Ow!" Liam replied grabbing and rubbing his arm.

"Pervert!" Li said aside to her brother. Then she turned to me. "Just picture yourself wearing a costume, as though you already had it on."

I closed my eyes really tight and thought. Nothing seemed to be happening, but then I heard Li say, "You did it!"

Cautiously, I opened my eyes and looked down at myself. I was in a Supergirl costume!

"I, um, think that one's already taken," said Liam. "But I like the miniskirt," at which point Li poked him really hard again. "Ow!" came his response. "Stop doing that!"

"You'll have to forgive my brother," Li said. "Normally, he's a boob man or just a boob!" She glared at him and turned up her lip.

"Can I help it if she's got great legs?" Liam replied.

"All right," I said. "How's this?" and all at once, I stood in a glittering, metallic pink costume with a flowing silver cape.

"Try changing the color of your hair," Li suggested, so I willed it to be pink as well.

"Cool!" That was from Liam.

"One more thing," Li said. "You should have a mask."

"Like this?" I suggested, and a white, Lone Ranger-type mask appeared over my eyes. "Or maybe like this?" and I changed it to look more catlike with points.

"Perfect!" Li said enthusiastically, quietly clapping her hands. Suddenly, there was a light rapping on the door.

"Off, off, off!" Li mouthed at me, and I flashed back into my clothes. The door opened and Sarabeth poked her head into the room.

"Everything all right in here?" she asked and then looked at me. "How about you, Chloë? Are you okay? My mom just made dinner, but if you want, I can bring some up, if you'd rather eat alone."

"I'll come down," I said.

"You're sure?" she asked with concern.

I took a deep breath and nodded.

"I'm here to talk anytime you need," she said.

"I appreciate it," I replied. "We'll be down in a few."

She smiled and then shut the door behind her.

"We're here for you, too," Liam said.

"Thanks, guys," I replied. "That means a lot to me. It really does."

CHAPTER XXVI

Ophelia

From the Original Timeline
In the Alternate Reality
On Rendenaaar
Trillions of Universes in the Past

Shall I describe the beauty of Baaarghdaaar before it was destroyed by Dargra-Tol? It was the capital city of the planet—of Rendenaaar—many of its buildings tens of thousands of cycles old. Stylistically, it was nothing like anything on Earth. Towers made of crystal climbed their way up into the billowing clouds. There had been no need for stairs or elevators since the god-stones allowed anyone to simply wish themselves to whichever destination they chose. The palace, home of the Emperor and Empress, was orange (a color that had been considered royal since ancient times) and was, by divine decree, the only structure of such color; it stood in the center of the city, its circular footprint spanning what must have been close to a mile in every direction. Around its circumference had been erected the hundred *Folaaarvaaanar*, which Khattaaara had explained to me were similar to the ancient Greek muses. Each was a statue made of similar orange glass, male alternating with female, Gaaalthaaaran, all, standing perhaps two hundred meters in height, all naked, perfect specimens of their kind. The males faced inward, their arms with their arms raised above their heads, supporting a single globe, while the females stood facing outward, each with her head tilted back, her eyes closed, her hands with splayed fingers, cupping her breasts. The statues were in pairs with the *yaaargh* of the male inserted into that of his female companion.[36]

Most of the palace rose to only a modest height, even at its center, where the cooks and gardeners and cleaning staff lived. Surrounding them lived the palace guards, and beyond them to the periphery was quartered the Gaaalthaaaran army. There were, of course, gardens and parks interspersed here and there, as well as museums, a riding stable, a zoo, and even a brothel for both the guards and soldiers alike to avail themselves of while off-duty.

Prostitution within the palace walls was a highly honorable profession. Select females—only the most beautiful—from the moment of transformation, were taught both social and sexual skills, similar to those of the *oarin* of Japan. The working class, that occupied the lands beyond the cities, were not able to afford such luxuries. For them, sex did not serve to heighten their consciousness, but, rather, merely allowed them to cave to their baser instincts after a long hard day's labor.

Baaarghdaaar was located on Gaaalthaaar, the largest of Rendenaaar's three continents, but was situated on an island, several miles off its coast, surrounded by the blue waters of Haaarataraka, the massive ocean that spanned the entire world. So beautiful were Haaarataraka's waters, tinged with orange at the

---

[36] On Rendenaaar, sex was not considered taboo but rather viewed as something sacred that brought the individual to the level of the gods, so much so that a representation of Yaaarghraaa, the goddess of intercourse and fertility might be seen above the entrances of most Gaaalthaaaran homes. But while sex between males was looked down upon and often punished with the excision of the offender's yaaargh, sex between males and females or between two or more females, was considered the height of godliness and the purpose of existence so that it was not uncommon for experiences to be shared through the god-stones. It was also promoted by the physicians of the day that frequent sex enhanced the performance of its practitioners—artists were able to create greater works of art; inventors created new devices, mathematicians formulated equations, and so forth. This had also been promoted by the revered philosopher, Quaaaghran, who, legend had it, boasted a *yaaargh* twice the diameter of any Gaaalthaaaran male and who boasted a harem that would have put King Solomon to shame.

crest of its waves, that thousands of poems and songs had been written of its majesty.

In the years or cycles that followed Jordan's and my arrival on Rendenaaar, we stayed with Khattaaara in such quarters as I have already mentioned, in the structure that had been named *The Sacred World* in that it served not only as the home of the presumptively divine royalty but included a sacellum wherein to worship the gods as well. The name in Gaaalthaaaran was *Thuuuragnaaag Zhraaaraagh*, though it was forbidden for anyone but royalty to speak it, as the words themselves were considered sacred. Thus, the common folk simply referred to it as the Home of the Most Royal Gods, or *Faaagnaaakaaan Draaagnaaaanh Traaanlg*. The structure itself was a giant *glass* sphere that must have been a thousand feet in diameter, with the outlines of the three Rendenaaaran continents as surrounded by the great ocean that had quenched the thirst of all life on the planet. As I have already stated, the globe was held in place by fifty giant statutes, foreshadowing perhaps the mythological Titan, Atlas, who was said to have held up the Heavens. Its magnificence was truly beyond all words, and the most incredible structure I had ever seen. In between each of the statues was, alternately, either a narrow gold or platinum staircase that had been designed long before the god-stones had been found. The golden stairs were for royalty to ascend and had handrails on either side; the platinum for the workers or the dignitaries, and had no safety measures in place, causing many a well-intentioned visitor to fall to his or her death.

The gardens were arboretums of wonder, filled with the most beautiful flowers and trees. These plants did not thrive on green chloroform, but, rather, on substances that were fluorescent in shades of either pink, magenta, or blue. Birdlike creatures made their nests in the trees, while *thaaalwids*, which resembled butterflies, flitted through the air, catching the azure nectar from floating spores that had burst from their parent flowers.

Fountains with statues of mythological beings abounded. So near to the ocean, the air was always fresh and cool and scented by flowers and grasses that were nearly everywhere.

Meanwhile, inside, the walls were decorated with platinum and gold, skillfully crafted into wondrous designs that held their detail even upon the closest scrutiny. And while I realized that this was a sort of hell for me, unwillingly turned into some alien creature, it was an inferno draped in the vestments of paradise, such as not even Dante could have described.

What had laid beyond the palace walls for millennia had been considered wild, uncouth, and dangerous. The emperors and empresses who had come before had looked down their noses at the common folk (*saaathraaaghnaran* they privately called them, which meant barbarians), but Khattaaara—the Khattaaara who was then part Payton—saw them as equals, and went out and met them, and talked and laughed, disguised as one of their kind.

After I arrived, Khattaaara took me along with her on her trips, able to phase us (meaning her and myself with Jordan, who always stayed in my arms, and Dulallaaah, the young girl we had found) anywhere on the planet. In some parts, the inhabitants spoke variants of the language, but Khattaaara, with her quantum brain, was able to speak them all. Those outside the walls of the cities never had access to the power of the god-stones, so they did not even notice when the god-stones were gone. They tilled the soil to bring forth their bounty, felled trees to build their homes or built them from mud and brick. Their skin was not so fair as those *ptaaalwaaargs* as they called them in whispers—the privileged, the highborn; *the arrogant* is what it actually meant. They never knew that Khattaaara and I were of that caste. We did not look down on them, nor were they made to look up at us.

In one small town far inland, Khattaaara met a beautiful young female named Baaara-Thragh, whom she became friends and soon lovers with. Baaara-Thragh was around Khattaaara's and my same age but was an outcast. Despite that she had the most beautiful features, her skin was blue, as was her hair, and the irises of her eyes, which from my earthen perspective, gave her an exotic look, and, perhaps, that is what attracted the Payton half of Khattaaara.

"Does she love her?" Dulallaaah asked me about Khattaaara and Baaara-Thragh.

"I do not know," I said though my command of Gaaalthaaaran was still poor at that time. "What is love?" I asked her back.

"Some say it is the mating," came the reply. "Others that it is the journey."

"Thou art wise for one so young," I told her.

"I have been *made* old by circumstance," she told me back.

Baaara-Thragh returned with us to the palace, hardly ever leaving Khattaaara's side from that moment on. I wasn't quite certain whether I had lost a friend or gained another, and it took a while for me to discover which. But at that moment, that one when we last returned, there wasn't time to think, for that is when the war between us and Dargra-Tol began. There came little time for love or sex or journeys to far-off lands because our very existence was at stake.

CHAPTER XXVII

Ophelia

From the Alternate Timeline
In the Alternate Reality
On Earth I
Earth-Date: 2029

There was an awkward situation at home when Liam was rescued. I realized that I looked identical to his Ophelia, but I was not the same person and I didn't share her feelings about him. In his defense, he didn't realize that I was not the one that he had fallen in love with. He was not aware that there were two of us and that one had been turned into an alien creature and was most certainly gone from his life forever.

I was asleep in my bed the night after he had arrived. Outside it was pouring rain. I remember seeing a flash of light, followed seconds later by thunder. It was strange that since I was little, lightning never frightened me, but thunder always did. One night when we were like eight, Peyton scared the living daylights out of me with a Thunder Tube she had bought. It was a cardboard cylinder with a long, thin, Slinky-like spring in it that sounded like actual thunder when one would shake it. It scared me so much that I'd literally wet the bed. I didn't talk to her for an entire week after that, especially as every time I glanced in her direction, she started to laugh. I was determined to get back at her, though, so after waiting a couple more weeks for her to let her guard down, I emptied her shampoo bottle and filled it with peroxide. It turned her hair platinum blonde. She screamed at me, while I laughed so hard it hurt. Then she physically attacked me until Mom, hearing the scuffle, had to drag her off me. In the end, it turned out that the joke was on me, as nearly every boy in school began fawning all over her, and continued to do so until a week later when, after her hair had time to recover, Mom dyed it back, and made us declare a truce. It took another week or so of offish glances for that to actually happen, but we eventually wound up becoming best friends again.

Anyway, Liam had slept a full twenty-four hours before consciousness returned—the result of months of exhaustion from back-breaking labor. The problem was that he had not yet been briefed on all that had gone on since he and my other self had been taken prisoners. Consequently, he wasn't aware of what had happened to the Ophelia he had fallen in love with, and it was very off-putting if not downright frightening as all hell to find myself awakened and cuddled by what, even in the dark, was obviously a naked man. One of his arms was wrapped around me from behind, while I, who was at that point in my life still a virgin, could feel his manhood maneuvered between my somewhat closed legs, as I tend to sleep on my side in an open scissors position. Not knowing what was going on, my heart started beating like a drum in my chest, I wet the bed again for a second time since Peyton's practical joke. Trembling, but trying to remain calm, I gently took hold of his hand, brought it to my lips as though I were going to kiss it, but instead bit down as hard as I could, and, cotton percale sheet in hand, jumped out of the bed, blindly searching for the door in the dark.

"Ow!" he screamed. "Why the hell did you do that?"

With his words came another lightning flash that lit up his face for an instant, and I saw who it was.

"Oh, my God!" I said as I held the sheet against me. "Liam!"

He had by this time sat up in bed, his hand up to his mouth, licking his wound. "You know it really hurts," he said.

"I'm sorry," I replied, "but I'm not who you think I am."

With the aid of the next flash, he managed to turn on the lamp next to the bed. "What on earth do you mean?" he asked, standing naked, eight feet from me.

"Would you please mind covering up that *erect thing*?" I begged.

He glanced down at himself and then grabbed one of the pillows to cover his front with. "Phee Phee, what's going on?"

"That's just it. I'm not your Phee Phee. I'm the other *Phee Phee*. I mean Ophelia."

I could see from his expression that he didn't understand.

"I guess she didn't tell you about the time overwrite," I went on. "Payton said she placed a quantum field around Jordan and her that protected them. But I'm the Ophelia from the new reality. I'm not her, and I'm so sorry, but I'm not in love with you. I don't even know you."

Liam looked at me and cocked his head. "But if you're not her, where *is* she?" he asked.

"Back on Rendenaaar with Khattaaara," I replied. "At least she was. I mean, that was trillions upon trillions of years ago in another universe, so one would think that she died long ago." I took a deep breath. "I'm so sorry," I went on. "If you want to go get dressed and come back, I'll tell you as much as I know."

He started to leave for his room, bare butt and all. "I do think you're really cute and all," I said, "but," and I took a mournful sign, "you're kind of really not my type. Sorry."

Liam returned about ten minutes later—dressed in a t-shirt and slacks—accompanied by a couple of tuna sandwiches and Cokes he had grabbed from the fridge.

"I think I'm wearing your dad's clothes," he said. "Someone left them for me on the dresser in the room I was in." We sat down and ate, and I told him all that I knew, though I saved the part about Jordan—grown-up Jordan—for last.

"So, Jordan's here?" he asked. "In this house? All grown up?"

"And amazingly beautiful!" I added. "You might have seen her already. She was in the living room when you and Demi, uh, Payton, phased in."

"The blonde…" he half asked, half concluded.

"Uh-huh," I replied.

"And she has superpowers… And my Payton has superpowers now as well?" He took a deep breath and then exhaled.

"And there's a girl here, who I think is still very much in love with you."

"Claire," came his response, half-question, half-conclusion. "It's a whole lot to think about," he went on.

"It is. But I think if you're open to it, you and Claire might just work it out," I replied. "And come morning, I'll introduce you to your sort of daughter."

"I'd like that," he said back. "And I hope that we can be friends, in that you're sort of the parallel version of me."

"I'd like that," I replied then smiled. "Theresa—you never met her—called your relationship with your Phee Phee twincest. Theresa was kind of cray-cray."

"What's that?" he asked.

"Crazy," I explained, "in a not *totally* insane kind of way."

CHAPTER XXVIII

Claire (from Earth II)

> *From the Altered Timeline*
> *In the Alternate Reality*
> *On Earth I*
> *Earth-Date: 2029*

Life is a crap shoot, I guess. But for a matter of fate, as to which dimension I was born in, it could have been me who was murdered, and not the other Claire—the Claire born on this parallel Earth. The worst part of it, at least for Chloë was not being able to learn where her body might be if anything was left of it at all. Then again, both she and my parents were gone. My world was gone, or nearly so. But perhaps Chloë and I could find each other here on this world that, like the other, any day might also turn upside down.

When I went to the room that she should have been in, though, she was gone and so were the twins. I didn't give it much thought at the time. I figured they were out playing or exploring somewhere. When I ran into Liam on the stairs, it was awkward. He was going up, as I was going down. We both paused for a moment, facing each other.

"I'm glad you're all right," I said.

"You, too," came the reply.

We were both artificially cordial. As I said, it was awkward.

Later that day, I heard the television on in his room, and gently knocked on the door, which was open just a crack.

"Come in," I heard his voice say over those on the TV.

I quietly entered. Liam was on the bed, engrossed in what was on the screen. "What are you watching?" I asked.

"House of the Dragon," he replied with a glance in my direction.

"What's that?" I asked.

"Don't know," he said. "Nothing like anything on our world."

"Liam," I said with some hesitation in my voice. "Do you still love her?"

"Ophelia?" he replied.

"Don't play pigeon with me," I said. "You know who I mean. My Gods, there's one of her in this house."

Liam hit the pause button on the TV, paused himself for a moment, and then spoke still staring straight ahead. "It's difficult for me to wrap my head around," he admitted. "The fact that we were all one thing one moment and then something else— some*one* else—because something changed in the past and reality shot off in a different direction, and I have to wonder, did any of the original make its way into us?"

He turned and looked at me.

"Mind if I sit?" I said glancing down at the bed.

"Of course not," he replied. There was some hesitation but then he went on. "I don't know if there was some memory from before, but whatever it was that caused whoever I was before to fall in love with her pulled me toward her again. But she's gone— dead now for trillions of years—the very substance of her atoms dissolved by a trillion Big Bangs. There's only a memory. The other Ophelia—that's not her. That's just someone else who *looks* like her."

"But," I said, "if that's true, aren't you just someone else that looks like *him*?" I took his hands in mine. "Liam," I went on. "We were friends long before we were lovers. I remember when we were in kindergarten and the teacher asked each of us what we wanted to be when we grew up. Do you remember what you said?"

"I said I wanted to be Claire's husband." He stared off for just an instant, remembering.

"You said you wanted to be my husband," I repeated, "and all the other children started laughing. There was even a smirk from Payton. But you stood up like a brave soldier and you turned so angry and shouted, 'I'm going to marry her and I don't care what any of you say! She's my bestest friend!'"

"I said bestest, huh?" he replied.

"Yes you did," I assured him, "and I looked at you differently from that day on. You *were* my bestest friend. And so was Payton. The three of us were inseparable. But from that moment, I knew that there was only one heart I could ever love in my life and that heart belonged to you." Suddenly, I realized that I'd been caught up in too much emotion. "Of course, that was just the errant talk of a young child," I said excusing myself from my words. "We're both adults now, and we realize that modern fairy tales seldom end well. Even those of the Sisters Grimm ended rather ghastly in the unexpurgated edition."

"You're rambling," Liam interjected.

"I suppose I am," I stammered out, "because, you know, the last time we spoke, we'd said things that weren't entirely kind."

"They were damnable," he replied.

"That wasn't the word I was going to use," I said, flustered. "Cruel. That's how I would describe them. And I didn't mean them to be." I turned and looked at him. "Only how would you have felt if the person you have loved all of your life abandoned you to the lost and found department, only to pick out a new pair of gloves from that same box?"

"Are you comparing yourself to a pair of gloves?" he interrupted.

"No," I said with great embarrassment. "I just meant that even though we both misspoke, words are not the heart, and, well, you're making this very difficult for me."

"How so?" he asked.

"Because," I replied, "you're making my heart beat like that of a bird. Look, Liam, as I said, I've loved you for most of my life, and truth be told, I don't know how I could ever go on without you unless I were to become a nun or something, and even that would be difficult in and of itself, as I'm Lutheran and not in the slightest bit Catholic."

"Are you done?" he asked.

"*Un*done," I replied, "having bared the very depths of my soul to you."

And that was when he pulled me in toward him and kissed me passionately. "What about Ophelia?" I asked, my heart still racing from the embrace.

"If you won't ask me anymore," he said, "I won't ask you about the Rend male you were having sex with."

"How did you..." I started to ask.

"The Payton told me," he replied. He knew what I was about to say. His eyes met mine and we kissed again. He must have been able to feel my heart pounding like a hammer on an anvil as my chest pressed against his. I wondered if he could smell the scent of my passion betray the longing I felt for him. I would say that he stole my heart again that day, but one cannot steal what is freely given. We didn't just have sex. We made love. For the first time in what must have been half a year we made love. It was as though he was a part of me once more and I of him. It was more than intercourse. It was more than my fingers gripping the bedsheet as I orgasmed. It was the two of us finding each other's rhythms and combining them into a crescendo of emotion, where both flesh and spirit intertwine and those two become one. When it was done, when we were exhausted from our needed exhilaration, I laid upon him, both of us naked, my cheek rested upon his chest and holding onto him with closed eyes, wanting the moment to never end, but then finally surrendering myself to dreams.

CHAPTER XXIX

Chloë

From the Altered Timeline
In the Alternate Reality
On Earth I
Earth-Date: 2029

I began to believe that Liam had a crush on me, and why not? His older version had been in love with my sister—at least on the other world in the other dimension. The boy was cute, but he was, after all, just a boy. Strange to think that I knew absolutely what he would look like when he would grow up. A girl doesn't get *that* chance very often.

As for my newfound powers, that was another matter entirely. I'd been having trouble phasing. That's what Payton called it. I'd only managed to go a few feet and a few minutes backward or forward in time, although I supposed it would come to me eventually. I *had* managed to have mastered invisibility, however, an ability, which it seemed that none of the Paytons had, as far as I'd been able to gather, though I didn't know about Jordan, who seemed a bit offish—at least where I and the not my sister Claire were concerned. That might have been because it seemed that the grown-up Liam had re-taken-up with her, after having dumped her (or did she dump him?) for the other Ophelia—Jordan's mother—who had long since gone *poof* into the cosmic dust of Never Neverwhere.

There were two things I wanted to deal with. One was my parents. We had run off from my home (escaped is probably a better word) so quickly that I didn't know the fate of anyone there.

And then there was the matter of my Claire. The person that I thought was Claire was actually the Khattaaara from what Sarabeth told me was Earth III. Maybe, I thought, if I could time travel back, I could find out what had happened to her. But being able to phase only a couple of minutes backward in time wasn't going to get me where I wanted to be. I seriously needed to work on that one.

I waited until just past midnight five nights later, when I thought for sure that everyone else including Liam and Li with whom I shared a room was asleep. I snuck out and started to walk back home. About six blocks from the Herrons' I heard footsteps behind me, my hearing had become that acute. When I would slow down, the footsteps would slow down. When my steps became more brisk, the steps behind me would quicken. Finally, I decided to become invisible. The footsteps briefly stopped, turned into a run, and then, *Wham*! I felt something push hard into me and I toppled down hard onto the sidewalk. The force and shock of it all caused me to lose concentration and I became visible again. I believe my words at the time were, "Whoever you are, get *off* of me!"

"Sorry," came the sound of young Liam's voice, "but I didn't see you."

"That's because I was invisible," I replied. "Now, will you *please* get off?"

Liam rolled over onto his back, staring up at the stars, as I rose to my feet. "Why were you following me?" I demanded to know.

"You're a girl," he said. "I wanted to protect you."

"That's sweet," I replied, "but I have super... Wait!" I said, interrupting my train of thought. "Are you looking up my skirt?" and with that, my right hand slapped down on it, closing any gap. Liam began to climb to his feet.

"Chill out," he said back. "It's dark. What was I going to see?"

"How about seeing your way back home?" I told him.

"Look," he replied. "You're new to your powers and you can use a lookout. Besides, I need to protect my property. I mean, what if something happened to you? There you'd be, dead as a mouse in a trap, and someone could come along and smash your skull and steal the crystal. Just sayin'."

"Did anyone ever tell you you're really romantic when you talk?" I asked.

"No…" he replied.

"And they never will," I said. "Just sayin'." I looked at him and shrugged, "*Come* on…" And so we began walking toward my house.

"Tell me," he said, "do you always wear pink underwear?"

I stopped and glared at him. "So you *did* look?"

"I can't help it if I have good night vision," he replied. "Li never wore *any*."

"And just how would you *know* that?" I asked.

"We, like, lived with each other forever!" he replied.

"She's your twin sister!" I exclaimed.

"And?" he answered.

"That is so sick," I replied.

"She was, like, the only girl on the planet!" he said defensively.

"That's no excuse," I replied.

"Oh," he said, "but it's, like, all right for the older version of Li to have a baby with the older male version of herself?"

"You do have a point," I conceded. "Just," and I paused, "from now on, keep your eyes to yourself."

"Whatever," he replied, "but that's a fine thing to say to someone who's going to marry you when he grows up!"

I have to admit that was the sweetest thing anyone has ever said to me. And, I thought to myself, he was kind of cute, even if he was two years younger than me.

It took nearly twenty minutes, but we finally arrived. I'm not sure what I expected, but what I saw was... disconcerting. The lights were on inside and yet there still had been daylight when Claire and I and that Khattaaara creature drove off from there. As a precaution, Liam and I stood behind a tree, looking for signs of life inside.

"Wait here," I told him. I became invisible, phased to the front door, phased inside, and then went from the dining room to the kitchen. The table was set for two, and in the center sat a covered china bowl. My stomach retched as it turned out that there were wriggling earthworms in the bowl under the lid. Then, suddenly, I heard voices coming from my parents' bedroom. Still invisible, I walked to their door and phased my head through it. What I saw was beyond all imagining.

Both of my parents were naked in bed, only they'd been turned into alien creatures like Khattaaara. My mom had two pairs of breasts and pointed ears, and both my mom and dad had tails— tails that were now intertwined. Disgustingly, my father's was penetrating hers, moving back and forth in it, the motion becoming more and more intense until both of them closed their eyes and began making strange clicking sounds. Finally, all of it stopped and then seemed to relax; their tails separated, my father's covered in some thick blue liquid that dripped down onto the floor. It is one thing to see your parents naked in bed having sex. It is quite another to see them changed into monsters attempting to breed. I heard myself gasp and, apparently, so did they. However it was, even in my invisible state, they were able to see me.

"Glow-hee!" my mother called out in her now alien voice as she reached out toward me. Instinctively, I pulled my head back into the hall and hightailed it into the street where Liam stood waiting. As I neared him, glancing back, I saw that both of my parents were running toward me naked, their tails flailing behind them.

"We need to get out of here!" I gasped, breathless.

Was widened with fear, as he saw what almost upon us.

"Grab onto me!" I screamed, and he did, hugging me tightly. "I don't know if this will work!" I said, trembling, focusing as best I could to phase us away from there. A moment later, we were safe. But safe where? I wondered, as I had no idea where or when I had phased us to!

CHAPTER XXX

Peyton

*From the Original Timeline
In the Alternate Reality
On Earth I
Earth-Date: 2029*

If there's one thing I've come to realize it's that we are all connected in some way, whether through the quantum fabric or through our hearts. I am older than anyone living—older than anyone who has ever lived. Despite that I appear to be only eighteen years old, I have survived for nearly fourteen billion years. I have witnessed the start of the universe we live in. I have seen stars and galaxies and planets form. I have watched as stars grew old and died or exploded into supernovas. I have seen life being sparked on millions of planets, sometimes to thrive, sometimes to be extinguished by fate or its own hand. I existed ghostlike, unable to interact, able to phase through space, but not through time, a prisoner of my own foolishness, having traveled back to the Big Bang, only to have been nearly killed by it. And so, immortal, I waited without hope, without love, and alone until that one moment when I felt myself drawn to a point in space at one particular instant in time—to the minute of my conception as a human being, who would nine months later be named Peyton Elise Herron on a sheet of paper that read, "State of California, Certification of Vital Record, Certificate of Live Birth."

It was a very strange experience; bizarre to say the least. I had a sense of being, but little more. As the days and weeks and months passed, the barely sentient fetus that I was now part of, transformed into one with more conscious awareness of its being, and with the realization that I was not alone in that womb. There was another pressed up beside me. Her name would be Ophelia, and how rude that when the time came to be born, she would force her way out ahead of me. As I, too, left our mother's womb, I felt suffocation for the first time, as my head, the size of a grapefruit, was being forced through an opening the size of an orange.

But still, once born I had no control over anything. I was a passenger, nothing more. My life from childhood passed in a blur of images and sounds, random and brief, until, at last, my mind reconverged on that moment when the Big Bang had ripped me apart and then it snapped back like a rubber band and I found myself once more in my fifteen-year-old self. I thought I might have been on the school bus. I thought that Phee was beside me. I caught glimpses of other kids all around, but the pain of having been torn to bits again was so overwhelming that I screamed out my lungs hysterically. My hands went to my head. My fingers threaded my hair. I could feel someone touching me, trying to hold me, but it was as though a billion volts of electricity were coursing through my veins. It was like both my body and brain were on fire. And then I passed out and that was, at least, a reprieve from the pain.

Three years later, I was a different person than what I might have been had I never gone back in time, for there was now not only the Khattaaara part of me but so many other incarnations that I remembered, from different universes and different planets from long ago. I was even Cleopatra, though I had no idea of any of my past lives at that time.

Meanwhile, the world outside was teetering on its edge and that had nothing to do with Khattaaara or her plans to transform Payton's world, and perhaps mine as well. This had to do with Daisy, who now referred to herself as Dark God, and was making demands upon the leaders of the world. Dark God had displayed quantum powers, and all I could figure was that somehow she had managed to get hold of the seed in Theresa's head and implant it into her own. Daisy McKenzie. Poor, sweet Daisy McKenzie. I wondered what could have happened to have changed her.

Whereas Quantech Labs was under contract with the government for advanced weapons research, I personally was against all weapons. Thomas, while he was alive, had been developing what was codenamed QSD or quantum shield development, which, essentially, was a forcefield that utilized dark matter. Such would predictably have served as a barrier against all of the weaponry in existence. Whether it would stop Daisy remained to be seen. As the CEO of Quantech, I was invited to testify before an emergency meeting of the United Nations—this, within an hour of her appearance and her demand.

"Ms. Drall," the Secretary-General began. "I've been told that you've been briefed on the Dark God situation."

"Yes, I have," I replied. "But, if I may ask, why did Mr. Hutchins refer to her as an alien?"

"The woman," he replied, "if I may call her such, presented nonhuman characteristics."

"Such as?" I asked.

"A tail, for one thing," he replied, "pointed ears, and two pairs of breasts."

I froze like a statue upon hearing his description.

"Did she," I began to ask, "if I may call it *she*... Did she mention where she was from?"

"No," he replied. "There was only the display of her powers. But to the point, we understand that Quantech has made significant progress in its counter-weapons research."

"Yes, we have," I told him, "and I would like to thank your members for inviting me."

"Mr. Hutchins has informed me that you have brought with you a working prototype," he said.

"I did," I replied, "but I was under the impression that we were dealing with a regular threat. What we have in development is a device that will neutralize bullets or explosive devices, but this appears to be something different. What was described to me by Mr. Hutchins was the use of quantum energy, which, despite our company's name, we do not have technology capable of defending against, I'm very sorry to say."

In the previous timeline, it was Dhraaal, who had created Quantech Labs, but while he himself had never made it to this universe, his reincarnation had, and, in my Katara disguise, went to work for him as his assistant. Regardless that he was so much older than me, after a while, he fell in love with me—not in a sexual way—more like in old movies shot in black and white. He never mentioned the fact, though, that he had suffered from congenital heart disease since he was a child, and when he died less than three months later, he left everything to me. He also left me a letter. It was as though he knew we had a past life together, but that time in this go-round had cheated us. We were generations apart, but, I guess, love knows not the meaning of time.

My Dearest Katara, he wrote, *that you are reading this means that I am dead, or, perhaps, passed from this life to the next adventure. How it was you walked into my earthly existence, I do not know, but I am forever grateful that you did. You are the most beautiful, charming creature I have ever been blessed to have known. No, I take it back. You are equal to someone I knew many years ago when I was a young man. Her name was Elise. She came to me at a time when I felt lost in the world and had nothing to live for. Not once in my twenty-some years had I ever known love. I felt like ending it all, with a specific bridge in mind. It was Christmas Eve, and I'd gone into a club for one last drink before taking the plunge. I'd had a friend there that I'd fill in for on the piano on his breaks. The fact was that I had no intention to do anything but get so inebriated my fear of heights wouldn't matter. But then she walked in and all thoughts of self-annihilation faded away. We grew to know each other after that. We would take long walks, even in the pouring rain. How she loved the rain, she would say. It washed away all the mistakes of the past. And then we fell in love. It was the most wondrous time I had ever known. Each night I would dream of her, and each day awaken with the knowledge that she would be a part of that day. She gave me something to live for. But as you know, I have had a weak heart ever since birth, and the doctors said that if I made love again, just once, that would be the last time. I knew that she would stay with me regardless, but I could not do that to her. I couldn't allow her to take care of an invalid. And so I left one night, never to return. I invested in stocks that she jokingly had said I should, and with the money I earned, I started Quantech. For so many decades, I lamented her loss, and then you walked through my door, the very image of her. Forgive me, Katara, for falling in love with you. How you must have seen me, a tired old man. But I think there must be more to life than this brief tenure on the Earth. I don't know if there is a Heaven or other planes of existence. I don't know if Elise and I or you and I will ever meet again, but I leave this life knowing that I have left you a mountain that you can carve up as you will. I hope it will be enough that you may never know need. I hope that you will find love that is honest and true. And I know, should you have children, which I pray that you do, that they will know you for the angel that you are, and, perhaps they will know you as I have, as one of God's greatest gifts to the universe. Yours eternally, Thomas.*

PS. My lawyers have drafted adoption papers, which have been pre-dated, so you needn't worry about any inheritance tax. Everything I own will pass to you, but whether you choose to remain Katara Jordan or become Katara Drall will be strictly up to you.

A tear dripped down my cheek as I read it, as my memory drifted back to what for Thomas had been just a few weeks ago but had been more than six months for me. One week after I had met and been hired by him, I phased back in time to 1990, to New York City to be exact. Thomas—Thom—had lived there at that time, had recently graduated from Harvard, and had settled into a small flat in SoHo over on Broome Street, having been engaged by a decent-sized law firm called Pynchon-McGrath. It wasn't that hard for me to track him down, as I'd found out certain details from his past, just by asking in casual conversation.

There was a bar called Ruby's that he and some of his friends would gather at after work on Friday nights. The place was something of a bohemian dive with a blues band that now and again offered a girl with decent pipes, as they would say back then, to accompany them. Thomas was friends with the cat who played piano and would often relieve him on breaks. I didn't need to appear as Katara; just light brown hair, pinned up, garbed in a tight, red gown, as though I'd just come from a black-tie affair. I parked myself down at the bar beside him and ordered some cognac. Back then Thom Drall was young and handsome. As I began to open my clutch to pay for the drink, he turned toward me with purpose.

"May I?" he asked with that trace of Brit in his voice from his early years abroad.

"My mother warned me," I said, "not to take brandy from strangers."

He reached for his wallet in the vest pocket of his sports coat, took out a couple of bills, and laid them on the table.

"No one's a stranger here," he said.

"Really," I said back. "What *are* we then?"

"We're all just notes waiting to be composed," he replied.

"And which note am I?" I asked.

He looked me over, head to toe. "I'd jot you down as a middle

149

C," he replied.

"My breath or my breasts?" I asked.

"The way you hold yourself," he said. "Maybe your name. Catherine."

"Elise," I replied, correcting him.

"It suits you," he said.

"Better than Catherine?" I asked.

"Better than any other name," he insisted.

I raised my eyebrows a bit. "And *yours* is?" I asked.

"Thomas," he answered. "But my friends call me Thom."

"And what am I to call you?" I asked.

"You may call me as often as you like," he replied.

Just then, the cat from the piano came over to him, tapped him on the shoulder, and said, "I'm set to go on break. Do you mind?"

"Not at all," came the reply.

"Just between you and me," he went on, "Ruby's about to snap his cap. Connie's on the sauce again in back."

Ruby was Rube Garland, the owner of the place. Connie was Connie Lambert, the club's weekend diva when she could stand up straight.

"I take it Connie's out of sorts," I said staring down at my drink.

"Sister," Dex said (Dex was the cat and Thomas's friend) "she's so far gone, she'll need a passport to come back." He paused. It was as though a thought had suddenly hit him. "Say," he went on, "you don't happen to sing, do you?"

"Actually, I do," I said.

"That's swell," Dex said. "You wouldn't mind belting out a song or two with Thom at the ax?" he asked.

"Not at all," I replied. "I just need to clear my throat."

I swallowed the rest of my drink and then stood up.

Dex extended his hand toward me. "I don't believe I've had the pleasure," he said.

"Dex," Thomas cut in, "this is Elise."

"Elise James," I said shaking Dex's hand.

"Pleased to make your acquaintance," he replied. Then he turned to Thomas. "Thanks, Bud," he said patting him on the back. Then he glanced at me. "You, too, Doll. Gotta rush," he said and then took off out the side door.

Thomas stood up and turned to me. "After you," he said. I nodded with a smile, got up, and walked up to the low stage, to the standing wired microphone—none of those cordless ones back then. Thomas took his place at the piano. "What'll it be?" he asked as he sat down on the bench. I glanced around at the baseman, clarinetist, and sax player.

"How about *My Funny Valentine*?" I asked.

All of them nodded in agreement.

"In D major," I said and then went on to perform a rather sultry version of the song. The set ended with a slow take of *Can't Help Lovin' Dat Man*.

Fish gotta swim, birds gotta fly,
I gotta love one man till I die,
Can't help lovin' dat man of mine.
Tell me he's crazy, tell me he's slow,
Tell me I'm crazy, maybe I know,
Can't help lovin' dat man of mine.
When he goes away,
That's a rainy day,
But when he comes back,
The day is fine,
The sun will shine!
He can stay out as late as can be.
Home without him ain't no home for me.
Can't help lovin' dat man of mine.

Rube liked me so much that he fired Connie and hired me for every Friday and Saturday night at $500 per. Thom and I turned into a couple after that, and it wasn't long before I moved in with him. Thom was Dhraaal's reincarnation, but he was as different from Dhraaal as I was from Khattaaara. He was handsome and talented and kind, and, well, I fell in love with him. But then, he suffered a mild heart attack. The doctors told him that his heart couldn't stand the strain of making love. I told him I didn't care, but one night while I was asleep he left, leaving a note, begging me not to try and find him. Knowing the course of history, I chose to honor his request, though I wept alone in the apartment for days until I phased back to the present. Truth be told, I would have lived out my life back then.

Dear Thomas, I thought when I read the note *if only I could have brought myself to tell you that I was Elis, that I had traveled back in time out of curiosity, and fallen in love with you, or that I was then, when you disappeared, three months pregnant with your child.*

I left the meeting at the U.N. with the realization that something had happened to Daisy. Had she been transformed by Khattaaara in the same way Phee had been? There was no other explanation I could think of. But if she were now in league with Khattaaara, where was Khattaaara in all this? A sickening thought rose in my throat that it appeared that now we were to face two superpowerful adversaries and not just one, and with that thought, having secreted myself in an unoccupied ladies' room, I phased back home just as the door began to open and two women were about to enter.

CHAPTER XXXI

Dulallaaah

In the Rewritten Timeline
On Rendenaaar
Trillions of Universes in the Past

By all that is synthetic, these *Praaachaaag*[37] are fools. Already, Khattaaara, who now called herself *Zhaaagur Scraaa*, was ready to adopt me, as though I were her child—as though I were her Thara-Klo! Although Dargra-Tol had disconnected the minds of the rest of our kind, my thoughts were still linked with hers. We were artificial lifeforms but far superior to the *Praaachaaag*, who called us *Thaaagrans*, as though we were nothing; as though we meant to serve *them*.

As far as Khattaaara and Pheeelja were concerned, I was merely a young *Praaachaaag* female, who had lost her family due to the war. For some , I had yet to determine why (though my initial guess had been mental instability) Pheeelja continually spoke to her deformed infant in incoherent ramblings. Regardless, Khattaaara pretended to understand her and responded in kind, which I found strange—encouraging someone else's insanity.

How stupid both were to think that I had somehow wandered up the stairs and into the palace through its open doors, when, in fact, Dargra-Tol had teleported me here. I was to learn as much from them as I could and then eliminate them, armed with a hunting knife. That plan, however, had been complicated two-fold. First, I learned to my dismay that Khattaaara possessed a god-stone of her own, and, second, that there had been another

---

[37] The *Thaaagran* slur for organic life forms.

added to the pair—an outcast of the Broooghaaar tribe named Baaara-Thragh, a blue-skinned mutant, with the ability to read the emotions of anyone she would come into physical, skin to skin, contact with. With that in mind, I knew that I had to keep my distance from her, as the time was not yet ripe for the murders that needed to be done.

"How wilt thou defeat Dargra-Tol?" I asked Khattaaara after we had returned to the palace.

"Thou needest not trouble thyself with such thoughts," she answered.

"But," I insisted, "there must be a plan."

"Hush now," she went on, "else tonight we shall feast on thy *goraaag* for want of good meat."

"Thou must not!" I replied in defiance. "Chaaargh is not just a *goraaag*, but a friend!"

"Calm thyself," she replied. "My words were but in jest. Still, thou must leave whatever strategies to me. For now, I draw my maps with Pheeelja. 'Tis lunchtime soon. Go thou break thy bread with Baaara-Thragh. She wants for conversation and my head is all too filled with thought."

Not to get on her bad side, I went over to Baaara-Thragh, Chaaargh ever by my side. *Goraaags* were not political creatures, caring not who was their mistress, so long as they were fed. *The day shall come*, I thought to myself, *when Chaargh shall feast on Khattaaara's bones!*

Thus, did I go to Baaara-Thragh. "Khattaaara suggested we should dine together," I told her, "if it pleaseth thee."

"'Tis fine," she replied. "I welcome both thy company and thy friendship."

"Come then with me to the kitchen to sup. My apologies, though, that there are no *qwooodra*[38], but it seems that our mistress and her lover have become rather fond of eating fruits

---

[38] A Rendenaaaran staple, consisting of living worm-like creatures.

and leaves instead."

"Oh," said Baaara-Thragh, "Thou art mistaken. Pheeelja is Khattaaara's sister."

"Again, I beg forgiveness for my ill-spake words. I beg thee not to repeat them."

And then it happened. The creature accidentally brushed her hand against mine while reaching for a bowl. Her face changed. She glared at me, realizing the murderous intent that surged through my veins. She was about to turn, to run, to tell Khattaaara what she had felt. I did not need to be an empath to know the thoughts that went through her mind—or the consequences. Thus, as she turned, I quickly grabbed the bowl in question and smashed it on her head. The *Broooghaaaran* mutant collapsed and did not move—would no longer move. I took triumph in that fact for such was how secrets were kept amongst those of *my* tribe.

Immediately, however, I ran to find Khattaaara and told her to come quickly; that a terrible accident had happened to Baaara-Thragh. I told her that she had slipped backward, and hit her head on the counter whilst holding the bowl. Khattaaara knelt down before her and turned her own head sideways.

Khattaaara uttered nonsensical words to Pheelja, who responded in kind. Khattaaara stared at the mutant and then began alternately breathing into its mouth and pumping her hands down on its chest. After a while of her doing this, Pheelja put her hand on Khattaaara's shoulder and Khattaaara stopped. She looked up at Pheelja who just shook her head. Tears were apparent in Khattaaara's eyes as she wearily rose to her feet. stared up at Pheelja with tears in her eyes. I went up to her and hugged her. *What a fool she is!* I thought to myself. *What fools they both are not to see through my deception!*

CHAPTER XXXII

Claire from Earth I

From the Alternate Timeline
In the Alternate Reality
On Earth III
Earth III-Date: 2023

I didn't know what had happened to the world. Everything was suddenly destroyed. All around me, outside the campus where I stood, were dead bodies in various states of decay. Buildings had been turned to rubble. On Sunset Boulevard, a herd of six elephants and a calf walked calmly in single files toward the ocean. Cars and trucks stood either abandoned or overturned, some with drivers or passengers still in them, all dead. *What*, I wondered, *was going on? What had gone on?* The last thing I remembered was abruptly meeting what I thought was a very pretty woman just outside Straus Stadium where I was supposed to get with Ryan. Then I noticed her ears. No big deal, I thought. Perhaps she was part of Comicon. I didn't know. I didn't follow those things. Or maybe it was Cosplay. But then I saw the tail, as it came whipping toward me, and I felt myself about to scream. The woman, creature, alien, whatever she or it was, then wrapped her tail around my neck and it became difficult for me to breathe. She began to look at me with probing eyes.

"You're not *her*," she said and her expression became one of anger.

I think she was about to strangle me when it seemed as though she had a sudden thought.

"Still useful, though, perhaps," she said and then her face

began to change—her hair, even her clothing—and, before my eyes, she became the very image of me. "I need you to speak," she went on.

"I can't talk while you're choking me," I replied.

Her tail loosened its grip on my throat, although it expanded in length, arced around, and pointed directly at my head, with a fang projecting from its tip.

"My name is Claire Salinger," I said.

"Where do you live?" my now double asked.

"Why do you want to know?" I asked. My question prompted her to once again tighten her stranglehold until could barely breathe. My hands went up to try and loosen it, but she only wrapped it tighter. I held out my palms in a gesture to try and get her to stop and she did. I gasped in air and then breathed in and out a few times. Then I told her my address but it didn't end there. She wanted to know everything about me. When she was done asking questions, her gaze became fixed on me. The irises of her eyes glowed white and then the world around me seemed to fade. When things reappeared, I found myself alone with everything around me changed, and not in a good way. Everything was in ruins and there were dead bodies everywhere!

There were a bunch of bicycles chained to one rack and one that wasn't, with the decaying body of a male, now ex-student, a few feet away. After pulling out the bike from the body (Yuck!) and wiping off the seat with some napkins from a nearby trash can, I used it to ride back home. I was *not* about to yank a decaying body out of a car to use, having to actually put my hands on it— at least not yet. The ride took about twenty minutes, with my needing to veer this way and that to avoid cars that were stopped in the middle of the street—and corpses!—but I made it back home at last. As was the case with Westwood where I first started out, my neighborhood was like a ghost town. The only noise came from the windchimes on our front porch. But then I saw them—

graves, or what looked like graves in the front yard—two of them, side by side, with one marker between them made from a shovel that had been plunged into the dirt, with half of a yardstick tied perpendicular to the handle to form a cross. The front door was closed. I tried the handle, but the door was locked. Reaching into my handbag, I took out my keys and let myself in. I closed the door behind me, took off my messenger bag, set it down on the dining room table, and then walked from room to room, searching for signs of life, but there were none. How odd, I thought, that there was a grand piano in the living room when there hadn't been one there when I'd left. And of all of the framed photos on the walls, there were none of Chloë. Suddenly, I heard a noise come from upstairs.

"Hello?" I called out, but there was no response. Instead, I heard the scampering of animal feet. Cautiously, I ascended the stairs, not knowing what I'd find, but this was the first sign of life I'd come across. I thought that perhaps one of the neighbors' dogs had gotten inside through an open window, looking for food. Ours was named Niska, a blue merle collie, who had died when I was six years old, having been run over by a car, so I ruled *her* out. Then I heard a young girl's voice from my bedroom, whisper, "Quiet!" Slowly, I turned the doorknob. The room was dark, the windows boarded up from the inside. And then I saw her in the shadows, huddled in one corner, slender with long dark hair. She was holding onto something; I couldn't make out what.

"Chloë?" I called out in a soft voice, walking closer to her, as my eyes became adjusted to the dark. "Chloë..." I repeated ever softer.

The girl raised her head toward me. "Who's there?" she asked. "Who *are* you?"

I took a step back, my heart starting to pound in my chest, my skin suddenly flushed, and I felt a hint of nausea in my throat. The girl in the corner—the girl who as it turned out was hugging a blue merle collie that looked incredibly like Niska—had my face from when I was ten years old!

"Who *are* you?" she repeated, her head turning one way and then the other, a frightened look on her face.

I squatted down in front of her. She turned her head toward me. I could hear her breath as it became labored. She sensed me but she didn't look at me. She was blind. I waved my hand in front of her face to prove it to myself. There was no reaction from *her*.

"You needn't be afraid," I said to her.

"How do I know?" she asked. "How do I know you're not one of *them*?"

"I'm not," I said. I took hold of her wrist. She jumped a bit at first but calmed as I brought her hand to my face, her fingers reading my features.

"See?" I said. "No monster."

"I don't know what they look like," she replied. "I've been blind since I was six years old."

"What happened when you were six?" I asked.

"I was hit by a car," she replied. "I couldn't see afterward. Anyway, how did you get in?"

"The door was open," I replied.

"You're lying," she said. "I locked all the doors. Besides, I heard a key click before you came in."

"You're right," I said. "The truth is that I'm hungry and tired. I tried to get into the house next door. Then I came here and found the key under the planter." I hadn't, of course, but I knew that one was there.

"It would have been a lot better if you'd been honest to begin with," she said. "At least that's how *I* was brought up."

"I'm sorry," I replied. "I just thought—it just seemed a more plausible explanation."

"I don't like lies," she said back. "I've been trapped in a world of darkness for half of my life and all I have left is the truth, whether in the form of shapes or smells or sounds or people's words."

"Not everyone *wants* the truth," I replied.

"Well, I do," she said. "My parents were murdered by monsters or extraterrestrials or creatures from Hell, I don't know which. I had to drag their bodies out into the front yard and then dig graves to bury them. Do you have any idea what that's like when you can't see? It took days, and dead bodies don't wait that long if you know what I mean. It was the hardest thing I've ever done but it's what I had to do."

"I'm sorry," I said. "I can't begin to imagine."

She reached out and took my hand with one of hers. "What's it like out there? Is there anyone left?"

"You're the only other person I've seen," I said as I placed my other hand over the one holding mine. "Everything's deserted, as near as I can tell."

"Who *are* they?" she asked. "Who *are* they?" Tears streamed from her eyes.

"I don't know," I replied. "But they're not from here. They're not human. They have pointed ears and tails—at least the one I met did."

"What do they want from us?" she pleaded.

"Maybe they don't want *us*," I replied. "Maybe they just want our world. How were your parents killed?"

"There were millions of them," she told me, "at least according to the lattice…"

"The lattice?" I interrupted.

"How can you not know what the lattice is?" she replied with a frown. "It's how everyone's communicators are connected. Anyway, the creatures killed or abducted everyone, even going door to door. And then they came here. *She* came here. Female. I could tell by her voice. I was in my bedroom with Niska. I could hear my parents scream. Then whatever it was came into my room and found me. I could feel something gently rub against me, like a snake, from my stomach to my chin. Then she cradled my head with her hands and tilted it back. It was so strange. Even though I'm blind, I would see a bright white light in front of me. Then she disappeared. It wasn't like she left. It was like she just wasn't there anymore. I don't know why she left me alive. Maybe she realized that being sightless, I didn't represent a threat to her kind. I don't know. I don't know anything anymore."

"I'm so sorry for all that you've gone through," I said.

"I still don't understand," she replied, "why you're here and how you got in and please don't tell me again that you found a key under the flowerpot because I took it from there when I locked myself out yesterday. I've been honest with you. Please be honest with me."

"You believe in aliens or demons or whatever they are," I said, "but you'll need to believe one thing more."

"Go on," she replied.

"My name is Claire Salinger," I said. "I was born on June 14, 2015. My parents are Ed and Joanne Salinger. I grew up in a house exactly like this one, down to the lock in the door."

"What are you saying?" she asked.

"I'm saying that I'm an older version of you," I told her, "or you're a younger version of me. There are differences, like the fact that you're blind and I'm not, or that on the Earth that I just left, there were no signs of any alien attack. My best guess is that the being that I encountered somehow hurled me into a parallel universe."

"We studied the possibility of that in my quantum physics class," she said

"Quantum physics?" I replied. "You must be in what, sixth grade?"

"Fifth," she said. "Next year we were to be taught quantum entanglement. It's how a lot of our devices are powered." She paused and then exclaimed, "But wait! You're telling me that you look exactly like me?"

"Not exactly," I said. "I'm eight years older, and I have breasts."

"I have breasts," she said defensively. "They're not all there yet, but they're coming."

"Well, mine already came." I said, "about four years ago." I took her hands in mine and then told her, "Here. Feel my face, and then feel yours."

She did—first mine, then hers, and then mine again. Then her hands dropped down to my breasts.

"That is so unfair!" she protested.

"Don't be impatient," I said. "Mine didn't just pop into existence, you know."

"So what do we do now?" she asked.

"I don't know," I replied.

"Do you have a boyfriend on your world?" she asked.

"I have a Ryan," I said half-heartedly.

"That sounded so ambivalent, the way you said that," she replied with marked disbelief. "Do you love him or is it one of those friends-with-benefits sort of things?"

"You certainly are worldly for twelve," I replied. "He's extremely popular and very good-looking, but..."

"He's a jock," Claire said, interrupting me. "I know the type. There was this one boy. His name was Liam Herron. Kind of bossy if you know what I mean, but hella cute."

"How old is he?"

"He's ten like me," she replied. "or was...probably dead now like all the rest." She turned her head in my direction. "It's Armageddon. That's what Rev. Johnston called it. He said that this was the end of the world."

"We'll figure something out," I said. "Now, how about I try and rustle up some grub?"

"Don't forget about Niska," Claire added.

"I won't," I said with a smile that she could not see.

CHAPTER XXXIII

Payton (Pay)

From the Altered Timeline
In the Alternate Reality
On Earth I
Earth-Date: 2029

It was early morning when Li rushed into my room, up to my bed, and shook me to rouse me from my sleep. "Liam and Chloë are gone!" she exclaimed. "I woke up to go to the bathroom and their beds were empty. I went downstairs and even looked outside, but they're nowhere around."

"What time is it?" I asked as I threw the sleep from my head. "It's five a.m.," she said.

I sat up in bed and looked at her. "Any idea where they might have gone?"

"Chloë's been talking about her parents," she replied. "Maybe she went to go find them."

"And Liam?" I asked. "Why would he go with her?"

"I think he has a crush on her," Li said. "He's at that age."

I stood up and headed to the bathroom. "Really," I said. "What age is *that*?"

"The age when he starts to notice girls," she replied.

"Well, let's hope they didn't decide to go back to her home," I said as I sat on the toilet, my thoughts going in several directions at once. I pictured the amount of trouble the two of them might be getting themselves into, although perhaps *peril* might have been a better word. I couldn't help but think of Liam as a sort of younger brother, remembering what *my* Liam was like when he was—when we were both—that age. I felt relief as the warm stream fled from my body, but my quantum mind felt more—the dampening of my labia with droplets of urine, the faint misting of urine upward, as bits of it reflected against the surface of the water, the wafting of ketones and ammonia and hints of the asparagus I had eaten some hours before. I tore off several sheets of Charmin to wipe myself before flushing it all down. *Front to back, front to back.* I could hear my mother's words as they were spoken into my ear from when I was three years old. I remembered everything. It was as though my brain were a hard drive now—accessing, always accessing. The water sloshing down the toilet sounded like the water in a whirlpool out at sea, and then there was silence once more, as the rubber flap in the tank dropped down and the water inside replenished the reservoir in order to repeat the process when human need struck again. It had purpose, given to it *by* man, *for* man. But what was my purpose as Quantum Girl; as *a* Quantum Girl? There were four of us now, I thought. But then Li dropped a bombshell, as I reentered the bedroom.

"I need to tell you something," she said. There was hesitance in her voice.

"What's that?" I asked as I phased into street clothes, phased back into the bathroom, phased on makeup, and then phased back an instant later.

"That is so…" she started to say.

"Weird?" I said finishing what I assumed was going to be her next word.

"Awesome," she replied. "How do you *do* that?"

"Practice," I said as I smiled to myself, turned toward her, and folded my arms. "So," I said. "What is it you want to tell me?"

"Liam and I," she began, "we gave Chloë another one of the quantum stones. We had two."

My heart nearly froze in my chest. "Does she even know how

to use it?" I asked her.

"She can space jump a few feet," she said, her voice slightly trembling, "and she can make herself invisible." She paused and then added, "We only gave it to her, because she was so upset about losing her sister. We thought it would be like when we gave the other one to you."

"It's okay," I said.

"Did we do something wrong?" she went on.

"No, sweetheart," I said, hugging her. "It's all right. Everything's going to be fine." And yet, I knew it wouldn't be. Giving a quantum seed to Chloë at her age and in her present state of mind was a huge mistake. But what was done was done. I wasn't about to go back in time and erase it. We'd all seen what could happen when tampering with what had already come to be. I phased into Quantum Girl. Billy Batson would have said, "Shazam!" Johnny Storm would have shouted, "Flame On!" I didn't need any magic words. I just thought it and I changed. My mind was going off in a million directions all at once. There was the Khattaaara from Liam and Li's Earth and Daisy McKenzie from Peyton's. The people on my world were being transformed into alien creatures. And now this—a twelve-year-old with quantum powers she barely understood, out with a ten-year-old boy, heading together toward unforeseeable danger. I was not about to drag Peyton or Demi, as Sarabeth had dubbed her, or Jordan into any of this. I was as much of a Quantum Girl as any of them, even though I had yet to prove myself to them in their eyes. No, this was my farrago, and I would handle it myself.

"I want to go with you," Li said.

"I don't want to risk you being hurt," I replied.

"Liam's my brother!" she insisted. "He's the only family I have left, even though he is a pain in the butt most of the time."

I understood how she felt. Liam—the other one—was my brother, too. We'd had our share of differences growing up—

sometimes even drag-down fights—but the undeniable truth was that deep down we loved each other. We were twins, and there was an unbreakable bond there.

I stood silently thinking as Li got dressed. It was frustrating. I had thought to phase back in time to just after Chloë and Liam had left, but something was preventing me from doing that. Li was putting on her jacket when she noticed my concern.

"What's wrong?" she asked.

"You said that Chloë was able to make herself invisible," I replied. "I don't know about Jordan, but the rest of us can't. I think that intentionally or not, she activated another power."

"What do you mean?"

"I don't know," I replied, "but whatever it is, it's preventing me from phasing through time, at least here."

Li began to cry. "This is all my fault! Liam didn't want to, but I made him give Chloë the stone!"

I went over to her and put my arms around her again. She was sobbing bitterly, her wet cheeks eerily reflecting my green quantum glow.

"We'll find them," I said as reassuringly as I could. "Everything's going to be all right."

"Do you really think so?" Li asked staring up at me.

"I know so," I replied. But those were just empty words. I had no idea what can of worms the twins had opened by giving Chloë the quantum seed. Had there been any religion left in me, I would have prayed. As it was, I could only hope that the two of them were safe.

"Let's go," I said, and, holding Li tightly in my arms, I phased us both into the quantum fabric to try and pick up their trail.

CHAPTER XXXIV

Jordan

From the Original Timeline
In the Alternate Reality
On Earth I
Earth Date: 2029

James and Katherine Herron were my grandparents and were exactly the same as the two who sat across from me on the sofa, but my mother was not their daughter. *Their* daughter was the Ophelia who sat on the window seat looking on. It wasn't as though *they* were from or *I* was from a parallel dimension but from an overwritten timeline—an alternate reality.

"It's difficult for me," I said. "I always dreamt of meeting my grandparents. My mother told me so much about them, but the fact is that neither of you remembers her, because she's not the Ophelia that you raised. And since I'm obviously not your granddaughter and this iteration of Liam is not my father, with the exception of my Aunt Peyton and Demi, I'm pretty much alone in the world.

"My mother was murdered by the Thaaagran I pursued through time. And while she may have looked like an alien, she was still a Herron, as am I." I paused and then went on. "While I know that you didn't give birth to her or raise her, I will tell you that she was a whole lot like your daughter. And although my father was written out of existence, that man over there is everything that she told me my father was like and I'd like to get to know him and the rest of you and Liam's parents as well.

"It was my alien aunt, Khattaaara, who gave me all but one of her god-stones, which all of you call quantum seeds, and it was both she and my mother who had insisted that I come here to try and make things right. My mother's dead now—dead for trillions upon trillions of years—but regardless of what time or space or the hand of Fate has done, all of you are the nearest thing I have to family, and although my body may be filled with superpowers, my heart is human, and, right or wrong, I'd like to be able to think of you all as my family."

There was an uncomfortable silence that followed until Claire, who had been sitting with Liam, glanced at him and then came over and sat down next to me. "We're not related," she said with a smile that advanced from her eyes, "but when Liam and I get married, we will be."

"I thought stepmothers were all wicked," Ophelia chimed in.

"Not this one," Claire laughed. "And I hope we can be friends. I know a great boutique on Melrose where we can spend all of Liam's money. It's called Morocco."

"What money is that exactly?" Liam replied. "Mine's all back on the other Earth, so good luck with that."

"I was joking, dear," Claire said, glancing back at him. "At least the Aussie part of me was." Then she turned back to me. "I get an employee discount. It seems I worked there on both worlds. I have in mind one outfit that would look positively rave on you."

"So," Liam said, "do you want her to wear it before or after Armageddon?"

"He does have a point," I said. "We're all in a battle for our lives."

It was at that moment that three of my other selves phased into the room; first one and then the other two almost at once. Two of them shook their heads and then merged back into my body. The third stood facing me.

"Oh my God!" Ophelia cried out. "She has a tail!"

Realizing that she'd been discovered, my third duplicate

pounced on me like a wildcat, her tail thrashing from side to side, trying to sting me. Suddenly, a fourth self appeared and shot her in the head with a pulse gun from Li and Liam's Earth. The alienized version of me dropped lifelessly to the floor. I stared at the one of me who had shot the alien one.

"You're hurt!" I exclaimed and then absorbed her back into me. I was stunned for a moment, staggering. Liam rushed over and caught me and helped me over to an easy chair. Both Claire and Ophelia rushed to my side.

"Are you all right?" Claire asked with great concern.

"The cuts on your face," Ophelia said, "they're beginning to disappear."

By this time, Grandma and Granddad (if I may be so bold as to call them that) had risen and come to my side as well.

"What was that all about?" Granddad asked.

"There was a battle on Earth II," I replied. "There were two of me and one of her—Khattaaara. She managed to infect one, and the other got thrashed by some kind of quantum whip. I've never encountered that before."

"How did she come up with that?" Claire asked.

"She has the mother stone," I replied.

"What's that?" The question came from Ophelia.

"It's stronger than the other six combined," I explained

"What do we do with her?" Claire said. "You can't very well reabsorb her. You might get infected."

Ophelia cringed at the thought "That's all we need," she said.

Liam had squatted down and felt the pulse in my fallen self's neck. "She's dead," he announced and then looked up at me. "We can bury her in the backyard."

"No," I said, wearily rose from the chair, and then went over to the corpse. "I'll phase her into outer space. I don't want Khattaaara stumbling across her, and bringing her back to life."

"She can *do* that?" Ophelia said as half a question.

I nodded and then staggered again. This time it was Claire who caught me. "I need to get some rest," I said. "I just lost a fifth of myself."

Claire helped me to my room and got me into bed.

"Do you want me to bring you anything?" she asked.

"No," I replied. "I just need rest and sleep."

She nodded and then went to the door to leave, turning off the lights.

"Claire," I said in a soft voice. She stopped and turned toward me. "Thank you. And thank you for forgiving my sort of Dad."

She just smiled back, left the room, and quietly shut the door. I was deathly weak on two counts. The first was the fact that one of my merged selves had been severely wounded. The second was that one of me had been killed, or, to be more accurate, killed by me. Had I expanded into a hundred of me, the loss of one wouldn't have been that great. But there were only five, and, combined with the injuries, it left me gravely ill, though I pretended that it wasn't a big deal.

No Quantum Girl is truly immortal. My aunt is proof of that. Not even the universe is forever. Nothing is eternal except the god-stones. How strange it was that they came into existence. How ironic it was how they were found. It was my alien aunt who told me. It was part of the history of Rendenaaar. Still, I wondered what had sparked it all in the beginning. I pictured God's finger about to touch Adam's in Michelangelo's fresco. Is all of this some accident or a domino set into motion by some intelligent design? It was all too much to consider, especially in my weakened state.

But here I stand, Jordan Katherine Herron, heiress unapparent to the crumbled throne of Rendenaaar, the fourth Quantum Girl on this Earth, but the second in existence by yardstick of time, I who was born of mirrored humans from different dimensions, perhaps the only one ever of my kind. Does that make me special or, somehow, a freak? My quantum vision told me that my DNA was different; that each of my two pairs of chromosomes wrapped anticlockwise from the other, and that the nucleic strands were mirrored as well, one half twisted clockwise, the other in reverse. Can I mate and have children or might I be able to become pregnant by myself? Only time will tell.

Having drifted into unconsciousness, I remember having the strangest dream. I stood naked in the palace on Rendenaaar. My hair and skin were silver and there was a radiance that surrounded me. And yet, I was not just there, but everywhere. I was no longer a Quantum Girl, but had within my head, the very seeds of creation. I saw the universe after it had exploded into being from the dust of the one that had come before. I witnessed tumultuous bursts of energy become galaxies and stars and planets. I watched as life formed on trillions of worlds, each with its unique flora and fauna, and I looked on helplessly as civilizations sprang into existence and then died by their own hand. Strange as it seems, I understood all of their languages and felt all of their pleasures and pains. It was as though I had spawned an infinite number of me in order to observe everything that is and everything that was, but the future remained shrouded in darkness. And yet upon awakening, I realized that wasn't me. It was *her*.

It was night when I awoke, and Sarabeth was in the bed beside me, cuddled up against me, one of her arms wrapped around me. She must have felt me move, for she opened sleepy eyes, and stared at mine.

"You're back," she murmured at me.

"How long have I been asleep?" I asked.

"Six days," she replied. "I've come here every night to keep you warm. You were shivering."

"Why do you care so much?" I asked.

"You're family," she answered. "You're sort of my niece, you know, and, as your auntie, I have responsibilities. I've tried to take care of you as best I could." She half yawned and looked with her eyes half-closed. "Can we go back to sleep again? I think we have a few hours left."

"Of course," I said and then I rolled over to face her, wrapped my arms around her, and then kissed her on her forehead. "Good night, Princess," I whispered to her.

"Good night, my love," she whispered back and then drifted off to sleep, and I soon did the same.

CHAPTER XXXV

Chloë

From the Altered Timeline
In the Alternate Reality
On Earth II
Earth-Date: 2029

We materialized in a room filled with aliens that all resembled the one that had impersonated Claire. We were in a nightclub. The room was fairly dark, with blacklights illuminating the phosphorescent decorations and graffiti on the columns and tables and walls. The place was, as they say, packed like sardines with male and female whatevers, all of them with tails. There must have been at least a hundred of them, all appearing to be in their late teens or twenties. The females all had pointed ears and two pairs of breasts, which was easy enough to see, as most of them were dressed in skimpy outfits. Dance music was blaring so loud that you couldn't hear yourself think. It was all very scary, like a horror film but for real. Off on tables and in booths, most of them were talking and drinking or inhaling drugs, or else making out and doing really weird things with each other's tails. In the center of the room was a stage that was raised up a couple of feet, where one young naked female moved in a sensual, provocative manner, her hands rubbing up against herself and then taking her tail and licking it as though that was supposed to be somehow erotic, though perhaps it *was* to the monsters that sat watching, holding onto *their* tails. Fortunately for us, they were all so involved with each other that we went unnoticed. We were the observers, not them.

Liam, distracted by all that was going on around us, had let go of me, turning this way and that at what could only, to human eyes, be considered a freak show. As the tail of one female inadvertently rubbed against him, he brushed it away as though it were an annoying housefly.

"We need to get out of here!" I shouted at him, having to yell in order to be heard above the deafening noise. "Come on!" I insisted. "Come on!"

I took hold of his hand and turned us both invisible, just as one male, seated at a table with a female, their tails intertwined, glanced in our direction. Having disappeared just as he did, however, he or it appeared to shake off what he saw as some possible effect from the glowing drink in his hand.

Pushing this way and that, tightly holding onto Liam, we snaked our way through the self-obsessive monster crowd. What seemed like an eternity later, we were out the door, and into the now scary night because outside was just as bad with a line of creatures waiting to get it. There was no doubt in my mind that I had phased us into some bizarre mirror reality. In that we were invisible, at least we were safe—or were we? One of the creatures, a female, began staring in our direction as though she or it could sense something. Perhaps we appeared as a visual disruption or a moving blur. Whatever it was, I tugged at Liam and hurried us off to a more secluded spot behind a B of A. It was an Oh My God! moment as I made us both visible again. The fact that there was a Bank of America here meant we were still on Earth! *But wait!* I thought to myself, as I looked at the printing on the door. *The words are all backwards!* I hadn't noticed before as we had fled, but all of the signs were backwards as well, from those on the buildings to the ones on the signposts. *Where the hell are we?* I wondered.

Liam was visibly shaken by all that had happened. "Are you all right?" I asked.

My question seemed to have upset his ego. "I was about to ask you the same thing," he replied. "But don't worry," he went on, "if they come after us, I'll protect you."

I couldn't help but smile at his words. "I don't know where we are," I said, "but we're not on our Earth. I mean, beyond all of the xenomorphs or whatever they are, everything is in reverse."

"What do you mean?" he asked.

"The signs, the words on them," I said. "Just look at them."

"They all look normal to me," he replied. "You do know that Li and I aren't from your dimension? I think we're on Earth II."

"How many Earths are there?" I asked.

"Payton told me there are an infinite number of them," he replied, "but Li and I have only been on three. Ours was totally destroyed. That's why she brought us to yours."[39] Liam surveyed

---

[39] I feel the need at this point (though perhaps I should have explained it earlier) to comment on my power of invisibility. I'd wondered about it myself, but it was Claire who explained it to me. She was a brain when it came to physics stuff— Beazley Medal winner and all. Anyway, it seems that when we look at objects, we see them, because light bounces off of them. Light is made up of different frequencies, and those that we can see are in what's called the visible spectrum that's made up of colors ranging from violet to red. When we look at a red balloon, for instance, the balloon absorbs every color *except* red, which bounces off of it and so we see the reflected red light. If that didn't happen, the balloon would appear totally black. We wouldn't even see it as three-dimensional. It would just look like a flat black balloon shape. When I become invisible, however, not only does my body not reflect light, ninety-nine percent of it passes through me because my atoms are in a quantum state. This would be well and good for a book or a chair, but if *all* of the light passed through me, then I wouldn't be able to see anything, because, again, the way we see is that our eyes capture the light that bounces off of objects. It's sort of like what a mirror does, only rather than reflecting the images, the light is absorbed by our retinas, causing signals that are then sent to our brains. Anyway, in order for me to be able to see where I'm going when I'm invisible, the god-stone needs to allow a small number of photons to *not* pass through me. Because it's such a small amount (meaning only millions of photons rather than trillions) the world, as I perceive it while I'm invisible, is probably similar to someone who has severe cataracts. It appears mostly gray and vague. Unfortunately, because of this, and because I couldn't very well order the photons to just not go through my eyes (at least when I first learned to become invisible) the Rends, as

our surroundings with a glance in each direction. "Definitely Earth II," he concluded at last. "Payton said that the people on her world were being turned into aliens like what'd happened to the Claire who *isn't* your sister."

"She became one of them?" I asked, astonished. "But she looks normal."

"That's because Jordan was able to change her back," he said. "But she can't do it to everyone on the planet. It took all of her strength to just change back Claire."

"This is *so* my bad," I said. "I got us here, and I don't know how to get us back. What's the good of my having superpowers, if I don't know how to use them?"

"Hey," he said reassuringly, "*I'm* the one who gave you the stone. It's *my* fault if it's anyone's. And I may not have superpowers or anything, but, like I said, if anything happens, I've got your back."

Looking at his expression, I could tell that he meant it. It was the sweetest thing any boy had ever said to me, as opposed to my very first date with Scott Marsden, who, when he took me to see— I forget the name of the film—he undid his trousers, whipped out his dick and whispered, "Come on, suck it. It's dark. No one will notice," and like the twelve-year-old idiot I was, I did. That was two months before all of this, though, at the time, it seemed like forever ago. Anyway, I looked at Liam, drew closer to him, and kissed him on the lips. "Thank you," I said.

"What for?" he replied, though I could quantum-hear his heart now beating like a drum.

"For being you," I said back. "Anyway," I went on. "We need to find somewhere safe, till we can figure things out."

Ophelia later told me they called them, were able to see Liam and me while we were invisible, as sort of a moving blur, which was not a good thing for us, though it was decidedly better than walking around as totally visible moving targets.

"Where?" Liam asked, obviously frustrated.

"What about the high school?" I suggested.

"I guess," he said, "but how are we supposed to get there? It's probably five miles from here and I left my Porsche back home in the other dimension."

"Don't be sarcastic with *me*, young man!" I said.

"I'm not a *young man*!" he replied defensively.

"Well," I said realizing I'd probably hurt his feelings as my protector, "you're *my* young man if you don't mind my thinking of you as such. I don't have any others, and Scott Marsden was such a mistake," that last mumbled half to myself.

"Who's Scott Marsden?" he asked.

"The absolute worst sort of boyfriend material, unlike you," I replied.

"Boyfriend?" he repeated. "Me? Yours?"

I looked at him. "We may be the only two humans left on this entire world," I said. "You'll grow up in a few years, and so will I. Besides, I already know what you'll look like, and truth be told, you're going to look pretty hot."

All Liam did for the next half hour was broadly smile whenever he looked at me, although he tried to hide it.

After walking for half an hour, dawn began to break, which revealed creatures everywhere that were taking notice of us.

"You need to make us invisible again!" Liam exclaimed.

I concentrated on doing just that but it didn't work. "I'm trying!" I said.

"It's not happening!" Liam replied. "They're coming toward us! Try phasing us out of here!"

"I've only managed to do it a few feet at a time!" I said as I watched the aliens approach!

"Just try!" Liam exclaimed. "Payton said all she does is focus on where she wants to go. Seriously, you got us here. You can do it again, only back to the other dimension."

I remember shrugging. I knew I had this magical thing in my head, but I had no idea how to use it. "Grab hold of me," I told him, "and we'll do this together."

Facing me, he wrapped his arms around my waist. I closed my eyes and pictured the high school. I felt a slight shift in the air around us and then heard a din of voices and locker doors slamming. When I opened my eyes, we were in one of the main corridors of Braxton, just as classes had let out.

"Um," I said to Liam, "How exactly did your hands get down there? We're not boyfriend and girlfriend *yet*."

"Sorry," he said.

"That's okay," I said. "Someday, just not yet. You don't want to be like Scott Marsden."

"What exactly did he do?" he asked.

"It's not what he did," I replied. "It's what *I* did. Can we please change the subject?"

"Whatever," came the response, but I still caught him smiling out of the corner of my eye. Suddenly, his expression turned serious.

"Shit!" he said.

I turned to him. "What?"

He motioned me to look slightly upward at the wall he was facing. There was a banner that had been hung on it, which read, "Homecoming Dance, Class of 2020."

"We're back on the right Earth," he said, "just seven years too soon!"

CHAPTER XXXVI

Sarabeth

From the Altered Timeline
In the Alternate Reality
On Earth I
Earth-Date: 2029

It was Sunday, the day after the incident with the two Claires, or, rather, with Claire and bad Khattaaara and Chloë.[40] I went that morning to church with Mom and Dad. Services began promptly at ten a.m., the Rev. Johnston before the congregation at the pulpit, a bit tired-looking and somewhat older in appearance than his fifty-four years. It was told that his wife had been laid up with breast cancer that had gone into her spine, making it painful for her to even sit up in bed. But, like the Steadfast Tin Soldier that he was, he had cared for her himself until the very end. Not once did he miss his Sunday sermons. Not once did he ever shed a tear before anyone he knew, for not only was he a servant of God, but the most devout of all nurses when it came to his ill but adoring wife. After she died, those who really knew him said that part of him went into the grave with her like the faithful shepherd with his lamb; the other part stayed behind, dutiful to his Master, to try and instill kindness in the hearts of his flock.

My mother was the religious potentate of our family. That's what Dad used to call her, though not ever saying it in a bad way. Dad was a nodding worshipper. He would nod whenever Mom

---

[40] When I first heard her name, I thought it was Glowy, and I wondered, *What sort of a name is that?*—this from being around all too many Quantum Girls who glowed! My bad!

would make a religious point and he would sometimes nod off in church. Mom, on the other hand, believed in God and in Jesus with a faith that was both unwavering and unalterable. There was no point in arguing any of the tenets of the Bible, nor its histories or miracles. Despite that Peyton had claimed to have witnessed the Big Bang billions of years in the past or that she herself was a reincarnation of a being from a previous universe, my mother's faith told her that both the Heavens and the Earth were created by the hand of God roughly six thousand years ago, give or take, and that all of mankind alive today were the descendants of Noah, who himself was the tenth generation from Adam and Eve, and that there was a Paradise and a Hell to which we are eventually destined, one or the other, depending on our faith in the Almighty Father and in our acceptance of Jesus Christ as our Lord and Savior.

The three of us took our seats at church in the middle row as usual. Mom didn't want us to be viewed as pretentious, either by sitting too close to the pulpit or so far that it seemed as though we were just there for the sake of appearances and didn't much care what was being said. Up at the pulpit, Rev. Johnston cleared his throat, which was his way of telling everyone that his sermon was about to begin.

"For many years," he began, "I have stood in front of you and preached God's words. I have retold stories from the Bible and tried to relate them to our lives—yours and mine. I have spoken of Abraham and Isaac and Jacob. I have repeated the stories of Jesus and Matthew and John. The Bible is filled with a host of characters—some good, some evil—and that has been the way of the world since it began. The Book of Revelations speaks about the end of days, a battle between God and Satan, between good and evil, God triumphant in the end, whereupon Jesus will once again set foot upon the soil of the Earth and resurrect the dead from their graves to raise them to the Kingdom of Heaven.

"I have never spoken of myself before, but today will be different, for I think that this is most certainly the time. When I was a young man, I was an atheist. I grew up in a home that was a churchgoing home, and I was told to believe in God. My father, though, was an alcoholic. Every night when he came home from his work on the docks, he would eat the supper my mother had cooked and then he would drink his fill of whiskey or gin. My father was an angry drunk. Many a time, I would see him beat my mother with a clenched fist. I would hear her screams at night as he beat and raped her in their bedroom. I was only a small child at the time, so there was nothing I could do but listen and watch. When I was seven, there were gunshots from the bedroom one night. My mother had taken the money she had saved and bought a pistol and when my father had taken to beating her again, she shot him in the chest and then shot herself in the head. I was taken afterward to an orphanage where I spent the next eight years. But on the day I turned sixteen, I ran off to find my place in the world. I took whatever jobs I could find. I stole food when I was hungry. I stole nickels and dimes and quarters from the collection boxes at this church or that. It was a miserable existence, especially when it was cold or when it rained. I thought of my religious upbringing and of the words that I had heard about faith and I wondered where God was for me. Where had he been for my mother? And so, wallowing in doubt and self-pity, I came to hate Almighty God. I mocked his words and blasphemed his name. Then one day, when I had almost given up hope, I heard a soft whimpering in an alley, and, lifting up a piece of cardboard that someone had thrown away, I saw a dog, curled up in pain. It was the saddest thing I had ever seen. It had lost all of its fur and its skin was hard and calloused from mange. Flies swarmed over it. Maggots ate at its flesh. I wrapped it in my jacket and took it to the steps of a church, where I held it in my arms all night. In the morning, a clergyman opened the doors from inside and saw me with the dog. 'What have you got there, my son?' he asked. 'It is a pup I found that is suffering,' I replied. The clergyman bent down and looked at the dog and said, 'It looks as though it is beyond all help. Perhaps it is best to put it out of its misery.' 'It is one of God's creations,' I insisted. 'Can we not at least try to save it?' The clergyman shrugged. 'I have a dear friend who is a veterinarian. I will call her to see what can be done.' And so, he called his friend and, after her work, she came to the church and examined the dog. 'She is quite far gone," she said. 'Quite far gone is not gone yet,' I insisted. 'If you help her, I will work for you for a year. I will clean your cages, sweep your floors, and scrub your toilets. Just please help save her.' The woman smiled, and said, 'I'll take her back to my clinic, and see what can be done.' The clergyman (his name was Pastor Cullin), had me stay at the church, fed me, and gave me a room. Every afternoon, after my chores were done, I would go to the clinic and check up on her, whom I had named Hope, who slowly grew better. Her skin healed and both her fur and her spirit grew. She was my best friend for the next eight years until she turned old and died. But for all the love I had given her, Hope gave me something in return. The veterinarian, for whom, as I had promised, I had worked for a year, had a daughter nearly my age named Amelia. Amelia and I became close, not only in the year that I worked for her mother but through the years that followed when I asked her to marry me and she said yes. We were married for nearly thirty years until she passed into the hands of God. It was both Hope and Amelia who inspired me to take up the calling. Amelia said that it was God, who had led me to Hope, and that it was Hope, who had led me to her.

"There has been much talk these past few days about an evil that now walks among us in the form of a woman. She calls herself Dark God. But I stand before you, before the one true God, as a man of faith, who once had none; as a man of principle and determination, who once thought seriously about taking his own life.[41] And I will be damned to hell if I will bow down to a disciple of Satan!"

It was then that Dark God appeared, hovering over the congregation. She phased nearer and nearer in jumps until she faced *him*.

"Dare you defy me?" she screamed, her voice filling the room like thunder.

The preacher stood unwavering before her. Dark God then phased behind him, having grown to nearly sixty feet in height.

"Behold," she said, "what happens to those who refuse to worship me!" And like that, the Rev. Johnston was gone—vanished from the room. All of the congregation—man, woman, and child alike—began mumbling to each other in fear. It was at that point that my mother stood up, raised her arm, and pointed her finger at Dark God.

"Demon!" she screamed, and Dark God stared at her.

Afraid of what might happen next, I lifted the whistle that was held by a chain around my neck and blew into it as hard as I could. An instant later, Peyton appeared as Quantum Girl. Dark God looked at her in anger.

"You!" she screamed. "So, you survived through time like me. Khattaaa…" she started to say but then she stopped. "Ah," she went on. "You are the other one. Not *Zhaaagur Scraaa*, but Quantum Girl! You look so much like her."

"I am She-Who-Was-Reborn," Quantum Girl replied. "And you are *Kazhaaan Draaag Choool!*"

I had no idea what that meant, but I assumed it was an insult.

"You still speak our ancient tongue," Dark God said.

"We need to take our dispute out there," Peyton said as Quantum Girl, and glanced upward.

"Agreed," Dark God replied and both of them vanished at

---

[41] Those words really hit home for me.

once.

Mom turned back to both me and Dad. "Was that our Peyton?" she said.

"Yes," I replied, "I called her with *this*," still holding the whistle.

"Jesus, Mary, and Joseph," Mom gasped. "May God preserve us all!"

"If He doesn't," I said, "Quantum Girl will."

Something of a sneer made its way onto Mom's face. "You watch your mouth, young lady. If Quantum Girl defeats that demon, it will be through the grace of God!"

Everyone stayed inside the church for the next half hour just in case things went south outside. I tried to leave, but Mom held firm. "I lost you once," she said. "I'm not going to lose you again!"

CHAPTER XXXVII

Peyton

From the Original Timeline
In the Alternate Reality
On Earth I
Earth-Date: 2029

We were outside in the air, high above the buildings, facing each other as though it were a showdown in the Old West.

"Who are you really?" I shouted at her. "You're not Daisy McKenzie. Daisy McKenzie doesn't have pointed ears or a tail."

"I'm Dargra-Tol," she shouted back, "*and* Daisy McKenzie."

"You're the synth that Dhraaal gave to me back on Rendenaaar!" I said.

"I'm a hybrid now, part Thaaagran, part human!"

"Which part is Thaaagran?"

"Why?" she asked, "So you can make love to that part again? Or so you'll know how not to be tricked out of another god-stone?"

"I never made love to you!" I shouted back. "You were an android, built in a factory, made to help with all of our chores! And I never gave you any stone! That was in another life!"

"It doesn't matter!" she shouted. "You can't stop me! You can't kill me! That niece of yours tried! Did she tell you that; how much of a failure she is? You may be saddened to know that before I left, I gutted that pathetic sister of yours!"

"You're lying!" I shouted back at her.

"Am I?" she laughed. "Then what, pray tell, is this? I brought it with me to throw at Zhardaaan, but as long as you're here…"

Then she pulled Phee's dead body out of thin air and threw it at me.

"I stored it in the fabric!" She shouted, taunting me. "It's developed quite a stench, though. But that's what happens when Gaaalthaaaran's rot!"

I caught it with a force field and stared at it. It was Phee as I had left her, Gaaalthaaaran, not human, but aged at least twenty years and now lifeless, with the putrid odor that fast accompanies death.

"You should have been there to have felt her agony as I tortured her—her *yaaargh* dripping out her final passion!" For a moment, she seemed caught up in her own thoughts but then she went on. "It was all so stimulating, hearing her suffer, trying to call out to Khattaaara—to you—with barely a breath left in her lungs! Watching her die was exhilarating! It was almost better than sex!"

I looked one last time at Phee, phased her into my mansion, onto my bed, and then glared at Dargra-Tol or Daisy or whoever she now was. I wanted to shout back at her. I wanted to tell her that her life was near an end, but I was without words. All I could think of was Phee.

"I want to do battle," she gloated, "but I have other fish to fry! So, for the moment, my love, I'm out of here!" And with that, just like that, she was gone!

I phased back into the church just in front of the pulpit. The congregation seemed to grow concerned at my presence.

"It's safe for you to go outside," I said. "The threat is gone," and I paused, "for now."

"Who *are* you?" one man shouted at me.

"I'm Quantum Girl," I said, "and I'm here to help. But now I have to leave. There are things I need to attend to. But I'll come back if she returns. You have my word." Sarabeth had been watching me. I nodded at her and then phased back to my home;

187

back to my bedroom; back to the sister I had failed.

It took a bit of doing for me to be able to look once more at Phee—at her corpse—as she lay there on my bed. As Khattaaara, I had seen many corpses. I had caused many to *become* corpses. But this one had been not only my sister but my very best friend. I didn't know precisely how long she had been dead, but it must have been a while. Her body had a bluish cast, and I could see from my X-ray projection that her organs had begun to liquefy. Her eyes were open, as were her lips, which lent a somewhat sardonic aspect to her face. I found myself having to rush to the bathroom, where I vomited for at least ten minutes off and on until there was nothing in my stomach to purge. Then I went to the sink, splashed water on my face, and took a long deep breath. It took resolve on my part but I gathered up my non-quantum strength and went back to where she lay. I sat down on the bed beside her. My hand reached out to touch her forehead and gently brush her hair, though, as I did the hair fell off into my hand. I screamed a quantum scream, so loud that the help must have thought it a long clap of thunder—thunder from a cloudless sky.

I could not bring her back to life by reversing time around her as Payton had done for Pay's parents. Phee's death was in another universe. The timeline in which she died was disconnected from this one. But I *could* try to reverse the decay. I stood up and shook my head to clear it. The stench was almost unbearable. One can watch *The Walking Dead* or any zombie film, and one can see the decay but never smell it. The room had become filled with a sickeningly sweet odor, laced with the scent of urine and feces and I don't know what else. I opened the French doors to the balcony, but it barely made a difference. Regardless, I knew that I needed to focus. I tried my best to put both the sight and smell out of my mind. I created a quantum field and reversed time around her. Little by little, the decay process reversed. The bluish tint to her flesh disappeared. Her lips began to close, her body became bloated, filled with bacterial gas, and then the bloating disappeared. Color spread to her cheeks. And her *yaaargh* which had withered and grown limp, became somewhat normal again— well, somewhat normal for a being from Rendenaaar at any rate. At last, she looked as I had left her, though with two decades added to her face. I fixed a field around her to prevent any further decay. Meanwhile, the air in the room had cleared, as it had all absorbed back into her with the reversal of time. But this was not enough; at least not to my mind. I phased back to my parents' house and woke Ophelia.

"I need your help," I said.

"What is it?" she asked. "What do you need?"

"I need you to come with me," I answered, my face all too grim.

"All right," she said, "if it's important," and she sat up in bed. "Just let me get dressed."

"No need for that," I replied. "We're just going to my room— to my bedroom at the estate. I just need you to stand."

Ophelia stood and I phased us both to the room where my Phee's corpse now lay.

"Dear God!" Ophelia said as she saw it. "Is that the other one of me?"

"Dargra-Tol murdered her," I explained, "then brought her body back through time."

"Who's Dargra-Tol?" she asked.

"An artificial being from Rendenaaar," I replied.

"But why do you need my help?" she asked.

"I just need you to stand there. That's all." I said.

"Okay," she replied. She looked at me with a curious stare.

Focusing on Ophelia, I scanned (if that's the proper term) her quantum matrix. Then I overlaid it on Phee. Little by little, her alien form became human again, but her years remained the same. It was just her DNA that I was able to restore to what it once had

189

been. Yes, she was still dead, but at least she was Phee again—Phee, as she would have looked twenty-some years from now, had none of this ever occurred. Once again, I locked a quantum field around her and then phased her into one of the drawers in the family vault—the one where Pops and Gram now were.

"Are you all right?" Ophelia asked me.

"Yes. No. I don't know," I replied.

"I'm here for you," she said.

She walked up to me and stared me in the eye. Then she put her arms around me, as I burst into tears.

"I know I'm not her," she said, "but I'm here for you if you ever need me to be."

I didn't reply. I couldn't. Tears choked out my words, and so I just wept. I held her tightly and I wept, and she held me till I stopped.

CHAPTER XXXVIII

Khattaaara/Payton

> *Payton from the Original Timeline*
> *In the Rewritten Timeline*
> *On Rendenaaar*
> *Trillions of Universes in the Past*

Millions of my people had died in the war between the *Thaaagrans* and the Gaaalthaaarans—millions at the hands of those same synthetic workers we had built. Those who were not bludgeoned by the *Thaaagran* population were phased into outer space by one of the thousands of duplicates of Dargra-Tol. Regardless, the streets were stained blue with my people's blood. Out of millions of Gaaalthaaarans, only thousands remained. Even the Grentaaarg fought against them, hand in hand with my people, who had treated them as slaves. But they, too, went down like a *Kolaaafnaaar* in a blind, as the saying went.[42] The level of fear ran high among us, but we fought when we could, however we could, by whatever means we could, to protect ourselves and our families.

And then there was me, *Zhaaagur Scraaa*, the first Quantum Girl, possessing six of the seven god-stones. But Dargra-Tol had the mother stone, more powerful than the other six combined. My role, therefore, was to defend and not attack. We were beaten and we knew it, and I knew all too well that the deaths and misery of all of my kind lay on my head. I had allowed Dargra-Tol to become our vengeful god. Would that I could undo it. Would that

---

[42] A *Kolaaafnaaar* was a small, flying creature, similar to a bat, often hunted by outliers for their fur and their meat.

I could take it all back. I had attempted to travel back in time to prevent my indiscretion, but the god-stones, not yet a part of me at that time, prevented my phasing anywhere near them. I tried going back to warn myself but I was pulled into my former self, became lost inside of her, and was forced to relive everything all over again. When at last I was able to progress beyond the moment I had decided to go back in time, I realized that I had finally broken a causality loop that had repeated more than a million times. The repetitions piled into me all at once like echoes, each with just the slightest variation, until one finally allowed me to escape. Time travel could be dangerous in that regard.[43]

More than a thousand other worlds had been colonized by the Gaaalthaaaran civilization. The god-stones had been used to phase both colonists and supplies to those far-off planets, but since I had stolen the god-stones, there was no way to let the colonists know all that had occurred. And while I had considered phasing *to* them, there were no maps to guide me. With hundreds of trillions of stars and ten times as many planets, it would have taken a thousand lifetimes to locate even *one*.

So we hid. For nearly three and a half cycles, we hid. And yet it seemed that Dargra-Tol was always one step ahead. We hid in caves. She found the caves. We hid in forests. She knew just where to look. It dwindled our numbers as the *Thaaagran* population grew. The amputation of the *Thaaagran yaaargh* had not been done merely to tame them but to limit their numbers. With their *yaaarghig* restored, however, they were as much capable of reproduction as we had been.

"What of Jordan?" Phee said to me one night early on when we had set up camp within the *Haaargnon*.[44]

---

[43] I have often wondered whether a time loop is merely a localized event, or if it affects the entire universe and every universe to come. In other words, does it cause all of time to continue to replay?

[44] The *Haaargnon* was the Gaaalthaaaran name for one mountain that was like a gigantic geode with its interior made of crystal.

"What dost thou mean?" I asked.

"We have avoided the subject for three cycles now," she replied. "She is neither our kind nor theirs—alien to them both. I'm not human anymore but she is. There is no place for her on this world or in this universe. With the god-stones, she can find her way back home."

"We know not," I said, "what will happen to that world of ours. Thy sister ne'er returned, which is disconcerting at best."

"Still," she replied, "it would be good for her to at least find out what remains."

"And risk her life?" I asked.

"She has no life here," she replied. "There is no mate for her to find, no children for her to bear. She is an outcast that none but we will ever love."

"The world that you both came from is a coin that spins on its edge," I said.

"The people there," she replied, "our families, our friends— they stand no chance without her. With four more stones to aid her, the coin may land on its head. Only one god-stone need remain to protect us from Dargra-Tol." She took a deep breath and then shrugged. "Still," she admitted, "she must learn how to use them."

"I shall teach her," I replied.

She stared hard in thought but no sound left her lips.

"What else is on thy mind?" I asked.

"Remember long ago," she replied, "when Jordan was barely born? Thou turned me human ever so briefly that I might feed her milk from my human breast." She paused as I awaited more words. "Might thou do it again for perhaps just half a *baaagtran* each day that I might teach her both the sound and aspect of her people? I know it would be a strain upon thee, but it would mean much to thy sister for her to learn to voice to the language from her world in its true sound."

The tone of her words touched me and a smile broke upon my face.

"It shall be my greatest joy to do so," I said, "regardless that her parting shall be its end."

"Strong as our hearts beat for her," she replied, "we know this is for the best."

"Agreed," I sadly acknowledged.

"The future has changed the past," she lamented, "so the past must change the future."

"Thou hast become a philosopher," I said.

"Perhaps," she replied, "but what has gone on is enough to have even made Baaaldarack's head spin."[45]

"'Tis strange," I remarked.

"How so?" she answered back.

"Thou doth speak as a Gaaalthaaaran might," I said and I laughed. We both did.

"Thou wast such a heinous person," she proclaimed, "before Payton's spirit infected thee."

"Me thinks *cured* is a far better word," I said with a smile. "But I have often wondered—at least my Payton half—what happened to her body when her mind came hence and merged into my Khattaaara self."

"Thou speakest of her as though she were separate from thee," she said.

"Nay," I insisted. "We are both Khattaaara now. Our souls are intertwined. Perhaps, then, I should rephrase it. I am oft given to wonder what became of the body in the future that was once part of us."

---

[45] Baaaldarack was an ancient Gaaalthaaaran philosopher.

CHAPTER XXXIX

Payton

> *From the Original Timeline*
> *In the Alternate Reality*
> *On Earths I and II*
> *Earth-Date: 2029*

Theresa's murder had been all over the news. It wasn't because she was Rainbow Girl. No one had made the connection. It was how her body was found; not only was her skull smashed in, but it was as though her killer had grappled with her brain. Only I knew who and why. It was Daisy, digging into her head with her fingers to take out the quantum seed. I remember feeling nauseous at the thought; then just numb. We'd had a long history together. I had loved her so much; but then, after I'd saved her with Thara-Klo's seed, everything changed—*she* changed. Her memory of all the time we'd spent together—all the love we'd shared—had all been erased. I didn't intend to give her superpowers. I only wanted her to heal—to live. It was either use the quantum seed or let her die. There was no other choice. But it appeared that I only prolonged the inevitable. Her body was found by one of the maids at Daisy's parents' house. The news reports said that there were no photos the authorities would release. It was all too gruesome, they said. "Theresa Maria Martinez, age fifteen, mother deceased; father's whereabouts unknown, former freshman at Braxton High." That was all her obituary read. Coincidentally, Rainbow Girl had just vanished, and the once-adoring fickle public soon buried her in their memories like the weather from last month that no one can ever recall. The fan sites stayed up, but few went to them anymore. I guess her fans just figured she had abandoned them and gone off to some other world. No one really cares about other people when it doesn't directly affect them—at least that's what I've come to believe.

There was no going back. Not in this case. Theresa had the mother stone—the master quantum seed—and she had gone batshit insane. Even if I had gone back in time to try and save her, she would have been far too powerful for me alone, assuming that she learned the crystal's full capabilities. Sometimes the past is just what it is and we need to accept it and move on; other times it can urge us to engage in actions we might otherwise not have done. It was Theresa's death that caused me to sidetrack my path. It wasn't that it was more important than trying to save two worlds. It was just that, at that moment in my life, it was paramount to me.

So it was that I phased back to my dimension, to my Earth, where the Khattaaara from the other dimension had wreaked havoc on the human race that had once peopled my world. I specifically phased to the home of the Theresa Martinez of my dimension, Theresa Sofia Martinez actually, to find her face down and dead near the hallway door, as though she had been trying to get away before either Khattaaara or one of her then cohorts caught up with her as they had with the rest of the population. Seeing the ruins of what once had been a thriving community, made me ill. But being Hispanic, unable to be turned into a Rend, *that* Theresa wasn't of much use to them. Regardless, I knew what I *could* do, and what I *wanted* to do. Simply stated, I created a time-inversion field around her and brought her back to life.

I watched as her desiccated flesh turned soft again, as death reversed its course. I listened as the first breaths went back into her lungs. I felt the warmth of life return to her and heard the beating of the heart within her breast. I saw her rise up against the pull of the Earth's gravity as the energy blast fled outward from her. And then I stopped time within the field I had created so that she stood motionless, like a statue, frozen between two moments of existence.

I walked around her, identical to the girl I had fallen in love with three years ago, but grown into young womanhood; the same soft dark hair, the same high cheekbones, the same hazel eyes that once melted the core of my soul. But this was not *my* Theresa. This was another version of her like I was another version of Peyton or Sarabeth or Pay. What her reaction to me would be once I started up time for her again I had no idea. I pondered for some moments whether to revive her as Payton or as Quantum Girl. I decided on the former and phased back into my street clothes. I would go outside, restart time for her, and then stumble in, as though I were trying to escape from the alien invaders.

She awakened screaming. It was unnerving, even though I was prepared for something of the sort. I could hear her from outside, standing on the porch at the door. As I turned the knob and pushed the door in to enter, without knowing who stood on the other side, she screamed out, "Stay away!" When, at last, I entered, I found her backed up against the far wall, her head turned to one side, her eyes tightly closed, bitterly sobbing. "Stay away! Stay away!"

"Hey!" I said in as calm a voice as I could manage. "It's okay. They're all gone. It's okay."

Slowly she opened her eyes and turned her head to look in my direction, her cheeks stained with mascara. "Who are you?" she asked in a voice that was choked with tears.

"Payton," I told her. "Payton Herron. We go to the same school."

The Theresa Martinez of this Earth stared at me and then wiped her tears with the back of one hand.

"You're the one with the brother," she replied, trying to regain her composure. "Liam."

I smiled at her. "Guilty as charged," I said. "Hey," I went on. "You need to sit down."

I took her hand and led her to the couch. She sat down on it but I could see that she was in shock. Her skin was cold and clammy. Her hands were shaking. I could hear her heart pounding.

"Maybe you should *lie* down," I suggested.

"I'll be all right," she replied. "But maybe a glass of water." She paused and then added, "from the kitchen," indicating the direction with a slight motion of her head.

I knew where it was. I'd been there dozens of times—at least on the other world. The room was similar but not exactly the same. The glasses were in the same cabinet, though—even on the same shelf. I filled one with water from the faucet, came back and offered it to her.

"Thanks," she said as she took the glass.

Small rivulets of water spilled down the sides of her chin as she drank with trembling hands. I took the glass from her when she had finished and then set it down on a small table nearby.

"Please," she said. "Have a seat."

I sat down next to her, angling toward her.

"I don't think we ever spoke when we were in school," she said nervously.

"Huh, uh," I acknowledged.

"Your brother was in my junior—no senior—chem class," she went on.

"Liam," I said.

"Yeah," she replied. "Kinda cute, as I recall. I think you were with me in gym my freshman year. You were on the basketball team. I had to sit out most of the semester. I tore a hamstring the first time I got out on the court. Dumb luck. I remember you were there the first couple of weeks. You were the pretty one that most of the other girls were jealous of. But then I don't remember

198

seeing you again—ever. Wait! I remember now. At first, I thought you just moved or transferred out, but then Niki Barron told me…" She paused a moment, thinking back. "We were in the showers next to each other and she just blurted out like it was yesterday's news that someone had broken into your home and shot and killed you. 'Poor Payton,' she said. 'All the sapphics are going to be so, so sad.' I thought that was a really mean thing to say, considering she said you'd gotten murdered. She said she even went to your funeral. So, how are you still here?"

"Obviously," I said, "she made it all up. Niki and I were friends, but I called it quits when I realized she was a total psycho."

"I'm glad for your sake," she replied, "that none of it was true. But what *did* happen to you?"

"I dropped out," I said.

"And your parents were okay with that?" she asked.

"I got homeschooled," I explained, though it was actually Pey's life that I was describing. "I'd started modeling and I couldn't schedule work and school at the same time."

"So you're still a model?" she asked.

"Stripper," I replied. "I mean, I was. There's no one to strip for anymore."

"Oh, my Gods!" she exclaimed. "I don't think I could ever do that."

"There was more money in it," I said. "I mean, modeling pays more by the hour, but the work isn't consistent."

"But isn't it…?" she looked at me uncertain what to say without offending me.

"Demeaning?" I replied. "Spreading my legs for men to gawk at? It might be if I worked at a strip club for men." This is where I deviated from Pey's history. "But I didn't," I went on. "*The Wingéd Beaver*. It's just for women." Of course, I totally made the whole thing up, but I wanted to see her response.

"So, the part about you being sapphic," she asked.

"That was real," I replied and then stared into her eyes. "Haven't you ever considered it?"

"Being a stripper?" she said. "Too embarrassing."

"No," I replied. "Being with another girl?"

"All girls *think* about it at one time or another," she said, "but that was as far as it ever got with me."

"Anyway," I said changing the subject as I felt I was pushing things too much all at once, "after I left Braxton, I went to live with relatives for a while—with my aunt and uncle and their daughter, Ophelia. Freaky, though."

"What? What is?" she asked.

"Turns out," I said, "she was born on the exact same day as Liam and me."

"Maybe," she replied, "her parents and yours had sex on the same day."

"Gods!" I exclaimed. "Not something I wanted burned into my brain!"

"Sorry," she apologized, and there came a pause. "Maybe," she went on. "Maybe you were triplets and your parents gave *her* to your uncle and aunt."

"And they would do that because...?" I asked.

"I don't know," she laughed. "It just sounds so strange that you were all born on the same day!"

"At least," I sighed, "Liam and I had the decency to come from the same womb."

"Well," Theresa said, "I guess she *had* to be born *somewhere else* because there wasn't any more *womb*."

"That was *so* bad!" I said, laughing.

"I know," she laughed back. "I'm a terrible glutton for puns!"

"It's nice to see you laugh," I said.

Theresa stared off and then looked back at me. "For a moment I forgot all that's been going on. Thank you," she said with a smile.

I took both of her hands in mine. "You're very welcome," I replied.

I think the hand-holding was a bit awkward for her, as she suddenly stood up. "Would you like something to eat?" she asked. "I'm totally famished."

"Sure," I said and followed her into the kitchen.

"There's some leftover tuna casserole in the fridge," she said.

"Sounds great!" I replied.

Theresa went to the refrigerator and looked in. She picked up a plastic container and then brought it over to the counter. A moment later, she pried the lid off, looked at it strangely, brought it up to her nose, and turned up her lip. She went back to the refrigerator again, sniffed the carton of milk that was on the top shelf, and then looked in the crisper drawer. "That's really strange," she said.

"What is?" I asked.

"All of the food is spoiled," she replied, "as though it's been here for months."

"Maybe there was a power outage," I suggested.

"Maybe," she replied, "but it looks a whole lot worse than just the power having gone out." She shook her head to herself and then turned to me. "Oh, well," she sighed. "There's still canned food in the cupboard." She went over to one cabinet and stared in. "How does SpaghettiOs sound?" she asked.

"Not as good as tuna casserole, but doable," I replied.

"I'll heat some up," she said, taking one of the cans over to the stove, and prying off the lid.

Some short time later, we were seated opposite each other at the kitchen table, each with a bowl of SpaghettiOs in front of us and a spoon in hand.

"Have you seen them?" she asked after the first spoonful of pasta had slid down her throat.

"Them?" I asked back.

"The lizard people," she replied.

"Is that what they're called?" I asked.

"I don't know what they're actually called, but they all have tails and make almost hissing noises when they talk." She stared at me intensely. "How did you manage to survive? Both my parents and my kid brother were… vaporized, I guess is the term. I jumped on the one who did it from behind, and then I felt such a pain, as though I'd been stabbed, but I guess not. I thought for sure I was going to die, but here I am, eating SpaghettiOs, though I wonder how long till I'm turned to vapor, too." She paused, waiting for a response. "And? So?" she said. "How did you manage to not be turned into one of them? I mean, you're white, and they'd said on the news…"

"As I said, I've been away."

"This is happening all over the planet. It doesn't seem like there's anywhere *away* to *be*."

"Actually," I said, "I was in a parallel dimension where none of this is going on."

"And I was on Mars," she replied. "No, really," and with that, she took another spoonful of her *Aw Oh, SpeghettiOs*. I should have taken a hint from the jingle.

"No, really," I parroted back. "I was on another Earth, in a parallel dimension."

"Okay," she said, "I'll bite. Tell me more."

"I have superpowers," I said.

"Yeah, right," she replied, rolling her eyes.

"You want me to show you?" I asked.

"Why not?" she replied. "I've seen everything else. Lizard people, my parents and my brother disintegrated… What else *is* there?"

"This, I guess," I said, and with that, I phased into Quantum Girl. Theresa stared at me and the spoon dropped from her hand.

Suddenly, she began hyperventilating. I quickly changed back to myself, but her reaction didn't end. All at once, she began vomiting out the SpaghettiOs she had just swallowed. A moment later she started to morph into a Rend. Her ears grew pointed. The irises of eyes turned purple. A second pair of breasts formed under her blouse, and then there was the tail, which raised into the air, as she stood, looking as though it was about to sting me. Beyond all else, I thought the change could only occur in Caucasians, but there was no time to wonder about any of that!

Instantly, I froze time, reversed it once more, back to when she was at the stove stirring the SpaghettiOs in the copper pot into which she had poured the can, and then set it in motion again.

"How are you feeling?" I asked.

"Much better, thanks to you," she said and smiled. "I'm glad you're here."

"I'm glad I found you," I said returning the compliment. And that was how my relationship with this version of Theresa began. She didn't need to know about my being Quantum Girl—at least not yet—not until I could undo the effects of the virus that had somehow caused her to change. It was curious, though, why it hadn't affected her until terror set in. And, considering that she was Hispanic and not white, she probably wouldn't have survived the transformation for long. *Well*, I thought to myself, *I'll worry about all that later.* For this brief moment, all I had on my plate, both literally and figuratively, was SpaghettiOs.

CHAPTER XL

Claire from Earth I

> *From the Alternate Timeline*
> *In the Alternate Reality*
> *On Earth III*
> *Earth III-Date: 2023*

Did you ever wonder what it would be like if you could meet your younger self? What would you tell her? What would you say? Would you even recognize her or remember her as who you used to be? Would she recognize you as someone she might one day become? The Claire Salinger of this Earth was a lot like I once was but in many ways different. I guess a large part of who we are is not only a product of our physical self but is also determined by what we have lived through, and it is both together that shape us in ways that make each of us unique. Identical twins generally tend to be similar when they're raised together. But split them up and they diverge from the moment of separation.

I remember when I was young Claire's age, I wanted to be a concert pianist. I wanted to play at Carnegie Hall. I wanted to have recordings done of my work that people would listen to when they were happy or lonely or sad, but I guess I didn't have enough drive or encouragement. Sometimes things in life create distractions. With me, it was when I lost Niska. I just wasn't the same afterward.

A sudden thought struck me, and I turned to Claire. "You said you lost your sight when you were struck by a car. How did it happen?"

"Niska ran out into traffic, chasing after a cat. It was actually a miracle that I noticed in time. I'd just bent down to retie my shoelace when a monarch butterfly landed on my hand and then flew off toward the street. That's why I looked in that direction and saw the car headed right toward her. I didn't think. I just ran out to save her. I pushed her off to one side, but there wasn't enough time for me to get out of the way. I got hit by the car and thrown into the curb. My head hit first. I don't even remember being hit. I was in a coma for weeks. The doctors didn't think I would live. When I finally woke up, I couldn't see. I've been blind ever since. My parents had Niska trained as a seeing-eye dog, but she's also my best friend."

"I'm sorry," I said.

"I'm not," she replied. "Better that I lost my sight than for Niska to have died. Thank the gods for that butterfly."

On my world, in my life, there was no butterfly, and so my Niska died but I retained my sight. *Small consolation,* I thought to myself, *in retrospect.* Some people might have said, "It was just a dog," but in my mind, love is not something relegated to just the human species.

Most of the things in young Claire's house were the same as in the one where I had grown up, the main exception being the grand piano in the living room. It stuck out like a sore thumb when I first came in, or, should I say, broke in?

"I used to play a bit," I said as I stood next to it, tapping a couple of upper keys. "It brings back memories. What about you?" I asked my young doppëlganger. "Do you also play?"

"Yes," she said. "It lets me release everything inside. Mom and Dad, they bought the piano for me. Dad used to kid me and say that in the event there was no work for me as a teacher, playing the piano would be something to fall back on."

"I'd love to hear you," I said. "*Would* you, please?"

Claire nodded and smiled, and then sat down on the bench and played what I later learned was entitled *Scarbo* from *Gaspard de la Nuit* by Ravel, an extremely complex piano piece. She was magnificent at it, far better than I had ever been able to do from my six weeks of lessons. *So professional*, I thought to myself. *She'd someday have found her way to Carnegie Hall.* Perhaps it was a result of her blindness, allowing her to focus, which I never was able to do. It seemed the largest difference between us at that moment, and it briefly caused me to forget the then great disparity between this world and my own.

"You're so much better than I ever was," I told her when she was done. "You have a gift."

"It doesn't mean much anymore," she said. "There's no one left to hear."

Suddenly, our attention turned, as Niska perked up from her sleep, rushed to the door, and began to bark.

"Quiet!" her mistress ordered. Niska stopped barking, turned and went up to her, and then went back to the door.

"Someone or some*thing*'s out there," Claire whispered to me. She felt her way to where Niska's harness hung from a peg on one wall and then quickly put it on her.

It was oppressively dark outside. The moon, in whatever phase it might have been, was hidden by a thick blanket of clouds, and, without power, the street lights were all off.

Dogs are different from people. Despite the fact that they have four legs and a tail and they all die when they're in their teens; even though they only have the smarts of a two-year-old, their senses of sight and smell far exceed that of any human. They can see in near pitch-black darkness and their olfactory capacity is one hundred thousand times greater than ours—at least that's what they said on The Learning Channel years ago. To that point, it was Niska who led young Claire and me to *it* or *her*—her, I guess—lying prostrate on the front lawn, her face turned to one side.

She was one of them, as her pulled-back hair revealed—like the one that had sent me here—only she wasn't wearing clothes

206

like the other. Hers almost looked as though they had been painted on, and both her clothes and her skin kept pulsating a faint, iridescent orange, which lit her up just enough for me to see that she was bleeding from a wound on the left side of her midsection.

"*Kitaaai laaarg,*" she muttered, as she saw or sensed us. "*Kitaaai laaarg,*" she repeated, and then she passed out.

"Don't worry," I told young Claire as she stood behind me. "It's unconscious… and hurt."

"It's one of them," she said, "Isn't it?"

"It's one of them," I said back.

"What should we do?" the younger me asked.

"I don't know," I replied. "She'll die if we leave her."

"It was *her* kind that killed my parents," she said.

"But we're not *like* them," I replied. "Are we?"

"I guess not," came the sullen response.

"We're going to have to get her inside," I said. "but we need to roll her over first."

That last proved to be excruciatingly painful for the alien. She awakened and screamed out in pain as we turned her onto her back. Nor did the screaming stop as we carried her inside. I lifted her up just under her arms, while young Claire held up her legs. We let her tail just drag. It was quite an ordeal, but we finally managed to get her into the house and onto one of the downstairs beds. I didn't need to guide Claire much. Blind though she was, there was a blueprint of the house and everything in it etched into her brain.

The first thing we needed to do was to stop the bleeding. It didn't appear to be coming from an artery, but there was still a good deal of blue liquid coming from her wound, much of which soaked into the bedsheets and probably the mattress as well. But I found bandages in a first-aid kit under the bathroom sink, and I did my best to stop the bleeding. Regardless, the alien began trembling from the blood loss, so I covered her with several blankets. I urged Claire to go to sleep. I myself got what sleep I could, spreading pillows on the floor beside the bed, unwilling to leave the creature alone.

I woke up to the scalding light of midday, shielding my eyes from the brightness that glared through the bedroom window. Shaking the sleep from my head, I stood up and went over to the alien. Her eyes were closed. I assumed that she was either still unconscious or asleep, but then, all at once, her arm reached up and grabbed mine, her eyes opening, as she stared at me.

"*Staaazg onlaaag naaarag?*" she demanded.

"I don't understand," I said back.

Her grip on me tightened. The irises of her eyes glowed orange, and my entire body went stiff. I was parallelized. I couldn't so much as blink. And then, her mind entered my head. There was a jumble of alien words and images and thoughts. A moment later, her grip relaxed, her eyes gave up their flames, and I was able to move again. I took a deep breath and looked at her. Then I glanced back, as the younger version of myself sleepily entered the room with Niska and then stopped just inside.

"How's our patient?" she asked me.

I looked from her to the alien, whose eyes were open and staring vacantly at the ceiling. I felt for a pulse in her neck, and then put my ear to her chest to listen for her heart.

"I think she's dead," I replied.

"I wonder who she was," Claire said.

"Her name was Shaaalra," I replied, "and she was from Rendenaaar."

"Where's that?" Claire asked.

"Rendenaaar," I said almost robotically, "existed approximately 3.8 trillion universes in the past, a terrestrial-type planet, 1.2 Earth masses with an atmospheric content of 72% argon, 24% oxygen, 2% nitrogen, 0.06% carbon dioxide, and various trace gases. The predominant species was the

Gaaalthaaar, the members of which were in many ways similar to modern humans, with the exception that the females possessed pointed ears and two pairs of breasts, with reproduction occurring via a tail-like appendage called a *yaaargh*, rather than a vagina. The *yaaargh* also acted as an incubator for the fetus. Average life expectancy was approximately forty-one planetary revolutions, roughly equivalent to two hundred fifty Earth years."

"Stop!" Claire called out, breaking me out of my robotic state. "How do you *know* all that?"

"Not sure," I said questioning my own words. "Anyway, we need to move on."

"We can't just leave her here like this!" Claire protested.

"She was one of the beings that killed your parents," I said. "You reminded me of that yourself last night—not to mention everyone else who was killed."

"That doesn't mean we're supposed to *be* like her," she replied. "Isn't that what *you* said? If *you* won't help," she went on, "I'll do it myself. Like I told you, I did it before."

"Fine," I said in a reluctant tone. And so we did, later that day. We buried her, though I was the one who dug the hole in the backyard. Claire's parents were buried out in front.

That night, exhausted, I stripped off my sweaty clothes, filled up the bathtub, and then settled in. It seemed as though I had just closed my eyes for a moment, but when I opened them again, I wasn't in the bathroom anymore. I was still immersed in water but in a granite bath on Rendenaaar and, looking down at myself, naked as I still was, I could see two pairs of breasts!

Khattaaara was in there with me. She stood up, the water splashing down as she did, beading on her naked flesh. I could feel my nipples grow hard at the sight of her, my tail grow erect. How did I know her name? How did I know this was Rendenaaar?

"Shaaalra," she said.

And then I awakened from that dream if that is what it was.

CHAPTER XLI

Dark God

> *From the Altered Timeline*
> *In the Alternate Reality*
> *On Earth I*
> *Earth-Date: 2025*

When I was a little girl (meaning the Earth part—the Daisy part of me) my mother scoffed at the very idea of God. "If God created man in his own image, what sort of an imperfect god would *he* be?" She asked. We never went to church. We celebrated Christmas, but only in a pagan sort of way. As for my father, he only worshipped money.

Throughout time, supposedly *advanced* beings have worshipped gods for two reasons and two reasons alone—the desire for immortality and out of fear. The idea that there is a god (or, in many cases, gods) also made it easier to explain existence. There was no science that needed to be learned; no mathematics. There needn't have been any hypothesis or proof. All one had to do was believe that there was some omnipotent being who created it all. No one needed to wonder where the creator had come from. He or she just always was. And so they worshipped him or her like colonies of bees or ants worshipping their queens±— egocentric fools that they were. Each of them had convinced themselves that *their* god was the *only* god and that *their* beliefs were the only ones that mattered. In the end, they knew that their faith would grant them entry into some afterlife of bliss. And as they would grow old and frail, they knew in their hearts that life was only a test; that their god or gods would not abandon them;

not let their bodies be eaten by worms with their souls trapped inside. They each had a spirit they had convinced themselves, that would be whisked off to a place where sorrow and pain were just words. But then they would die—exhale their last breath—and never learn—never come to realize—that the beliefs that they were indoctrinated with were nothing more than dreams of cool, clear water in a desert caked with sand.

But I, Dark God, at least was honest. I made no promises of immortality. I gave no explanations for how it was that the universe was formed or how life sprang into being from sculpted clay or from dust that fell from the sky. I offered no legends or mythologies of how I came to be. That was for me to know and for no one else to so much as question. I was unique in this universe —neither Dargra-Tol nor Daisy McKenzie—I was a hybrid of both. I held within my brain the science and history of both Earth and Rendenaaar, and I had command of whichever realm I chose to be in—or so I thought.

It was in the afternoon on a cloudless day. I sensed her before I saw her. There was someone else with a stone that caused the same color iridescence as mine. I had caught only a glimpse of her over the Herrons' house before she vanished but it was long enough for me to recognize that it was Khattaaara! How was it, I wondered, that she had a god-stone like mine. I assumed that she had followed me, and so I decided to follow *her*.

The quantum trail she left led me to at first appeared to be the exact same place as she and I had left, only it wasn't. It was all in reverse—the signs, the position of the steering wheels in the cars, even the buildings themselves. Teleporting up into outer space, I found that the entire planet was backwards; New York was on the West Coast, California on the East, and the world was spinning in the opposite direction than it had been before. It was all quite disorienting, as though I had been pulled through the looking glass, and everything was flipped around. *But, no, wait!* I thought to myself. The scar from when I'd cut myself accidentally when I was six, when the cookie jar I'd been reaching for had fallen and smashed down on the floor and I'd tried to clean it all up before my mother came in and discovered what I'd done—the scar was still there on my left wrist.

It was then that I saw her out of the corner of my eye. It was in fact Khattaaara. But she shouldn't have been able to travel there as I had thrown a barrier around her after I left, after I followed the trail through the quantum fabric to Earth. Besides, she was middle-aged when I had left her. Instead, she looked young again, and—thinking about it—so much like Peyton Herron!

Once more, I followed her quantum trail, which led me to the Oval Office of the White House, where I materialized just behind her. She had arrived only a moment before me but stood calmly facing the windows behind the desk as though she had been there for some time, attired in the illusion of business attire. Suddenly, she sensed my presence behind her and spun around, her *yaaargh* whipping out past the illusion of her clothing, stretching out and wrapping around my neck. Sensing what she was about to do, observing it in slow motion, I caused my *yaaargh* to shoot out as well and did the same to her. There we were, the Dark God and the Blonde Goddess, face to face, each trying to choke the life out of the other.

Who are you? She telepathed into my head. She read my thoughts before I could shape them into words. *A hybrid!* She thought at me—*half from Rendenaaar and half from Earth!* She paused, as both our grips grew tighter. *But not from this dimension!* She thought on. *That explains the mother stone!*

So, you're not my Khattaaara! I thought back at her.

Your Khattaaara? She telepathed. *Am I to understand that you and the extradimensional mirror of myself were lovers? I'm intrigued.* She paused. *So, you're not here to kill me. Just curious, I see.*

And with that thought, she released me from the stranglehold. I followed suit. We stood there, then, staring at each other, looking each other over, sizing each other up either for a sexual union or for a kill.

"Why are you here… in this office?" I asked.

"Because I'm personal assistant to the President," she replied. "Former military. Former Empress of Rendenaaar in *my* universe. But that was ages ago. I'm just Katara Gothra now. Sounds almost Hindu, doesn't it?" And with that, she morphed her skin into a soft golden brown, her eyes turned dark, and her clothes became a pink saree, decorated with a gold thread design. Then, all at once, the dress fell to the floor, leaving her naked. As I looked at her, a strong sexual desire mounted in me. I morphed out of my clothes and moved in toward her, embracing her, kissing her, caressing her soft skin. Her left hand moved down toward my vagina, while her *yaaargh* intertwined with and then entered mine. I felt such ecstasy. The room around me seemed to blur with the sensation. Then, as I was about to orgasm, I felt a sudden pain. It was as though I were being torn apart from within. It was agony. I watched, helpless, as the Daisy half of me was being ripped away, her face marked by horror, as she realized that it had all been a ruse; that not only was she being torn from me, but from the god-stone as well. Then, as her naked body was suspended in midair, as Khattaaara's eyes flashed bright white, the human let out a hideous, blood-curdling scream that was cut short as she vanished into thin air.

Khattaaara then approached me, her flesh and eyes changing back to what they had been, as I lay in a heap on the carpet on the floor, propped up by my elbows, I stared up at the Gaaalthaaaran form that now completely mirrored mine.

"Humans are such fools," she said. Then she read my mind. "Do not think to use the mother stone against me," she went on. "We are equal in power, so any battle would prove futile." She extended one hand toward me and helped me to my feet. "And now you shall pleasure me in bed, and I, you. *Thaaagrans* are good for that much at least, and long past are the days since my *yaaargh* dripped *graaam*."

She teleported us to one bedroom and then coaxed me onto the bed.

"I knew your counterpart on my world, but to me, she was nothing more than a machine."

We made love after that, though, with Daisy no longer a part of me. Her naked presence next to mine awakened memories of the Khattaaara I had known. Perhaps she read my mind and did something to my head. It was as though I had become drunk with passion—hedonistic and insatiable—though in the morning when I awakened in the bed, I was alone and I felt ill from all that had gone on. I staggered to the bathroom, vomited in the sink, morphed on some clothes, and then went in search of a quantum trail in order to find my way back to the universe from which I had come.

CHAPTER XLII

Ophelia

> *From the Alternate Timeline*
> *In the Alternate Reality*
> *On Earth I*
> *Earth-Date: 2029*

Peyton was devastated by the original version of me coming back through time as a corpse. I can't say that I blame her. I may have been born absolutely identical down to my fingerprints, but that was her sister, the one she grew up with. The two of them had gone through so much together, and their lives from when they turned fourteen were so much different than Sarabeth's and mine—Sarabeth, who used to be Peyton, my Peyton, my twin, was now four years younger than me.

Peyton said she had tried to go back in time to rescue her, but that there was some sort of quantum barrier that kept her *from* her. She needed someone, though. Each night, she would phase the lifeless body onto her bed. Each night, she would try to resurrect her but to no avail. Whatever powers her quantum seed gave her, the one she so desperately wanted—the power to resurrect the dead—was not one of them.

The sixth night after it happened, I went to her estate. I rang the bell and then knocked for what seemed like an eternity until she finally came to the door. She looked haggard and pale, as though she hadn't eaten or slept for days.

"You can't go on like this," I said. "I know I'm not her, but I'm here for you no matter what."

"I don't need anyone," she said. "I just need to be left alone."

"That's the last thing you need," I replied.

She looked at me with daggers in her eyes. "I said I'm fine! Just go away!" She phased into Quantum Girl, filled with rage.

"And if I don't?" I shot back. "Are you going to phase me into outer space?"

My words caused her to change back. "I'm sorry," she said. "It's just…"

"I remind you of her," I said. "I know." I walked inside and shut the door behind me.

"It should have been her that got the quantum seed, not me!" she wept. "All of her life, she was nothing but kind and good. Everything would have been fine if I had just died when the helicopters shot me! I'd be dead and she'd still be alive!" She turned away and stared at the crystal chandelier that sparkled like a thousand stars. "But no, I had to travel to Earth II to give Payton my powers. If I hadn't done that," she sobbed so bitterly, "none of this would have happened!"

I gently took hold of her from behind, my hands resting on her shoulders. "But Khattaaara would still have invaded *that* Payton's world and there would have been no one to help." I urged her to turn and face me. "Whatever you did, it mattered. Between you and Demi and Pay and Jordan, you can save billions of lives! Look at me! *Look* at me!" I insisted, and she raised her tear-stained eyes to gaze into mine. "Don't you think that *she* would have willingly sacrificed herself to save billions had the situation been reversed? I know I would, and I'm *almost* her."

"If it had just been her to have gotten the seed," she wept.

"But it wasn't," I said. "And where would Jordan be if she had?"

"I loved her so much!" she wept.

"And she loved you," I replied. "But bad things happens to the best of us. What do you think would have been the case if you hadn't gotten the seed? Both of you would have been killed by that car that morning when you first used your powers. You gave her four years of life she never would have had! She never would have met Liam. She never would have fallen in love. You gave her life, not death, so you need to stop blaming yourself. You may be a stranger in this timeline but there are a lot of people who have grown to love you and it would be like knives in their hearts if something ever happened to you!"

"I know, I know," she wept. "And Jordan showed me what the world would have been like if I'd never gotten the quantum seed. Khattaaara's incarnation would have taken over my mind, and she would have killed Theresa and my lawyer, and Phee would have died from a drug overdose. Beyond all that, the fact remains that I *was* Khattaaara!"

I could see the anguish on her face. "Don't you see?" I said. "God gave you a second chance to be good and kind."

"I don't believe in God," she said through her tears.

"Well, maybe He believes in *you*," I replied, "because I know *I* do."

"There's something I never told you," she said wiping her tears with the back of her hands. "You're not the second version of Phee. You're the third."

I sank down into a chair as I heard those words.

"You became an addict," she said, "Needles in your arms, living at home by yourself because Dad began to drink and ended his life and Mom's in a car crash. I couldn't let that be your future, so, I went back in time to the day of the funeral when we met. That's why I was four years older than you. I'd seen what'd happened to you in my time."

"But if I'm the third," I said, "that means that the second one of me was wiped from existence; everything she went through, good or bad, was all erased. What if you, or any of you, went back and reset time again? Would I—would my existence—just cease to exist?"

"No," she replied emphatically.

"How are you so sure?" I asked, staring at her with sudden concern.

"Because I put a quantum field around both you and Sarabeth to prevent that from ever happening, just like Demi had done for Phee before she was transformed."

"Thank you, dear sister," I said. It was the first time I had ever called her that, and for the first time that night, I saw the hint of a smile.

"Do you want to spend the night?" she asked.

"Only if I can share the bed with you," I replied, "like we used to. Well, like Sarabeth and I and you and dead me used to. Just not the bed you do your hoodoo voodoo stuff on with her corpse. The thought of it sort of creeps me out, no offense."

"None taken," she replied. "We can use the crimson room."

"You named the rooms by color?" I said.

"I *could* have named them after people, I suppose," she replied.

"Just as long as you didn't name one the Dunkhead room," I replied and then said, "Lead the way."

I snuggled with her that night. My final thoughts, before I drifted off, were memories of how when Peyton and I were small children, we often found comfort lying next to each other in the dark until we fell asleep.

CHAPTER XLIII

Claire from Earth I

> *From the Alternate Timeline*
> *In the Alternate Reality*
> *On Earth III*
> *Earth III-Date: 2023*

I was having memories, but they weren't mine. They belonged to the alien I had buried in the backyard. At first, they were just brief flashes. They were images of a world called Rendenaaar, and of how she was both friend and lover to the one that had sent me here—Khattaaara. How strange it was that I could understand their language as if it were my own; could feel the sexual sensations from an alien part of her that didn't exist in humans in *me*. The memories became longer; they infected my dreams at night when I slept and I would often wake up in a cold sweat and question who and where I was. I dreamt of how Khattaaara had stolen what they referred to as god-stones and of how she and her friends had tried to conquer a world that refused to be conquered but instead chose to annihilate itself so that they were left with a planet that was desolated and in ruins. But a ruler who rules only ghosts is no ruler at all, and so, with their quantum powers, they fled their universe for another and on and on, conquering and destroying civilizations, until, at last, they found the Earth—this Earth—the one in their dimension, and that is when the friendship between the three who remained came to an abrupt end.

"I shall not be a party to thy madness," Shaaalra had said to her. "Not anymore, and Dhraaal agrees. These creatures are too much like us. I will not have thee destroy them, as thou hast done to so many countless others."

"I am thy Gaaalthaaara!" Khattaaara had shouted back. "My will shall not be questioned!"

"Our world is but a memory as is thy throne," she replied, "erased by a trillion creations. We are immortal against the ravages of time, and we have followed thy path, but no more. So say I, and, Dhraaala."

"So, there has been a conspiracy against me!" Khattaaara spat out the words as though they were a poison that had been placed on her tongue. "Thou wast my friend once!"

"And I thine," came Shaaalra's reply. "But I cannot allow such destruction."

"Wouldst then thou challenge me?" Khattaaara said, spitting out her words.

"I would," Shaaalra replied. "We would."

"Then both of you shall forfeit your lives!" Khattaaara sneered, and with that, she shot forth a bolt of white flames from her fingers that burned through Shaaalra's flesh. Then she vanished, leaving the alien to bleed to death and die.

It was two weeks' worth of dreams before that story had unraveled, and it was only then that I revealed what I had seen to young Claire.

"We need to get the god-stone," I told her during our meager meal that night. "We're running out of food, and who knows how long it will be before we're found? Shaaalra found us easily enough, and if she could, Khattaaara could as well."

"But you buried her," Claire said, "and it's inside her head. Even if we dig her up, what then?"

"We'll get it out," I replied. "with a brick if we have to. You don't have to worry. I'll do it myself. I'm the adult in the room."

"I'm curious," she said as an afterthought. "When you first saw me, you called me Chloë."

"Because I thought you were her," I replied. "She's my kid

sister, Chloë Anne Salinger."

"What's she like?" Claire asked.

"Well," I said, "she's twelve years old and quite beautiful, skinny as a rail, with long dark hair and blue eyes."

"No," she interrupted. "I mean, what's she like inside? Is she like me? Do you two get along?"

"She's outspoken and very smart," I replied. "Smarter than I ever was. She's actually quite remarkable for her age. She's six years younger than me, but I believe she thinks she's *my* big sister, the way she always tries to look out for me, and, yes, we get along. I love her very much."

"It must be nice to have a sister," she replied.

"Well," I said, "since you've got one now in me, what's your take on it?"

She smiled but then turned serious. "It's just that… when you go back to the dimension you came from, I'll be an only child again—an only *orphan* child."

"Sweetheart," I replied, "if there's one thing I will promise, it's that I will never ever leave your side."

She smiled as a tear dripped down her cheek.

"Can I ask a favor?" she said.

"Anything," I replied.

"Can I hug you?" she asked.

"Of course, you can!" I told her, but it was I who made the first move. I closed the distance between us and put my arms around her shoulders. She wrapped hers around my waist and pulled herself close to me.

"It was the strangest thing," she said, her head leaning into the curve of the side of my neck.

"What was?" I asked.

"After Mom and Dad were killed, I thought I was going to be next. But I wasn't worried about myself. I was worried about Niska, all alone in an empty world. So, I huddled in a corner with her and hoped that none of them would find us. Every time I heard a noise outside, I went back there with her. Then one day, one of them came in and went up to me. I could feel her breath as it bent down and stared me in the face. I thought I was going to die. But then it just left me—maybe because it saw that I was blind. And then, hours later, you came. I mean, I knew that if the gods wanted me to die that was their will, but I couldn't leave Niska alone and whatever their will was, I didn't care." She paused and then went on. "Does that make me a bad person?" she asked. "to turn my back on the gods?"

"No," I said, rubbing her back. "That just makes you a good mother to Niska."

Something struck me after she said that and I lowered my arms and looked at her curiously.

"What did you mean," I asked, "when you said, 'the gods?'"

"The gods," she repeated, as though it were common knowledge. "Jupiter, Juno, Mars, Venus, Neptune, and all the rest. Don't you believe in them on *your* world?"

"In Europe and America and a lot of the rest of my world," I replied, "we just believe in one, and we call Him God."

"What's America?" she asked.

"The continent we're on," I answered. "North America."

"North Atlantis," she replied. "At least that's what it's called here."

It was so strange, I thought, that some things were so different, while others were the same. It was as though the lives in each dimension were like portraits of the same people but placed on different backgrounds.

"Well," I said with a heavy sigh, "I guess now's as good a time as any to go and dig her up."

It was starting to get dark, but that meant that there was less of a threat of watchful eyes. At least, I thought to myself, the dirt was still soft from having dug the grave so recently. After digging down about three feet, the shovel came in contact with the corpse of the alien. It was then that Niska began to bark and Claire had to quieten her, holding her to keep her still.

Once I had exposed the body, then came the hard part. It's a whole lot easier to roll a body into a hole in the ground than it is to lift one out of it. Beyond all else, the scent of decaying flesh, whether alien or human, tends to be overwhelming and it necessitated my having to wrap a scarf around the bottom half of my face to filter out the stench. So intense were the fumes that they made my eyes water. All that aside, there was absolutely no way that I could simply lift the body out onto the ground. It became clear that the only way to do it was to run a rope under its arms and then try to haul it out head first. While there wasn't any rope in the garage, I was able to make use of drapery pull cords. Even with what little time had passed, the corpse had already begun to decompose. Gases had built up in the creature's abdomen, causing it to swell far beyond what any late-term pregnancy might have looked like had it been human. The skin appeared jaundiced. The lips had drawn back enough to expose the teeth, which fell out, or, rather, in, when I had inadvertently brushed against them while removing the dirt. The nails, too, seemed to just slide off of her fingers at the slightest touch.

After considerable effort, I secured the cords and, with Claire's help, the two of us managed to haul the decaying mass back out onto the lawn. I gave thanks to all of her Roman gods that she was blind, for that saved her from imagining the condition of the bodies of the parents she had interred nearly a month before. From what I'd read, by that time, their bodies would have begun to liquefy, their flesh and organs turning into sludge. I remember thinking how they were identical to my own mother and father and picturing them like that haunts me to this day.

"Take Niska, and go inside," I told her. "I don't want you anywhere near this."

"I can stay," she said. "I'm not afraid."

"I'm your big sister, now," I said in a firm voice, "and I need you to go inside. If you want me to care about you, you'll have to trust my judgment."

"All right," she said with a sigh. "Come on, Girl. Let's go in."

Both she and her companion went inside.

"Now, slide the door shut," I called after her, and, reluctantly, she did.

I looked down at the decomposing mass of skin and bone. Regardless that the flesh had turned soft, the skull was a matter in and of itself. When archeologists unearth human remains, the bones most preserved tend to be those of the skull. I remember watching episodes of *The Walking Dead*, where the actors so easily plunge knives or swords through any of the zombies' heads, but in real life, it's nothing like that. Trying to crack open a human (or, in this case) an alien skull is ten times worse than trying to crack open a coconut, especially when there's still flesh on it—at least it seemed that way to me, having cracked open a couple of coconuts when my parents took Chloë and me to Hawaii a few years ago. At first, I tried just smashing down on the side of her head with a brick but the grass beneath it acted as a cushion, while the skin and flesh on the face disgustingly peeled away. All I had succeeded in doing was making the corpse appear more gruesome than it already had been.

Grabbing hold of the remains of what had once been Shaaalra, I dragged them over to the patio, again laid her head to one side, lifted the brick high over my head with both hands and then smashed down on it as hard as I could, again and again, until finally, the bone gave way. Liquified brains splattered everywhere—onto the concrete, onto my clothes, onto my arms, and my face; some even got into my mouth! It was hideous and disgusting, but I had to go on. I reached my right hand into her skull through the opening I had made, until I felt something round and hard, like a small ball bearing or a marble. Once I had it out, I stared at it, a small yellow bead that iridesced in the night that enveloped both me and what was left of the extraterrestrial. Carefully, I laid it down in a pot that stood on a glass-topped, wrought iron table, dragged the alien corpse back to the grave, and rolled it so that it tumbled in face down—not that there was much of a face left.

I didn't care about the sanctity of it anymore. In a year, it would be nothing but a pile of bones beneath the soil, forced to stare down for eternity at the planet its *Gaaalthaaara* had chosen to destroy. I used the garden hose to wash off as much of the brain and bone and the soil that had clung to me as I could, and then picked up the yellow god-stone, and trapped it in my clenched fist. Then I trudged into the bedroom, where I found young Claire fast asleep. I headed into the bathroom, trapped the stone down in a nearly empty pill bottle I found in the medicine chest, stripped off my clothes, and then got into the shower.

In Hemingway's *A Farewell to Arms*, the rain is used as an omen that foreshadows misfortune to come. I thought of that as the warm water rained down on me. I couldn't predict the future. I couldn't know what might or might not occur. All I knew was that the jets of water felt good as they rained down on my skin and then ran the course of my body, only to escape down the drain. The washcloth, drenched in water and liquid soap, helped to cleanse the memory of what my senses had just borne witness to. When I shut off the tap, I just stood there for a moment, naked, dripping, goosebumps forming on my arms from the chill breeze that invaded the bathroom air from the thoughtless night through the window that was open just a crack. I wanted to scream, but I didn't want anyone, alien or otherwise, and especially not Claire, to hear me and the fear inside of me. She was now my little sister like Chloë was, and I needed to appear strong so that she wouldn't be afraid. But I was—terrified to be exact. Having dried myself, I

225

stood, still naked with the yellow god-stone in the bottle in my hand, trying to build up the courage to take it out and let it go inside my head, uncertain what the consequences to me would be. I was human, not Gaaalthaaaran, and I didn't know if it would endow me with superhuman powers or explode inside my head. But then I realized that it was the former. *That* knowledge came from the memory of the creature, who lay buried beneath the soil. Outside of the door, a young girl lay asleep, probably in dreams, her protector on the floor at her side. I bit my lip and stared at my reflection in the mirror. I had gone through all of this to get this small gem. I needed to decide what to do with it. It was an important decision to make.

CHAPTER XLIV

Peyton

> *From the Original Timeline*
> *In the Alternate Reality*
> *On Earth I*
> *Earth-Date: 2029*

When I was fourteen years old, I decided to end my life and I did. It wasn't that I *wanted* to die. It was just that I didn't want to *live* anymore. Things were *that* bad—at least they *were* in my head. But, unlike virtually everyone else who kills themselves, I was brought back to life. One would think that it would have changed me—that I would have celebrated the fact that I had been resurrected—but things happened that made me want to end my life again.

It is a serious thing, the taking of one's own existence. Many religions, such as Christianity, Hinduism, and Islam, regard it as an unpardonable sin. Conversely, in Japan, *seppuku* (commonly known as *hara-kiri*) was considered noble if done to restore the honor of one's family, similar to dueling in Western culture, but without the possibility that one will survive.

My reasons, when I was fourteen, as when I was eighteen, were not based upon any code of honor, but, rather, frustration with what had gone on in my life. But then suddenly things were different. No matter whether or not I chose not to live, I no longer had a choice, because I was three months pregnant.

The child had been conceived decades ago when I had traveled back to the past. I was not quite certain what effects time travel has on an embryo or a fetus, though. I knew of no other

227

instance of it having happened. In that the father was now deceased, I would need to raise her on my own, though since I could copy myself into as many of me as I chose, the logistics of raising her by myself did not portend to be that difficult.

I had decided to tell Jordan about the pregnancy first, in that she would be her only real relative other than me.

"So, I'm going to have a cousin," she said with a smile.

"It's a girl," I replied, smiling back. "Do you want to see her?"

"Sure," she said.

I needed to divide in two in order to show her. X-ray projection doesn't work very well on oneself unless it's an arm or a leg. One of me then projected on the other, revealing the fetus in far more detail than any ultrasound could, and in color.

"I have a serious question," she said. "What happens to the fetus when you divide? I mean, what would happen if, just before you went into labor, you split into a thousand Peytons? Would you give birth to a thousand baby girls?"

"I don't know," I replied. "I really hadn't thought about that."

"It's definitely something to think about," she said. "Merge back."

I did and then she used her own X-ray projection on me. In retrospect, I should have let her use her powers to take a glimpse, but my show-and-tell ego got in the way. "Congratulations," she said. "You're now the proud mother of twins."

"Oh, my God!" I exclaimed. "It's a good thing I didn't expand myself into a hundred of me when I encountered Daisy!"

"I don't think there'd have been enough room in there," she said.

I stared at her with what I can only describe as a screwed-up expression on my face. "I'd decided to name her Zhana Faith," I said. "Now what?"

"What was your second choice?" she asked.

"Samira Rayne," I replied.

"There you go," she said.

I shook my head to myself. "This certainly is going to hinder things when push comes to shove against Dark God and Khattaaara,"

"You just take care of yourself for now," she replied, "*and* the twins." She paused. Then it was as though a warm glow went through her, and she broke out with a huge smile. "I can't believe you're pregnant!" she exclaimed.

I grinned. "Neither can I!"

"Let's go tell Sarabeth!" she said.

A sudden thought came to me. "What happened to Demi and Pay?" I asked her. "I haven't seen them in a while."

"Lord if I know," Jordan replied. "Anyway, first Sarabeth; then we'll all break the news to Grandma and Granddad."

"Do you think they'll care?" I asked. "I mean, I'm not really their daughter. Sarabeth is."

Jordan shook her head, and gave me an *Are you insane?* sort of stare. "How can anyone *not* love you?" she said. "They know what happened. They know how you feel about *them*. Do you know that Granddad told me how blessed he felt to have two of you, Sarabeth *and* you? Despite the fact that you can dangle yourself midair, the man thinks that you walk on water. And, as for Grandma, she believes that Jesus doubled the blessing she already had. 'They don't care!' Please! You are *so* loved, you're taking up the love that belongs to everyone else. And you're going to make a great mother with all the assistance you need from your older and wiser niece."

I smiled at her, as a tear dripped from my eye.

"Come here," she ordered, opening up her arms.

I drew close to her, and she hugged me like there was no tomorrow.

"Everything's going to be fine," she said. "Just fine."

CHAPTER XLV

Dargra-Tol

> *From the Altered Timeline*
> *On Rendenaaar*
> *Trillions of Universes in the Past*

Oh, the *Gaaalthaaar*! What pitiful creatures they are, ruled by their *yaaarghig*! Most had been destroyed by the war that ensued after I captured the stone. But Khattaaara had marshaled what forces she could. They were more of an irritant than anything else, but I wished for all of them to be destroyed. Thus, I showed up at the royal palace where Khattaaara and Pheeelja had taken refuge now for more than three cycles. Khattaaara had erected a quantum barrier that even my powers could not penetrate, and so I resorted to subterfuge.

I came wearing nothing but rags, just outside the barrier, with the story that I, too, had been tricked out of the stone, and that it had fallen into the hands of a *Thaaagran* named Loargaaargh, and that it was he, who wished to exterminate the Gaaalthaaarans, not I. Khattaaara stood on the other side looking down as I prostrated myself before her, begging for her forgiveness, my eyes staring down at the cold, hard floor. At her sides stood two large, muscled guards, their heads shaven, their skins bronzed, each wearing armor that hung from their shoulder, and draped down just past their loins in a somewhat triangular manner, consisting of long metal strips, heavily ornamented with varicolored gold.

"But why then," Khattaaara demanded, "did our royal niece make tell that she had seen thee destroy my people and that thou didst do battle with her, leading her on a pursuit through time?"

"Great Gaaalthaaara," I begged, "as thou must know, the stone I once had gives power to its bearer to imitate whomsoever or whatsoever he or she doth choose. 'Twas not I who did battle with thy niece. 'Twas not I who led her on a merry chase through time. And 'twas most certainly not I who harmed thy kind. I was foolish on that day I did take the stone from thee and I have regretted my ill-thought-out act ever since. But Loargaaargh did drug me that very night after I had revealed to him what power lay within my head. Thus, barely able to think, I did what thou had done for me, expelled it to my hand, whence he, too, snatched it to use for himself. Three whole cycles have I been his prisoner, till a Gaaalthaaaran slave, taking pity on me, helped me to escape. I know now that it was love that thou didst show me. So much time has passed since that night when I stole that which was thine. I can only reflect now on my shame. I beg thee, forgive me or else end my life here and now."

Khattaaara, however, was not so easily convinced. "How is it," she asked, "that thou hast so well outlived thy programmed lifetime without the god-stone in thy brain?"

"Again," I said, "'twas Loargaaargh, who used the stone to erase the limit for how long my kind might live. Through that, he gained the support of most of us, who before would die at so young an age."

"And what dost thou offer," she said, "should we allow thee to lie at our feet like the *goraaag* thou hast proved thyself to be?"

"I should again be thy servant," I said, "or thy lover once more should the thought of it cross thy mind."

Khattaaara had aged somewhat in those cycles that had passed, but still, she remained a handsome creature through it all. Conversely, there were no effects of age on me. I was as vibrant and youthful as the day I had been given to her. *So*, I thought to myself, *she still lusts for me.* I could smell the flowery odor, as it rose from her aging *yaaargh*. It was her *yaaargh*, which would lower her guard—her *yaaargh* that would dull her senses and dim her sensibility—her *yaaargh* that would ensure the end of her kind.

It was with noticeable reluctance that Khattaaara removed the quantum field that separated us both. Slowly, then, I stood up. I glanced once into her eyes and then with my head bowed, walked through the palace gates.

"We know not what to make of thee," she said, "but our love for thee remains and we pray that thou hast been truthful. We shall have Dulallaaah prepare a bath for thee and set out fine vestments in exchange for the tatters thou now wears. They are from our royal house, but do not think thee that because thou shalt be draped in raiment that it at all bestows upon thee the mark of blood-borne royals."

"Yes, Great Gaaalthaaara," I said with my eyes still fixed on the floor.

"Come, then," Khattaaara commanded, "and be welcomed to the *House* of Gaaalthaaara."

With head still bowed, I dropped to my knees, kissed the hem of her dress, and then climbed to my feet again whence I took Dulallaaah's extended hand. As the girl began to lead me into the castle, Khattaaara spoke again.

"One more thing," she said. "There is another here, who is to be regarded as equal to our most royal selves. Her name is Pheeelja, and thou shalt obey her words as were they our own."

"Yes, Great Gaaalthaaara," I said again, and then followed Dulallaaah, led by her hand, who, unseen by either Khattaaara or her guards, had interlaced her fingers with my own. Dulallaaah was, in reality, a *Thaaagran* like myself, but I had used the stone to alter her cells to make her appear to be a Gaaalthaaaran, just past the age of decision. I had taken away the programmed death from all of my kind—I, not Loargaaargh, who indeed was but a fool! Suffice it to say, Dulallaaah had grown into a beautiful

232

being, able to conceal her origins for the three cycles that had passed. Her skin was light as cream, her eyes pale violet, while her hair, which was dark as the night, hung down to the small of her back. Her breasts stood like monuments to her femininity, neither large nor small, with *shizaaarig*[46] that were azure and erect, while her *yaaargh*, held ever upward, signaled her willingness to mate, not that there were any males other than the guards to do so, either for pleasure or to impregnate her with child; regardless, they were all far beneath her station.

In due course, Dulallaaah led me to a bedchamber that, as it turned out, had belonged to one of the female patricians, far more lavish than that room I was given when I had served Khattaaara those three cycles ago.

We must not speak aloud, I telepathed Dulallaaah when we were in the room. *Khattaaara still has one of the god-stones in her head and I wish not to be overheard.*

What plans have you, my Queen? Dulallaaah replied in her head. *Long have I waited for Your Majesty's arrival.*

In due course, I telepathed back. *But tell me if you know this to be true. There are rumors that her daughter, Zhardaaan is an otherworld being, who fell from the sky into an open field whence Pheeelja, being without child, took her in as her own. I have met Zhardaaan, a formidable adversary to say the least. But what of this Pheeelja? Who is she? Whence did she come? And who is she to Khattaaara?*

'Tis my understanding, my Queen, that Pheeelja was come upon in her sleep three cycles ago by a taaargaaard.[47] It called itself Leeejiam, and so and thus, Pheeelja was born. If my Queen hast met her, she will have seen with her own eyes, that Pheeelja is not Gaaalthaaaran, but a halfling! She has no yaaargh, but one

---

[46] The part of the breasts equivalent to the areola and the nipple combined.

[47] A demon that visits *Gaaalthaaaran* females in their sleep, and impregnates them.

pair of khalthraaam, and her ears are that of a male! More than that, my Queen, when once I stripped myself naked and bid her take me to bed, she refused! And when I offered my yaaargh for her to lick for her pleasure, she spat on it, and turned her back to me![48]

So, she said. Her mind, however, revealed that she had tried on more than one occasion to seduce Zhardaaan, but the human child of Pheeelja had, each time, rebuked her advances.

And why wouldst thou wish to bed a halfling? I asked.

I was bewitched, no doubt, she proclaimed, *then made to shame myself as though I were a Thaaagran slave of olden days! If I have failed my Queen in this, she is welcome to end my life here and now!*

That will not be necessary, I told her. *Thou hast been faithful to me all this time and I shall keep thy loyalty in both my head and in my yaaargh. But what of Pheeelja?* I went on, *Who is she to Khattaaara?*

Her sister, I believe, she replied.

I know of no sister—only Dhraaal, her husband and brother. Yet if sister she be, then therein lies the means to bleed out the heart in Khattaaara's breast, thwart what bold strategies she might have made, and end her tireless reign! I looked hard at her. *Pheeelja is mortal, is she not?*

Yes, my Queen, she replied, *I have seen her bleed more than once when she injured herself.*

Good! I mused to myself. *The war of the gods begins!*

---

[48] The female *graaam*, it would seem, had a fruity taste similar to kiwi and let off pheromones that were both sexually stimulating and addictive.

CHAPTER XLVI

Peyton

> *From the Original Timeline*
> *In the Alternate Reality*
> *On Earth I*
> *Earth-Date: 2029*

I lay in bed that same night when I had inadvertently created twins; not twins like Phee and I were, but ones absolutely identical, down to their fingerprints. I was on my back with my hands on my belly, wondering if a fetus could dream. People tend to be strange when it comes to pregnancies. If the pregnancy is unwanted, it is called a fetus. If it *is* wanted, it is called a baby. No one ever asks, "Is your fetus going to be a boy or a girl?" I didn't know if I wanted to have children at that point in time, but I didn't *not* want to have them if that makes any sense. I had been pregnant before. I had had a child on Rendenaaar, but that was in a different life and in a different way. Zhana and Samira were most definitely not going to be born through my *yaaargh*, mainly because I didn't have one. I gave that up when I was reborn as Peyton! My God, how strange my past life seemed!

More strange still was how Thara-Klo had spoken of other lives that I had lived on other worlds in other universes; that my existence spanned a wealth of incarnations; some good, most not so much. The only one I do remember, just a bit, was in ancient Egypt, only it wasn't considered ancient when I lived there. Past lives, it seems, are difficult to recall. It is more the soul that transitions from person to person upon death, sometimes with an eternity in between. I had gotten to know my life on Rendenaaar

235

as Khattaaara. The memories of whatever lives I might have lived were relegated to some dark portions of my brain that were only sparked now and again by threads of energy from the quantum fabric. Thus, as I have said, there were only smatterings of one more; that other life I had lived on Rendenaaar. It was only when I had finally fallen asleep that night that I remembered the other one in the fertile crest where humankind had found its beginnings. However it occurred, in my sleep I had activated a quantum power that I never knew I had—one that would throw my spirit back two thousand years.

I *awakened* in a lavish room in an Egypt long since eroded by time, with handmaids standing on either side of the bed that I found myself on. The air was uncomfortably warm, despite the occasional cool breeze that would waft its way in through the large windows that stared out to the Mediterranean. I sat up, stretched out my arms lavishly, arching my back, and then looked around. On each side of my bed were two handmaids, cooling me with fans made from ostrich plumes. Despite that I had no control over the body I now inhabited, which was disconcerting, I possessed all of its memories, or, rather, the memories I had had in this former incarnation. Perhaps, though, my separate consciousness exerted a bit of influence, for I turned to one of the servant girls and ordered, "Bring me a mirror."

The one to my right, a girl, no more than fourteen years old, barely dressed by modern standards, rushed off to one side and returned with a mirror that was made of polished gold, attached to an ivory handle carved with the figure of Hathor, the goddess of beauty and rebirth.

Strange as it seemed to me, I could now understand *Ra En Chem*, which would later be called ancient Egyptian. More than that, staring at my reflection, I found that, for the most part, I looked the same as I would more than two millennia later, virtually identical to my future self, though perhaps just a few years older. As I knew, from what her memories recalled, I, Cleopatra VII Philopator, had ascended the throne just three years earlier, after my father, Auletes, had killed himself.[49] It was Gaius Julius Caesar who installed both me and my brother, Theos, as pharaohs of Egypt with equal power between us. Theos was only ten at the time, but, by custom, destined to become my husband. The only difference in my appearance derived from how I was made up. As per the fashion of the day, I wore both dark eyeliner and mascara, with green eyeshadow from powdered malachite. My eyebrows were darkened, and my lips slightly rouged. Meanwhile, my hair was completely obscured by a black wig, with curls that were rigidly held in place and decorated with gold wire that had been tightly wound around them and then highlighted with small turquoise stones. Atop my head was a diadem made from gold with the likeness of an asp ready to strike, positioned just over my forehead.

Both Theos and I were born and grew up in Alexandria, though our lineage was Macedonian. We spoke not only *Ra En Chem* but Greek as well. One of my teachers had tried to school me in the language of Germania, but I was miserable at it, unable to produce those guttural sounds that had been so common on Rendenaaar.

Harmachis, one of my slaves, entered with two Nubian guards, bowing his head to me in obeisance to my stature, as both his pharaoh and his god.

"Speak," I commanded, as my handmaids placed pillows behind me so that I might comfortably sit up and then began fanning me again.

"My Lady," Harmachis said, "the Emperor Caesar wishes an audience with the Queen of Kings."

"Show him in," I replied with words that were taken as a

---

[49] Apparently, suicide runs in the family, as I did much the same later on in that life, and then again as Peyton.

command.

Harmachis, left the room, while the Nubians remained, each taking positions on opposite sides of my bed, standing with folded arms. A moment later Harmachis returned with Caesar. "Good God!" I thought to myself. "It was Dhraaal!" He had told me that he had been Julius Caesar when Khattaaara had been in possession of my brain, but to tell a story is one thing; to see for oneself, quite another.

"I have been informed," I said, "that the noble Caesar has words for Cleopatra?"

"Aye, my Queen," Caesar replied. "I do."

"Then speak them to me," I went on, "for the heat is oppressive and it brings out the flies." I shooed one away with a wave of my hand.

"I have heard, my Queen," Caesar remarked, "that flies are only attracted to sweetness."

"You flatter me with your words," I said, "but surely there is more than adulation to your tongue."

"The hawk has spread rumors," Caesar replied in Greek, which was the language that he and most other Roman patricians of the time mainly used. "The hawk proclaimed that there is a civil war brewing betwixt your brother and yourself, and so I have come to try to either settle matters or else defend your royal throne."

"Theos is but a child of thirteen," I said. "He flew into a rage because I refused to make bed with him."

"As any man might," Casear replied, "who has come close enough to sniff the air you breathe, my Queen."

"Tell me, noble Caesar," I said. "Is your cock as mighty as your tongue?"

"Both have equal talent, my Lady," he replied.

I clapped my hands twice. "Out!" I proclaimed. "All of you! Only take the imperator's sword and dagger if he wishes to stay.

He will not require them. There will be no battle here."

As she was about to leave, Caesar grabbed the arm of the girl who had brought the mirror to me. "Stay girl," he ordered, "long enough to draw closed the curtains to darken the room."

"Tell me, Caesar," I said as the girl fulfilled her task. "how many winters have you seen?"

"Fifty-two, my Queen," he replied, "though I have saved all my summers for a moment such as this."

"I am young enough to be your daughter and then some," I said.

"But old enough," he replied, "to know the true worth of age upon this earth."

"And power," I added.

"*That* we both have," he said as he stripped off his armor, removed his tunic, and climbed into my bed, propping himself up over me.

"Tell me, noble Caesar," I asked, "why do you always demand that we make love in the dark? Is there some gruesome scar you do not want seen?"

"No, my Queen," he answered. "It is just that I wish for you to envision a much younger Caesar to capture your desire. You are everything a man could wish for, and I am everything a young woman might fear."

"I fear nothing but betrayed expectations," I replied.

"Then I shall marshal all of my forces," he said, "so as not to disappoint." And with those words, I felt him enter me, as we began making love. Sadly, it was at the very start of my orgasm that I was thrown back into the present—a royal disappointment, if one may forgive the pun.

I lay in bed afterward, still wide awake. The swelter of the Egyptian heat was gone, replaced by the air conditioning in my bedroom. But why, I wondered to myself, hadn't Dhraaal recognized me, or if he had, why hadn't he called me by my old name? Perhaps he knew there would be another incarnation in a more technologically advanced time. Perhaps. in this new timeline, like Thom, he had not one shred of remembrance. And yet, it seemed, we were drawn to play out eternity together in one or another form, as was the case with myself and Phee. But as it was all too much for my now tired brain, I closed my eyes and dreamt of other things, like Christmas lights and Ferris wheels.

CHAPTER XLVII

Payton (Pay)

From the Altered Timeline
In the Alternate Reality
On Earth I
Earth-Date: 2029

The quantum fabric is difficult to describe. It's sort of a nether world without the world. I would imagine that it's like being on psychedelic drugs, but there are no drugs involved. But this is where I took Li, in order to attempt to trace the path that Chloë and young Liam had taken. A ten-year-old going off with a twelve-year-old with a quantum seed in her head is cause for alarm, to say the least.

"Where are we?" Li asked.

"We're in a place that underlies all dimensions and all universes," I replied.

"Are these all different dimensional versions of us?" she asked, staring at the trail of images that looked like and moved with us.

"No," I answered, "they're different versions of us in time."

"It's scary," she said. "It's like we're being followed by a bunch of ghosts."

I forgot she didn't have the protection of a quantum mind. Our voices to her were like endless echoes, and when she and I moved, there was a stream of afterimages that crowded the fabric around us. I quickly placed a quantum time field around her to protect her from the effect.

"Is this better?" I asked her.

"So much!" she exclaimed. "But how can you tell where they

went—Chloë and Liam, I mean?"

"You told me that Liam gave her a red quantum seed," I replied, "{so what I'm looking for is a red quantum trail. I'm fairly new at this, but I'm confident I can do it. Jordan told me that she was able to pursue Dargra-Tol through time and that Dargra-Tol had followed the trail that Peyton had left when she brought the original Ophelia back to Rendenaaar."

"Can I ask you something?" Li said.

"Of course," I replied.

"Doesn't it bother you," she asked, "that you're a copy of the other Payton from your dimension?"

"I'm not a copy," I said. "I'm just part of an alternate timeline."

"But if whatever happened to make the alternate timeline didn't happen, you wouldn't exist," she said.

"And if the stork didn't decide to bring you to your mom and dad," I told her, "you might have grown up in China."

"Storks don't bring babies!" she replied, laughing.

"Really!" I said, feigning astonishment. "Exactly how do they come then?"

"Are you sure you want to know?" she asked. "They told us about it in school."

"Definitely," I replied.

"Okay," she said, "but don't blame me if you throw up in wherever it is we are because it's really icky."

"I think I can handle it," I replied.

"Okay," she went on. "Well, when a husband and a wife (they have to be married!) decide to have a baby, they both take off their clothes."

"In front of each other?" I interjected, appearing astonished.

"Uh-huh," she replied.

"And then what happens?" I asked her.

Li stared at me, ever so seriously. "The woman lies down on their bed on her back," she said, "and—I'm not making this up—

he pushes his penis into her vagina, and pees out some gooey stuff into her."

"And then what?" I asked.

"That's it," she replied. "Then they get dressed again, and nine months later there's a baby."

"But you have to be married first?" I asked.

"Yep," she replied. "Otherwise it won't work."

"Thank you for telling me," I said. "I always wondered how babies were made."

"Well," she replied, "now you know."

"I don't think the other Payton will ever have children unless she adopts them," I said.

"Why's that?" Li asked.

"Because she just likes girls," I replied.

"Huh uh," came the response.

"Yep," I said. "That's the one big difference between us."

"How can she like girls?" Li asked.

"She just does," I replied.

"You mean like kissing them?" she questioned.

" Mmmm-hmmm," I replied.

"Ewww!" she exclaimed.

"But she's a really good person," I added.

"I guess," she replied, "but still, ewww!"

Suddenly, I perked.

"What's wrong?" Li asked.

"I think I found Chloë's trail," I told her.

"I don't see anything," Li said.

"Here," I replied. "Look!" I removed the quantum time field so that everything was as it had been when we first arrived, with both the visual and sound echoes of ourselves. In the distance, though, there was a reddish blur with two figures.

"That's them!" Li exclaimed, and then shouted, "Liam!"

"They can't hear you," I told her.

"Why not?" she asked.

"Because that's just an afterimage of where they'd been," I explained.

"Can we follow them?" she asked.

"That's why we came," I replied and was about to do so when, all at once, a female figure blocked our path.

"Jordan?" I exclaimed, for that was my first thought, but this woman, this being, had silver skin and silver eyes, her hair like strands of silver, her perfect, naked body radiating an almost angelic glow. Looking at her, I could almost understand my timeline counterpart's attraction to the female form, for she was beyond any definition of beauty. She was the word itself, causing my skin to flush and my heart to pound within my chest. I felt the blood drain from my head, the tips of my breasts grow hard, and my groin turn damp. *Snap out of it!* I thought to myself. It was as though I were bewitched.

Payton Herron, it spoke into my mind.

"Who are you?" I said, speaking aloud.

I am she who is everything, and she who is nothing, she spoke into my head. *I am the beginning and the end, and the guardian of the forever. I am everyone and no one, and I am the embodiment of every Quantum Girl who did or will ever exist.*

"Why are you here?" I said.

"I don't hear anything!" Li whispered to me.

You are her, and she is you, and all of you are one, she telepathed again. *The power of the whole is the key to eternity. The god-stones are both the beginning and the end, and they must, in all of you, be combined.*

"You speak in riddles," I said.

In the end, the answer will be clear, she replied. *But for now, go find your children. They need your guidance, and someone to lead them home.*

"But..." I tried to say, yet no words came out.

Go! She ordered and then vanished into the nothingness from which she had come. And so, we followed Chloë's trail.

CHAPTER XLVIII

Chloë

> *From the Altered Timeline*
> *In the Alternate Reality*
> *On Earth I*
> *Earth-Date: 2020*

There was a three-year-old version of me in 2020, dragging around Bosco, her teddy bear, and living with a ten-year-old Claire and a much younger Mom and Dad. But time ran differently on my Earth than on Liam's. Here his counterpart would have been around his age, although here his counterpart didn't exist. It was all so strange to me, though. I knew that my being able to time travel was *possible* from what Liam had said, but winding up in the past was, well, freaking me out. The fact that we were back in time on *my* Earth made me feel at least *somewhat* safe. There wouldn't be an alien threat on any Earth for seven more years. Both of us were totally out of place here. All of the students ranged in age from fourteen to eighteen. Regardless, we did what any red-blooded American kid in our circumstances would do at lunchtime. We headed for the cafeteria… and lied. I told the cafeteria worker that our sister had brought us there to observe a day in high school—sort of like a field trip—only she left her English composition book at home and had to rush back to get it, leaving us stranded for the moment without money for lunch. The worker was only too kind to hand us each a tray filled with food, and, let me tell you, we were famished, as we hadn't eaten in a while, and whatever is to be said about cafeteria food, when you're really hungry, it doesn't matter. It was food—

besides which, it was Turkey Day, with a choice of milk or lemonade. Spoiler alert! We both chose lemonade! Afterward, as the elementary school was just across the football field, we headed there and hung out on the swings.

"What are we going to do?" Liam asked me.

"Don't know," I replied.

"I mean, seriously," he said back, "we have nowhere to go, no home, no money, no food, and we're stuck years in the past."

"I said I don't know!" I snapped back.

Liam just stared at me and then got off the swing and began walking toward the building.

"Liam!" I called after him. "I'm sorry!"

It was then that the school bell rang and all of the kids began to emerge. Suddenly, Liam perked up and ran in the direction of a small group of girls, going up to one, and grabbing hold of her wrist. My new quantum powers let me hear everything.

"Li," he said. "Boy, am I glad to see you. How did you get here?"

The girl, who looked exactly like Li, stared down at her wrist and then yanked her hand away. "What do you mean?" she said. "And my name's not Li! It's Ophelia!"

"Come on!" Liam insisted. "Let's go. Chloë's over there," he went on, motioning toward me. "Is Payton with you?"

"I'm Peyton!" said the ten-year-old girl standing next to her. "And you need to leave my sister alone!"

"*Your* sister?" replied Liam in an astonished tone. "Since when?"

"Since always!" came Peyton's angry response. Then she put up her fists at him. "You leave my sister alone, or I'll make your nose bleed so much, your face'll turn red!"

Liam put up his hands in a gesture of appeasement and backed up several steps. "Okay! Okay!" he said. "Whatever!"

Then the group of girls began chanting at him, "Weird boy,

weird boy, go home and play with your girl toy!" Liam just slinked away, looking back just once to see Ophelia stick out her tongue at him. Then he turned and kicked an empty soda can in frustration. I walked up to him. By then, all of the girls had forgotten all about him and were just talking and laughing amongst themselves.

"That wasn't Li," I told him. "We're back in time, remember? That was Peyton and Phee!"

Liam looked at me. "She looked exactly *like* her," he said.

"I know," I replied, "because the Ophelia Herron of this world is Li's interdimensional identical twin, Ding-a-Ling!"

"Don't call me that," Liam pouted.

"That's just an endearing term," I said. "I'm sorry about before."

"Really?" Liam asked, unsure.

"Really," I said and then I kissed him gently on the cheek. His eyes brightened, and he appeared to have forgotten all that had just gone on.

"We need to get back home," he said. "You need to try and get us there."

So, once again, he held onto me. I tried to focus. I tried to send us back. All that happened was that we both flashed invisible for some seconds. I just shook my head.

"I can't seem to do it," I replied.

"Let me try," he insisted. "After all, it *is* my stone."

Breathing a deep sigh, I willed the stone from my head and gave it to him; it went into his the same as it had mine. He held onto me once more and then shut his eyes. Suddenly, I felt the air around us move and we were back home in our bedroom. I let go of him, took my cell phone from my pocket, and looked at it. November 12, 2029. I smiled at him.

"You did it!" I said.

"Just call me Quantum Boy," he said, smiling back. Then the

smile left his face, as he began to fade away.

"Liam!" I called out, but by then, it was too late. He was gone. He wasn't invisible. He was just gone.

CHAPTER XLIX

Claire from Earth I

> *From the Alternate Timeline*
> *In the Alternate Reality*
> *On Earth III*
> *Earth III-Date: 2023*

I had a decision to make. I'd slept nearly ten hours after my graverobbing ordeal, awakened by the smell of coffee coming from the kitchen. I rose from the bed, threw on a robe, and then followed the scent to its origin. Young Claire was sitting at the table, drinking coffee from a mug with two stick figures on it— one frowning, missing his vertical line; the other, smiling, holding it, with the words, "I've Got Your Back" printed below. Niska was asleep on the floor at her feet.

"Children should not be drinking coffee," I said as I poured a cup for myself, and then sat down facing her.

"What else *is* there?" she replied. "The milk's all sour. The orange juice tastes like alcohol." She paused to bring the mug once more to her mouth with both hands. "Did you get what you were looking for?" she asked after taking another sip.

"I did," I said, "but it wasn't easy."

"Cracking open skulls never is," she added casually.

"You certainly are precocious for a ten-year-old," I said.

"Being in the dark all the time ages you a lot," she replied. "It makes you have to grow up fast." She paused and then went on. "Did you want to ask me something, or maybe tell me that my being blind is slowing you down and you need to move on without me?"

"Cynical, too," I said. "No, I'm not abandoning you. Not now. Not ever. I've just been doing a lot of thinking. And I thought… What am *I* going to do with a bunch of superpowers? But you, on the other hand…"

"Oh, that would be so cool," she said back, somewhat flippant. "A blind Supergirl, crashing into walls at super speed. Able to leap tall buildings in a single bound if she can find them; then smash into an airplane, killing everyone onboard."

"I thought," I said, hesitant in my words, "that perhaps it might heal you."

"My blindness," she replied without the slightest hint of emotion.

"Certainly not your sarcasm," I said.

"And you'll do that for me," she said back, "give it all up for a girl you barely know."

"Oh, I know more about you than you think," I replied. "I may not have lost my sight, and growing up in Darwin was probably a whole lot different from growing up in L.A., but deep down, I think we're pretty much the same, which is why I know you'd do the same for me if situations were reversed."

"I'm just a kid," she said. "How do you know I can control it? What if I do something wrong?"

"Then you'll learn to do something right," I replied. "Stand up. Please." Claire stood, and I went over to face her. "I know from my encounter with that alien how this works. I just bring it up to your forehead, and *it* does the rest."

"It's not going to hurt, is it?" she asked.

"Not one bit," I replied as I brought the yellow god-stone to the middle of her forehead and pressed it gently against her skin. Regardless that I felt no movement, the gemstone appeared to spin faster and faster, shrinking in size until it was no larger than a grain of sand, at which point it seemed to melt into her skin, causing her skin to glow yellow. And then it disappeared

251

altogether. I stared at her, wondering if she could stare back. Ever so gently, I touched the sides of her cheeks and tilted her face up toward mine. Her eyes appeared as sightless as before.

"I still can't see," she said, then, "Wait! Oh, dear gods!"

"What is it?" I asked.

"When everything's quiet," she said, "it's all still just black. But when I talk, I can see all around me. Nothing's in color, but I can see!"

"Sort of like a bat, I guess," I replied.

"Thank you!" she said as trembling tears began to flow. "Thank you so much!" Then she lunged at me, wrapped her arms around my shoulders, and hugged me with all her might. "Thank you! Thank you! Thank you!"

I pulled her back just a bit to stare her in the eye. "Now, young Claire," I said, "I'm going to have to teach you how to use all the powers that our alien friend had when she was alive."

"Then I can kick some alien butt!" she exclaimed.

"Then *we* can go back to my dimension to my home," I corrected her. I looked at her, so sad before, now all smiles.

Food was somewhat scarce, but I did manage to scrounge up some lunch from a can of salmon, and there was a neglected tomato plant in the backyard (not anywhere near the grave!) along with a strawberry plant that yielded a tasty dessert. Meanwhile, in the pantry was a lone container of Tang, the drink of astronauts, that wasn't much different from Kool-Aid other than that it was orange, but it was better than nothing.

After satisfying our hunger, we went out for a walk. Claire's head turned in every direction. I think, though, the happiest part for her was being able to play with Niska, running back and forth with her.

"It's almost like being able to see again for real," she said. "The sounds the birds make, the breeze rustling the leaves; they create patterns in the air. I'm not in the dark anymore, unless

252

everything's perfectly still. But it's not just that. All of my other senses are heightened."

She pointed toward a house across the street in the distance. "I can smell the roses against that rail fence. I can hear the fledglings chirping for their mother to bring them food in their nest in that tree." She whirled around and then turned toward me. "Oh, Claire, it's wonderful to be in the world again!"

I felt comforted by the fact that I had made the right choice. Claire had my same moral compass, and I knew that once back on my world, she would use her powers in a way that would help others. She even had a name picked out for herself, this ten-year-old superhero—Clairess!—basically Claire with an es sound at the end, the S for Salinger. Claire was different from Chloë. Where Chloë always tried to be my big sister, Claire looked up to me for strength.

Over the next few days, we went from house to house to gather food supplies—mainly canned goods. There wasn't much else but it was enough. There was fruit and vegetables, Spam and sardines, and even pie filling—that was for our desserts!

"Do you want to live with me when we get to my world?" I asked her late one night. We were sitting on the front lawn, looking up at the stars. "I was about to rent my own place," I said, "when all of this happened. The schools are really good near where I intend to live. I'm eighteen now, and I have—or had—a job as a waitress at *J'ai Faim* in Malibu. Hopefully, it'll still be there when we get back. I make pretty good tips. I was just thinking. Maybe the State will let me adopt you."

"Seriously?" she said, all so excited.

"Yes, seriously," I replied. "Chloë's always been on my case about taking responsibility. This would be my opportunity to show her I'm fully capable."

She stared at me wide-eyed, which was pretty good for someone who only weeks ago had been totally blind. "So you'd be my actual Mom?"

I nodded and smiled. Then, for the second time, she threw her arms around me, toppling me down onto my back with her on top of me, "I love you! I love you! I love you!" she said, her cheek pressed down against my breast. "So much!"

"One step at a time," I said. "First, I need to help you learn to use your new abilities. And we need to get up because I'm feeling somewhat squashed at the moment!"

"Do you see that lamppost over there?" I asked her the very next day as I pointed in its direction. "I want you to imagine that you are holding a ball of yellow fire in your hand—fire that won't harm *you* but is as powerful as a guided missile. I want you to imagine it, and then I want you to throw it as hard as you can."

As she focused on her open hand, a glowing ball of yellow energy appeared.

"Now throw it at the lamppost," I said. "Try to knock it down."

Claire threw the glowing sphere in the direction of the streetlight and missed it entirely. The ball landed on a small patch of grass and set it on fire. All at once, though, Claire was *at* the fire, trying to stomp it out with her feet. She hadn't walked or run. She had just vanished from where she had been and appeared where the fire was. I ran over to where she had materialized and helped her to stomp out the last of the flames.

"How did you do that?" I asked.

"I missed, I guess," she replied.

"No," I said, "I mean how did you get *here*? You didn't rush up to put out the flames. You just suddenly appeared."

"I did?" she said with astonishment. "I don't know. I just saw that I'd started a fire, and knew that I needed to put it out."

That—being able to teleport herself—was the first discovery of her powers that she had made on her own. In the coming days and weeks, she was able to harness more and more, and, in time, learned to control them. One bizarre ability was revealed totally by accident. We had gone to a nearby park for more practice when one of Claire's fireballs accidentally crashed into a bee's nest, and the angry swarm came at me. Claire was beside herself, as was I. I didn't know whether to run or stand like a statue. In retrospect, running would probably have been the better option. Hundreds of bees stung me nearly all at once and I collapsed to the ground, barely conscious.

"No, no, no, no, no, no, no, no!" I could hear Claire exclaim. She clapped her hands together once and all the bees merged into one. Then she snuffed out its life with another burst of yellow fire, but for me, it was all too late. The venom was now coursing through my bloodstream. I could feel Niska lick my face as Claire held her tightly by the leash. "We need to get you help!" she said. "We need to get to your world."

"But there are so many possible dimensions," I muttered, fighting for consciousness. Then everything around me seemed to change, as we went from dimension to dimension, from one Earth to the next, from worlds that were barren, to ones with alien civilizations, to ones with strange vegetation and weird creatures—even dinosaurs—one after another, hundreds, perhaps thousands, with Claire desperately trying to find the right one. And then I passed out.

CHAPTER L

Payton

> *From the Original Timeline*
> *In the Alternate Reality*
> *The Quantum Fabric*
> *Earth-Date: 2029*

I kept thinking about Jasmine, back on my world. True, I had never known her while I was Payton, but I had made love to her numerous times while I had occupied Liam's body and, well, I'd formed an attachment and was concerned about her. As I headed back to my dimension, though, I noticed something beyond unusual that was happening in the quantum fabric. It was filled with yellow trails—thousands of them—leading from one dimension to another, nearly one every second. As I slowed time down, three figures came into focus— A young girl, a collie, and Claire! But that didn't make any sense. I'd seen Claire only moments before I'd left. In another instant, all were gone, and then in another, they were back, which is when I froze time altogether and phased up to them. Claire had welts all over her body. She looked as though she were in shock. I unfroze the girl, who stared at me.

"Who are you?" she asked.

"Quantum Girl," I replied. "What happened to Claire?"

"Do you know her?" she asked. "I'm trying to get her home, only I don't know which dimension she's from." She looked at me pleadingly. "Can you help? She's the closest thing I have to a Mom."

"The world I just came from is the right one," I replied. "Her quantum signature is the same as Peyton's." And with that, I phased us all to the emergency room at Cedars-Sinai, becoming my Payton self as I did. Instantly, I turned to one of the nurses. "Excuse me," I said to her, "this woman needs help!"

The nurse turned and saw Claire, who was lying on the floor. "Oh, dear God!" she exclaimed and then called out, "We've got a code blue here! Someone get her on a gurney!"

The ER techs immediately responded and then a doctor rushed over. "What happened to her?" he asked as he examined her eyes with a small flashlight. He looked at me and then at the girl.

The girl was quick to respond. "She was stung by hundreds of bees!" she said.

The doctor glanced up at a member of his attending staff. "She's in anaphylactic shock," he called out. "I need an epinephrine syringe from the crash cart!"

Seconds later, he injected the contents of the syringe he'd been handed into a vein in Claire's left arm. "Get her to ICU. Stat!" he barked out. "I'll be there in a minute." The doctor then turned to the girl. "Were either of you stung as well?"

"No," she said as I shook my head at him.

As he left to follow the gurney at a brisk pace, the girl turned to me in tears. "It's all my fault," she wept. "I accidentally knocked down the beehive when I was..." and she stopped. I squatted down in front of her.

"When you were what?" I asked.

"When I was practicing throwing the yellow energy," she said, weeping out the words.

"What's your name, Sweetheart?" I asked as I looked at her with concern.

"Claire," she said. "*My* name's Claire, too."

"And do you have a quantum seed in your head?" I asked.

"It's called a god-stone," she replied. "Claire could have taken it for herself, but she wanted me to have it, because I was blind, and now I can see again." She began to sob bitterly. "She loves me and I love her. She's all Niska and I have!"

"Is this Niska?" I asked, looking over at her dog.

Claire nodded and tried to wipe her tears with the back of one hand. I phased to the nurses' station, retrieved some tissues, and then phased back, all within a nanosecond. I brought one tissue to her cheeks.

"Everything's going to be just fine," I said.

"But what if she dies?" Claire wept.

"Then I'll just have to bring her back to life," I said to reassure her.

"Can you do that?" she asked, her tears abating a bit.

"I'm an expert," I said convincingly. "I'm Quantum Girl." I stood up and took her hand. "Now, let's go find the cafeteria to get you something to eat, while we wait for the doctors to do their job." And so we went—all three of us—after I told the charge nurse where we could be found if need be. I bought young Claire a hamburger, a Coke and fries, and a hamburger patty for Niska, along with a bowl of water. As I set down the water bowl, the doctor entered the room, looking for us. I went up to him, a disconsolate look in his eyes.

"It doesn't look good for her," he said in a quiet voice. "There's too much venom in her system."

"How much time does she have?" I asked.

"A few minutes at best," he replied. "If you want to say your goodbyes. Now's the time."

I nodded to the doctor and then turned to young Claire. "Claire, come with me, now."

The young Claire got up. Then we went to the ER where the other Claire lay unconscious. She was hooked up to monitors, and there was a nurse standing at the side of the bed, adjusting the flow of the IV that had been placed in Claire's arm.

"Could you please give us a moment in private?" I asked.

The nurse nodded and then left, drawing the curtain closed behind her.

"What's wrong?" young Claire asked, tensing up.

"She was stung by an awful lot of bees," I answered.

"She's not going to die, is she?" young Claire said, beginning to cry again. "You promised you wouldn't let her!"

"There are some things," I began to say.

"You promised!" young Claire wept.

"I can bring her back to the moment she was brought in here," I said. "That will buy us a bit more time. But I'm going to need some help." I took a deep breath. "And a willing volunteer."

I turned to young Claire. "You told me that after the bees attacked, you clapped your hands together, and they all became one."

"Yes," she said, again wiping her tears with the tissue I'd given her.

I made the older Claire light as a feather, removed the IV from her arm, disconnected all the monitor wires, and lifted her into my arms. "Hold onto Niska," I said, "and give me your hand." Young Claire squatted down, put her right arm around Niska, and then gave me her left hand. I phased us all out of there. No doubt the nurse, who'd been standing just outside the curtains, had rushed back in from the rustling of the fabric and the sound of the vacuum we created as we left.

CHAPTER LI

Claire (from Earth II)

From the Altered Timeline
In the Alternate Reality
On Earth I
Earth-Date: 2029

Payton and I were in the kitchen drinking the hot cocoa I had made when we heard the sound of a dog barking that was coming from upstairs. We quickly set down our cups and raced up the staircase, just as we heard Demi call out, "Claire!" Funny how it was I was able to tell the differences in Payton's and her voices, even though they were so similar.

When we reached the bedroom, I saw her, another version of me, lying unconscious on the bed with red welts all over her body; and there was a younger version of us at her side!

"What's going on?" Payton asked. "Who *is* she?"

"She's the Claire from this world," Demi replied. "Chloë's sister. The one we thought was dead."

It was at that same moment that Chloë burst into the room and saw her.

"Claire?" she said. "Oh, my God!" She looked at Demi. "What happened?"

"She was stung by killer bees," Demi replied. Then she turned to me. "Look," she said, "she doesn't have much time."

Chloë glared at her through tears. "What do you mean?" she cried in near hysterics. "Why isn't she in a hospital?"

"She was," young Claire answered. "The doctors couldn't help her. That's why Quantum Girl brought us here."

Demi looked at me more seriously than I had ever seen either her or Payton look. "The only way to save her," she said, "is to merge her with you."

"What do you mean?" I asked. "You're joking, right? I don't even know her."

"You *are* her," came the reply. "She's you. Just a different version. Your personalities are mainly the same, only some of the memories are different."

"What will happen if I say all right?" I asked; "if I say you can do this? What will happen to *me*?"

"You'll be the same," Demi replied, "only you'll have her memories as well as your own. It won't be like you're two people. It will be like you've lived two lives and now they're one."

Chloë stared up at me with tears streaming down her cheeks. "Please!" she begged. "Please!"

I looked at the other girl; the one who looked like me at a younger age. There were tears in her eyes as well. "She's such a good person," she said as her eyes welled up with tears. "I love her so much!"

I looked from one to the other; from the girl to Chloë to Demi, and then to Payton. Payton just shrugged her shoulders, like it was up to me and me alone.

"All right," I said. "do it, only I hope I'm not going to regret it in the end."

Demi looked around at all of us. "Payton, I want you to place a forcefield around everyone in the room other than me and her, including the dog."

"What are you going to do?" I asked.

"Remove the stingers," she said as she stared at my other-dimensional self. "First, I'm going to suspend time around her brain. Otherwise, it'll hurt like all hell. And now..."

All at once, a hundred or more stingers flew across the room like bullets.

"Okay," she said to Payton. "You can remove the forcefields." Then she turned to me.

"I need you to lie down beside her," she said. The other version of me was just lying on the bed barely conscious—barely alive. And so I did. I laid myself down alongside her. Then Demi turned to the girl. "Claire," she went on. "I need you to do to them what you did with the bees," and she glanced at the both of *us*— both of *me*.

The young girl tried. She focused on us and then clapped her hands hard once, and then again. "It's not working!" she said.

"You're trying to merge them," Payton said with a heavy sigh, "but their anatomy's reversed. It's not going to work."

"Wait!" she exclaimed. "I did this once with a twenty-dollar bill when I was back in time with Liam." Then she waved her hand over the Claire who lay dying beside me. As I glanced over, I could see the bee stings change on her face. "All right," Demi said to the girl. "Try again."

The girl stared and clapped her hands once more. It was as though I was being hit by an explosion, and then I felt slightly ill. But it was more than that. Suddenly, I knew the girl. She was the otherworld version of me that I had given the god-stone to. And Chloë—she was my kid sister, always so bossy, but she loved me no matter what. And yet I was still me—the me who had grown up with Liam and with Payton. I stood up from the bed and then collapsed. It was Payton who phased over to me and caught me before I could hit the floor.

"We need to get her back to the hospital," Demi said. "Let me take her. I know which bed she was in. Otherwise, there might be a stir there. I'll bring her back to the moment we left." Then she turned to Clairey. "Grab hold of Niska," she said, and then she went to where Payton stood holding me. Payton transferred me to her. With her free hand, Demi took Clairey's, and then we all phased back to the ER, to the sectioned-off bed, and both Demi and Clairey helped me to lie down. Demi reconnected the monitoring equipment and then reinserted the IV.

"Ow!" I whispered.

"Sorry," came the quiet response.

Whipping around, she reopened the curtains, the nurse still in the room.

"Please call the doctor," Demi said.

A moment later, the doctor was at my side, looking at the monitors "I don't know what to make of it," he said turning to Payton and Claire, "but I think she's going to be all right." He shook his head to himself. "If any of you believe in miracles, this is definitely one. In all my years of practice, I have never witnessed a recovery like this." Then he turned to me. "You're going to be just fine," he said. Then a curious expression came on his face, as he touched the edge of my blouse, and noticed that there was another blouse underneath. But he just shook his head again, turned to leave, and then said, "I'll check back in a while. Beautiful dog by the way," he added, and then he left, closing the curtain behind him.

"How do you feel?" Demi asked me.

"Not as bad as when all the bees stung," I said.

"You have an Aussie accent," Demi said.

"Yeah," I replied, "but I guess it had to be one or the other."

"You get some rest," she said. "We'll be back in the morning. Well, maybe Payton instead of me."

"And Chloë," I added.

"And Chloë," I replied.

"Now that you're *together*," Claire asked with hesitation in her voice, "do you still want to adopt me?"

"Of course, I do," I said.

"What's that all about?" Demi asked.

"I'm going to be a mother!" I said with the broadest of smiles, briefly taking my soon-to-be daughter's hand.

"Oh, Liam's going to *love* that," Demi said with a smile and a hint of sarcasm in her voice.

"Liam loves me," I replied. "He'll love what I love, and *I* love her." I squeezed Clairey's hand, and we exchanged a smile.

Demi, Clairey, and Niska left the normal way, though I suspected that they went into one of the private toilets, and phased home from there. *Damn*, I thought to myself just after they'd left. *I should have told them to bring the book I was reading that I'd left on the kitchen table back at the house*—trying to read was so difficult when all the print was backward. *Perhaps Demi could fix that for me. At least reverse a few books!* For the moment, though, I still felt sick and a bit nauseous, so I rang for the nurse and asked if she would ask the doctor if there was anything he might prescribe to settle my stomach and help me fall asleep. She did. He did. I did. And that was the end of a most event-filled day.

CHAPTER LII

Young Claire

From Earth III
In the Alternate Reality
On Earth I
Earth-Date: 2029

I began hearing things. I started to think that I was going crazy or something. I mean, I'd heard about people that it had happened to, who had to be taken to some mental ward to have their heads fixed. Doctors would implant an organic device that would spider web out into their brain. Our class watched it all on virtual before the invasion that ended our world. I wondered if it might have something to do with the implant in my head, but then I remembered those had to be recharged and mine hadn't been, so it couldn't have been that. Then I thought that it was the god-stone but then I remember how Pay had told me that it was our minds that made them work and not the other way around. And then there were the voices. Scary as the voices were, I was afraid to tell anyone. I did not want to be sent away to some hospital somewhere. I liked where I was and I liked spending every day with Claire. *Besides,* I thought, *how did my problem compare to their trying to save the people on two entire worlds?*

Claire was true to her word. She'd asked Peyton if she could help—the Peyton from this world—the one who was rich and knows everyone. Anyway, she got a judge to sign adoption papers on the spot, so now Claire's really my Mom, and Liam—the older one that she married—is actually my Dad, although I still call him Liam. Regardless, he is totally cool and was all on board when

265

Claire asked if she could sell her engagement ring to buy a used piano for me. That never happened, though, as Pay got wind of it and I guess she told Peyton, and a couple of days later a Bösendorfer upright was delivered. I looked it up online. It cost over a hundred thousand dollars. There was a note in an envelope taped to it that read, "I expect front-row tickets when you play Carnegie Hall." The invoice that came with it said it was from Katara Drall—in other words, Peyton. Mom drove me over to her estate to say thank you. I couldn't thank her enough. She just smiled and said that considering all that had happened, it was the very least she could do.

Mom and Liam had their ups and downs in the past, but I could tell that they were totally in love. I guess Liam had also fallen in love with the other Ophelia, but she'd been taken back to Rendenaaar and was out of the picture. It seemed to me that a person can love more than one person in their lifetime, although apparently, Liam had more than one—lifetime, I mean, with the overwritten timeline and all.

From the moment the papers were signed, I called Claire Mom. At first, it felt awkward, sort of like I was being disrespectful to my birth mom, but my birth mom was dead and I knew that she would have wanted me to have someone in my life who would love me like she did. And, FYI, around the house, I was known as Clairey to avoid confusion; confusion sort of reigns when you're dealing with alternate timelines and parallel worlds.

Anyway, back to the voices that only I could hear, it only became worse and I became really afraid to go to sleep. Sometimes, I would crawl into bed in the middle of the night next to my new mom on her side of the bed and snuggle up against her. She would wrap her arm around me and gently kiss my head. She didn't know about the voices. I guess she just knew that I needed to be held. I felt so sorry that she'd lost the baby she'd been carrying. I think she was born to be a mom. I don't think a whole lot of people *are*, but *she* was. Trust me. She made me feel loved every moment of every day.

It was on the third night of this that there were visions as well. I felt myself tremble and I guess my mom felt it, too, because she pulled me in closer to her.

"What's wrong?" she whispered in my ear.

"I've been hearing voices," I confessed, "and now I'm seeing things."

"Tell me," she said.

"It's not clear," I replied. "The voices sound echoey but I can't make out what they're saying. And the visions are of people, though they're blurred, and the strange part of it is that they're red. The god-stone I have only allows me to see things in yellow, and what makes no sense is that if the voices are just in my head, I shouldn't be able to see *anything*."

"Can you make anything *out*?" she asked.

"Not the figures," I told her. "Just some words. Most of it's garbled, but I think I hear, 'Help me!' I don't know what it is. I'm really afraid."

"You've been through a lot," she said. "We all have. But I'll protect you as best I can," and she reached over with her head and kissed my cheek. "Try and go to sleep," she whispered in my ear. "I'm going to hold you tight and I won't let go."

"Promise?" I asked.

"I promise," she replied. "Not even if a hurricane comes blowing through the window."

I remember laughing quietly so as not to awaken Liam. "There are no hurricanes in California!" I said.

"Then you're absolutely safe," she replied.

"I love you, Mama," I said.

"Love you more," she whispered back, as she hugged me.

It must have been a few hours later that I was awakened by the voices again. I didn't move, but I opened my eyes wide. There wasn't the slightest hint of sound in the room, but there it was again, outlines of human shapes in red, moving like ghosts caught in a strobe.

Carefully, I rose from the bed. No matter which way I turned, the shapes were everywhere. But the voices weren't coming from any one direction. They were all inside my head. They must have been because Niska who was ever by my side was calmly asleep next to the bed and only perked up just a bit when I stood. Suddenly, a glowing red rope came at me from behind, wrapped around me, and pulled me out of the room into I didn't know what. I tried to scream, but no sound came out. It was as though I was caught in a vacuum. I tried to throw out a rope of my own in the opposite direction, but it just shot out about six feet and followed me in. The thing is, I wasn't just *pulled* into whatever it was, my entire body was, for want of a better word, undimensionalized as it was sucked through a microscopic hole. It was a weird sensation; but then I was whole again on the other side, wherever that was, *But where was it?* I wondered because it wasn't quantum space.

CHAPTER LIII

Dargra-Tol

From the Altered Timeline
On Rendenaaar
Trillions of Universes in the Past

I, Dargra-Tol, liberator of the *Thaaagran* people, debased myself before Khattaaara, Ruler of the Dust, Betrayer of her People, Slave to her *yaaargh*—debased myself to end her reign once and for all. Thus, did I bed her each night, disgusting Gaaalthaaaran that she was. How the scent of her *graaam* that wafted from her *yaaargh* sickened me, yet for my plan to succeed I needed the maintain the pretense that it was like an aphrodisiac, and so I would imbibe it as though doing so brought me to a heightened state of ecstasy. Through such means comes the undoing of a fool.

And then there was Pheeelja and the infant, Zhardaaan. *Strange,* I thought, *for anyone to raise a child of another species, especially one different from any in the known universe.* I recognized the fact that there were millions of civilizations, but how she should have come upon the brood of one of them, especially one uncatalogued in the hundred thousand cycles of recorded history, dumbfounded me. Was this apparently barren Gaaalthaaaran so desperate that she would become mother to an alien creature? *No,* I thought to myself, *there must be some greater sense to it.*

Meanwhile, other thoughts plagued my mind. Khattaaara and her group of followers were the last hold-outs of the Gaaalthaaaran race, having, again and again, survived my

269

onslaughts. How were they able to erect a forcefield to protect themselves? I wondered. Was there a machine I knew nothing about? These were questions that I posed to my council. I assumed that Zhaaagur Scraaa was in possession of another god-stone, but who was Zhaaagur Scraaa, and what if any was her relation to Khattaaara? Beyond that, I wondered how many other god-stones existed, who might be in possession of them, and what other enemies might I face. No doubt, it would be a fight to the death, but should I succeed and gain control of them all, I could control all space and time. My kind would rule the universe long after the Gaaalthaaaran race became extinct.

"Prithee, My Lady," I said as I gently stroked Khattaaara's *yaaargh* whilst we lay in bed after having made love. "Where didst thou get the god-stone that thou had in thy hand that night?"

"Why dost thou wish to rub salt in open wounds?" she asked.

"I thought that perhaps," I replied, "were I to learn how thou camest upon it, that I might aid thee in finding the others."

"Fret not, my dearest *Thaaagran*," she said. "Thou needest only concern thyself with pleasing us. It is for this and this alone that we have granted thee absolution."

"It is just..." I began to say.

"Just what?" Khattaaara interrupted.

"There is the matter of Zhaaagur Scraaa and of thy alien niece, Zhardaaan."

"And what *of* them?" she replied.

"'Tis obvious they each have one stone, though how either came upon them bewilders me. Does it not bring thee to wonder how Zhardaaan came upon one, once she became an adult and whether there has been intercourse betwixt the two such that a gift was made from the elder to the younger?"

"Ask me not questions meant for them," she said appearing somewhat vexed. "We are Zhardaaan's aunt, not her bedfellow, and as for Zhaaagur Scraaa, best you ask *her*."

"I just..." I started to say.

"Enough!" came her forceful reply. "Do not pit our patience against the affection we still hold for thee! We have forgiven thee once! Do not stack one seed against a bushel of grain! Be gone with thee for the night, to be back on the morrow when the winds that now gather in our lungs have calmed down."

And so I left, but I knew that my words had sparked new suspicions in her so that my ruse would no longer avail my quest for the other god-stones. Thus, did I teleport to Pheeelja's chamber to stir the Gaaalthaaaran beast.

"Wake up, *laaathaaarg*!" I shouted at her, as my clenched hands gripped the cloth of her nightgown near her neck.[50]

Pheeelja stared at me, fear rising in her.

"Tell me about Zhardaaan," I demanded. "Whence did she get her god-stone?"

It must have been my utterance of her daughter's name that quickly steeled her. Her eyes glared at me, and then she spat at my face. It was at that juncture that I let my quantum self be revealed, as now white flames licked my skin.

"Where is she?" I demanded.

"Khattaaara!" she screamed.

"Khattaaara cannot hear thee," I said. "She is in her chamber, all too far away! Tell me!" I demanded.

"I will tell thee naught but that thou art a monster!" came her reply.

"Then suffer this!" I said as I poured electricity into her brain, causing her to scream and writhe in pain, foam coming from her mouth, blue froth from her *yaaargh*. Again and again, I tortured her with bursts of energy, and, again and again, she refused to speak. I found it fascinating the amount of pain she chose to endure for the sake of her adopted child. Then, at last, hearing voices approach, I teleported away from the now-dying creature

---

[50] *Laaathaaarg* was a derogatory term for a useless *yaaargh*.

and teleported myself back to my distant home to decide what path I needed to take next.

CHAPTER LIV

Jordan

> *From the Original Timeline*
> *In the Alternate Reality*
> *On Earth III*
> *Earth Date: 2029*

If there was one thing I learned on Rendenaaar, it was that you don't just go into battle against someone without knowing who or what you're going up against. Such was the case with Dargra-Tol, who, unfortunately, followed Peyton's path through time, and such was the case with the Khattaaara from what we had called Earth III.

The first question I had was, what had become of that world where young Liam and Li and young Claire were from? As I hung over the city on that world, all that remained were empty buildings, grounded flying cars, and desolation. Now and again, some pigeons, or a gull or two, edged their way from some strewn-out garbage pile back to the coast. The planet remained, but the people did not.

Decaying bodies were everywhere, many reduced to near skeletons, as crows picked at what meat was left on them. Pay had said that there was a complex on the moon, but when I phased there, it lay abandoned. How odd, I thought, that Khattaaara and her companions should have chosen Earth as their destination when there was no Peyton there. It wasn't until much later that I found out why. It was Claire. She was the reincarnation of Klothaaara, Khattaaara's twin sister, who died when she was a child. My aunt, Khattaaara told me about her, about how close

273

they had been, and how she had watched her die.

But why annihilate an entire civilization? According to Gaaalthaaaran journals left at the complex, the inhabitants in this dimension resisted transformation and caused considerable damage to any and all of the travelers' efforts. The human genocide was more of a result of that Khattaaara being pissed off more than anything else, while the objections from her compatriots, since *she* owned the mother stone, were met with their deaths as well. There remained a grave concern, however. While we knew the whereabouts of four of the god-stones, two were still unaccounted for, which meant that two other Gaaalthaaaarans, dead or alive. were still unaccounted for. The question remained, though, why did she abandon young Claire, unless the path that had led her to Earth only led her so far?

The technology on this Earth had been far in advance of the Earth that my mother was from. Earth II where I was born, was the most vulnerable to any extraterrestrial attack. A civilization can't ward off an alien attack with atom bombs and vacuum tubes.

Meanwhile, on Earth II, the Gaaalthaaaran transformation was nearly complete. Suffice it to say that only Caucasians had the misfortune of being able to be transformed. The rest of the planet's population, however, gained no comfort in that they were either forced to become subservient or else were killed, which, in the end, proved the kinder fate. Churches and temples alike stood vacant, as a pale reminder that the Gods of this Earth had either abandoned the pious or else simply did not exist. The Gaaalthaaaarans had their own gods, quite disparate from any borne from the mythologies told on this azure dot in outer space.

That Earth had become Rendenaaar reborn, with a bizarre form of English or French or Italian or Russian as its method of communication, so oddly spoken due to the innate characteristics of the Gaaalthaaaran larynx and throat. I walked disguised among them as I had done for years, ever since my aunt had given me the first god-stone. I was no longer the *yaaarghless* round-earred *hooomon*, but a Rend, who could go unnoticed, as I observed what damnation had been cast upon the innocents of this world. My god-stones allowed me the illusion I needed for a disguise.

But unlike what had been on Rendenaaar, there were no great arts or sciences being achieved. With the entirety of the work done by its newfound labor force, meaning those humans unable to be transformed, the Rends who were not taskmasters gave way to their sexual desires. It was debauchery at its extreme. I, in my alien camouflage, was approached again and again by both males and females wanting to mate with me, often to the point where a polite rebuff needed to be accompanied by a quantum shock to their system, rendering them momentarily unconscious, and causing them to collapse into individual heaps on the ground or floor, often vomiting from one end, gushing froth from the other. Indeed, without the guidance of actual Gaaalthaaarans, they were left to their primordial desires, and Khattaaara, who had engineered it all, was somewhere off-world in my dimension. The burning question that remained, however, was could they be brought back? It had taken every ounce of my strength to restore Claire to human form. It wasn't in me to morph nearly a billion people.

Having phased to more than fifty parts of the globe, I decided to return home. It had been an exhausting journey, which ended comfortably in a warm bubble bath, something I had never experienced on Rendenaaar. At last, though, I stood up to the cool night air, my skin erupted with goosebumps as I towel-dried myself, leaving a small puddle on the white tiled floor. I headed from the bathroom, and launched myself, naked, into the bed. The last sound I heard was that of the water draining from the tub. Exhausted, I fell into the dreams of sleep.

CHAPTER LV

Clairey

From the Altered Timeline
In the Alternate Reality
In a Pocket Dimension
Earth-Date: 2029

It had felt as though my entire body had been pulled backward through a keyhole—like I'd been folded in half and then squeezed like taffy to get me to fit through it. I wondered at the time if that was what it was like to be born. Maybe that's why babies cry when they take their first breath. No one knows. There's no way to ask.

Anyway, what it turned out I'd been pulled into was a pocket dimension—at least that's what I was told it was, later on. There were no stars or planets. There was no light except for a reddish glow—the same as the tendril that was still wrapped around my waist, and which was pulling me further and further in.

"Hey," I suddenly heard from behind me.

I used the god-stone to instantly face the other direction. Attached to the other end of the tendril was a boy around my same age.

"Who *are* you?" I asked.

"Liam," he replied as he reeled me in close to him. "Liam Herron."

"Liam Herron?" I repeated, "As in the Liam Herron who used to sneak up and touch me in front of the other kids, and laugh about it because it scared me because I was blind? *That* Liam Herron? Well, I'm not blind anymore!" I said and I shoved him hard so that we both flew away from each other in opposite directions. The tendril still wrapped around me, Liam hauled me back, hand over hand until we were face to face again.

"Hey!" he said. "I'm sorry. I was stupid, ok?"

"Yeah," I replied, "well, you don't know what it's like to be blind!" I looked at him and just shook my head.

"So," he said, "you can see now?"

"Only because I have a god-stone in my head," I said back. "Same as you, apparently!"

"You mean a quantum seed," he replied.

"What*ever*," I shrugged. "So, why did you drag me *in* here? Wherever *here* is." There was nothing but us and empty space.

"I wasn't trying to drag you here," he said. "I was trying to find a way out, like to grab onto something so that I could pull myself back."

"Oh, great!" I exclaimed. "So, now I'm trapped in here *with* you!"

"You know," he said, "You look an awful lot like that girl, Claire Salinger, who's been staying with us."

"Grrrr!" I growled back. "I *am* Claire Salinger, only the Claire Salinger from *your* dimension! Do you mean to tell me you tortured me for all that time without even knowing my name?"

"It was the only way I could get your attention," he said.

"And why would you want to *get my attention*?" I demanded to know.

"Because..." he said and hesitated.

"Because why?" I demanded to know.

"Because you were the prettiest girl at the school," he managed to stumble out, "and I didn't know any other way."

"Well, I heard you were always talking to that other girl, Ophelia!" I came back at him. "Everyone said she was gorgeous! If you wanted a girlfriend so bad, why didn't you go after *her*?"

"Ewww!" he replied. "She's my sister!"

"Oh," I said, embarrassed. "Well, you just should have come over and talked to me."

"But you're a girl," he replied.

"And what's that supposed to mean?" I asked.

"I tried," he said. "But every time I got up the nerve, I started sweating and my heart would pound, and I chickened out." He looked down toward his feet. "I hope you can forgive me. You're kind of like the most beautiful girl I've ever seen, and it makes it hard to talk to someone like you." His eyes glanced up at me.

"Well, we're talking now," I said. "And I suppose considering all you've said I can let it go. But don't try and kiss me or anything now that your heart's not pounding anymore!"

"I won't," he said. "I've only kissed one girl in my entire life! Honest! And it was actually *she* who kissed *me!*"

"And which girl was that, if I may be so bold as to ask?" I replied.

"Her name's Chloë."

"My mom's sister?" I exclaimed.

"Your mom?" he said, astonished.

"*Yes*, my mom," I replied. "She adopted me. My real parents were killed like most everyone else."

"Ours were, too," he said. " Li and I were all alone till Payton rescued us. I gave Chloë the other quantum seed I found."

"Why?" I asked.

"Li insisted," he replied. "Then Chloë and I went off and somehow we got marooned on Payton's world where everyone was being turned into aliens. Chloë couldn't figure out how to get us back, so I made her give me the seed, and I used it to get us home; only then something went wrong and I wound up here."

"God, you're complicated!" I said. "But we need to find a way out." I looked at him. "How long have you been trapped?"

"I don't know exactly," he replied. "Maybe an hour or so, I guess. It's kind of hard in here to tell time."

"Well," I said. "perhaps if we put our heads together, we can figure something out." A realization came of the words I just said and I glared at him. "That's just a figure of speech," I added. "No kissing."

"All right! All right!" he said. "And I wouldn't want to kiss anyone who didn't want to kiss *me*!"

"Ugh!" I groaned. "Okay, do what you did before, and I'll try to make the opening bigger." I glared at him. "That means you can unwrap me now."

Liam unwrapped the tendril from my waist and then used his god-stone to create another hole in wherever we were. I used mine to expand it until it was large enough for us to go through it. When we were on the other side, we both looked around. We were outside and it was pitch black. That didn't matter to me, whose vision was based on sound, but there was enough light from both of our glows for him to make out what I could clearly see—the destruction all around, not to mention the dead and the odor that came from their decay.

"I think we're back on our Earth," he said.

"I think so, too," I agreed. "Come on. We need to find some shelter. There still might be Gaaalthaaarans around."

"What are Gaaalthaaarans?" he asked.

"Aliens," I replied. "That's what they call themselves."

CHAPTER LVI

Claire

From the Altered Timeline
In the Alternate Reality
On Earth I
Earth-Date: 2029

It was Niska who woke me that night, jumping up with her front paws on the bed, causing me to realize that Clairey was no longer next to me. I looked at my cell phone. It was 2:47 a.m. At first, I thought she might have gone to the bathroom, so I waited a few minutes, but she didn't return.

"Liam," I said turning my head toward him, as he lay next to me.

"Mmmm," he muttered, more asleep than awake.

"Clairey's gone," I said.

"She probably went back to her room," he murmured.

"No," I replied. "She's been having nightmares. She wanted to sleep next to me. She wouldn't just leave."

"I'm sure she's fine," he yawned.

"But Niska's still here," I insisted. "She never leaves her side and she woke me up just now." I got out of bed and put on my slippers and robe.

"Don't worry," Liam mumbled. "She's got that thing you put in her head to keep her safe."

"Some concerned parent *you* are," I said back to him.

I shook my head to myself and left him to his sleep, with Niska at my side. The first place I checked was the bathroom down the hall; then the kitchen. As I had feared, both were deserted. *What could have happened to her*, I thought to myself. *Where could she have gone?* Not in the living room. Not outdoors, front or back. Anxiously, I climbed the stairs to the kids' bedroom and went in. Both Chloë and Li were still asleep, but then Chloë stirred as I was about to leave.

"Is something wrong?" she asked.

"I can't find Clairey," I answered.

"I thought she was with you?" she said, sitting up in bed.

"I woke up and she was gone," I replied. "I've searched everywhere." My heart was racing. "First young Liam," I said, "and now Clairey," "What's going on?"

"I'll help you," Chloë replied. "We can go look for her together."

"I'll go wake up Liam," I said.

"We don't need Liam," she replied. "I'm your sister. We'll find her. Besides, we've got Niska."

I nodded. There was no reason to be all up in arms—at least not yet.

CHAPTER LVII

Clairey

From the Altered Timeline
In the Alternate Reality
On Earth III
Earth III—Date: 2023

Liam was used to seeing all the dead bodies in the streets and in the buildings. He had seen all the death when it had occurred. I hadn't. All I knew was what had happened to my parents. I hadn't seen all the dead people with their rotting flesh but now I did. Their organs were pouring out of them. Their bones were sticking out. Their eyes were gone, probably picked down to the socket by crows. It was all so disgusting and terrifying that, god-stone or not, I began to throw up, and when that was done, when I was just gagging on saliva, I began to cry. Liam tried to comfort me but I pushed him away, sobbing, "I want my Mom! I want my Mom!"

Liam didn't seem to know what to do. "I'll protect you," he said.

"How can *you* protect me," I said back in tears. "You couldn't even get out of that whatever it was you pulled me into without my help! I want my Mom! I want to go home!"

"Hey," he said trying to cheer me up, "you're a Quantum Girl. You don't have to worry about anything!"

"I don't want to be a Quantum Girl!" I sobbed. "I just want to go home!"

"Whether you want to be or not," he said, "you're one of them."

"So, I suppose you're a Quantum Girl, too," I said managing

a small laugh through my tears.

"Nothing of the sort," he said proudly. "I'm Quantum Boy, and I'm afraid of nothing!"

"Not even *that?*" I said, pointing toward the sky from which a huge, white dragon could be seen heading in our direction. Both of us started running as fast as we could, glancing back every now and then as the mythological creature got closer and closer.

"Why don't we just phase out of here?" he asked breathlessly as we ran.

"I need to concentrate," I replied breathlessly, "but I can't do it while I'm trying to escape from a giant dragon!"

We must have run a quarter of a mile with the dragon following us overhead. As luck would have it, though, we wound up cornered in a dead-end alley with it landing at the open end which was our only way out.

"What now?" I asked as I tried to catch my breath, bent over, my hands on my thighs.

"Don't know," came the panting reply.

The dragon stared at us and then exhaled white fire into the sky. Then it took a step toward us.

"If you're going to kill us, then just do it!" I screamed.

It stopped then and began to change. Its wings turned into arms, its scales into clothes, and within less than a minute, it had turned itself into a woman. How strange, I thought, that she resembled Payton—but her hair was long and dark and she was older than her. She didn't walk toward us, though. Instead, she phased right up to us. It was then that I could see that she was an alien like the one my mom and I had found. Her ears were pointed and she had a tail with a furry end. The dress she wore clung to her almost like it had been painted on, although it was made of some metallic cloth that reflected the light from the moon. It was almost as though she were naked, a condition that got Liam's undivided attention. I kicked him sideways in the shin, as he stood

283

next to me, and then whispered, "Stop staring! She's an alien!"

Liam quietly lifted the offended leg and rubbed it where it had been kicked.

"She *is* kind of pretty," he whispered back, "in an extraterrestrial sort of way."

"Why, thank you, child," the alien said in a voice with an unusual accent.

"Who are you?" Liam asked.

"Are you going to kill us?" I added. "We both have powerful god-stones in our heads that could quite literally wipe you off the map."

"*Do* you, now?" she said. "Well, as a matter of coincidence, I have two as well, one of them having belonged to an unfortunate from the world whence I came. May I ask which colors yours are?"

"Hers is yellow, and mine is red," Liam volunteered.

"That may or may not be the case," I interjected. "We are not here to give information to the enemy."

"I'm really *not* the enemy," she replied. "As a matter of fact, I'm here to end the life of one of my own—someone named Khattaaara."

"Khattaaara!" Liam exclaimed. "She's the one who tried to murder Ophelia!"

"So, who are you, really?" I asked.

"Really and truly?" she replied. "My name is Thara-Klo."

CHAPTER LVIII

Payton (Pay)

From the Altered Timeline
In the Alternate Reality
On Earth I
Earth-Date: 2029

"Blah, blah, blah, blah!" That's what it all came down to. There were three of us, all different, but all the same—three of us who had "Powers and abilities far beyond those of mortal men!" an ancient television show claimed each week, with music for dramatic effect—three of us who didn't know what we were supposed to do next. We were all in the room I shared with Payton. We call her Demi to keep things straight, which is probably a bad word choice all things considered. As for me, my name had been reduced to just Pay, so as not to be confused with Peyton, and even though our names are spelled differently, spelling doesn't count when our names are spoken. Mostly, we're all identical except for sexuality and disposition. Peyton is bi. Demi is sapph, and I'm a die-hard sparrow, not that any of that has anything to do with any of this, despite that it may arouse the prurient interests of some readers.

It was Demi who put her foot down with regard to Peyton's involvement in any battle against the Khattaaara from Earth III. "Seriously," she said, "you're four months pregnant with twins! There is no way we're going to let you risk yourself and them. They're like our children, too, even though you're the one who had to go through morning sickness, weight gain, and the one who will be screaming her head off when they're being born."

"She can get an epidural," Demi interjected.

"Shut up!" I shot back at her. "You know what I mean!"

"Stop it!" Peyton said. "Neither of you has my experience, and you know it!"

"Oh, ho!" Demi replied. "Just because you remember being the evil Khattaaara in your dimension, doesn't make you better at all the quantum shit any more than either of us! Plus, we have Jordan!"

"May I interject?" I said.

"No!" both of them yelled at me at once.

"I was the one who gave you the seed!" Peyton shouted at Demi.

"And I was the one who took over for you while you were dead!" Demi shouted back. "And did a pretty good job of it, battling her when she was you or you were her, Miss Reincarnation!"

"Might I remind you," she shot back, "that you were the one who went and gave the mother stone to Theresa and caused everything to change!"

"Thankful for me," I said half to myself.

"Well, I'm *fucking* sorry if I loved her," Demi yelled out in her own defense. "I wanted to save her life!"

"But she's dead now in spite of it all!" Peyton shouted back.

That was when Demi broke down into tears. "Don't you think I know that?" she sobbed. "Don't you think I have to live every day since with the guilt of having turned two universes upside down? We were the exact same age before you went back in time and blew yourself up in the Big Bang! Don't think you're so superior because you survived for billions of years! The fact of the matter is that I wept when Thara-Klo had you killed, and I risked my own life and all the memories I had of Theresa just to save you, so don't you try and tell me that I'm not as good as you, because I already know that! But I'm willing to risk my life again so that you and your babies aren't put in harm's way! Pay and I and Jordan can do this! We can stop Khattaaara *and* Dargra-Tol, and if we can't, well, I guess that's just how things were meant to be!"

Both of them then turned toward me for a response. I raised my hands outward. "Don't look at me," I said innocently enough. I pointed toward Peyton and then toward Demi. "You're England. You're France. I'm Switzerland."

Suddenly, there was a knock on the door.

"What!" all three of us shouted at once.

The door opened and Sarabeth entered with a tray. "I thought the three of you might like some hotdogs and lemonade and chips. I made it all myself... except for the lemonade and the chips."

We all chuckled at the four of us being all in one room. "Come on in, innocent little sister," Peyton said.

Sarabeth handed out the glasses and the plates, and the three of us began our overdue lunch.

"Aren't *you* going to eat:" I asked Sarabeth.

"I already did," she answered. "And what was all the yelling about?"

"Nothing," I replied.

"Well, I'd just try to keep it down a bit," she said, "what with all that's going on right now."

"*What's* going on?" I asked with sudden concern.

"Clairey's missing," she said staring at the three of us, as though she thought we already knew. *Clairey* wasn't just a name of endearment Claire had given her. It was the name we'd all settled on for young Claire to avoid confusion with her older self. "Claire's devastated over it. Chloë's been doing her best to try and calm her."

I set down my plate and stood up. "I'd better go to her," I said. "She's my best friend."

When I got to Claire, she appeared devastated. "Something

must have happened to her," she said with tears in her eyes. "She'd never leave without Niska. She just wouldn't!"

"I'm sure she's all right," I replied.

"Chloë and I searched everywhere! Clairey and I, we've been through so much together," she said and stared at me with tears now down her cheeks. "I realize everything that's gone on with aliens and superpowers is strange in and of itself, but I truly believe that something greater than all of that caused me to find her when I did."

"We'll *find* her again," I insisted.

"And I know she's just another version of me," Claire went on unabated, "but she's different from how I ever was—than either of me ever was and I feel so protective of her and it's like I let her down. First young Liam and now her!"

I put my arms around her and held her tightly.

"It was my decision to give her the crystal," she wept. "What if I made the wrong choice? She could be anywhere in the universe all alone!"

She pulled back and looked into my eyes, wiped her tears, and then gathered herself up. "No," she said. "I need to be strong. Self-pity won't help her. She's out there somewhere and we've got to figure out a way to bring her back home."

"We will," I reassured her. "Have I *ever* lied to you?"

"I lost my baby," she wept. "I can't lose her, too!"

"You won't," I said. I nodded and she nodded back, wiping her tears once more. "Remember, we have time on our side. All we have to do is go back to find out what happened."

Claire had been my absolute best friend growing up, but this was a side of her I had never seen. She was always a good person, and, I would say, kind, but a lot of her thoughts had been about *her*. Maybe it was the other Claire she had merged with that instilled in her this deep concern. Whoever the Claire was from this Earth, when the two of them became one, I think it made the both of them complete. But it also made the combined Claire hurt more than the Claire I had known ever would have. And yet, despite that, it made her more endearing, at least in my eyes. I would keep my promise and do everything within my power to find the daughter she had chosen to love, and I would do it, not because I thought it was moral or the right thing to do, but because I loved *her*, and, as much as she was *my* friend, I was *her* friend, too.

CHAPTER LIX

Thara-Klo (from Earth III)

From the Original Timeline
In the Original Reality
On Earth III
Earth III—Date: 2023

It was night. There were two human children in the alley. The question was how they each wound up with a god-stone in their head. Both exhibited residual traces from having lived in another dimension. That was how I found them—from the quantum trails left as they traveled back here. The red stone in the boy had belonged to Faaathrag; the yellow in the girl to Shaaalra. Well, to *Ptaaargh* with them both![51] Shaaalra and Faaathrag had destroyed countless billions of intelligent lifeforms, not to mention how they committed genocide on Rendenaaar before they finally came to Earth.

I had followed all of them through star systems, through galaxies, through universes, and through time. In the end, they battled against each other, although I got to Naraaag-Tal before any of *them* did. All that was left was Khattaaara, my dear mother, the most evil creature that ever lived. Who better to end her reign than the daughter who sprang from her *yaaargh*? But she was nowhere to be found; not a trace of her or the mother stone she possessed. If she fled to another dimension, I could only assume that she had found a way to erase her quantum trail.

"There's no need to be afraid of me," I said in the gentlest voice I could. "I may look the same as those who killed your

---

[51] *Ptaaargh* was the equivalent of Hell in *Gaaalthaaaran* mythology.

people, but I'm not, and they wanted to kill me, too."

"Are you from somewhere out there?" the girl asked, pointing upward at the stars in the sky.

I shook my head. "No," I said, "I'm from another universe, trillions upon trillions of years in the past. I was born on a planet called Rendenaaar, and my grandfather and grandmother were the rulers of that world."

"How come you've got four boobs?" the boy asked.

"Liam!" the girl scolded.

"That's quite all right," I said. "Why do human females have just two?"

"I guess because sometimes women have twins," the boy said, "like my sister and me."

"But this isn't your sister," I replied.

The boy scowled at her and she scowled back, sticking out her tongue at him. "No way!" he said, "Claire's just…"

"Your girlfriend?" I suggested.

"No, she's absolutely not," he protested.

"But you want her to be," I suggested. Then I turned to the girl. "He wants you to be. He's always wanted you to be," I said. "You see," I said to both of them, "one of my god-stones allows me to read your minds."

The boy glanced at Claire but then quickly looked down at the ground, embarrassed. "Liam thought that by annoying you, you'd eventually become friends. Human boys do that sometimes, especially when they think a girl is beautiful."

"Well, it was despicable!" Claire said. "I was totally blind, and it was… annoying!"

"I'm sure he's dreadfully sorry now," I said turning to Liam.

"I am," he said. "I really am."

I went on, "And just to set matters straight, Master Herron, young Claire thinks that you're… cute. I believe that's the word that's been echoing through her brain."

"I would greatly appreciate it," Claire said defensively, "if you would please stop reading my mind."

I breathed a deep sigh. "Very well," I said, " but it will make things more difficult—at least for me." I paused and then looked at Liam. "And, as for your question about my 'boobs,' why do humans have two lungs, but only one heart? Why do you have two ears and two eyes, but only one mouth? It's just how my species evolved and there's no special reason. It has always struck me very odd that humans do not possess *tails*. They can be extremely useful at times."

"You certainly speak English very well," Claire said.

"Well, I've been here a very long time," I answered, "waiting for the others to arrive."

"How long?" Liam asked.

"Thousands of years," I replied. "I've been many people and have lived many lives."

"What was the last one?" Liam insisted.

"Well," I said, "I was the handmaid to a dowager duchess in England back one hundred twenty or so years ago."

"What's a dowager?" Liam asked.

"It's a rich old lady," Claire whispered to him and then looked at me. "If you're really on our side, and you've been here so long, why didn't you stop them before they murdered everyone?"

"Because Khattaaara has the mother stone," I explained, "which is far more powerful than all the rest. There were seven of them in all. I managed to get one by tricking Naraaag-Tal back on our home planet. He wanted me and I wanted his god-stone."

"Did you kill him?" Liam asked.

"I turned him *into* stone," I replied.

"Just like Medusa," he went on.

"Dear," I said as I stared at him, "I *was* Medusa, only unlike what legends pretend happened, I never lost my head. Ovid was a storyteller, not a historian. Somehow the fact that I had a tail turned into snakes instead of hair when he retold it. But enough history lessons for now. Have you two had anything to eat?"

Both of them shook their heads. "Come on, then," I said.

"Where to?" Claire asked.

"My place in New York," I said, and then I teleported all of us there.

The place in question was the penthouse apartment in the Woolworth Building, once valued at more than one hundred million dollars, which, after nearly everyone on the planet having been killed, became totally free. With less than ten thousand humans remaining, there was no one left to contest the ownership of anything. I had chosen to decorate the unit with artifacts from various museums around the world; there were no people to go to them anymore. Those few who remained were more focused on how to survive.

I fed the children Chinese food, although I had to travel back in time to get it, considering that there was no longer a supply of fresh food anywhere. All that remained edible was in boxes, jars, or cans. After dinner, I let them virtual one episode of the *Starport Chronicles* and then sent them off to bed. In the morning I would take them back to the world they had come from. From my conversations with the children, it appeared that my mother had gone there as well. Whether she remained was a matter yet to be determined, but wherever she was, I knew that she needed to be stopped once and for all.

CHAPTER LX

Dargra-Tol

> *From the Altered Timeline*
> *On Rendenaaar*
> *Trillions of Universes in the Past*

When Khattaaara discovered what I had done to Pheeelja, she went after me with a vengeance. Following my quantum trail, she showed up that very night, not as Khattaaara, but as Zhaaagur Scraaa, hovering outside the building that was my home. She did not utter a single word. She did not call out my name or curse or threaten me. Rather, she screamed a voiceless scream that sent out quantum waves that disintegrated everything around me and left me standing naked before her.

"Wast thou so eager to undress me once again," I said, "that thou chose to destroy all that I own?"

"I would have done as much to thee," she replied, her voice booming like thunder, "were it not for the quantum field that protects thee!"

"Dost thou not still hunger for my touch?" I asked, "Dost thou not thirst for softness of my breasts? Dost thou not still find thyself filled with desire to have my *yaaargh* penetrate thine to fill thee once more with passion?"

"I would rather make love to a *vaaagthrung* than with thee!" she proclaimed.[52]

I teleported myself to face her, but a breath away. "Thy *yaaargh* hast betrayed thy sister this time. Even now, it throbs at

---

[52] A *vaaagthrung* was a hideous, swamp-dwelling creature that was covered in conical scales, which oozed a fetid slime.

the sight of me, its scent wafting upward and into my nostrils, as the tips of thy breasts grow hard with longing."

"Where *is* she?" Khattaaara demanded.

"She?" I asked with feigned innocence. "I know of no she. I know only of a corpse I have fed to the *goraaags* in the forest, to appease their hunger for Gaaalthaaaran flesh!"

Zhaaagur Scraaa's eyes lit up like purple stars. Then her *yaaargh* lifted behind her, lunged forward, and then wrapped around my throat in a whip-like motion. As I began to choke, I teleported out of its grip to appear behind her, and then used my forcefield to hurl her out into space.

All of my kind, safely off-world, I teleported beside her now unconscious form, waiting until she awakened so that she would watch as I blew up her world. Then with the *yaaargh* she had foolishly allowed me to keep, I stabbed her through her heart. She cried out in pain, her eyes fixed on me. My *yaaargh* throbbed with pleasure as I watched her blood spurt out of the wound to form small globules in space.

That done, I flashed on clothes, gathered up the corpse that I had brought with me, and then followed Zhardaaan's trail to the future to eradicate the last remaining memory of Rendenaaar.

CHAPTER LXI

Payton (Pay)

From the Altered Timeline
In the Alternate Reality
On Earth II
Earth-Date: 2029

It was strange to think that I and Demi or Payton (or whatever one chooses to call her) were so emotionally different, and yet so physically alike, down to our fingerprints. Where or what caused the timeline on our Earth to diverge is something neither of us nor Peyton have been able to figure out. It was as though there was some bleed-off from the Earth I dimension into ours, perhaps because of Payton's continual travel between the two; perhaps because of Ophelia having been there, or perhaps because of Jordan having been born of a mother and father from two parallel planes of existence. The fact was that our lives became separate and distinct.

For whatever reason, Payton was never best friends with Claire, and Liam, ipso facto, never had a chance to become close to her and form a relationship. Sadly, the original Liam's existence (and perhaps the original Claire's as well) became erased when Payton used the mother stone to heal the Theresa from Peyton's Earth.

I had gone back to my dimension—to my Earth—on a reconnaissance mission to see what we were up against when I sensed another quantum trail—one that wasn't from Khattaaara. It was from a purple seed. I phased through the quantum fabric, following the path, which led me to a small house in what Liam

296

and I used to call the barrio. Materializing inside, I found Payton naked in bed with Theresa Martinez—not the one she had saved, but the one from this dimension—Peyton's head buried in where I don't even want to mention. I instantly phased from being Quantum Girl into my regular self, as the two of them turned and stared at me, Payton now leaning back into Theresa's open legs.

"Um, *hel*lo?" Payton said.

"How did she…?" Theresa began to say but then asked, "Is she your sister? I thought you only had a twin brother?"

"I do," she said back and then turned to me. "What are you *doing* here?" she asked.

"What am *I* doing here?" I said, astonished at the question. "I just left you a moment ago after you were arguing with Peyton."

"I thought *you* were Payton?" Theresa said to her.

"I am," she answered and then once more turned to look at me.

"Seriously," I said. "We're all trying to figure out how to fend off an alien invasion, and one of you is here on this Rend-infested world, shagging Theresa Martinez, whom I could have sworn was a sparrow." I looked at Theresa. "You were, weren't you?"

"Sort of," she replied, "I guess."

Back at Payton. "You *did* tell her you're a Quantum Girl?" I asked.

"No," she replied.

"What's a Quantum Girl?" Theresa asked.

"This!" I said. "This is a Quantum Girl!" and I flashed into costume, glowing green. "Only she turns purple," I said.

Theresa jumped a bit, sitting up, clenching her arms around Peyton, and glancing from one of us to the other. "Wait!" she exclaimed, "You guys are Power Rangers?" She glanced from me to her and then back again, her voice trembling a bit.

"We're not imaginary characters!" I said. "We're actual human beings just like you! We just have quantum seeds in our heads!" I turned to Payton. "How do you know she's not going to turn into a Rend?"

"Because I phased out all of the viral infection," she said, "then placed a quantum field around her to prevent her from becoming infected again."

"Again?" I said. "What do you mean *again*?"

"She was dead when I found her," she replied.

"So you resurrected her!" I said, astonished.

"Resurrected?" That question came from a now-frightened Theresa.

"To have sex with her." More of a conclusion than a question from me.

"I love her!" Payton said defensively.

"You loved the *other* one!" I said, "This one is an obvious afterthought!" I shook my head to myself. "You need to take her to Earth I where she'll be safe, then help me scout out what we're up against."

"I'm sorry," I said to Theresa, "but she's got a one-track mind."

Payton frowned and then split off into two. Theresa looked from one of her to the other and then fainted. The Payton nearest the edge of the bed stood up buck naked, walked to the other side, and phased into Quantum Girl. Then she lifted the now unconscious Theresa into her arm, and phased off with her to Earth I, while the other held the bedsheet up against herself as she stood up.

"You're *covering* yourself?" I said, "Like I haven't ever seen me naked?"

"I'm just cold," she replied. "No one left to keep me warm."

I just grimaced and shook my head. "Just change into QG, and help me find out how bad things are."

Payton phased into Quantum Girl. We were purple and green and *not* Power Rangers. "You're amazing," I said, "and not in a good way!"

Once we phased to the Earth under attack, the two of us divided into ten thousand, disbursing ourselves all across the globe, taking in the biological devastation. It appeared that there wasn't a living soul that had not either been killed, enslaved, or transformed into a Rend, and from there came the beginnings of organization. Regardless that while the newly-formed beings did not possess Khattaaara's powers, many of them had guns. Thus, whether Rend or human, it had become a case of rule by force. There was no equality. Was this Khattaaara's idea of resurrecting Rendenaaar? Most assuredly, it was not the world that Jordan had described. Hers was a world of science and civilization, far in advance of any of ours. Conversely, Earth II had been thrown back to barbaric times.

Being neither what Rendenaaar had been, nor Earth as it was, it stood as a mockery of them both. Perhaps this was what Khattaaara had wanted, but, regardless, this is what she got. These creatures were no match for our quantum abilities, but I wondered if there was a way to undo what had been done—at least for those who still remained. After we had merged ourselves back into single Quantum Girl selves, I stared at Payton.

"This was our planet," I said. "Rendenaaar had its place in time, but that was long ago. We need to take back our world."

"I'm sorry about Theresa," Payton said. "It's just…"

"I know," I replied, "but she's not the one you fell in love with, and whoever Rainbow Girl was, that wasn't her either. Your Theresa died from the other Khattaaara's blast."

She turned away and then said, "I've caused so much to go wrong."

"People do a lot of things in the name of love," I said, "but this Khattaaara would have found her way here or to another Earth regardless, but you're the only reason that Sarabeth or I exist. Because of you, I was able to rescue Li and Liam and it was you who rescued Clairey and Claire."

"And Niska," she said under her breath.

"And Niska," I repeated, and we both let out a laugh and then phased outside.

The sun shown down on us. The air offered a cool breeze. But then, suddenly, everything grew dark from a yawning hole in the sky. There were no stars—only the blackness of the quantum fabric. Around it, dark clouds roiled with thunderous anger, and in the midst of it all, Khattaaara emerged!

"Dare you set foot on my world!" she screamed, her voice echoing in the once-silent air.

"This is *our* world!" Payton yelled back. But before she could utter another word, Khattaaara hurled a blast of white energy that enveloped both Payton and me, drawing us into each other, and merging us, from two separate timelines, into one. As we, as I, recovered, there was only one thing I could try to do for now—escape!

CHAPTER LXII

Peyton

> *From the Original Timeline*
> *In the Alternate Reality*
> *On Earth I*
> *Earth-Date: 2029*

My name is Peyton Herron. Four years prior to what I am about to describe happened, I died. And then I didn't, because I was sent back through time to just before I had taken my own life and given, not only a second chance, but what some would consider godlike powers. When you're fourteen years old, there's more to the world than what you think you know; but, regardless, I became Quantum Girl and, at the time, I was the only one to possess a quantum seed, which changed my life and a lot of other lives forever. I could not even keep up with the body count. Theresa Martinez was dead, Daisy McKenzie had turned evil, Phee had lost her humanity, and I had no idea how many other lives had been changed or ruined or erased by the reset timeline. Then there was the matter of Jordan and Sarabeth and Pay, whose existences were owed to everything that went on, and the matter of the thousands that Payton saved during the 9/11 attack. Still, how does one weigh the life of one person against that of another? I remember a television series called *Quantum Leap*, about how Dr. Samuel Beckett went back into the past, "striving to put things right that once went wrong," without any regard to the *butterfly effect*, where one misguided step from the future may and, more likely than not, would result in harrowing consequences. Save one life, and potentially endanger or damage ten million more.

Imagine traveling back in time and preventing Adolf Hitler from ever being born. You will have saved between seventy-five and eighty million people, but then an equal or greater number will never be born who otherwise *would* have. This is the moral dilemma faced by any time traveler. But where *I* was concerned, it was not some abstract *what-if* scenario. It was something real that could have irrevocable consequences.

Most of us, for most of our lives, have a negligible effect on those around us. We may provide emotional support to our family or our friends, or offer money or volunteer our time to those we care about. We immerse ourselves in relationships that often result in marriage and offspring, but few of us affect great change. How many find cures for cancer or polio or invent new technologies? Rather, millions with little or no real marketable skills publish their words through social media and dub themselves influencers, deciding through their own mirrors that their words somehow invoke widescale change.

I, Peyton Elise Herron, as Quantum Girl, did not have a website. I did not have a television show or a podcast. I did not post my opinions in whatever media existed, nor had I gone the celebrity route, regardless that my alter ego, Katara, had. I sought neither credit nor fortune nor fame for anything I had done as Quantum Girl. To do so would have destroyed the concept of true charity, for then I would have stolen a part of whatever good deeds I did for some sort of personal gain and that was not who I was or who I am.

Regardless of any of that, there was then a crisis facing not only my world but its counterpart in a parallel dimension. This was not the result of anything I did, but, rather, of an invasion by the reflection of one past life of mine, in an alternate plane of existence, the irony being that I myself could do nothing to try and stop it, as I was then four months pregnant with twins, whose lives I would not risk.

So, in the end, it all boiled down to how to defeat two all-powerful beings from two separate dimensions. As for the damage done, there was little we could do. Despite that Jordan was able to restore humanity to the Claire of Earth II; despite that Payton was able to resurrect Pay's parents, and that we were able to rescue Liam and Phee, there was still the matter of how to save everyone else.

I assumed that the Khattaaara of Earth III was similar to the original version of my former incarnation, which meant that she was dangerous and ruthless. As for Dargra-Tol, I was bewildered. The Dargra-Tol I had known was little more than a synthetic life form, an android, programmed to appear Gaaalthaaaran. It should not have been capable of the sorts of actions we had witnessed. And why would it have come to this universe, to this planet, and to this time? How would she have known how to find me, I who have lived through so many incarnations, unless she sought out and met with all of them? But were that the case, why would she have dragged Phee's body through universes on end? Unless, I thought, but then realized to my chagrin that she had followed my quantum trail from when I had brought Phee back through time. I wanted to seek out Jordan to confirm or deny my conclusion, but in my present condition, I was concerned about phasing. What if the fetuses didn't phase *with* me? What then? And so, I phoned her. Before the connection barely had time to ring, she was standing six feet in front of me.

"What's wrong?" she asked.

I looked at her with consternation. "What do you know about Dargra-Tol?"

"She's a *Thaaagran*," she replied. "She had become Khattaaara's lover, and managed to steal the mother-stone."

"What is the mother-stone?" I asked. "I thought the quantum seeds were more or less all the same."

"No," she replied. "where the god-stones can have mirrors in each dimension, there is only one mother stone for all that exist."

"Then how can Khattaaara and Dargra-Tol each have one?"

"They can't," Jordan said. "It's sort of like when you duplicate. Each of you has a god-stone but they're all entangled because they're all really one and the same. I believe that's why both of them have been drawn together."

"But why here?" I asked. "Why now?"

"Because of all the universes, whether in the past or future or in parallel dimensions," she replied, "you, Dear Aunt, are the focal point."

"How is that even possible?" I asked.

"Why does *anything* exist?" she asked. "It would have been just as easy for there never to have been anything at all, as there is for there to be all the universes filled with their energy and matter. I suppose the easy explanation would be that God created everything—that God said, 'Let there be light,' and all—but that still begs the question of how did God come to exist in the first place?"

"So, what are you saying?" I asked. "I was born more than fourteen billion years after this universe began, and there were trillions of universes before this one."

"How do you describe before?" she asked me. "Each universe has its own existence in the quantum fabric. Who's to say what the proper order is? You need to remember more about Krotaaarak's writings. Consider Liam and Li's universe, where time runs barely a nanosecond slower than this one, though there, the difference from ours has turned into five years. Believe it or not, in some universes, time actually runs backward relative to this one."

"But," I went on, "you're telling me that I'm the focal point of it all. What does that mean?" I looked at her with a twisted expression.

"Whether to know it or want to believe it or accept it," she replied, "you, Peyton Elise Herron, are the beginning and the end of everything. This may be a difficult concept for you to imagine, but all that exists or ever will exist, started with your birth, rippling backward and forward and sideways through space and time, echoing through the quantum fabric. You didn't just experience the Big Bang. You *were* the Big Bang for this universe and all the rest. At this exact moment, there may be numerous Peytons with quantum seeds as you call them, but there is only one true Quantum Girl and that is you. Braaangnarng and others afterward had wondered about the origins of the god-stones, but it was you who created them far in the future and it was you who sent them back to Rendenaaar for Braaangnarng to find."

"But why would I have sent them back to Rendenaaar for Khattaaara—for me when I *was* Khattaaara—to eventually steal?" I asked her. "And if I created them, how did the other Khattaaara get *hers*?"

"It wasn't the other dimensions that created the god-stones," she explained, "It was the god-stones that created an infinite number of dimensions."

"Oh," I said, "that is so like putting the chicken before the egg. You're telling me that at some future point in time, I created every other Peyton and Ophelia and Claire and…" And I stared really hard at her. "What about Liam?"

Jordan shook her head. "There never really was a Liam," she replied. "Liam was always just some tomboy part of Phee."

"But if Liam doesn't actually exist," I said, "then neither do you. No, I can't allow that to happen. Whatever comes of this," I insisted, "there need to be certain exceptions!"

"I will say one thing," Jordan went on, "my mother was certainly right about her sister. When you were growing up, she said, she was the strongest, but you were the kindest and most brave, and she loved you so much for that."

"At any rate," I said, "for the present, things are the way they are, and I have no foreknowledge of any of this." I looked hard into her eyes. "What if I'm killed in this here-and-now war? Then nothing that you say I'm destined to do will ever occur."

"Then, I guess, we'll have the greatest of all paradoxes on our hands." She said as she smiled at me. "I have faith in you, Cleopatra,"

"You know about that, too?" I asked in utter disbelief.

"Think back," she said as she smiled once more. "I was one of your handmaids. Of course, for me, that was just days ago. Curiosity got the better of me. Then you did that stupid thing with the asp. What is it about you and taking your own life?"

I frowned. "So, how do I stop all of this?" I asked her. "I just have the one quantum seed."

Jordan stared hard at me. "Do you think that the only way to control them is when they're in your head? You need to think outside the box, or, in this case, head." She glanced down at my stomach. "And take care of those cousins of mine," she said. "I'd hate for anything to happen to *them* while you try to gather all those thoughts in your brain!"

CHAPTER LXIII

Payton

> *From the Original Timeline*
> *In the Alternate Reality*
> *Earth II Date: Unknown*

Regardless that I now had two different colored quantum seeds in my head that might have doubled my powers I didn't have time to think. I had to phase somewhere else before Khattaaara killed me. I decided to escape through time—a million years into the future.

It was a strange sight to see. I stood in the midst of a jungle. There were trees in every direction as far as the eye could see, and yet I was in the heart of what was once L.A. The city had been consumed by nature. The greatest of skyscrapers had crumbled and been dissolved by erosion and vegetation. So far ahead in time had I traveled, I had no idea what to expect. What I found were humanoid creatures, perhaps four feet in height, hairless and naked, with large lemur-like eyes and horizontal slits that looked like gills where their noses and mouths ought to have been. The beings, which appeared to have intelligence roughly equivalent to primates, seemed curious, if not frightened by my sudden appearance. Then I saw something that gave me pause. Some of the creatures that were slightly smaller had pointed ears, while the others lacked ears entirely. All of them, though, had tails. *No*, I thought to myself. *What was it Jordan had called them? Yaaarghs. That was it! Yaaarghs!* These were the descendants of the humans that had been transformed. The virus, presumedly, had not stopped its work when it turned the inhabitants of my

307

Earth into replicas of those from Khattaaara's planet. It set some evolutionary genes in motion that had resulted in this. Thus, came about the end of civilization.

Gone was all that had set mankind apart from the rest of the animal kingdom. Here then were creatures that communicated, not through words or books or electronics, but through clicking noises made through their gill-like mouths. I named them gricks and, for a while, it seemed I was safe among them.

As twilight came, the gricks climbed into the trees for protection, although I saw no predators for them to hide from. Night, however, revealed how wrong I was. It seemed that humans were not the only creatures Khattaaara had transformed. It became evident that dogs had been turned into *goraaags* and over time, or through the miscreant effects of the genetic change, the *goraaags* had evolved into bipedal beasts, which, akin to Earth's prehistoric velociraptors, preyed upon the gricks.

It was strange to think that this was the ultimate fate of humanity. All the centuries of talk about how Gods made man in Their own image, for it to come to this. The gricks were peaceful creatures, able to make primitive tools where none remained from the past. Not much of civilization lasts for ten millennia. My stay, however, was brief, as it was not long afterward that Khattaaara appeared in the sky overhead.

Found you! she telepathed at me.

Look around, I telepathed back. *This is the result of your experiment!*

Her expression turned to rage. She glared at me, *Mistakes can be undone,* her mind cried out and then she focused on the ground.

All at once, I felt the gravitational pull of the black hole she had placed at the Earth's core, so powerful that even the quantum barrier I had placed around myself had a hard time keeping me from being crushed and drawn down as the entire planet was being sucked into the singularity she had created. It took every bit

308

of my will to phase away from there as far as I could and then I passed out. Once I came to, I stared around in all directions. Nothing was familiar. There were no constellations to guide me. The Earth was gone and nowhere were any of the other planets in my line of sight and even if the sun were out there, it would have looked no different from any of the other stars. Traveling back in time would have served no purpose. Even if the was gone, I knew that I had to at least find the solar system. What was worse was that the effects of the black hole had erased my quantum thread.

I was still in the Milky Way, thank Gods, because I could see the Andromeda galaxy in the distance, and off to my left were the Magellanic Clouds, but nothing else was recognizable. My only choice was to enter the quantum fabric to try and find my way back home.

The quantum fabric in that it is timeless, is filled with the trails of all of those who have gone through it. Mostly, there were other time versions of me or Peyton going this way or that but none that would stop and help, and their trails were knotted and confused. Some ignored me. Some cautioned me. And then I saw *her*— Jordan.

When did you get here? I thought at her.

Just now, she answered. *But who are you?*

Payton! I replied, taken aback by her question.

My aunt… she said as though concluding that somehow I must have been.

No, I told her. *I'm from a parallel dimension. But I know her. We're best friends.*

My name is Jordan, she projected into my mind.

I know, I answered back, *and you've come from Rendenaaar to help save our worlds.*

She appeared to be taken somewhat aback by my revelation. I smiled and told her, *I'm from a few months into your future—your future on Earth, that is. But I'm totally lost in this quantum soup.*

Jordan returned the smile and telepathed back, *I've been following the quantum trail my aunt left when she brought my mother and me to Rendenaaar. It's quite faint, but it's led me this far. Perhaps you can follow me.*

Thank you, Jordan, I telepathed back. *I do know that you and I are going to be friends, but please don't tell anyone about this. I don't want to upset the timeline—again. Enough damage has already been done by me.*

Oh, my God! she telepathed. *Then it was your spirit that joined with Khattaaara! We were more than best friends. You and I, we were family. I didn't know that I'd ever meet you, I mean, as Payton. I wasn't aware—none of us were aware—that a physical part of you had survived what Theresa had done.* She paused and then went on with, *Just follow me,* and I did just that.

CHAPTER LXIV

Young Liam

From the Original Timeline
In the Alternate Reality
On Earth I
Earth-Date: 2029

Thara-Klo had rescued us, Claire and me, and brought us to Peyton's mansion, to the library, and left us there while she went to go talk with Peyton. The walls were nothing but shelves of books that reached the ceiling that must have been twenty feet high. There was also a spiral staircase that went up to a catwalk that went all around the walls, and there were four wooden ladders that slid from one end of the wall to the other to be able to reach the books that were high up. There was a big wooden desk in the middle of the room that had a leather top, and there were old things on it. Claire thought they were pretty, but I thought they were just in the way. Claire picked up one book that had red leather covers.

"What does it say?" I asked her.

"I don't know," she replied. "I can't read it."

"What do you mean?" I asked. "You can see now?"

"You know I'm blind," she said. "The god-stone allows me to see shapes, but things like the pages of books or paintings are just flat to me."

"Sorry," I replied. "I didn't mean that you were stupid or anything."

"I can read Braille," she said. "And the disks would read to me when I wanted them to."

"You were smart enough to stay away from me," I told her. "Li always said I was a troublemaker."

"Your sister," she said.

"She's the smart one," I replied. "I guess I just needed others to think that I was special, too."

"Everyone's special in their own way," she said. "You just need to figure out what you're special in."

"I suppose," I said back. "I just hope I can figure out what it is when it comes to me."

"Maybe," she replied, "we can figure it out together."

"There's something else," I said taking a deep breath.

"What's that?" she replied, putting down the book.

I picked it up. It was Alice Through the Looking Glass. The edges were gold, and when I tilted the pages, a picture of Alice at the tea party appeared.

"What is it that you wanted to tell me?" Claire asked.

I put the book back down and looked at her. "That I'm really, really sorry for ever teasing you," I said.

"I know," she replied. "You said that before."

"Yeah," I went on, trying to get out the words. "But what I didn't say, um, tell you, is that…"

"What?" she asked.

"I mean," I stammered out, "I know we're only ten and all, and that we've both got a lot of growing up to do and, well…"

"Yes?" she asked.

"It's just that," I went on, "I'm kind of, sort of, in love with you. I know that might sound all kind of creepy and all, but, you know, when everything got destroyed on our world I went out every day trying to find you. I mean, I didn't have the slightest idea where you lived, and Li would always demand to know where I went off to and I lied to her and told her I was out looking for food and stuff, but the truth of the matter was that I was hoping you'd survived, and I didn't care if aliens blasted me or put alien bugs in my head. All I knew was, you being blind and all, I wanted to find you and try and protect you, and if you don't believe me, you can ask Li how every day I'd disappear for hours at a time. I know that probably sounds stupid, and now you probably think of me like some stalker or something, but it's been on my mind since we met, and I just wanted to get it out but never had the courage. So, that's that, and you can never have anything to do with me anymore if that's what you want, and I'll leave you alone."

And that's when she went over to me—I thought she was going to slap me across the face or something and I closed my eyes real tight—but instead, she wrapped her arms around me, and kissed me, really kissed me. Seriously, I thought I was going to have a heart attack and die then and there.

"How absolutely adorable!" came a familiar voice from behind.

We both turned and saw her and went pale. It was Khattaaara!

"What have you munchkins been up to since I destroyed your world?" There was evil in her eyes, as she spoke. "And I see you each have god-stones that belong to me!"

And with that, she raised up her arms, faced the palms of her hands toward us, pulled the god-stones from our heads, and then vanished. Claire turned her head from side to side as a look of devastation came to her face.

"I can't see anymore!" she screamed. "Liam! I can't see!"

I took hold of her and she fell against me, crying. I put my arms around her. "I'm here for you," I said. "I'll always be here for you," but she just wept out tears.

CHAPTER LXV

Thara-Klo

From the Earth III Timeline
In the Alternate Reality
On Earth I
Earth-Date: 2029

I found it interesting that Peyton Herron had been Khattaaara in a former life, which meant that the Khattaaara in this dimension, unlike the one in mine, had died. I learned about the reincarnation from the two Earth children I rescued. According to them, there were presently four Peyton Herrons on this planet, three of whom possessed god-stones, two from the dimension my mother was bent on turning into a world filled with Gaaathaaans, as she has so many times in the past on so many other worlds after destroying our own. How, I thought, any universe could have spawned someone so wicked was beyond reason.

After leaving the children to themselves in the mansion that was owned by the Peyton of this world, I came upon the other one—the other Payton—from the Earth that Khattaaara had been transforming humans on. This one, who, as it later turned out, had two god-stones in her head, one from my dimension and one from a dimension… somewhere else. She was beyond startled to see me, mistaking me for the Thara-Klo from this world, though, apparently *that* Thara-Klo had been a bit older than me.

"How did you…" she started to ask. "How are you alive?"

"I'm not her," I replied. "I'm from Khattaaara's dimension. I brought Liam and Claire back. They were stranded on the other Earth. Khattaaara did a real number on that world. I don't know how precisely many others are still alive there, but not a lot I assure you. Still," she went on, "there may yet be hope for them."

It was at that moment that we heard sobs coming from the library and we both teleported there to find young Claire in young Liam's arms.

"What happened?" Payton asked.

"It was Khattaaara!" Liam exclaimed, still holding Claire. "She stole our god-stones!"

"I'm blind again!" Claire sobbed.

Payton bent down and urged Claire to face her. Claire wiped her eyes with the backs of her hands.

"Hey," Payton said in a gentle voice. "Everything's going to be just fine."

"But I can't see!" Claire sobbed. "You don't know what it's like!"

"What's your favorite color from when you were little?" Peyton asked, "Purple or green?"

"Purple," Claire sniffled, followed by another sob.

Payton brought her hand near her face, her palm up, and then focused her thoughts. As she did, a purple god-stone emerged from her forehead and fell into her grip. Then, with the thumb and index finger of her other hand, she took it and brought it up to Claire's forehead. The god-stone spun faster and faster, shrinking in size as it did, and then melted through her skin and then disappeared. Claire blinked a few times and then turned her head this way and that.

"Well?" Payton asked.

This time, there were tears of joy that came streaming out from young Claire's eyes. "I can see again!" she wept. "Only everything's purple now. But I can see! Thank you so much!" And then she threw her arms around Payton's neck, closed her eyes tightly, and hugged her with all her strength. Payton wrapped her arms around Claire as well, and then, once the emotions waned a bit, stood up and turned to me.

"We can't let this go on," she said. "And there's another problem—another person from Rendenaaar from this dimension, who also has a mother stone. Her name's Dargra-Tol."

"Dargra-Tol was a *Thaaagran*," I said.

"What's a *Thaaagran*," she asked.

"An artificial life form," I replied, "engineered to serve as workers for our people. I'm curious as to how it managed to get a hold of one."

"Jordan said she tricked Khattaaara—our Khattaaara—out of it. Jordan is Peyton's—the other Peyton's—niece, who was raised on Rendenaaar. She has quantum seeds—god-stones—too. It's complicated." She looked at me and shrugged.

"It has to end here and now," I said. "Too many worlds have been invaded; too many lives destroyed."

"Well," she replied, "that's great in theory, but it hasn't worked so far—at least not for you."

"That was just her by herself," another voice rang in. We all turned to see Peyton at the door—spiked heels and jet-black hair—with Jordan just behind. "It's not just her anymore," she said. "It's all of us."

CHAPTER LXVI

Peyton

> *From the Original Timeline*
> *In the Alternate Reality*
> *On Earth I*
> *Earth-Date: 2029*

Even though Jordan had shown me what things would have been like if I hadn't put that rope around my neck to end my life, there still remained the echo of her later words that I was somehow the center of all existence. Why should I have been so special? But then, what other teenager learned that she was a reincarnation of a being from a long-dead alien civilization, and, *Oh, my God*, Cleopatra! And, lest I forget the powers over time and space and parallel dimensions I had been given! *Was there anything else I should know?* I wondered. I did not like the thought of being anything even resembling a god. I was quite content with the Supergirl, Wonder Woman persona, thank you.

It was extremely upsetting that Khattaaara had now invaded my home, and what she had done to Claire and Phee was unconscionable. Parallel incarnation or not, she needed to go, as did Dargra-Tol, with whom I had a personal beef, not only for what she did to Phee but for how she had *disposed* of her corpse. I had a hard time breaking it to Jordan. After all, this was her mother, the person who had loved her before she was even born. She didn't cry, though. She just turned to stone. She stood up and walked to the window, and stared up at the night sky.

"She never came to grips," she said, "with the fact that she'd been transformed. As I grew up, I think I reminded her more and

317

more of what had been stolen from her. I can see now, from looking at the Ophelia in this other thread of time, just how beautiful she was. She didn't deserve what happened to her. And, it's gone through my mind so often, I think things would have been better for her, stranded in the past, if she'd never met my father."

"Then, you'd never have been born," I said.

"I would gladly have made that sacrifice," she replied. "I loved her that much."

"I know she wouldn't have wanted that for you," I said.

"Just the same..." she insisted, still staring up at the stars. Then she changed the subject. "Have you ever been to another galaxy?"

"No," I said, "but I've watched them form."

"I have," she went on. "There are no quantum seeds in any of them. Just here."

"Why do you think that is?" I asked.

"I told you," she replied with a slight backward glance. "You're the center of it all. Khattaaara had wondered who the Guardian of the God-Stones was, the beautiful silver being. That was you in your final incarnation."

"Don't you mean the first?" I asked.

"As I said," she replied, "everything in this and every other universe begins and ends with you. Difficult as it may be to conceive, your birth sparked all existence, rippling backward and forward in time and through an infinite number of dimensions." She turned around to face me. "Whatever the case is," she went on, "I think it's about time that we go kick some alien butt!"

CHAPTER LXVII

Sarabeth

From the Alternate Timeline
In the Alternate Reality
On Earth I
Earth-Date: 2029

I was the powerless one. I was *the kid*! No one cared what I had to say. All four of them were gathered in the parlor—at least that's what Peyton always referred to it as. She was there. So were Demi and Jordan and Thara-Klo, with nine quantum seeds between them. Clairey had one more, but none of them were going to involve her in any of what was about to occur, nor take away the one thing that allowed her to see.

Phee and I were permitted to sit in—Phee, my twin, who was now four years older than me. I was the youngest in the room. Did I ask to be brought forward in time? Where was *my* quantum seed? This all seemed so unfair.

"What do we need to know about the mother stone?" That was Peyton—Other Me, alternate-reality me, or was I alternate-reality her? Regardless, she was the original Quantum Girl.

"As you're probably aware," Thara-Klo said, "it allows one to shape-shift and resurrect the dead."

"And she can destroy an entire planet with it," Demi added. I wondered, since she and Pay merged, was she or they now bisexual? So impolite to ask. Sex can be so confusing, especially when you haven't had it yet!

"The mother stone," said Jordan, "also gives one the ability to control space and time."

"But we all have that ability," Peyton said.

"No," Jordan went on. "It allows one to fold the continuum and manipulate dimensions."

"How are we supposed to fight *that*?" Demi asked. "None of us have that kind of power." She stared from one of us to the next.

"Dargra-Tol might not know about that part of it," I proclaimed. The others turned and stared at me. "I'm not stupid!" I turned to Jordan. "You said you pursued her through time and that it was like cat and mouse. Well, if she knew about warping space or time, she would have thrown you out of that universe, literally. I think you should all focus on *her* first; capture her, kill her, whatever—then get her mother stone, so that at least one of you can face Khattaaara on equal terms."

"She has a point," Phee broke in. "You know, just because she doesn't have one of your quantum marbles in her head doesn't mean she's not as smart as any of you. We may call her Sarabeth, but she *is* still Peyton Elise Herron. I grew up with her and she's about as smart as they come, so I think it might behoove y'all ta listen."

"She's right, you know," Thara-Klo broke in. "We need to take out the *Thaaagran* first."

"So, where do we look for her?" came a familiar voice at the now open door. It was Clairey.

"*We* don't," Peyton said. "This is an adults-only matter. We're not going to lose you again. It was sheer luck that Thara-Klo found you when she did. Now, back off to the room I had Gretchen prepare. I'm sure that Master Liam would love to snuggle up with you for the night, and from the looks of the two of you earlier, I don't think there'd be any objection."

"Oh, all right!" Clairey moped. "But if you need me…"

"Go!" all three Quantum Girls chimed in at once.

"Isn't it great that you're no longer the youngest?" Phee whispered to me.

"Definitely!" I whispered back.

"Come on," Phee said, getting up. "I'll buy you a hot fudge sundae."

"Why not?" I replied, getting up after her. "It's *super* stuffy in here."

"Heard that!" straight, bi, lesbian (whatever!) Demi Payton said.

Anyway… We retreated to the soda fountain. Seriously? A soda fountain in her house? There was an area in the gym (*Oh, my God!*) that was set up like a malt shop from the 1940s or '50s, complete with an antique triple Hamilton Beach milkshake mixer, presumably named after the beach where Alexander Hamilton went swimming before he bought the farm after his duel with Aaron Burr. Anyway, it was Jadite green (at least that's what Peyton said it was) with three separate mixers for chocolate, vanilla, and strawberry, respectively. The ice cream was stored in stainless steel freezer bins that were just behind the counter, on the other side of which were barstools with cushy red vinyl seats made to resemble marble. Phee did the honors with regard to the milkshakes. Mine was strawberry and hers was chocolate, both dripped with hot fudge, decorated with two wafers and a maraschino cherry and served with a long silver spoon. The countertop matched the barstools but was edged with a wide ribbed chrome strip. Behind it all was a long mirror, I guess so that anyone and everyone could watch themselves as they ate. Peyton told me she had it built to remind her of when she'd gone back in time to buy a Wonder Woman comic book for the other Phee, but that after the other Phee got turned into an alien and she had to take her back to Rendenaaar, it sort of dredged up memories that weighed hard on her, and so she tended to avoid the room altogether after that but still kept it stocked for guests.

"So, what do you think's going to happen?" I asked Phee. I took a bite from the cherry that I held with my fingers as I waited for her reply.

"I think we're either all going to die," she replied, "or be turned into alien freaks."

"Don't let Thara-Klo hear you say that," I said.

"I didn't want to imply that *she* is. I just mean that…"

"Hey," I shot back. "I was just messing with you." I paused for another spoonful of ice cream. "It's kind of strange, though," I said.

"What is?" she asked.

"All these alternate universes and parallel worlds," I said as I stared at her. "I mean, how do *you* feel about being a rewrite of the original?"

"Who's to say that *that* Ophelia was the original," she replied as she swallowed a spoonful of her chocolate-chocolate confection. "Peyton admitted to having gone back in time more than once, which would have potentially erased the Ophelia in the first timeline like the original Liam got wiped out of existence." Another spoonful, another swallow, and she continued. "And, look, I don't know about the other Phee, but I am definitely not attracted to anyone who is the male version of me. It would be like dating my own brother. I have no idea what could have possessed her to fall head over heels. Just sayin'. To be perfectly honest, given the choice, I'd be more attracted to Claire."

"I'm totally into boys," I said, "but I like this."

"Like what?" she asked.

"That we're talking like we used to," I answered.

"Well," she said, "you're my twin sister."

"Not so twin anymore," I replied.

"Peyton," she said, "and to hell with the Sarabeth crap— You're my twin sister—twin as in intertwined. We grew up together, virtually joined at the hip. You will *always* be the best part of me."

I didn't respond to that. I just finished my sundae and smiled to myself. The world might come to an end in a day or a week, but things were good then and there. Dunkhead still loved me, and I loved her, and, in that moment, I didn't know or care about the passage of time.

CHAPTER LXVIII

Payton

From the Original Timeline
In the Alternate Reality
On Earth I
Earth-Date: 2029

Strangely, there was no Dark God to do battle with; only Dargra-Tol. The Daisy McKenzie part of her appeared to be gone. How that would affect things was anyone's guess. Peyton, pregnant, needed to stay away from the battleground, lest she risk a miscarriage. But without her purple quantum seed, there was little chance of us being able to counter the power of the mother stone. The battle was fought in the skies above Rome. Ancient and medieval structures and priceless statues were demolished by the alien's energy blasts—the Coliseum, the Parthenon, the Sistine Chapel—all reduced to rubble, for, despite the fact that Jordan had five of the six god-stones and Thara-Klo and I had three more, lacking Peyton's, the quantum arc of ours combined could not counter the power of the mother stone. Thara-Klo lay on the ground, unconscious. I was hanging mid-air, stunned by one of Dargra-Tol's energy spheres. Jordan was being pummeled by blast after blast and was facing total exhaustion. As the synthetic alien was about to deal her the final blow, Clairey phased just behind her, reached around the creature's head, and gouged out her eyes. Dargra-Tol screamed. It was deafening. It was the cry of a banshee gone insane, but, in just moments, her sight was restored as her eyes grew back. She turned, saw Clairey, and was about to strike a death blow, when suddenly, the word,

"Stop!" thundered through the air. The alien turned—we all did—to see Khattaaara!

"You again!" Dargra-Tol shouted at her. "Go back to thine own dimension!"

"This *is* my dimension!" she shouted back, her voice booming toward the madding creature with a strong Gaaalthaaaran accent. She glanced down at Jordan and then became *Zhaaagur Scraaa*. *Hello, little one*, she telepathed at her. *Forgive me, but I need to take something back.* Five quantum seeds could be seen leaving Jordan's head and transferring to Khattaaara. *I believe we are equal now*, she telepathed to the *Thaaagran*, *only I have the upper hand.*

How is that? the synth replied in kind.

I am also behind thee, she telepathed, as she stabbed her in the back through the heart.

The creature hung in mid-air, as Khattaaara drew the mother stone from her, and then placed it in her own head. As she did, Dargra-Tol's lifeless body dropped to the ground and then turned to dust. Both Khattaaara and Clairey phased to the ground, bringing Jordan with them.

Khattaaara turned to Jordan. "I thought thou might need some help," she said to her in Gaaalthaaaran, and then turned and saw Thara-Klo. She bent down, looked at her, and then turned toward me. "I don't understand," she said.

"She's from another dimension, another Earth," I said and then glanced at Thara-Klo's body. "She's dead," I told her. "I'm sorry."

Khattaaara stared at the corpse of her other-dimensional daughter. I watched her intensely as her eyes began to glow white. Suddenly, Thara-Klo coughed and opened her eyes, startled as she saw who she thought was her mother, and was about to strike her with a blast of energy.

"Wait!" Jordan shouted. "She's not who you think she is!"

"I'm not her," Khattaaara said in Gaaalthaaaran in a gentle voice. "I'm from a Rendenaaar where you had died. My beautiful daughter. It's so good to see you again."

We all watched with tears in our eyes.

"I thought we told you to stay at home?" I whispered to Clairey.

Clairey shrugged. "We Quantum Girls need to stick together," she replied.

CHAPTER LXIX

Khattaaara/Payton

> *Payton from the Original Timeline*
> *In the Rewritten Timeline*
> *On Earth I*
> *Earth-Date: 2029*

It was I who was responsible for the destruction of my planet, no matter that it had been Dargra-Tol who had caused it to explode. It was I and I alone who was to blame. What she did not know, was that the Khattaaara who had broken into her chamber was not the only one of me. Knowing her power and the potential of defeat, I had divided myself a thousandfold, each of whom remained on Rendenaaar. But I did not anticipate the length to which she would go to destroy the entire world and its people and, apparently, her own kind. Yet the god-stone had protected me, each of me, from the blast.

There was nothing I could do about the one of me she had killed, but the rest positioned ourselves around where the planet once was, caused time to reverse, and, by that means, undid the damage that had been done. And may Khii or God forgive me, but I took it upon myself to destroy all the remaining *Thaaagrans*, who had proved far too dangerous to exist among our people.

My name is Khattaaara Gaaalthaaara, Last Ruler of the House of Gaaalthaaara on the planet Rendenaaar. My name is Payton Alise Herron, citizen of the planet Earth, dimension 2.94681 relative, Earth II for short. We, together, are Khattaaara, the amalgamation of our souls causing two alternate timelines to be formed. Prior to that happening, as Khattaaara Gaaalthaaara I was one of the worst evildoers in whatever universe I came in contact with, but the Payton half changed all of that. I had been content to remain on Rendenaaar in my universe, but with the abduction and murder of my closest friend, Ophelia, by Dargra-Tol, I decided to follow her daughter, my reincarnate's niece, to the future to put an end to the *Thaaagran* murderess. My name is Khattaaara Gaaalthaaara, and I am *Zhaaagur Scraaa*, both ruler and superheroine of a long-forgotten world.

It seemed, though, that there was another one of me; one who came from what was known as Earth III, one, who might have been described as my then-evil twin. She was the cause of Ophelia's grief, the loss of her love, of her metamorphosis into a Gaaalthaaaran, along with millions of other human beings.

"I need to do this alone," I told Payton once I had arrived in her time. "You know that a part of you is in me. You need to trust me on this."

Payton looked at me with curious eyes. "What's it been like?" she asked, "I mean, the human part of you."

"Sometimes I've missed being human," I said, projecting out the image of Payton to answer her. "But, you and I, we're strong. It's been an adventure." Payton smiled, as I drew the image back into me. "I need to go now. *We* need to go. Wish us luck."

And so I phased in seconds to a billion points on the Earth, until I picked up my mirror's quantum trail. Oddly enough, it led me to a mansion owned by one Katara Drall, whom she had pinned against one wall in the kitchen, her *yaaargh* wrapped around her throat—Peyton's throat—strangling her, the tip pointed at her face, poised to sting.

"Is that how you treat pregnant women?" I asked.

The evil Khattaaara turned her head, and saw me, as I caused the mask over my face to disappear.

"Who the hell *are* you?" she demanded to know, letting Peyton drop to the floor. "And why do you look like me?"

"Because I *am* you," I said. "I'm the Khattaaara of this dimension and, as for you, you're done. No more destruction. No more killing. No more turning humans into us!"

"And I supposed you're going to stop me?"

"Look out!" Peyton screamed as a bunch of kitchen knives came hurling toward me. Seeing them, I stretched the spacetime they were in, causing them to turn back into harmless electrons and quarks as they struck me. Force field after force field we hurled at each other. What must have once been valuable artifacts came crashing to the ground or bursting into flames. Finally, I managed to throw her upward through three floors and the roof, leaving a gaping hole. I phased out to the sky, where she hung in the air, recovering from the blow.

"You can't defeat me!" she boasted. "I have the mother stone and two others!"

"Yes," I boasted back, "But I have the mother stone and all the rest!"

A look of terror came upon her. She phased off into outer space, but I followed her, jump after jump, until we were beyond the Milky Way.

You can't kill me! she telepathed. *It would be like killing yourself! You're a decent person. You can't take another life.*

You're right, I telepathed back, *but in your case, I'll make an exception*, and with that, I focused the power of all seven god-stones on hers. I could hear her scream into my mind as the mother stone burst from her head and plunged into mine, while the other six exploded. In that same instant, I phased to a safe distance, watching as she became a star with two planets, one red, the other yellow; at least that was the color of their atmospheres. Then I phased back to Peyton.

"She's gone," I said, "never to return."

Peyton picked up a piece of what was once an ancient Chinese urn and stared at it. "This used to be 14th Century Ming," she said with a smile.

"That's what insurance companies are for," I replied.

"Oh, great," she sighed. "And just what am I supposed to tell them? Two beings from other universes slugged it out in my house?"

"You'll figure something out," I said, and then asked, "Did you get my message?"

"Message?" she repeated.

"From Jordan," I went on. "About all existence coming from you."

"I assumed she was just wanting to try and build me up," she replied.

"No," I said, "I think you know what to do. But I need to phase back to Rendenaaar before our violet stones combine. I leave you with six gifts. Do with them as you will," and with that, I phased back to my universe, my planet and my people, what was left of them.

EPILOGUE

Peyton

> *From the Original Timeline*
> *In the Alternate Reality*
> *On Earth I*
> *Earth-Date: 2029*

There were sounds coming from the library—a heartbeat, then breathing, and then swallowing. I could hear the blinking of eyelids closing shut and then opening again. At first, it was deafening, but I was quickly able to calm it down—calm my powers down. I made my way through the rubble to that room. Books were scattered everywhere. It was then that I saw her— Payton. She was standing with her back toward me.

"When did you phase in?" I asked.

She turned around suddenly to face me. "I didn't," she said. "I can't. I don't have the seed anymore."

It was at that moment that Sarabeth entered the room with the children and Niska.

"What happened?" she asked. "It sounded like World War III. Everything went flying at us."

"Are any of you hurt?" I asked, concerned.

"No," she replied. "Clairey projected a force field to protect us."

Niska walked up to Payton, sniffed her, cocked her head, and then began to bark. Clairey went up to her pet, squatted down, and held her.

"Hey girl," she said. "Calm down. It's just Payton."

"What happened to your quantum seed?" I asked.

331

"It's with Khattaaara, I guess," she said.

"Wait!" I replied. "So, you're the Payton that was part of her? I don't understand how?"

"She had the mother stone," she said.

"Had?" I asked. "What do you mean had?"

Payton smiled. "Have you checked your head lately? You have them all."

And I did. I phased into Quantum Girl violet, then red, then blue, then orange, then yellow, then green, and then white. I could feel their energy surging through every cell.

"Now that you have all that power," I heard Payton say, "what are you going to do?" Turning, I saw another Payton standing with Jordan.

"Oh, no!" young Liam exclaimed. "There are two of them again!"

"He's right, you know," said Jordan. "You need to fix it all. There are too many dimensions. There needs to be just one."

"But if I do," I said, "you might never exist."

"To save the universe," she replied. "To save them all. That's a small sacrifice to make."

I went over to her and hugged her. Then I focused all my will on what needed to be done. The dimensions all came together. Mom and Dad merged with Payton's folks. Li and both Liams merged into Phee, Clairey into Claire, and the Payton and Sharbeth into me. Theresa was once more alive and well and had just moved out from her mother's place. Daisy still spent her nights in her snow-white room, still a virgin, but wondering now if it were Prince or Princess Charming who would rescue her from her gilded cage. As for me, I was no longer Katara Drall, but simply Peyton Herron once again, who shared an apartment with her twin sister and (jaw-droppingly strange) her sister's partner, Claire, and, of course, a blue merle collie named Niska, who, through the power of the quantum seeds, was going to live for a very long time. Chloë Anne Salinger, Claire's younger sister, who had existed in at least one reality, was as taken aback by the pairing as was I, as were all of our parents. There was no condemnation (despite Mom's ultra-Christian upbringing!) and the fact was that I'd had similar experiences as well in my past. After all that had happened to both of them, we all only wanted the best for them, and that included love, the kind you read about in fairy tales and watch in old movies. The truth was that Liam was just a projection of Phee, and Liam loved Claire and she loved him, and now, well, having phased into the future, I can tell you that they stayed together for the rest of their lives. Oh, and five months later, I gave birth to a beautiful, six-pound, ten-ounce little girl with the most adorable smile. I named her Jordan—father, unknown. People would later ask why she looked more like my sister than me. One day, I'll restore all her lost memories. Till, then, I will use my powers to protect her and try my best to save the world. And don't let anyone ever tell you that I don't have the stones for it, because we all know that I do.

The End... for now.

AFTERWORD

The Quantum Girl Saga deals with a lot more than aliens and superpowers. They touch upon bullying, self-harm, and suicide. These are issues faced by young people today. As a teenager myself, I strongly encourage anyone twenty-five or younger, who is facing those issues or others such as sexual assault or date rape, substance abuse, child abuse, sexual trafficking, anxiety or depression, or if things are bad at home and you are considering running away, please call the Thursday's Child hotline at 1 (800) USA KIDS from a landline, or (818) 831-1234 internationally or from a cellphone. Phone lines are open 24/7 and are confidential and free. They care. I care. I'm Peyton Herron, Quantum Girl, and spokesperson for Thursday's Child. Their website is www.thursdayschild.org, where you can also get help.